TAINTED
Creek

BY

KC KEAN

Tainted Creek
The Allstars Series #2
Copyright © 2021 KC Kean

This book is licensed for your personal enjoyment only.
This book may not be re-sold or given away to other people. If you would like to share this book with another person, please purchase an additional copy for each recipient. If you're reading this book and did not purchase it, or it wasn't purchased for your use only, then please return to your favourite book retailer and purchase your own copy. Thank you for respecting the hard work of this author.
All rights reserved.
This is a work of fiction. Names, characters, places, brands, media, and incidents are either the product of the authors imagination or are used fictitiously. The author acknowledges the trademark status and trademark owners of various products referred to in this work of fiction, which have been used without permission. The publication/use of these trademarks is not authorised, associated with, or sponsored by the trademark owners.

Cover Designer: Bellaluna Designs
Content Editor: Valerie Victoria
Proofreader: Elemental Editing & Proofreading

Tainted Creek/KC Kean – 1st ed.
ISBN-13 - 9798533982009

To Grandad,

My first love, my absolute king.

May you win on the horses and continue to be confused by what it is I actually do.

Thank you for showing me how to love, and what a marriage should look like.

From your eldest Princess.

I'm sick of letting the people in this town bleed me dry, I have nothing left to give. Not an ounce.

- Eden Grady

KC KEAN

PROLOGUE

Emptiness.

KC KEAN

ONE

Eden

Standing on the edge of the cliff with the ragged rocks below, I let the wind tousle the wisps of stray hair around my face as the salty sea air fills my lungs.

I pull my gray hoodie a little tighter, watching as the waves crash and bubble below, the sound settling my soul a little as I hear giggling in the distance. Being here creates a sense of calm I can't seem to get anywhere else. The ocean is my sanctuary, but it doesn't stop the dark thoughts from clouding my mind.

I wonder what it would feel like to plunge into the

depths of the ocean, to let the riptide push and pull me around, not giving me a choice in the direction I take or whether I'll even resurface.

I could live with that.

I'm too emotionally drained, my head a fucked up mess with all the crap piling up on top of me. I'd love to go back to being the seventeen-year-old, fun-loving girl who only had to worry about practicing safe sex and making sure her phone was charged.

Now I'm lost in a metaphorical sea of lies, secrets, and douchebag Allstars. Knight's Creek seems to have it all, I just don't actually want *any* of what it has to offer.

"I have a brother," I whisper under my breath.

After spending my whole life as an only child, the words feel foreign on my tongue. But it's not just anybody, it's Archie.

Archie Freemont is my brother. *Twin brother.*

If I thought my life had gone to shit in White River when my father died, then Knight's Creek pushed me over the edge of sanity. My life feels as though it's no longer my own.

And they knew, they *all* knew, including Archie.

Just like that, the trust I had in him is gone. At least

that's what I keep telling myself, but my soul misses him already. The guilt in his eyes as Roxy goaded me, with Xavier encouraging her, will be forever etched in my mind.

Tobias had taken me home after someone had tried to kidnap me during the Allstars' football game. I'd woken in Xavier's bed, finding candid pictures of me scattered across his wall as I lay wrapped in his navy and gray sheets, but when I walked out to see him around the bonfire on the beach on Saturday night, he wasn't the same guy from just hours earlier.

No. He was someone else entirely. He was officially the Xavier Knight I'd been warned about. The guy who had a wall dotted with my pictures was gone, and in his place remained the fucking devil himself.

The confusion on both Tobias's and Hunter's faces said enough though. They had no clue what had caused the switch either, but I refused to stick around to find out.

After reading someone's shitty attempt at writing an obituary for me, I forced myself up off the bathroom floor and dialed the only number I felt safe enough reaching out to.

"De-de, 'um on!"

Holding my hair off my face, I glance over my shoulder

to find Cody reaching his hands toward me, his blond curls blowing in the wind as he smiles up at me. Bethany holds him tightly against her chest with concern in her blue eyes as she watches me.

If there is anyone almost as mad as me right now, it's Bethany—Ryan, too, by default. She is the only Asheville who I don't think is an asshole at the moment, but she's technically a Carter anyway since she's married to Ryan, and that definitely boosts my trust in her. I'm also glad she doesn't push for any kind of conversation that involves her brother.

I can't stop the soft smile that instinctively transforms my face, making my worry lines and sad eyes disappear as I put on a brave front for Cody. It's like he can sense when something is wrong, and the last thing I want is for this little boy to feel my anguish.

"Are you ready to head back?" Bethany asks, pointing to her SUV in the parking lot, and I nod as she lowers Cody to the ground and he charges straight for me.

Quickly picking him up before he gets too close to the edge, I balance him on my hip as I follow Bethany's lead. Cody snuggles in, and I happily absorb his innocence and joy, basking in his comfort.

It's been three days since everything went to shit, and this little man has distracted me like crazy. Bethany refuses to let me simmer away in private, letting my anger get the better of me, which is why we're even out here to begin with. She said it had something to do with my body needing vitamin D and fresh air, but I know it's because she recognizes how much I love the ocean with the amount I've talked about it.

Although, this is not the kind of D I need right now, but I don't say it, even though I'm sure she sees the snark in my eyes.

Bethany holds the back door open, letting me secure Cody in his car seat before I get in on the other side and settle beside him. No shotgun for me when there's this handsome little man to sit next to. We're travel buddies for life now, apparently, and I just can't bring myself to argue against it.

"De-de, a bo-bo," he mumbles as I clip him in, and I know he wants his blue bobbly blanket and a nap.

It's crazy how I can understand a two-year-old who doesn't have his full vocabulary more than I can understand ninety-five percent of the population in this toxic town.

I fall back into my seat as Bethany starts the drive back

to her house, and I can already sense her need to quiz me again now that Cody is already half asleep.

I've managed to put something or someone between us each time, stopping any deep discussion from occurring, but I know she's close to calling me out. The craziest thing is, I know she isn't trying to pry, she's just caring for me when no one else is here to do so—my mother included, but I can't get into that yet.

My phone vibrates in my pocket, breaking my eye contact with Bethany in the rearview mirror. I reluctantly pull it out. It's one of two people, the same two individuals who have called me repeatedly since I ran—Charlie and Archie.

I can't speak to either of them, not even Charlie since I know she's so close to Archie. Her messages have promised girl time and declared that I'm her priority, but I've been burned enough by this damn town. The whole damn place is tainted with scandal, and I find myself at the center of it.

"Lou-Lou" flashes across the screen, catching me by surprise. My gaze flickers back to Bethany's, a frown marring my face as I bring the phone to my ear, surprised to be hearing from her.

"Hello?"

"Long time no talk, girl. What's been going on?" Her cheery voice rings through the phone, and a sense of familiarity washes over me.

"Straight to the point, huh?" I reply, already missing her sense of crazy. My current inability to smile like the world is made of rainbows is apparently noticeable, since she remains quiet when she doesn't hear my usual snark, prompting me to speak again. "So much, Lou-Lou." I sigh. "There are no words for how upside down things are right now."

"What could possibly be so shitty about living so close to the ocean, Eden? Aren't there any hot boys for you to enjoy? I know you don't do repeats, but at least it's a distraction."

That's a much more loaded question than she knows. I haven't spoken to her since I first pulled up outside of Archie's home, and even though it wasn't all that long ago, *a lot* has fucking happened.

Pinching the bridge of my nose, I take a deep breath as my eyes fall closed. "We need to catch up, Lou-Lou. I don't even know where to begin."

"Eden? Is everything okay?" Lou-Lou questions as I lean my head on the headrest and glance out of the window as Knight's Creek passes us by. I can feel Bethany's eyes flicker to me while Cody snores lightly beside me as I try to find the right way to answer Lou-Lou's question.

"It'll be fine, Lou-Lou. I've been through worse. Listen, I have to go, but we need to arrange a girls' weekend soon, okay?"

"For sure. You know I'm going to be there for your birthday weekend. Send me your address, alright?"

Before I can respond, the line goes dead, and I'm left gaping at a black screen as Bethany chuckles from the front seat.

When I cast my gaze her way, dropping my phone into my lap, she masks her amusement.

"Friend?" she asks with a smile on her lips, and I nod.

"One from where I lived previously," I respond, glancing down at my phone as a text message comes through from Lou-Lou demanding my address, but I shut it off, not knowing which one to actually give her.

"You mean a decent human being, not some b-i-t-c-h from this stupid town?" she remarks with a grin, and I chuckle at the fact she still spelled the swear word out when Cody is sleeping.

"That would be correct," I reply as she pulls into her

curved driveway, which leads up to a stunning three-story mansion with a huge fountain made of pebbles out front. The cream exterior and terracotta roof make it feel like we're in Europe, while the lavender flowers, cypress trees, and ceramic tile steps only add to the Mediterranean vibes.

Jumping out of the SUV, I notice a bright red sports car parked to the left that wasn't there when we left. I watch as Bethany gently unbuckles Cody from his car seat, careful not to wake him as a voice booms through the security speakers hidden around the front entrance.

"Who goes there?" The voice is deep, growly, and deafening, but neither of us worry.

"That mothertruckin' man gets on my damn nerves," Bethany grumbles as Cody blinks awake.

"Ah shit," quickly follows through the speakers as Ryan realizes he woke Cody.

Laughter bursts from my chest at their antics and the way Ryan is secretly a big goofball under all his hard, security man exterior. The way he shivers at Bethany's irritated tone is brilliant. They are so in love, it's beautiful and ridiculous all at once.

"You guys make me want to barf. I'm going to run and hide before I catch your lovey-dovey germs." I grin as Ryan opens the front door and races down the steps, wrapping Bethany and Cody in his arms and smothering them in kisses. They are perfection. Everything about them and the bond they share just works.

"Oh, someone's waiting out by the pool for you," Ryan calls just as I reach the door, and I freeze.

It can't be *them*. There's no way. I've heard nothing at all not from Xavier, not from Tobias, and not even from Hunter. Even though Bethany told me they know I'm here, they've been radio silent, and I'm not ready for them to suddenly show up now. Not when I'm happy with the space I have.

I've enjoyed hiding out here and not going to school. The teachers send my work via email, although my gut tells me it's only allowed because the Allstars authorized it. I still haven't heard from my mom, who offers no further details even when I texted her. I asked her to confirm the truth about Archie and now it suddenly feels like my little bubble of peace I've been living in has officially burst.

Someone's here, and I already know what the topic of conversation is going to be—the fact I'm not Eden Grady, but Eden Freemont. Whatever that fucking means.

As I move through the den, the cozy atmosphere

beckons me to put a movie on and relax, but I continue into the open kitchen before stepping out of the tinted glass doors. My eyes instantly fall to the blond guy sitting with his head in his hands by the pool, raking his fingers through his hair as he fidgets nervously.

Archie.

That must be his car outside. Something clearly worked in his favor if he has a car again. Shaking my head, I stop my train of thought. It's no concern of mine.

It's a lot warmer here than it was on the oceanside cliff, so I shrug my jacket off, leaving me in a pair of leggings and a crochet-knitted white t-shirt which I borrowed from Bethany.

My sandals clack against the cobblestone steps, drawing Archie's attention, and my heart hurts the second our eyes meet. Betrayal, loneliness, and the throbbing reminder that he is apparently my family, my twin, pounds in my head.

Quickly rising to his feet, he steps toward me but freezes on the spot, second-guessing his approach, and he should. A part of my brain wants to dissect him, pull him apart, and compare our so-called similarities, but the other part of me can't bear to make it real.

I fold my arms over my chest and stare him down as he

gapes at me, trying to find something to say.

"What are you doing here, Archie?" I ask, deciding to put him out of his misery, and he sighs.

"You wouldn't return my calls or texts, and I didn't know what else to do," he mutters, his arms hanging helplessly at his sides, and I scoff.

"There's a reason for that, Archie."

"I know. I know, Eden. I just…I've been going out of my mind worrying about you, and I didn't know what else to do."

"You fucking wait for me to answer, even if I choose to never speak to you again. You can't force my hand. Don't you think that's already happened to me enough?" I shout, cringing at my language when I know Cody is in the house.

"I know. I'm sorry, Eden." I watch as he takes a deep breath and laces his hands together at the back of his head as he looks to the sky, his eyes squeezing shut.

Four days ago, I would have been doing anything within my power to wipe that pain from his eyes, anything, but I can't see past my own red haze of anger over his lies and betrayal.

He's my brother. My *twin* brother. He knew. I didn't. It's as simple as that.

Who is our actual mother? Or our father? Did my dad die or is he hiding out at the Freemont house doing nothing to reach out to me?

Dropping into the closest wicker chair, I swipe a hand down my face.

"I'm going to need some time, Archie. I don't think I've ever trusted anyone the way I trusted you, and although now it makes sense why, you still lied to me by hiding a secret big enough to shatter my soul." My words make his face scrunch in discomfort, but he doesn't argue, knowing I'm not wrong as my eyes water and I fight the urge to cry. "The ease, safety, and comfort I felt around you is gone. If I'm ever ready to listen to what you have to say, I'll let you know."

"Please, cookie, I—"

"Don't, Archie. Just…don't, okay? I can't deal with this right now," I interrupt, closing my eyes as I tilt my head back to face the sun as I try to clear my mind.

"Nothing has to change, Eden, I…"

Anger boils in my gut, and I'm back up on my feet in an instant, my fists clenching tight as my nails dig into my palms.

"Everything has changed, Archie. Everything! You were

my rock in this toxic town, but now, everything is tainted. You're no different than them with your lies and secrets," I yell, refusing to let my tears escape as my emotions get the better of me.

"No, no, no, no," he chants, stepping toward me, but I hold my hands up in protest, and he pauses barely a foot away from me. "Please, Eden, let me explain," he whispers, his face and neck blotchy as he tries to control his own emotions.

I shake my head. "Nothing you say right now will make a difference." My statement is final, determined, and leaves no room for discussion.

Hanging his head with his hands propped on his hips, he takes a moment before meeting my gaze again, defeat clear in his eyes.

"I'm sorry, Eden. I will be here whenever you're ready to talk." As he slowly moves toward the house, my brain screams for me to ask him to stop, but the words refuse to pass my lips. Just as he wraps his hand around the patio door handle, he glances over his shoulder. "Will I see you at school tomorrow?"

"It's not likely," I answer quickly, and he nods.

"I haven't spoken to them, but I can't imagine they'll

let you hide for much longer."

"I'm not fucking hiding," I growl, and he rubs his lips together nervously as he looks at the ground. "So if you do see those motherfuckers, let them know I couldn't give a shit about kids repeating their parents' woes. I'm sure one dictating Knight is enough for this town. I won't be a pawn in Ilana's games, and I certainly won't be a pawn in Xavier's."

With that, I turn, giving him my back as my fingers tremble.

Fuck. All my cool, calm zen from my walk with Cody and Bethany at the beach is now gone.

The boys of this town really fucking irritate me.

KC KEAN

TWO

Eden

I hit send on my email, submitting my English essay on *To Kill a Mockingbird* to Mrs. Leach, and then I flop back on the bed, a sigh falling from my lips.

An email came through from Mr. Bernard just before I hit send. It's Asheville High's principal informing me, in the most arrogant way possible, that my attendance is expected at school tomorrow.

"You won't graduate…Expulsion is on the table… Don't take this warning lightly. Fuck. Off," I grumble to myself with a sigh, reading over his bullshit words.

Fuck him and fuck the Allstars for pulling his damn puppet strings. It's embarrassing.

Blinking up at the white ceiling of my room at Bethany's, I know I need to figure this shit out, but where do I even begin? Archie is my brother. Who are my parents? Why does Ilana have a vendetta against me? And who the fuck killed my dad?

It seems like whenever I get one step closer to understanding why I was brought to Knight's Creek, they have already made a move to send me three steps back.

I hate that I pushed Archie further away yesterday, but I just can't deal with the pain he causes me. I know he has some answers, and the look on his face told me he's willing to share, but how much will I actually believe anyway? I dread to consider what else he could lie to me about, even if a part of me still wants to trust him without question.

I also need to figure out what I'm actually going to do with my life for the immediate future. I can't keep staying here. As nice as Bethany and Ryan are, I'm in their way and they have their hands full with Cody. They don't need to worry about taking care of a teenager or the drama I come with.

Fuck. I have a strong urge to bury my head in the

sand and pretend my life didn't go from bad to worse, but my dad would be turning in his grave if I let Ilana or the Allstars break me.

They obviously tried to break him, my mom, God, even Archie's parents—or my parents? I don't know—but I won't let myself become another one of their victims. I don't break easily, and that won't change for these psychotic fuckers.

My phone vibrates on the bedside table, and I roll my head to the side, staring at the offending device as I find the energy to get up. Grabbing my phone, I feel my heart stall in my chest as "Mom" flashes across the screen.

Scrambling to answer her call, I swing my legs over the side of the bed as I sit up. As much as I want to hear her voice, a part of me is furious she's taken so long to get in touch with me.

I don't speak as I hit the green button, waiting for her to talk first. She owes me that. Silence fills the line as I take in the room around me. Pale yellow walls make the space feel homey and cozy, and the white furniture and double sleigh bed sitting in the center of the room make it the perfect guest room.

God, it feels more like home than the Freemont house,

even if it isn't beachfront.

"Eden? Are you there?" My mother's voice filters through the phone, her tone a mixture of annoyance and concern.

"Is it true?" I ask, crossing my legs as I get straight to the point, disregarding any pleasantries. I'm sure she's seen my many messages and heard my voicemails repeating the same thing with my pitch ranging from quiet anger to enraged yelling.

"Eden, what's been going on?" she asks after a long pause, playing coy, and it pisses me the fuck off.

"Mom, I need you to tell me if it's true," I repeat slowly with exhaustion, the weight of the words heavy on my tongue as my pulse throbs in my ears. I'm greeted with silence for what feels like an eternity until she utters one single word.

"Yes."

It's barely above a whisper, yet the ramifications are earth shaking. I struggle to swallow, choking on any response I may have had. *Finally* hearing a piece of truth from her is overwhelming me more than I expected.

Catching my breath, I bite my lip hard as my eyes focus on my trembling hand.

"So, just for clarification, you forced me to move to your toxic hometown and stay in some stranger's house until I found out I was living with my fucking *twin* brother, all while keeping this to yourself?" Before she can even respond, I find all the anger that's been building inside me. Continuing before she can get a word out. I stand from the bed and pace beside it. "Do you know someone wrote a fucking fake obituary for me and I don't even know if the details are correct? Who is actually my mother and father, Mom?"

"I'm so sorry, Eden," she murmurs, repeating the same apology as Archie, and it rubs me the wrong way.

"If you were sorry, you would explain it to me, Jennifer," I bite out, and she sighs heavily through the phone.

"It's not as simple as that, Eden. There is very little I can say."

I slam my hand down on the chest of drawers as I reach the bottom of the bed in anger as she offers me no further details into my actual life.

"You're lying! Screw the consequences, Mom. Tell me something, anything…please," I plead desperately.

"The consequences are your life, Eden. I can deal with you hating me as long as it keeps you breathing."

I pause at the rawness in her words. I can understand her reasoning, but it still leaves me no better off. Dropping back down onto the bed, I feel even more alone than ever before. I thought…I thought this would be the end of the secrets with my mom, but she's giving me nothing.

"Tell me something real about who I am or why we were separated," I whisper, desperate for anything to hang on to.

"You know who you are, Eden. No matter what, your father and I will forever be your parents. Richard and Anabel are amazing. I miss them so much. I know you're safe with them. You'll *always* be safe with them."

Wait? Doesn't she know?

"Mom, Anabel died…from cancer. It's just Archie and Richard at the Freemont house." I hear her breath hitch as my words sink in.

"Oh God, no," she sobs, her voice thick with emotion, and I can feel her pain from here. "Poor Richard, and Archie too. Dear God. I love you, Eden, so, so much. I'm sorry I've been a terrible person at showing it. I wish I'd proven it to you sooner." Her cries get louder as my own eyes gloss over.

I don't know what to say or how to comfort her, and it

boggles my mind how the point of this call has completely flipped on its head. I know it's no use pushing her for more when she's in this state, full of self-loathing and pity.

"I'll let you go, Mom. I know it's a lot to take in, but can I ask you one more question before you go?"

"Of course, I just can't promise I can answer it." I strain my ears, hoping to hear anything around her, but there is nothing but silence coming through the phone.

"I know there is always something bigger at play in this town. Were you forced to separate Archie and me?"

Silence greets me. I even have to check my phone to make sure she's still there when she offers me another one-word response that holds a lot of weight.

"Yes."

When I eventually drag my mopey ass downstairs, I hear Bethany in the massive open kitchen. It's her favorite place in the house, so I always know where to find her, but this time I just wanted to sneak in, eat, and sulk back to my room.

This kitchen is the kitchen of my dreams, with all white cabinets and marble countertops, stainless steel top-of-the-line appliances, and a center island that's the perfect focal point where everyone instinctively gathers. The far wall is lined with windows, offering a perfect view of the outdoors while lighting the room.

"Hey, Eden. I'm sneaking some Ben and Jerry's while Cody is napping. Do you want some?" she inquires, and my desire to sneak away is instantly replaced with the need to devour ice cream with her.

"What flavor are we talking about here?" I question as I find her bent over with her head stuck in the freezer. She pops up with an unopened tub of Phish Food. "You have yourself a deal." I grin, my body already relaxing as I grab two spoons from the drawer at my side. I don't want Bethany to see my anger or sadness, I've already put her in a bad enough situation as it is, and I don't want to cause a rift between her and Hunter, so I'm working hard to keep my emotions under lock and key. Sometimes, though, it's just easier said than done.

"Come sit," Bethany murmurs with a wave of her hand, and I climb onto the stool opposite her, a sigh passing my lips as I try to relax. "So, I had the pleasure of a delightful phone call from my brother earlier," she states, spooning the delicious ice cream into her mouth as I freeze in place.

I try to act unaffected by the mention of Hunter, but I can't help it. Hurt and warmth fills my veins at the mere mention of his name. Wetting my lips, I try to take a discreet deep breath, but apparently I fail because Bethany shakes her head at me with a roll of her eyes.

"That sounds nice," I finally say, shoving far too much ice cream into my mouth as soon as I do, instantly getting brain freeze from the overload of chocolatey goodness.

She scoffs in response. "It was anything but nice. Have I ever mentioned that he's a dick?" I almost choke on my ice cream as she practically growls, and I'm afraid to ask what happened, but there's no need to because she continues on. "Can you believe he called to tell me I *have* to send you back to the Freemont house? And that I *have* to make sure you know you are expected at school tomorrow?"

Her words don't surprise me, not even a little bit, especially since I received the email earlier from the principal.

"It's okay," I mutter, scrunching my face in annoyance as I try not to react.

"No it fucking isn't," she bites out, taking a huge spoonful of ice cream in anger, and I just gape at her. "You better believe I told that little shit that *he* might think he's the boss of this town just because he's an Asheville, with his two idiot friends, but he will never, and I mean *never*, have control over me or you."

With a heavy sigh, I place my spoon on the countertop. "I don't want to come between you two, Bethany. I know you mean a lot to each other. I'll get my things and—"

"Are you not hearing me? I told that fuck nugget to fuck off. I'm the older sibling here, and that trumps everything." She waves her spoon around as she talks, flicking ice cream everywhere, but I keep my mouth shut as I sit in complete awe of her.

"I hear you, Bethany, but he's your brother. Take it from someone who didn't know she had one until three days ago—trust each other and be there for one and other no matter what. You and Hunter have a bond, and I want no part of damaging that. I feel played," I admit, watching as she gives me a soft smile.

"I promise you, me standing my ground is nothing new in our dynamic. Hunter is always trying to overrule me, but we both had the same childhood. If anything, he got out sooner, and *I* don't act the way he does." There's more to that statement than I can comprehend right now, and I don't wish to know anything more about Hunter or his stupid Allstar brothers. "There must be a reason he called about it though."

"Well, we're in Knight's Creek, remember? There will be some twisted secrets and lies intertwined amongst it all, forcing everyone's hand as usual," I grumble, rolling my eyes, but I know it's true.

"That is so fucking true, Eden."

A cry startles me as the baby monitor on the counter echoes around the room. Bethany appears disappointed and exhausted all at once as she gazes longingly at the ice cream, clearly hoping to have had more time to dig into my problems.

Before she can do anything, I'm up and out of my seat, heading for Cody's nursery as she sings her thanks from behind me, her mouth full of ice cream again.

Stepping into Cody's blue and green nursery, filled with all different kinds of toys and pictures, I instantly look at the handsome little blond as he offers a sleepy smile and reaches his hands out for me.

"Hey, Cody," I murmur, lifting him into my arms, and he clings to me like a monkey—his signature move when he's still waking up—and I revel in it.

Nothing makes me feel better than a hug from this little

guy. I somehow seem to forget all my worries and concerns when he's in my arms. I need to figure out how to bottle him up. I've never really been around young children before, but his pure innocence calls to my darkened soul.

I take a seat in the rocking chair by the window, sitting in silence as Cody wakes. While I watch the cypress trees blowing in the wind, I try to wrap my head around the fact I'm bringing trouble to Bethany's door.

That was never my intention.

"Hey, I heard my little guy crying," Ryan says as he steps into the room. Cody's little blue eyes widen with joy when he sees his dad, and he immediately jumps from my lap.

"I left Bethany to eat ice cream so I could steal his cuddles," I murmur with a smile as I watch them embrace. Ryan looks over Cody's head to meet my gaze and grins before clearing his throat. They look like two peas in a pod when they are together like this.

"I kind of know what's going on with you and the stupid fucking Allstars, but I just want to reiterate that you can stay here as long as you need. I hate this town, and I know what it feels like to not have grown up in it. We don't see it the way others do, all the manipulation and the complete shit show that this town is."

His words bounce around in my mind. I never considered that others wouldn't see things the way I do. All the lies, secrets, and orders are natural for the people who spend their whole lives walking around wearing rose-colored glasses.

"Thanks, Ryan." I offer him an appreciative smile before slipping from the room.

I feel stuck between a rock and a hard place right now.

I know I should leave, and I need to formulate a plan, but I want one more day in the bubble that is Bethany's home pretending like the outside world doesn't exist. When I run, I'll go back to being all alone again.

Taking the stairs two at a time, I step into my room and close the door behind me as my phone vibrates on the nightstand. As much as I don't want to speak to anyone, I can't help but look to see who it's from, and I find three new text messages from Charlie.

Charlie: Please come back, Eden. I miss you.

Charlie: No one will tell me where you are. Please, can you just let me know you're

safe?

Charlie: I broke it off with Archie. I was waiting to tell you, but I thought you should know I'm not okay with all of this.

Fuck.

Now I'm fucking everything up for her too. How do I always make a mess of things, even when I'm trying my hardest not to?

TOXIC CREEK

THREE

Xavier

The hustle and bustle at Pete's does nothing to improve my mental state. People laughing, babies crying, and the clanging of pots irritates the hell out of me. I want to scream at the top of my lungs for every motherfucker to get out so I can think. Think, in peace without all their noise and distractions.

Sitting in our usual booth, I try to smother my annoyance as I remember the last time we were here. Eden sat across from me as she took a call from her mom who warned her about the Knights. Me. My mother. My family.

She barely hesitated as she ignored her mother's warnings, and at the time, it stirred something inside me.

And what did I do? I shit all over it. I tore it all down piece by piece before I could even figure out what I felt. She should have listened to her fucking mother. I *am* my mother's child, after all.

"Three waters and a double stack of pancakes for each of you. Are you sure you don't want anything, Xavier?" Linda asks as she places our food on the table, pulling me from my thoughts.

I shake my head. "I'm good. Thanks, Linda," I murmur, reaching for my water, and I don't miss the concern written on her face as her blue eyes stare me down, her frown lines appearing as she does.

"Don't worry about it, Linda. He's beating himself up for being an absolute cunt. He'll get over it. He always does. Don't you, Knight?" Tobias remarks before stuffing a mouthful of syrup soaked pancake into his mouth with a smug-ass look on his face. I don't respond since I can't find a strong enough argument to stand by.

Clearing her throat, Linda ruffles her short blonde hair, the pixie cut making her look at least ten years younger than she is.

"Well, you know we're always here if you need to talk, but I do hope it doesn't involve that pretty blonde, Eden. I like her. I can already see the pain in her eyes. We don't need to add to that, now do we?"

She saunters off, not realizing the sucker punch she just gave me with her words, but I do nothing, say nothing.

Hunter continues to stare down at his plate, offering nothing to the conversation, but at least he isn't throwing insults my way—although his silence is never a good sign.

The front door flies open, the glass vibrating as laughter and shouts fill the whole diner, and the cackle I hear tells me exactly who it is—KitKat and Roxy. Great.

"Oh look, *your* new girl is here," Hunter sneers, finally breaking his silence, and I flip him off as I take a sip of my water. I don't miss the way he says *your* girl and not *our* girl like he did with Eden, and it feels like another kick to the stomach.

"What's wrong, X, don't like the truth? Didn't you claim her at the party this weekend? You know, when you went ahead with your shitty plan without discussing it with either of us?" Tobias adds, stabbing his fork in my direction as he gets his point across, and I sigh.

"We've been over this," I retort, but that only makes

him scoff. Before he can respond, the giggles get closer as the fucking party arrives, led by the two worst gold diggers in town.

"Xavier, baby, you've been avoiding me at school again. I don't like it," Roxy singsongs, dropping down into my lap with her tits barely covered and her skirt rising up her thighs. I glare at her before pushing her off me, and I almost laugh at her comical expression as she falls ass first to the floor, a yelp escaping her lips as she does.

The diner quiets around us as the other customers glance in our direction, or more specifically, Roxy's. She's splayed out on the floor with her miniskirt around her waist, showing her panties, and her crop top nearly revealing her tits too. She's a true spectacle.

"Xavier," she whines, at the exact same time KitKat does, but the guys with them just snicker, which doesn't surprise me. Billy and his friends on the football team are not part of our inner circle for a reason.

"Fuck off," I growl, not watching as KitKat helps Roxy to her feet before placing her palms flat on the table.

I'm about to respond, but Hunter beats me to it. "Can't you take a fucking hint?" he snarls with fire in his eyes as annoyance and anger build within him. It's rare to see

Hunter like this, but everyone knows when you do, it's in your best interest to back the fuck off.

I'm ruthless on the daily, while Hunter locks all his anger up until it's too late, and Tobias...well, Tobias plays everything off with cutthroat jokes and insults, throwing his weight around when necessary, but I don't think I've ever seen him lash out before.

Without a word, they all sulk off to a table on the other side of the diner where Linda is waiting, a scowl firmly in place, but I turn my attention away from them, not offering the group any more of my attention.

"What's wrong, Xavier? Trouble in paradise?" Tobias jibes as he pushes his empty plate away with an innocent look on his face.

I shake my head. "You're being a dick. If you want Eden so badly, I'm not stopping you," I grind out, making him squint at me.

"Are you fucking stupid? We stick together, brother. Through and through. It's your motto more than ours," he spits before scoffing. "It just pisses me off a little that *you made the fucking bed*, Xavier, and now we all have to fucking lie in it." He glares at me, his jaw tight.

"Ain't that the truth," Hunter mutters, and my hands

fist in my lap as I take in the raw emotion written on their faces.

"I don't know what else you want me to say."

"That's the problem, Xavier. I don't really want you to say shit. Every time you do, things seem to get worse." He slams his fist on the table, rattling the dishes and spilling water from the glasses. "Everything has always been a group decision, a team plan, but your mother said jump, and you asked how high," Hunter continues.

Bracing my elbows on the table, I drop my head into my hands as I rub my temples.

"Do you want to get out of this town? Do you want to leave it all behind without a backward glance? Because that's what she was offering. She knows about Ohio State. Either I toe the line with her or end up stuck here in Knight's Creek forever."

"That's bullshit and you know it," Hunter counters. This same argument, again and again, is starting to get on my fucking nerves. "You took the easy way out. Why is that?" he challenges, and it irks me that I'm allowing my emotions to show.

Sitting back in the booth, I remove my hands from my face and glance out the window, acting impassive as always, and Tobias snickers.

"You've shut him down again, Hunter. He's not going to admit to shit now."

"What's that supposed to mean?" I growl.

"It means you don't even see yourself playing God with our lives just like your mother does," Tobias replies with a smile as he leans forward on the table, his words cutting like a knife to the chest, just like he wanted.

Any response I have is interrupted by the sound of my phone ringing on the table beside me, my mother's name flashing across the screen.

"Speak of the devil, and she shall arrive," Hunter mumbles as I contemplate answering, but I would rather deal with her wrath than their butthurt feelings right now.

I hit the green button to accept the call and lift my phone to my ear.

"Mother," I greet, waiting for her voice to grate through the line.

"Xavier, do you want to explain why Eden Grady still isn't where I want her to be? A toy is not a toy if you aren't playing with it."

The thunderous expressions on both Hunter's and Tobias's faces tell me they can hear every word she's saying, even with all the noise of the diner surrounding us. At least I won't have to repeat myself.

"We know exactly where she is," I respond blandly, even though my heart pounds in my chest.

"Hmm, so do I. How are Bethany and baby Cody?"

My blood chills at the underlying tone in her voice, and Hunter's face starts to turn red with anger. Nobody threatens them. Nobody. Not even my own mother.

Maybe I should have had this whole stance with Eden, too, when it came to this bitch, but like Tobias said, I already made my bed in haste. Now I have to stick with it.

"What do you want, Mother?" I bite out, scrubbing the back of my neck as Tobias remains deathly still.

"I want her back at Asheville High, and I want to watch her break under your touch. How did she take the news about her dear brother, by the way?"

"I'll get it under control," I grind out, and she hums down the line.

"Don't let me down, Xavier. You know what's at stake."

The line goes dead, but it takes me a moment to pull the phone away from my ear as I try to get my emotions in check.

I hate being under her thumb, but here we are.

"I swear to God, Xavier. If she goes anywhere near—"

"She won't," I growl, shutting off Hunter's rant as I raise my hand. "I'll fucking make sure of it, okay? I won't let anything happen to them."

"Like you wouldn't let anything happen to Eden?" Tobias chimes in, snickering in annoyance, and I want to beat the shit out of him. He's not fucking helping the situation right now.

"Let's hope she takes the hints we already sent via Mr. Bernard and Bethany, and she shows up tomorrow."

"And if she doesn't?" Hunter asks, and I shake my head.

"Then we fucking go to Bethany's and pull her out kicking and screaming whether she likes it or not," I answer, and they both nod in understanding—probably because they just want to fucking see her. They have no self-control at all.

I'm dead to her anyway. The look in her eyes when she muttered those words to me before she turned and walked away from all the drama that surrounded us will be forever etched into my brain.

I go to stand, ready to leave, but the next person who walks through the diner doors makes me pause, and I lean farther back in my seat as he heads straight toward us, dropping down beside Tobias as he joins the table uninvited.

This fucker knew. He knew all along. Which explains a lot actually.

"We are all so fucking screwed because of you, Knight," Archie growls, his arms braced on the table as he stares me down, pain swirling in his blue eyes that remind me a lot of Eden's. Another piece of the jigsaw we were all missing.

"There's nothing for me to be screwed over, Arch—"

He slams his hand on the table, making the plates and cups rattle, he leans forward even more as he tries to get closer to me, his face turning red as he does.

"Shut the fuck up, Xavier. Do you even know what you have done? I told you that day you showed up at my house that I choose *her*. Every. Damn. Time. Not you, not the team, not my own fucking life. *Her.* Did I know five minutes before she turned up at my house? Yeah, yeah, I did. Did I see the fucking despair in her eyes? Yes, which is why she matters above all else. My sister is learning the hard way how twisted and fucked up the people in this whole town are, and you had to let that information come from someone else. Did your mother tell you to do it?" His voice breaks a little at the end, his emotions getting the better of him as I stare him down.

I watch as a vein pops on his forehead as anger and desperation play out across his face. Hunter and Tobias just glance between us, not getting involved or shutting him down for talking to one of us like this, and I know deep down it's because I fucking deserve it. But he doesn't need to know that. I need to remind him of his place, just like everyone else. Clearly, Eden made us all a little fucking weaker, and I refuse to let it continue.

"I suggest you get the fuck up from my table and out of my sight before I remind you who you're talking to," I state calmly, matching his stance as I lean forward on my arms. "I don't give a fuck about you or your so-called *sister*, Archie. You've said your piece, which is much more than others would get, but now you need to leave. You knew too. Remember that, Archie. You said it yourself. You can blame me, I couldn't give a shit, but you were at fault also."

He glares at me, as do Hunter and Tobias, and when he sees I mean every single word that came out of my mouth, he slams his fists down on the table before standing.

"I intend to be a barrier between you and her. I warned her about you when she arrived. I'll protect her from you now. You have my fucking word on that, Knight."

I watch as he storms from the diner, shoulder checking anyone in his path, and all I can think about is how I hope he means it, because there's no stepping back from the path I've taken now. She's going to need somebody.

TOXIC CREEK

FOUR
Eden

"Again, again, De-de!" Cody screams, splashing the water as his arm floaties keep him afloat in the pool, and I grin. I love it out here, with the palm trees and free-form pool continuing the Mediterranean vibes out back.

The second this little blond-haired, blue-eyed rascal woke, he completely disrupted my sunbathing session, but I can't even seem to complain. He has this infectious way of putting a smile on my face, boosting my mood, and right now, I'm feeling extra good.

I didn't show up to school today like the Allstars clearly wanted, and I felt empowered with Bethany's backing. We spent the day doing absolutely nothing except gossiping, reading, getting someone to come and give us matching pale pink mani-pedis, and soaking up the rays of the sun.

I wanted to make the most of my time with her, especially since I've decided I can't stay here anymore. She's important to me. I won't put them at risk, and I won't submit to this damn town, so tonight, I leave. No looking back, and no worrying about the consequences.

"Say please, Cody." Bethany laughs as I scoop him up into my arms and he shakes his blond curls, sending water everywhere.

"Please! Please!" he squeals, and I happily oblige, lifting him out of the water with my hands under his arms before dropping him into the pool. His armbands stop him from fully submerging, causing a little wave of water to whoosh over his head instead, and he cries out in delight, frantically rubbing his eyes so he can find me again.

"It's time for a break, little man. We can have ice cream," Bethany calls out from where she's perched on the edge of the pool, and he kicks his little legs as hard as he can to get to her. There's no complaint on his lips because he has to get out since ice cream is on the table.

Swiping my hair off my face, I take a moment to enjoy the sun. The pool is the perfect temperature, not too hot, and not too cold, but I'm definitely ready to dry off on a lounger with an ice-cold drink, and ice cream sounds perfect since we've been out here for some time.

"I'll grab the ice cream if you save me a spot on the loungers, Cody," I offer, and he claps his hands as Bethany lifts him onto the tiled side with her.

"I'd say that's a deal," Bethany says with a chuckle, and I couldn't agree more.

Climbing out of the pool, I squeeze as much excess water from my hair as possible as I step into my flip-flops. Otherwise, I'd slip on my ass as soon as I stepped onto the kitchen floor with wet feet.

The house is quiet as I head inside. I know Ryan is at work, holding some big security meeting, and their personal chef has already left for the day, so it's just the three of us. I wonder if we could kick Ryan out and I could keep the pair of them to myself?

The grin that takes over my face instantly vanishes when I remember everything else going on outside of this bubble and why that wouldn't actually be safe for them.

Safe for me? Yes. Ryan is amazing at what he does, but I won't put them at risk.

Pulling open the heavy freezer door, I stare in awe as I see the variety of popsicles and ice cream flavors available. I should have probably asked them what they wanted before I came in, but I didn't expect there to be over ten different options to choose from. Chocolate, strawberry, raspberry. You name it, they've got it.

Spying a blue cooler beside the freezer, I decide to take a few of each to let Cody and Bethany choose for themselves. It'll give me a minute to decide too.

I close the lid on the cooler and lift it over my arm as I nudge the freezer door shut with my foot, then I take the same path back to the pool area.

As I near the open glass doors leading to the outside area, my skin prickles and goosebumps trail up my arms as I hear Cody laughing nearby. He doesn't sound like he's in danger, so why would I feel…I freeze on the spot, the reason for my body's reaction glaring back at me.

Hunter. Tobias. Xavier.

Fuck. I should have known the Allstars wouldn't have let me go against their *rules* without making an appearance. I was naïve for feeling safe and protected here.

I gulp hard, trailing my gaze over each of them, taking in the three hot guys who had slowly started to get under my skin before they continued to turn my life on its axis. Again.

I refuse to feel vulnerable in my black two-piece swimsuit when I feel their eyes on me.

Tobias sits on the lounger I was heading for, shirtless, with his top tucked into the waistband of his denim shorts. His black wool hat is firmly in place as he stretches out, his blue eyes burning every inch of my body as he stares at me, but I can't pinpoint what he's feeling.

Xavier stands with his arms folded over his chest, his reflective aviators in place. His biceps bulge beneath the sleeves of his navy top as I watch his jaw grind from here. He's clearly unhappy with me, but what's new?

Hunter's blond hair is brushed back off his face as though he's been running his fingers through it. His white shirt clings to his body as his denim jeans hang dangerously low on his hips. I watch as he darts his gaze between Bethany and me, holding Cody in his arms as he tries to decide where to aim his wrath, but I can't help but melt a little as he smiles down at Cody, not letting the current standoff affect the little guy.

Straightening my spine and tilting my nose up in the air a little, I saunter outside, gripping the small cooler in my hand as I walk to the right of the pool. I feel their eyes on me with every step I take as I purposely take the long way around to reach Bethany.

"I told you to leave, Hunter," Bethany mumbles, trying to keep a smile on her face as she does so she doesn't upset Cody, but he simply scoffs. She glances my way with guilt in her eyes, but this isn't her fault.

"And I'm quite sure I told you her ass had better be at school today, but here we are." He doesn't take his eyes off Cody as he speaks, letting Cody tickle his hand, none the wiser to the tension surrounding him.

"*Her* has a name, and I already spelled out exactly what I thought of your tone yesterday. That doesn't give you the right to show up here. This is *my* home, Hunter, *mine*. You don't get to come in here and disrespect me."

Bethany jabs her finger around as she talks, standing her ground, and as much as I love her defending me, I don't want to cause any tension between them. Maybe one day I'll be able to be selfish and let people destroy their relationships with others to protect me, but I just can't do it. It's not who I am. Maybe it's because my rock was always my dad. We didn't even argue, and now he's gone.

I have so many regrets already, I don't even know where to begin with them.

Dropping the cooler at my feet, I reach out and squeeze Bethany's shoulder, but she doesn't budge.

"It's okay, Bethany, honestly. They can say whatever it is they came here to say, and then they can leave. Their egos won't let them leave us alone until we hear their thoughts and opinions, so we may as well get on with it."

"Are you sure?" Bethany inquires, folding her hands over her chest as she continues to face Hunter. She looks at me out of the corner of her eye and I nod, making her sigh with concern before she turns her gaze to Hunter. "Fine. I'll take Cody inside, but I'm going to stand by the door. One wrong move from you, mister, and I'll kick you out on your f-u-c-k-i-n-g ass. Understood?"

She glares at him until he eventually nods and whispers in Cody's ear before passing him over to Bethany, who pinches Hunter's arm as he hands Cody over. He frowns as she smiles sweetly, and I have to bite back a chuckle. She is quite possibly the best big sister I have ever seen in all existence.

Nobody speaks as we watch her retreat indoors, cooler

in hand, and true to her word, she pulls Cody's high chair over by the door and takes a seat beside him.

"What bullshit would you like to talk about today?" I prompt, shrugging casually as I try to remain calm, even though my heart is pounding wildly in my chest as my nerves try to get the better of me.

"I only deal with facts, Eden. If you don't like them, that isn't really my problem, now is it?" Xavier sneers, and my hands instantly fist at my sides. The telltale bite of my fingernails digging into my palms calms me, so I don't start swinging at him.

Motherfucker.

His stance hasn't changed at all since I first walked out. I can practically feel the ice wall he's built around himself as his words continue to cut deeper than I care to admit.

Clearing my throat, I take a page out of his book, ignoring his question just like he did mine. "Are you going to enlighten me as to why you're here, or am I going to have to guess? I'm never really sure with you, especially since you only give information when it suits you and never out of the goodness of your heart."

"Well, I see you two still love to be at each other's throats. Excellent," Tobias comments, clapping his hands as he grins at us. "But we're here to get you back to Asheville High starting tomorrow, Eden. If you don't feel comfortable returning to Archie's, you could stay with us."

I stare at him like he's grown a second head, slightly surprised to see a glimmer of hope in his eyes. A bubble of laughter passes my lips before I can stop it. "Is that a fucking joke? I don't know what's the worst of two evils. I've already answered you regarding returning to school. Do I need to repeat myself? Because if so, I will record myself saying it and hit the play button in the future. I don't have the time or energy to go around and around with you guys in another one of your games, and I *certainly* don't need to spend any unnecessary moments in your presence either." Glancing over my shoulder, I see Bethany watching us still, her hands on her hips as she nods at me, letting me know she's here.

"Sassy. How original. I don't think you'll like the consequences all that much if you don't, Eden," Xavier states in a bored tone, and it gets under my skin more than a growl would. His nonchalant attitude irritates me. I know it's a fucking lie.

"I think I've had enough of Knight's Creek's consequences, don't you? I don't get to be with my mom, someone here was responsible for my father's death, and surprise, I also have a twin brother and someone threatening me. Three strikes and I'm out, right? That's what I'm going with at least, so if you're done, you can leave."

Hunter sighs and reaches out to place his hand on my shoulder, just like I did to Bethany, but I quickly step back, watching as his arm drops to his side, secretly missing his heat instantly.

"Eden, don't you think it's a good idea to do as you're told since you literally just said someone here was responsible for your dad's murder? It doesn't seem wise for you to play with fire, especially not in your position."

Gaping at him, I bite my lip, trying to rein in my anger, but fuck it.

"Why? Are you going to do to me what was done to my dad? Do you need a play-by-play of what I was told, or were you there? Hmm?" I goad, stepping closer to him, my pulse ringing in my ears as I watch him shake his head.

"Eden, don't be—"

"Maybe. Are you willing to risk it, Eden Freemont?" Xavier inserts, cutting Hunter off with his sharp tone, leaving me speechless.

Was he…did he…I think I may be sick. I want to push him for more, but I know he'll only push back harder, and a dark part of me wants that, to drown in pain.

My hands tremble as I step forward, bringing us toe-to-toe, and his hand instantly goes to my throat, squeezing just enough to try and assert dominance over me.

"You are one sick motherfucker," I growl, my chest rising rapidly as I feel myself starting to hyperventilate, my mind swirling with the endless possibilities. "Do it then. Show me what was done to my dad. It seems like a much better option than being under your thumb," I bite out, water gathering in my eyes, but I refuse to give them the satisfaction of seeing my emotions get the better of me.

I am practically shaking from head to toe as Xavier stares at me in surprise, but before he can respond, Tobias wraps his arm around Xavier's chest from behind, stopping his movement, and Xavier releases me.

"That's enough, X," he warns before settling his gaze on me. "School tomorrow, Eden, or I'll come here and get you myself, threat or no threat. Don't push me. This is your final warning before we take matters into our own hands. You feel me?" His tone leaves no room for misunderstanding, but I say nothing as I watch them saunter toward Bethany. Not one of them looks back, so sure they have me exactly where they want me.

Well, fuck them. No one tries to spike fear in me to get me to do what they want. I've had enough. I'm done.

Tonight, I run.

TOXIC CREEK

KC KEAN

FIVE
Eden

Checking my room one last time for any stray items, I throw the duffel bag over my shoulder and pull the door shut behind me. It's a little after seven in the evening, and Cody is in bed. I already kissed his cheek goodnight, and I know Ryan and Bethany will be in the den, relaxing with a movie playing.

Taking the stairs slowly, my emotions at war in my mind, I drop my duffel bag by the front door as I go in search of the forever happy couple. Their love is like magic. They are so in sync with each other and understand their partner's needs. It's what love truly looks like. Even my parents weren't on this level, as if there was always something missing.

Heading down the hall, I glance at the family photos lining the walls, I can hear their laughter, leading me to the den just as I expected. I peek my head around the door and find them sprawled out on the sofa, with Bethany using Ryan as her personal giant pillow.

"Hey, sorry to interrupt. I'm going to head out," I murmur, forcing a smile to my lips as they glance my way. I don't offer any more of an explanation, but I see the suspicious crinkle between Ryan's eyebrows as Bethany smiles at me.

"No worries. You have all the codes, right?"

"Right," I answer, pushing my hands into my back pockets as I nervously glance around. "Thanks, Bethany. For everything, you've been amazing to me," I add, making her sit up, shaking her head.

"Always, girl. I wanted a sister, not some stupid fucking brother who thinks he's the don," she says with a grin, and I chuckle along with her.

Nodding awkwardly, I turn on my heel, my Converse squeaking on the hardwood floor as I call out another goodbye over my shoulder. I stop by the front door, sighing as I lift the duffel bag over my shoulder, when the sound of someone clearing their throat startles me.

Whirling around, I find Ryan leaning against the wall with a knowing look on his face as he nods at the bag in my hand, his demeanor surprisingly relaxed.

"You won't be back tonight then, huh?" he comments without judgment in his voice as he meets my gaze, and I offer a subtle shake of my head. His eyes light up with recognition. "Well, just know I'm not going to change the security details here. So if you ever need to return, it'll be as simple as your license plate registering or the security code, okay?"

"Will she be mad?" I ask, hating the thought of making her upset with me, but he shakes his head.

"At you? No. At the overall situation? Hell yeah. Have you met her?" I grin at his words, knowing they are one-hundred-percent true, as I unlock the door. "I mean it, Eden. This will always be a safe place for you. We are all too aware of what this town is capable of and how the people in charge operate."

"Thanks, Ryan," I whisper, stepping out into the cool night air. I've never felt more sure of my decision as I do now. These are good people. They have clearly had their fair share of Knight's Creek drama, and they don't need mine as well.

The door clicks shut behind me as I rush to my G-Wagon, climb in, and throw my bag on the floorboard of the passenger seat. My hands tremble a little, my nerves trying to get the better of me as I think of any repercussions from the Allstars or Ilana I would face for running.

Put the car in drive, Eden, and just go. Go.

I'm not going back to Archie's, and I'm certainly not going to stay with the fucking Allstars. That will only make me look weaker. I'll call my mom once I cross the border and am out of this fucking town.

Taking a deep breath, I start the engine, releasing a sigh as I push through my internal battle and slowly drive down the gravel drive. The gates open as the system recognizes my license plate, and I take a left, not really sure if that's the best way or not, but I'm all for finding out.

Linking my phone to the Bluetooth, I hit the start button, murmuring a quick, "Call mom," before I wait for the call to connect. My heart sinks a little when it instantly goes to voicemail, her voice filtering through the car. I try a few more times as I drive away from Bethany's house, continuing to get my mom's voicemail again and again, my heart sinking a little each time.

The sun is slowly starting to set in the distance, and I almost want to turn toward it and watch it set just one more time over Freemont Beach, but I have to stay focused. Coming to a stop at the next red light, I quickly turn on the sound system, my Spotify account linking instantly, and my latest playlist, "Fuck the Allstars," continues to blare through the speakers.

Demi Lovato's "Dancing with the Devil" filters through, resonating so deeply in my soul I think I might cry at the pain that transcends the song. I notice an SUV in my rearview mirror, but I don't think anything of it as the light changes to green and I take the road that will lead up and around town near Mount James and the waterfalls. By choosing the winding streets, I'll avoid going directly through town so no one will see me.

It's pretty quiet out in this direction, with pretty flowers and trees lining the road as I sing along to the radio. The only cars in the area are likely heading for a late evening hike or simply coming home from one, except...for the SUV that's still behind me.

I try to pay a little more attention to it, knowing it's the same black Jaguar SUV I've seen both Xavier and Ilana in—just like the one that was parked outside of our home back in White River when I was practically ran out of town. Apparently, the Knights have extra expensive taste, but my main concern right now is if it's one of them and if they are following me.

Don't be so ridiculous, Eden. It's just a fucking SUV.

Continuing along the road, I turn Demi up a little more as I pass one of my favorite waterfall spots. It's a shame this town is so stunning. I could have loved the area, just not the people in it.

I pick up a little speed since there isn't a car in front of me, and the SUV does the same. Taking a left, I head toward the other waterfalls, since I'm familiar with this road, to see if they take the same turn, which they do. It could be a total coincidence. It may not even be a Knight. It's probably some couple going for a hike with their cute dog or something, but they are not close enough for me to tell if it's a man or a woman driving, never mind if they seem familiar or not.

Stop overreacting, Eden. Xavier didn't mean that shit earlier... right?

The hair on the back of my neck stands on end as I

remember his taunt from earlier. *Are you willing to risk it, Eden Freemont?* The questions and emotions I have echo in my mind, distracting me when I really need to focus on the here and now. Whether I'm being tailed or not is more important than how the Allstars make me feel.

I test the SUV again when I take the turn away from the parking lot. My palms feel sweaty and my heart stalls as the SUV does the same, following me down the winding road that leads to the right.

I'm not too familiar with this part of town, but the road continues down the far side of the national park, the trees, flowers, and dirt paths all starting to look the same. I don't feel as confident as I did before, but I see a fork in the road, and I search for a street sign, not missing the complete irony of the current situation.

The smell of California Asters filters into the SUV as they line the side of the road, reminding me of the trail I took with Charlie and Archie, and I glance in the rearview mirror again, hoping for the SUV to be gone, but unfortunately it's not.

I feel sick. My gut tells me something isn't right as I try to gain more speed, touching forty-five miles per hour, but the SUV remains close. My gaze continues to flicker in the rearview mirror as the music blasts around me on repeat.

Spying a sign directly ahead, I read that the left leads to the Pacific Coast Highway, while the right will circle me back around to Knight's Creek.

I need to make a decision. Do I turn back and face their facade of a perfect town with the perfect people? I'd be forced to deal with their half-truths and deceit, and whatever it is they have planned for me. Or do I run? It would be my chance to get away from this fucked up town and people, and the consequences I always seem to face for being a Grady…or a Freemont…or whoever the fuck I am.

I try to see who the driver is again through my rearview mirror, but now I can tell the windows are tinted, and I can't focus on them and keep my eyes on the road as well.

Taking a deep breath, I choose a direction at the last minute, jerking the G-Wagon to the left as I stand by my decision to run. It continues over the red steel bridge that crosses over one of Mount James's rivers, opting to take my life into my own hands and get the fuck out of this place.

My fingers tremble as I squeeze the steering wheel tight, pressing my foot on the gas pedal and picking up speed since the road is clear. Hyperfocused on the asphalt ahead, I see the speedometer hitting fifty-five. Fear and paranoia take over as I panic, easing my foot off the gas pedal before I lose control from not focusing entirely on the road.

Continuing toward the bridge, I try to avoid the slight dip in the road, swerving a little to the right as the music quiets and the sound of my ringtone fills the car. I glance at the dash and see my mom's name flashing across the screen, so I rush to hit the answer button on the steering wheel as I continue to drive toward the bridge.

"Mom? Mom!" I yell, the fear in my voice recognizable in every syllable that leaves my mouth as the SUV moves closer to my bumper.

"Eden? Eden! What's going on?"

"I...I can't stay here anymore. I can't do any of this. Someone's fucking following me, and...and I'm scared, Mom, please. I'm near the interstate. Tell me where to turn, where to go...just anything."

The SUV surges forward, hitting my back bumper and sending me jolting forward as I try to keep the car straight. A scream rips from my throat as I start to cross the bridge towards the interstate. I have no idea how long this damn metal death trap is, but the quicker I get off it, the safer I'll feel.

"Fuck," I hear my mother mumble, and panic sets

in as I wait for her to say anything else. Taking a deep breath, she calls out my name. "Eden, I need you to listen to me. You need to turn the car around and go back to the Freemont house, okay?"

"Are you not listening to me?" I scream. "I can't do that, and I certainly can't when some SUV is trying to drive me off the road."

"It's going to be okay, sweetie," she whispers, and it sounds as if she tries to cover the phone, but I still hear her words loud and clear. "You need to back off my daughter right now. I don't give a fuck who is tailing her. If something happens to my girl, I will make you regret the day you were born. We're all playing your fucking games. Enough is enough." Her voice sounds deadly, a complete contrast to the soft and overly emotional woman I'm used to, but what confuses me even more is who she's speaking to. Especially since I could swear I hear a man in the background.

Fear forces me to slow down a little more, and I drop down to less than forty miles an hour. Panic continues to choke me as I practically pin myself back in my seat, gripping the steering wheel with everything I have.

"Mom, where are you? I can come to you, just please don't make me go back there."

Before I hear her response, the SUV moves to my right just as we come off the other side of the bridge and toward the on-ramp to the interstate, and I can practically taste the victory. I'm so close.

Suddenly, the SUV moves to the left, intentionally slamming into the side of my G-Wagon, and I swerve from left to right, the tires screeching over the pavement. I slam on my brakes, hoping to correct my direction, but I realize it's too late when the SUV clips the bumper of my G-Wagon again and I lose control. My head smashes against the driver's side window in a blur with the impact as the airbag deploys from the steering wheel, hitting me square in the face and muffling the scream lodged in my throat.

I helplessly let the vehicle play with me like a ragdoll as it rolls, finally rocking to a stop on the driver's side. Prying my eyes open when I sense the G-Wagon is no longer moving, I find my hands pinned to my chest and my foot still pressed down against the brake pedal as I stay frozen in place.

My head throbs, and I feel liquid trickling down the side of my face as I try to take a calming breath. I struggle to see anything other than the airbag and the gravel close to my head. Thank fuck it wasn't a moment sooner, or I'd have been down in the ravine.

I try to release the steering wheel so I can bring my hands to my head, but it's no use. It's like they are glued in place as I feel my breathing becoming more erratic. I can't see a thing, my body feels numb from all the pain, and the chaos transpiring around me makes me want to shut down, but I try to push through it all. I'm too scared to pass out.

Forcing my eyes open once more, I see nothing but the complete darkness like behind my eyelids from moments ago. I don't have enough energy to handle the aftermath of the collision anymore. I close my eyes, letting my head lull to the side, relaxing my body as I try to escape this nightmare in any way possible.

Even if it's through death.

As the world goes dark, all I can hear is my mom screaming my name. It suddenly feels ironic, hearing her voice as I slip into peacefulness. My mind goes back to the song playing earlier, hoping that once and for all my own dance with the devil is over.

TOXIC CREEK

KC KEAN

SIX

Tobias

Fuck. No.

No. No. No. No. No.

I spent the past hour giving Xavier and Hunter the silent treatment since they decided it was a good idea for us to go back over to Bethany's house and *politely* encourage Eden to listen once more like we didn't threaten her fucking life the last time we saw her. We're ridiculous.

Now...Now I don't think I'll ever be more grateful in my life that we ended up going back to see her again. Although my gut wishes I hadn't kicked up such a fuss, because then we would have been there sooner and she would never have gotten in her SUV—or I hope, at least.

My heart pounds in my chest as I sit propped between the two front seats. Xavier and Hunter are upfront in X's Jaguar as we continue to pick up speed behind the SUV that's following Eden.

"Call Ilana," Xavier yells for the third time as the phone rings throughout the interior, but it's not really a surprise when she doesn't answer again. "Fuck. Fuck. Fuck," he chants, slamming his hands on the steering wheel in frustration as my hands squeeze around the headrests.

What the fuck is even going on here?

"This is your mom, Xavier. You don't need to hear her say it to know it's fucking true," Hunter snarls, leaning forward in his seat with his elbows braced on the dashboard, his fingers clutching his hair as he watches the road.

"None of it fucking matters right now. We need to figure out how to get the SUV to back off," I shout, and Xavier growls.

"It would fucking help if we knew where she was actually heading."

Nobody says anything for a moment, but as she takes the bend veering to the left, the answer is right in front of us.

She's running.

From us. From this town. From everything.

I don't blame her, but it looks like Ilana is willing to go to extreme measures to keep her here.

"We wouldn't be in this fucking position if you hadn't been such a bitch about going back," Xavier argues, glancing at me in the rearview mirror, and I give him the finger. Fuck him. I'm already beating myself up enough, I don't need him to as well.

"What the fuck?" Hunter growls, leaning farther forward before pressing the button to slide his window all the way down.

"What?" I ask, watching as he leans out of the fucking window like a madman.

"They just fucking rammed her," he hisses as he falls back into his seat, his hands fisted as Xavier and I stare at him, processing what he just said.

Gazing out the front window, I watch as Eden starts to head across the old red bridge, her speed seeming to slow as if she's become more fearful. I punch Hunter's headrest over and over again, trying to let out the tension building inside me. I feel helpless, fucking helpless, and I have a gut feeling this is going to go from bad to worse, if that's even possible.

"We're going to have to try and run them off the road before they do it to her," Xavier says, his tone almost devoid of any emotion as he voices the only plan we could possibly have.

"Do it," Hunter demands.

Without another word, Xavier pushes his foot down further on the pedal, throwing me back in my seat, but we're too little too late. The SUV moves to her left and Xavier follows, but since she's dropped her speed it gives these assholes the chance to come up beside her again and ram into the back of her G-Wagon.

It all happens so fucking fast, it's almost a blur. One minute the SUV is in front of us, the next, both vehicles are turned on their sides. Eden's car is mere feet past the bridge, and smoke is starting to billow around her.

Xavier screeches the car to a halt as we all jump out of the vehicle. My heart pounds rapidly in my chest as adrenaline pumps through my veins. The sun has barely set, and the waning rays are the only light we have as we take in the scene before us.

I rush past the crashed SUV that we tailed, the one that was following Eden, hoping either Xavier or Hunter will take care of them as I search for Eden. They must have gone into the barrier on the right side of the road. Fuckers deserved it.

I run around to the front of Eden's G-Wagon, the windshield cracked in some areas and shattered in others. Eden is slumped over, the seatbelt holding her against the seat as her head lolls to the ground where her window is smashed. A trickle of blood flows down the left side of her face, the color bright against Eden's pale skin, and black and blue bruises are forming quickly around her eyes.

My fierce, beautiful soul.

Hunter called Ryan as soon as we realized what was going on, so I'm hoping he will have emergency services here as soon as possible.

Please, please, let everything be okay. I need her to be okay.

I startle as a woman cries out Eden's name. She must have her phone linked up, but I don't have time to respond to her. My priority is Eden, but I don't know how to remove her safely from the SUV, and I'm scared that if I try to pull her out, I'll hurt her.

A hand lands on my shoulder, making me jump, and I turn with my fist raised, ready to fight, but I pause when I see Ryan standing behind me.

"I need you to move out of the way, Tobias," he shouts,

as if he's repeated himself a few times and I haven't heard, but even now it sounds like a murmur in my ears as I slip to the side, watching as paramedics surround the SUV, my eyes trained on her as she doesn't move.

I search frantically for Hunter and Xavier, needing their support, and I find them by the SUV that hit Eden. There are two men dressed head to toe in black suits trying to fight against my brothers.

Those motherfuckers.

If I can't help Eden, then I'll help them.

On autopilot, I move toward them, watching as Hunter punches one of the men repeatedly, pinning him to the ground with his legs, while Xavier hovers above the other guy who is on all fours in front of him. Blood drips from the man's face, but he doesn't look anywhere near as close to death as Eden does, which only angers me more.

She doesn't deserve this. None of it.

I pick up my pace, and Xavier must hear me approach, because he steps to the side at the last minute, giving me the space to lift my leg and kick out like I'm going for a football. I hear the crack as my foot makes contact with this sick fuck's head.

He slumps to the ground as my chest heaves. I search

Xavier's gaze, noting he looks about as wild as I assume I do. The sound of flesh hitting flesh pulls my attention to Hunter, who is still unrelentingly beating on the other guy, so I hurry to his side, wrapping my arm across his shoulders to force him back.

He strains against me, trying to continue his assault, but I don't loosen my grip, and he slowly calms enough to stop fighting me.

"We need those pretty hands, brother," I remind him, resting my head against his shoulder as I try to calm myself down too.

"Where is she?" he finally speaks, his voice hoarser than usual, and I stall in my answer. I left her with Ryan, but I got a little too distracted with aiding in the beating these motherfuckers deserved.

Glancing back at Eden's damaged SUV, I see them gently placing her onto the stretcher, her neck in a brace, and I gape in despair.

"Fuck," Hunter rasps beside me as we watch them load her into the unmarked ambulance. Ryan approaches, a grim expression on his face.

"She's coming home with us," Xavier declares, his hands fisted at his sides as Ryan stops in front of him, staring him down.

"Yeah, because taking her to a place where Ilana has easy access is the best idea." Ryan rolls his eyes at us like we're stupid before casting his gaze toward the men on the ground. "Your mother's?" he inquires, focusing on Xavier who doesn't even snap back at Ryan's sarcastic remark because we all know he's right.

With a heavy sigh, Xavier swipes a hand down his face. "I honestly don't know, but it seems highly likely at this stage."

"I'll take care of them," Ryan responds simply, crossing his arms over his leather jacket, and Hunter nods. I have no idea what that actually entails, and I have no interest in finding out, although it seems Hunter is familiar with his brother-in-law's ways. I want to be with Eden. Fuck our bro code right now. She needs someone whether she likes it or not, and I want to be that person.

"I want to ride with her," I blurt out, and Ryan instantly shakes his head.

"You can come back to our house with us, but you fuckers are going to explain to me what you said this afternoon that made her decide she needed to run." With that, he turns on his heel, and I happily trail behind him.

I'd rather be with Eden, but as long as I'm not being pushed away, I'm not going to argue.

"I'll follow you in my car," Xavier calls out. "I need to call my mother."

"Fuck that, she won't say shit anyway," I retort over my shoulder, finding Hunter walking toward me too. If Xavier is surprised we're both climbing in with Ryan, he doesn't show it, but the tic in his jaw tells me he's aware there is most definitely a kink in our tight link right now. All for a sassy, beautiful, blonde girl with sparkly blue eyes.

I wordlessly sink into the back seat of Ryan's black truck, letting Hunter sit up front with him, and try to process what just fucking happened.

Someone, seemingly Ilana, just ran Eden off the road. Ran. Her. Off. The. Road.

Rage continues to build within me as the vision of the SUV crashing into her G-Wagon replays in my mind. I don't care what fucked up shit is going on here, I just need her to be okay.

Thankfully, Ryan stays right behind the unmarked vehicle, where I'm hoping the paramedics are tending to Eden, so I don't have to worry about her whereabouts as much. But my eyes keep darting around the roads, making sure there isn't another crazed vehicle chasing after her. It's difficult to see now that the sun's gone down, though, and I only have the car lights to guide me.

"So who wants to start?" Ryan rumbles, his eyes trained on the road as he waits for one of us to respond. I know exactly what he wants to know, but it's not really our thing to share details outside of the three of us. He's technically Hunter's family, so I'm leaving this decision up to him. When Hunter doesn't speak either, Ryan sighs. "You know I have surveillance set up around the pool, right? You can tell me, or I can just listen to it when I get back. Either way, I'll find out why she snuck out tonight with fear swirling in her big blue eyes like she was a completely lost soul."

His words hit me hard in the gut, but it annoys me slightly that this girl has somehow woven herself deep under my skin. I laugh, I joke, but I don't let *anyone* in. Finally having her beneath me has done nothing to quench my need for her. It was supposed to be sex, just sex, but right now, with Xavier's new obstacle in the way, I actually don't know where I stand for a change.

I guess it all depends on how strong Xavier's connection truly is with his mother.

Not that any of that matters anymore. She won't be

willing to even look at me again, not after this, because this definitely links back to Ilana, which connects to Xavier, leading to Hunter and me. I'm fucking screwed.

"We politely told her to be at school tomorrow before we took the decision from her hands," I mumble, and both Hunter and Ryan raise their eyebrows at me. Hunter because he knows, and Ryan because he can tell it wasn't said politely and that was not the worst of it.

Clearing his throat, Hunter finally speaks. "She asked if we were involved with her father's murder, and we didn't confirm or deny it. If anything, Xavier encouraged the idea, trying to goad her into submission." Well, that seems more accurate, I was just trying to sweeten it a little.

Ryan scoffs as he flickers his gaze between us. "I don't think she's into the whole submission thing since she's lying on a stretcher in the back of my company's ambulance. You're treating her just as you've been treated, but you, along with Ilana fucking Knight, are doing it publicly. She has *no* safe haven, *no* escape, and now you fuckers won't even let her run."

His knuckles whiten as his grip on the steering wheel tightens, and it surprises me how much this whole situation seems to bother him, but I don't really know much about his history. All I know is they went through a lot of shit together, Bethany and him, and Hunter treats him like family, says he earned a place at her side.

Neither of us denies his statement, but I never bring up my family history. Ever. So I keep my mouth shut, watching the world go by in a blur until we're pulling up to the security gates of Bethany and Ryan's home.

The blacked-out van continues around to the left of their house as Ryan puts the car in park in the driveway. I instantly hate the extra distance from Eden, but I keep my mouth shut, trying to remain calm as we step from the truck and Xavier parks his Jag beside us.

He has his phone to his ear, his eyes squeezed shut, and his face as red as a tomato as he talks to whoever is on the other end of the phone. I assume it's his mother, but when he swings the door open and growls, "Reza," his father's name, my eyes widen in surprise.

His family dynamic is nothing at all like mine. My father is the ruler, and my mother is the perfect Stepford housewife, whereas Xavier's mom runs the whole fucking town, never mind her home.

"This is too damn far and you know it, Father," he bites out before pocketing his phone, barely casting us as a glance as he prowls toward the front of the house.

We are quick to follow, not needing directions on where to go since Bethany's screams and shouts can be heard from outside the house.

"You are so fucked," Ryan mutters, and Hunter sighs, shaking his head as if knowing his fate as he walks beside me.

We turn to the left, the hallway leading to wide-open oak doors at the end, which is where the van is parked with two doors leading off the corridor on either side. The lights in the room to the right offer us another glimpse of Eden as the paramedics work their magic.

"You motherfucking pieces of shit. Did you do this? Did you fucking do this?"

Bethany comes charging out of the room, heading straight for Hunter as she punches his chest a few times, tears welling in her eyes as her emotions get the better of her, while Xavier, Ryan, and I all stand and watch.

Hunter doesn't put up a fight, letting her beat her frustration out on him until the tears fall freely down her face and she rests her forehead on his chest.

"Ryan, did this fucker have anything to do with the accident?"

"I mean, deep down, I want to say yes, just so you can punch him some more, but no. They are the ones who called me. They didn't do this, Betty."

"Don't fucking call me Betty right now," she grumbles in response, her mood relaxing instantly as Ryan steps up behind her, wraps his arm around her shoulders, and pulls her to him instead of Hunter. His six-foot frame is noticeable next to her small five-foot height.

"I've told them to run a full physical. She seems okay, and her vitals are alright. Fingers crossed she's just been knocked out and has a concussion. Anything more...I can't deal with the thought of anything more right now," she whispers, her face blotchy from crying, but she wipes at her cheeks, turns on her heel, and heads into the room as Ryan lets her go do her thing.

I have no idea what her thing is, or even where Cody is, come to think of it, all I know is I need to check on Eden.

"I need to see her," I murmur, sidestepping Ryan and moving into the room, trying not to be in anyone's way.

"No, not you," Hunter grumbles, and I glance at the door in confusion, but my frown deepens when I see Hunter standing in the doorway with his back to me and Xavier standing before him. "Fuck you and your stupid shitty decisions. If you hadn't gone all dark earlier, insinuating we had any involvement in her father's death, this wouldn't have happened. None of this would have happened. This is all on you. You can wait outside."

His tone is haunted, broken, and filled with rage as I simply stand and gape at them. It's rare to see Hunter lash out, even rarer for it to be aimed at one of us, but here we are, and I have to admit, I'm glad he seems to be feeling the same way I do.

Bethany cackles, but there is no happiness in the sound as she turns her laser glare on all of us. "No. Fuck you too, you little shit. I don't want any of you in this room if she wakes up. None of you deserve to be in here. Now get the fuck out."

SEVEN

Eden

Feeling the grass under my palms, I dangle my legs over the edge of the cliff, letting the sea breeze surround me. It embraces me, chilling me to the bone while warming me at the same time as I find my inner peace out here.

I don't know why I'm here, or where here is exactly, but like always, the ocean calls to me. The sun is bright in the sky, reflecting off the water below which foams and crashes into the rocks. The sound is almost hypnotic as it calms me.

"I should have known I'd find you here."

My head whips to the right, and I almost pull a muscle as I follow the sound of his voice. My mouth gapes open as I stare at him.

"Dad?"

His familiar grin spreads across his face as he takes the spot beside me, his eyes crinkling at the corners as his hand squeezes my shoulder, and it's like all my internal turmoil is settled with that single touch.

"How are you...Where...Am I dead?" I blurt out, rubbing my forehead as I try to jog my memory.

My dad snorts in response. "The way you're going, you're not far off. You seem to have taken 'living life on the edge' a little too far, don't you think?" His tone is soft, almost playful, but his expression is serious. This side of my dad is one I never really had to see since I was rarely one to get into trouble.

"There is so much going on, Dad. How did you even survive in this town?"

It feels like an eternity before he finally responds, his gaze fixed on the horizon just like mine, but I could sit here all day with him, forever even.

"Love. Love got us through everything."

Laughter bursts from my lips as I glance over at him. "That sounds like a totally crappy line from a totally crappy romance movie." My father laughs along with me, the sound like music to my ears as he ruffles my hair like he used to when I was a small child.

"*So I have a twin brother, huh?*" *I ask, the laughter cutting off, leaving unspoken words hanging between us, killing the happy moment. But even as I look at my dad now, I can't fathom him lying to me on such an epic scale, ever.*

"*I think you need to think about what I did for a living and maybe take a look at a photo album or two.*"

"*That's all you have to give me?*"

"*Eden Grady, I'm dead and a figment of your subconscious, you are answering for me.*" *I stare at him with my mouth wide open, unable to argue back at all.*

"*Well, if I die, will I stay with you? Then you can give me all the answers no one else is offering.*" *I turn to face him, and he cups my cheek, just like he did when I was an upset little girl.*

"*I'm sorry, sweetheart, but that's not going to happen today. I need you to survive, thrive, and beat the odds. You'll find your way. You always do.*"

My eyes squeeze shut of their own accord, and when I try to open them, my vision is nothing but darkness.

"*I love you, Eden,*" *he whispers around me as I try to cling to the image of my father, but the sudden assault of a glaring light wipes it all away.*

"Eden? Hey, Eden?"

My mouth is dry, my brain foggy, and my movement sluggish as I try to understand what's going on around me.

"Hey, it's okay. Take it easy."

Wait, is that…Bethany?

Taking a calming breath, I focus on one thing at a time. I try to swallow past the dryness, and then I feel the touch of a plastic straw at my lips. Slowly sipping on the water, I instantly gain some relief, and when I release the straw, I try to pry my eyes open.

It takes a moment, the light causing searing pain in my head as I blink open my eyelids. I groan as I come face to face with Bethany.

Her face lights up as her blue eyes glisten with tears. Grinning down at me, she calls out to Ryan, making me cringe in discomfort at the sound as he suddenly appears behind her.

Gingerly lifting my hand to my head, I press my fingers against my temple, trying to ease the pressure, but it's no use, and I feel the bandage on my face.

"Eden, do you know where you are?" Ryan asks, his voice like nails on a chalkboard, but I nod gently. I'd seen this room the other day when we needed a Band-Aid for

Cody, and I was stunned to find a fully equipped hospital room—another one of their many secrets.

"I'm at your house."

"That's right. Do you remember what happened tonight, Eden?" Bethany inquires, wrapping her hand around mine, and I try to focus on the last thing I remember.

"I, uh, was in my G-Wagon…I-I was running, Bethany, I'm so—"

"Don't you apologize, okay? I understand. *We* understand. I'm just glad you're okay," Bethany interrupts, relieving a lot of pressure from my chest as I admit what I was doing.

"Then…there was an SUV," I blurt, my heart rate increasing dramatically as pieces of my memory filter into my brain. My eyes scrunch shut as I feel the impact of the vehicles colliding all over again.

My hand falls to my chest as I frantically search the rest of my body, fear kicking in as I check for injuries.

"Hey, hey, Eden. It's okay, you're okay. Thankfully it's just a concussion and you'll be fine," Bethany rushes out, stroking her hand down my arm and soothing me as I search her eyes.

"Was it them?" I ask, emotion washing over me as I try

to tamp down my fear.

"Was it who?" Ryan questions, but I can tell by his expression he knows who I am talking about.

"They were there," he mutters, and a gasp breaks from my lips. "No! No, it wasn't them though," he adds quickly, concern in his eyes as he visibly worries over me before my mind can run away with itself, and I want to collapse with relief that it wasn't the Allstars.

I hate them, they are fucking dead to me, but I can still admit it would have gutted me if it was them who tried to kill me.

"Do we know who it was?" I finally query, feeling sick to my stomach, and the disappointed look on Bethany's face says it all.

"No," Ryan answers with a shake of his head. "I'm sure you can guess who we think it was, but it wasn't actually Ilana Knight in the SUV."

That doesn't surprise me, not at all.

"Who was in there?" I whisper, unable to stop myself from asking.

"Don't worry about—"

"Please, Ryan, you know how in the dark I've been kept lately, so please don't add to that."

He stares at me with understanding in his gaze as he glances at Bethany, who nods in agreement to whatever they are silently communicating.

"They looked like hired men, but the reason I say don't worry about it is because there will be nothing left of them to concern yourself with," Ryan responds with a sigh, gripping the back of his neck as he appears anxious about telling me the truth. I have to bite my lip to stop the gasp from leaving my mouth.

The way he said it makes me feel like things may be a little crazier than I anticipated, and deep down, I know this is one piece of information I don't actually want more details on regarding Knight's Creek. I'm also desperate to know what Ryan's job *actually* entails, but now really isn't the time.

"And why were the Allstars there?" I finally ask, trying to sit up in bed. Bethany fusses behind me, propping the pillows up as I move.

"B hasn't really given them a chance to explain, but I believe they are all still in the living room waiting for an update on your wellbeing."

I give Ryan a double take, his words catching me by surprise. They are here? *Still* here? I don't know how to feel about that.

"How long have I been out for?"

"Not long, you're okay. You have just been in and out for the past hour or so," Bethany responds, glancing over at Ryan who simply raises his eyebrows at her.

"Do you want them to explain for themselves, or would you prefer for me to get the details and come back with them?" Ryan inquires, and I take a moment to consider my choices.

"Let them in."

Hunter

Tapping my fingers on my thighs, I try to distract myself from the throbbing in my head as I play the latest rhythm I haven't been able to stop working on. Ever since I watched Eden fall apart as Tobias brought her to ecstasy out on the patio at our home, it's been stuck on repeat in my mind.

"I understand why they didn't want you in there, Xavier, but I have no idea why we had to be left out too," Tobias grumbles again, his leg bouncing as he constantly glances around the living room, before his eyes fix on the door that would lead us to Eden . Still, no one rushes out to say everything is okay, that *she* is okay.

"Maybe it's because we're the stupid fucking Allstars, and Bethany knows we stand together. She's protecting Eden, even from me, and I'm her brother," I answer, glaring at Xavier as he scoffs.

"How has some girl with the wrong last name and more drama than the rest of this town have us in such a fucking mess?" Xavier mumbles, his eyes closed as he leans back on the brown leather sofa, his hands clenched on his knees, battered and bruised just like mine. Let's hope that fucker can still throw a ball in the morning, but it'll all be worth it anyway.

"I'd say the mess is you denying that you feel anything at all and completely slipping back under your mother's thumb. Am I right, Hunter?" Tobias growls, but before I can respond, Ryan strides into the room with a phone ringing in his hand.

"Eden's mom keeps calling. What's her name?" he asks, glancing at us for an answer, and I frown at the device in his grasp.

"How did you get her phone?" Xavier questions, leaning forward, and Ryan rolls his eyes.

"One of the guys grabbed it from the car when they pulled her out."

Tobias suddenly stands, rushing to Ryan and snatching the phone from his hand before any of us realize what he's doing.

"Hello? Yes, this is Eden's phone...Uh, that doesn't matter right now...Tobias. My name is Tobias...No, I'm not a Knight," he answers, raising his eyebrows at Xavier as we all watch him pace in front of the huge television on the wall. Even Ryan just gapes at him. "I'm hoping she's okay, but no one is explaining...One moment." Covering the phone, Tobias glances directly at Ryan. "What state is Eden in? Momma Grady wants to know."

"She's awake, just a concussion and a few cuts and bruises, but she recalls everything that happened," Ryan mutters, swiping a hand down his face, and my heart stills in my chest.

"How long has she been okay for?" Xavier rumbles, rising to his feet as I do, and Tobias brings the phone back to his ear.

"I do apologize, Eden's mom...Oh, Jennifer, sorry. May I call you Jennifer? Thanks. Well, I am just now learning that Eden has suffered a concussion, but it's nothing I can't take care of…One-hundred percent I can bring the phone to her right now. Just one moment please, Jennifer."

With a grin on his lips, he races from the room, heading straight to Eden with Xavier, Ryan, and I hot on his tail. Rushing into the room on the right of the hall where we last saw Eden, I halt at the door as Eden and Bethany glare daggers at us and Tobias holds the phone to Eden's ear.

She's okay. Eden is really okay.

Watching her sit before me, awake, breathing, even glaring at me, fills me with fire.

Her blonde hair is thrown up in a loose bun on top of her head, and the area around her blue eyes is bruised, which must have been from the airbag. I hate seeing her skin marred like this and her head in a bandage, but as long as she's actually fucking breathing, we can deal with the rest.

I don't hear what she says to her mom since I'm too busy committing every inch of her face to memory, but when the phone drops to the bed beside her, I know Eden's full attention is back in the room. On us.

"Can you please give me a minute with these dickheads, Bethany? It won't take long," Eden says, and Bethany nods in agreement, giving the three of us her classic death glare before stepping toward the door, Ryan following closely behind.

"Just say the word, Eden, and I'll rip these little asswipes to shreds," Bethany mutters, and I take a deep breath, not letting my brotherly instincts take over, which makes me want to have the last word with her. "Stupid, little dicked, motherfucking shit-for-brains," she grumbles as the door clicks shut behind her, and I don't miss the smirk on Eden's lips at Bethany's little rant.

Awkwardly shuffling from foot to foot, I focus my gaze back on Eden, watching as she squeezes her temples.

"So are one of you going to explain why you happened to be present when I was ran off the road? Did you orchestrate it? Or were you there to make sure everything went as planned?"

My mouth falls open at her crazy questions and crazy mind as I stumble to respond, but Xavier beats me to it.

"If we were there to orchestrate it or see it through, you wouldn't be sitting here with just a concussion, now would you?"

"Will you shut the hell up?" Tobias yells, glaring at Xavier. "Your mouth is starting to get on my fucking nerves. You just keep making *everything* worse right now. So shut up or wait outside, Xavier." Giving Xavier his back, he steps up to the side of Eden's bed. "We were there because we were on our way over here to talk to you again, but, you know, like more politely. We saw you hightailing it across town, and when we realized the SUV was chasing you, it was too little too late for us to intervene."

Eden holds his gaze, searching his eyes for the truth as she nods subconsciously, processing Tobias's take on events.

"How...convenient," Eden replies, keeping any emotion off her face as she glances between the three of us.

"Very. You should have seen Hunter pummeling the fucker from the passenger seat, and I did the best run and kickoff of my life on the driver's face. Complete, total consequences for what they did. What they did to *you*," Tobias adds, detailing how my primal instincts took over and how he had to pull me off that fucker. Flexing my knuckles with dried blood on them, I still don't feel any pain, but I know I'll regret it in the morning.

Well, I won't regret what I did, but I'll regret not icing them sooner.

"You guys did what?" Eden exclaims with a frown as I move a little closer to the bed, Xavier stepping around to stand at the other side.

"That doesn't really matter. What matters is what you're going to do to get my mother off your back," Xavier murmurs, and silence follows his statement as everyone stares at him. How do we even respond to that? It isn't a lie.

"Huh, you mean your mother who makes killing off every Grady seem as simple as getting a mani-pedi?"

"That would be the one," I grind out, folding my arms over my chest as I try to figure out a way to shield Eden from all of this—Ilana's wrath, Knight's Creek, all of it.

"Do any of you have any idea how hard it is to want to defend yourself, only for someone to continue to tear you down, piece by piece, while fighting back only seems to bring you closer to death?" Eden sighs. "Actually, you know what? Of course you do. But that means nothing though, right?"

"That's all beside the point right now." Tobias tries to wave off her words, but that only irritates Eden more.

"There is going to be nothing left of me at this rate!" Eden yells. Clearly, she's a little overwhelmed with everything, and she squeezes her temples tighter as Bethany waltzes straight back into the room, unhappy Eden is getting all worked up.

"That's it, that's enough. You three can get out,"

Bethany orders, but none of us move.

"We're not leaving until we have a plan to get Eden back to school. That will at least keep Ilana at bay for the time being," I argue, glaring at my sister as she burns holes in my forehead.

"You can still stay here," Tobias offers, but Xavier steps closer to the bed, shaking his head in disagreement.

"She can't."

"Like hell she can't," Bethany retorts. "I don't give a shit about what your mom has to say. Ilana Knight can suck my tit for all I care. Eden can stay here."

Everyone starts to all talk at once, and no one actually notices the distress it causes Eden. Her blue eyes find mine, and even when she hates me, I can see the plea in her gaze to help her.

"Shut the fuck up," I yell, and silence falls over the room as I watch Eden, sweeping my arm out for her to speak. It almost looks like she may thank me, but the moment passes between us, and she remembers all too quickly that she hates us.

"I can't stay here, Bethany."

"No, you—"

"Bethany, please. You have been amazing to me,

beyond words, but I was running tonight because I couldn't stand the fact that I was putting Cody in the middle of this. I know you can handle yourself, just like Ryan can, but Cody...I just can't, Bethany." It catches me off guard to see unshed tears in Eden's eyes as she tries to stay calm, but what surprises me even more is that Bethany is doing the exact same thing.

The determination in Eden's voice when she speaks of wanting to protect my nephew stuns me. It stuns Bethany too, if the look on her face is anything to go by.

"You know you don't..." Ryan tries to reason, but trails off when Eden starts shaking her head. I glance at the guys who are standing and observing Eden helplessly as she makes her own choices.

"For my peace of mind, I can't. I'm going to go back to the Freemont house tonight, and I'm going to be at school tomorrow."

# TOXIC CREEK

KC KEAN

EIGHT

Eden

Standing on my balcony at the Fremont house, the familiar beach below, I close my eyes as I listen to the waves as the sea breeze blows against my face, the smell of the salty water surrounding me as the sun continues to rise in the sky.

I never thought I would come back to this bedroom, but here I am with the false appearance that I'm bending to their will so no one will attempt to take my life, or at least scare the shit out of me by running me off the road. If their goal was to put the fear of God into me, then they were pretty fucking close.

I had to swallow down bile as I unlocked the door last night, stepping into the Freemont house to find Archie on the sofa. He jumped up the second he saw me, his jaw on the floor as he took in my battered and bruised face, but the look in my eyes ensured he didn't take a step toward me. Even if I was much slower in my movements compared to usual.

His sunken shoulders, tired eyes, and helpless expression told me he was gutted, desperate to talk, but I'd been through enough, and his wants and needs were not at the top of my list of things to tend to. He can wait and fucking suffer like I had to.

The sound of the door slamming shut behind me pulled me from my stare off with Archie as Hunter marched up the stairs to my room. I followed willingly to put a little more space between Archie and me.

Once all the shouting had subsided at Bethany's house, she wouldn't let me leave without a chaperone for the night, bestowing the task to her trusty brother. I *unwillingly* agreed, but I had to stand my ground.

I am done running, done hiding, and I'm ready to take on this damn town. Whatever that actually means.

My phone buzzes in my hand, bringing me back to the present and drawing my gaze to the screen.

Charlie: I'll be there to pick you up in five minutes.

I don't bother to respond as I slip my phone into my back pocket, but it starts to vibrate again the second I do.

With a sigh, I check the screen again, only to find my mother's name flashing across the display. I must have spoken to her six times since the accident, which was barely twelve hours ago. Who knew almost dying would encourage a fucking conversation with her?

"Hello?" I answer, my eyes falling closed as her voice filters through.

"Hey, baby. You okay?"

"Yes. I already told you that this morning."

"I know, but don't you think you should take today at least before going back to school? You won't be over the concussion yet."

Glancing over my shoulder, I spy the now empty seat, which was filled with Hunter Asheville's body last night as he watched me sleep, making sure I was alright. When I woke this morning, he was gone, just as he promised me. At least he was able to keep his word on one thing. I'm sure the situation will be very different at school today, but deep down I appreciate him being here. It gives my soul crazy tingles when any of the Allstars surprise me, especially when it's in a positive way.

"The concussion is fine, I'm fine, and I refuse to be broken anymore. It'll only make me seem weaker and like an easier target. I think what we need to discuss is the fact that you suddenly have all this phone time for me when I've been desperate to speak to you over the past few weeks. What's going on? Is your captor suddenly letting you have your phone?"

Silence greets my snark until she mumbles, "Something like that."

I freeze at her words. "Mom, I was joking, are you..." My heart feels like it'll suddenly burst from my chest as fear creeps in at the edges of my mind.

"Don't worry about me, Eden. I'm fine too. Just...be safe, okay?"

"I will."

"I love you, Eden."

"You too, Mom," I whisper, ending the call.

I'm worried about her, about both of us, but I can't let myself sink into despair right now. I have to trust her word, even if trust seems like a hard thing to come by at the moment.

Stepping back inside, I close the balcony door behind me, the silence instantly noticeable. I barely slept last night. I'm not sure whether Hunter noticed or not, but every time I closed my eyes, I felt the air whooshing out of me just like it did in my SUV. My senses were constantly overwhelmed with the sound of glass shattering and screeching tires.

Now, I don't have a vehicle at all. Nothing. Which is why I reached out to Charlie this morning, asking for a ride, and she was happy to help. Realistically, Charlie knew nothing about Archie and me, if what she said was true, and I remember the shock on her face when I found out.

I need to talk to my mom about using my Amex card for buying a new car or ask her to wire me some money, but I'll save that chat for another day. It's going to take me a bit to get in the driver's seat again. I almost had a panic attack last night in the car ride over here, even though Hunter drove like I might shatter if he touched the brakes too hard.

Grabbing my bottle of water, I swallow down one of

the herbal remedy tablets Hunter gave me when he played the little knight in shining armor while I was on my period. I need them to take the edge off of what today might have in store, so I take an extra for good measure.

Stepping into the walk-in closet, I look myself over once more, scoffing at the state of my face. I have a couple of scrapes and bruises down my left cheek and two black eyes. My left arm is scraped up like my face, but everything is thankfully superficial.

I applied light makeup, barely covering the mess on my face, but let them see. Let them see the scars they are leaving on me. I don't care.

I've opted for a sleeveless, cropped white top with some high-waisted skinny jeans, white sneakers, and an oversized checkered shirt over it so it doesn't irritate my arm so much. After French braiding my hair to keep it off my face, I'm as ready as I'll ever be to face the day.

I head downstairs with my bag slung over my shoulder, and I'm not surprised when I find no one here. I heard Archie leave this morning, likely for football practice, and Richard is probably hiding from me now more than ever.

Charlie's white Jeep pulls up outside, and I take a deep breath before unlocking the front door and finding a smiling Charlie practically hanging out of her window. When she sees my face, shock flashes in her eyes as she sees the state of me. I had mentioned earlier there had been an incident, but she probably didn't expect *this*.

Thankfully, she doesn't say anything as I round the car and drop into the passenger seat as quickly and gently as possible with my eyes closed, refusing to glance out of the front window just yet. If I do, fear will kick in too swiftly and I'll start having a panic attack.

"So the look on your face tells me to keep this car ride to small talk only, huh?" Charlie murmurs, a soft smile on her lips, and I nod in agreement, unable to find words yet.

I expect her to pester a little, wanting something, anything from me, but instead she puts the car in drive and heads toward school while I keep my anxiety at bay.

Fixing my gaze on my lap, I try to ask her about the message she sent about her and Archie, but I feel like that'll be too deep before the day ahead.

"Drivers License" by Olivia Rodrigo plays through the music system, my heart breaking right alongside hers, for her. The way Charlie clears her throat tells me it's hitting a little too close to home for her, and it's kind of ironic she just picked me up from Archie's.

Wanting to distract her as much as myself from our emotions, I sit taller and glance in her direction. "So is there any school gossip I should know about? We both know there are some bitches there who probably had a lot to say."

Flickering her eyes my way, she bites her lip before nodding, training her gaze back on the road before she answers.

"I know you like to get straight to the point, so I'll do the same. You're a whore. You've been sleeping with Archie, along with the three Allstars. Your mom sold you out, and now you need to sell your body to get by, and the craziest of them all, I think, is that you're sleeping with Richard so you can be your own stepmom."

Well, okay then. I mean, some of them are creative, but it's not as bad as I was expecting.

"That is the pettiest and most disgusting load of shit I have ever heard," I blurt out, and Charlie can't hold in her bubble of laughter.

"Nothing says playground games like incest, right?" she adds, taking the last turn before the school parking lot, and I shake my head in astonishment.

"These people are fucking crazy. Did Pinky and Perky

start the rumors?" I ask, and she frowns at me.

"Pinky and Perky?"

"Yeah, the two bitches who really are trolls, with their brightly colored hair and desire to tear people down. Roxy and KitKat."

"That's fucking brilliant," she says around her laughter, and even though we're talking about crazy shit people have said about me, I feel a little lighter in Charlie's company.

I really feel bad that she seems to have put some space between her and Archie, and I will get around to addressing it with her at some point, but everything leaves my mind as she turns into the parking lot. I see the Allstars instantly, my eyes drawn to them like a beacon.

Xavier, Hunter, Tobias, Archie, and a few other guys from the football team stand on the path leading up to the school's stairs, all in their jerseys surrounded by cleat chasers in their full cheerleading uniforms, which makes me pause.

"Hey, if they are in their cheer outfits, why aren't you?" I question as Charlie parks the car two rows back, and I frown.

"Because I quit."

"You quit?" I repeat, turning to face her so I can make

sure I heard correctly.

With a heavy sigh, Charlie glances at me, her brown eyes searching mine as she finds the energy to explain, pushing her glasses up her nose in annoyance. "I either stayed on the squad and took part in bullying you, trying to tear you down, or I quit and stood by the one decent human being in this fucking town. I went with option B."

I gape at her in surprise. She hardly knows me, not like she knows these people, and they obviously have a lot of pull around here.

"Charlie, I..."

"I know what you're going to say, but I swear to you, hand on heart, there is not a single thing I know about you in some way, shape, or form that you don't already know about yourself. I have no secrets, no family lies that I'm aware of, and no desire to partake in breaking you."

Wow. The sincerity in her gaze catches me off guard, and I can't help but believe every word she says, yet I don't understand why, out of all the people here, I instinctively respect and trust her word.

"I was actually going to say *I* would always be option A, never B," I respond, trying to downplay what she just shared, and she rolls her eyes.

"Well, that's very true, but I have to admit, I was all prepared for you to question me as to why I decided that."

She pulls her brown hair back in a ponytail, a small grin on her lips, and I cover my mouth as I try to decide if she's a mind reader or not.

"That too," I finally murmur, and she turns to face me.

"Eden, my parents are good people and we live a good life, drama free, but I refuse to take the easy way out like they did. I won't stand by and let those trolls continue to hurt decent people. And since the one solid person you had on your side turned out to be a bigger asshole than you anticipated, you need someone, and that someone is me."

Dumbfounded, I nod in understanding as she steps from the car, containing my emotions, forcing myself to be completely calm as if she didn't just say all of that.

With a deep breath, I slide out of the Jeep, feeling eyes on me instantly.

"You don't look like the type to need a pep talk, but I can give you one if needed," Charlie tells me as she rounds the car in her denim jeans and Metallica tee.

I shake my head. She's right. I don't need her pep talk. I do perfectly well building myself up. It's just staying there at the moment that seems to be the problem. My mind is constantly all over the place. Who knew my father's death would lead to this chain of events? As if dealing with that heartache alone isn't enough.

Walking to the grass lined path, I feel eyes on me with every step we take, but I keep my head held high and my eyes focused forward.

"So it's my birthday weekend coming up, and I wondered if you still wanted to come to my family barbecue?" Charlie inquires, bumping her shoulder with mine as we walk, and I nod.

"Yeah, I could really use a chance to let my hair down and forget my life for a minute."

"I don't blame you, girl, and we'll work on my grandmother. If no one else is willing to talk, anything she may know about the Grady name may be of use."

"Thanks, Charlie," I murmur as the Allstars and all their little minions turn to face us.

Archie stares at me with guilt and the desperation to talk to me in his eyes, while Hunter observes me like I'm the new girl all over again—impassive, with his hands in his jeans pockets, like he didn't sleep in the chair in my room last night. His hair is desperately begging for someone to run their fingers through it, and it only agitates me more.

Tobias stands beside him, beanie in place, as he runs his tongue over his teeth, watching me like he wants to eat me alive even looking as rough as I do. He is hot as hell in his jersey and jogger shorts, the muscles in his legs flexing as he remains in place.

The roll of my eyes is paused as I meet Xavier's gaze. Anyone else would probably crumble under his gaze, having the ability to kill a man on the spot with his death glare, but I refuse to let him get inside my head, even if I can see the cords in his forearms bulging from here.

Fuck him. Fuck them.

"Oh my God! What the fuck happened to your face? I heard you liked it rough...but that's next level," Roxy shouts, gaining everyone's attention, and I force myself to hold back my retort. I want to smack her in the face, but the last time I did that, I was sent home, and my arm hurts.

Actually...that's a good idea.

Whirling around, I go to step toward her, but Charlie reaches her hand out, stopping me in my tracks.

"Don't let her win before you even step through the doors, Eden," she whispers in my ear, and it takes everything I have to turn around and head for the steps, all while they laugh and joke behind me.

Ultimately, she's right. Being sent home would only set me back in my plan to figure this huge game of chess out before I get the fuck out of town, and I need to at least make it look like I'm trying to follow Ilana's stupid fucking rules.

Hearing the bell ring in the distance, I quicken my pace with Charlie beside me as I take the steps two at a time. I draw in a deep breath, step into the hallway, and head for my locker. It's a new day. This is a new start and a fresh chance to get everything under control.

They can try to knock me down, I expect it, but they won't succeed.

TOXIC CREEK

KC KEAN

NINE

Eden

English and homeroom are surprisingly quiet. I'm waiting for someone to continue what Roxy tried to start earlier, but nothing has happened yet. I have my back up, my defenses raised, and I'm ready to pounce the second someone tries to push my buttons.

I've been on high alert since I woke this morning, knowing I would have to see the Allstars, but I became even more wary when I took my allocated seat in English, completely surrounded by the three of them. I caught the smug grin on Xavier's face, but I think the fact I played along with their little power play and showed up gave me a little breathing room. Even if I refused to make eye contact with anyone but Charlie. I wasn't willing to check on Tobias and Hunter either, in case they took it as an invitation to speak.

Now, I just need to get through science and history. Both of which won't include the Allstars since it was announced earlier that all football players are having extra training sessions for the up-and-coming game against their biggest rivals, the Vipers.

I can't help but consider showing up to the game and taking a seat in the away stands, screaming a big fuck you to all of them.

With Charlie's arm linked through mine, we walk into the science lab, and I take the chair beside hers since the class is much more condensed than usual with the football players out.

Mrs. Duffy stands at the front of the class, her thick brown hair pulled back from her face with a headband, her glasses perched on her nose as she timidly waits for everyone to take their seats.

Out of all the teachers I have, she is the softest, gentlest, but the sternest, and I don't understand how no one has tried to bend her to their will. Maybe I should ask for some advice.

"Okay, everyone, today we're going to be focusing on creating copper sulfate. I feel like it's the perfect time to do so since we have lost half of the jock boys, so you'll be easier for me to handle."

I can't help but chuckle at her words as KitKat and Roxy snicker behind me, clearly missing the eye candy to watch instead of actually learning anything in life regardless if it's useful or not.

The science lab is made up of ten rows of desks in pairs, with a walkway down the middle and windows to my right. I can actually see part of the sports field from here. I can't see any of the players yet, but maybe the bitches behind me can stare outside the entire class, because feeling their presence behind me doesn't sit well with me.

"There are lab coats and goggles for everyone on your desks. Please put them on straightaway so I can begin," Mrs. Duffy orders, and everyone slips them on wordlessly as she continues. "You should also find lab tweezers, a ring stand, an iron ring, a Bunsen burner, copper wire, sulfuric acid, a beaker of water, and a battery. We're going to do this step by step. Any questions?"

"Yeah, do we actually have to wear these goggles? They are really disgusting," Roxy whines behind me, and I refrain from rolling my eyes at the redheaded Barbie. There is more to life than what looks good. No fucking brains, this girl.

"Would you like to lean too far over the Bunsen burner and burn your fake eyelashes off, Ms. Montgomery?" the teacher instantly retorts, getting no response from behind me, and I internally give her a high five. "Excellent, we'll continue. If you all want to start your Bunsen burners first—I'm assuming you are all fully aware how to do that—then we can start measuring out the liquids. Girls, I'll only ask you once to tie your hair back off your face if you haven't already."

Turning her back to us, Mrs. Duffy lets us get set up, and Charlie instantly dives in to ignite the flame while I sit back and watch, letting her do her thing as I listen to Roxy and KitKat complain.

"Like fuck am I putting my hair in a hair tie. Does this bitch even know how long I spent curling it this morning?"

"Right, fuck that bitch." I can't help but snicker at their petty, self-centered attitudes as I roll the sleeves up on my lab coat.

"What the fuck do we even do here?" Roxy scoffs behind me, and I smother my smile as I glance over my shoulder to take a look at them, my goggles firmly in place as I shove my hands in the large pocket of the lab coat.

With their heads together and their eyebrows furrowed, KitKat manages to get the flame going before setting it down in front of her. Impressive. I almost feel like offering her a gold star for effort, but the sneer on her lips as she catches my gaze puts a stop to it.

"What the fuck are you looking at, orphan whore?" Unable to hold back my eye roll this time, I turn around, but not before she continues. "Don't roll your fucking eyes at me, bitch. Nobody wants you here. I don't want you here, Roxy doesn't want you here, the Allstars don't fucking want you. Damn, even your own dad's dead because he didn't want you either."

The blood drains from my face as her words sink in, and my heart wrenches with anger and pain.

"That's enough," Mrs. Duffy calls, but I don't hear her.

"What the fuck did you just say?" I murmur, turning to face her, and the snarky grin on her face only riles me up more. She doesn't respond, and I find myself on my feet as I brace my hands against their desk without even realizing

I moved, but they don't falter. "I said. What. The. Fuck. Did. You. Just. Say. To. Me."

Every word is punctuated with a near growl as she acts as though she's polishing her nails. My blood is boiling. I feel like I'm about to burst into flames. How dare she fucking mention my dad?

"I'm just saying the Allstars said you don't even know who your real mom and dad are, and Archie is your brother. I mean, instead of telling you the truth, your dad decided to kill himself. You probably would be better off dead with your dad."

That's it. I'm fucking done with this bitch getting under my skin.

Reaching forward, I grab a fistful of her purple hair, extensions and all, and drag her toward me. Fear and surprise mix in her expression as I pull her closer. "Listen here, you little cunt, you don't know shit about me or my dad, or anyone else for that matter, so you should keep your fucking mouth—"

"Fire! Fire!" Roxy screams, and I frown, glancing around as she shrieks, jumping up and down on the spot, and Charlie pulls me back.

Where the fuck would there be a—

Holy shit, I quickly release my hold on KitKat's hair as I watch the flames burn at her purple ends. What the fuck? When I jerked her toward me, I must have pulled her too close to the fucking Bunsen burner.

Staring in shock, I snort in surprise but quickly school my features as tunnel vision takes over and I focus on what I've done. I do nothing, say nothing, while the class is in an uproar with screams and shouts. KitKat bats at her hair, screaming like a banshee, but it continues to burn. The smell of a sulfurous odor saturates the air instantly.

"Stand back," Mrs. Duffy yells, a fire blanket held in her hands ready to throw it over KitKat, but Charlie steps up beside her, aims a fire extinguisher at KitKat, and fires the foam directly at her.

"No, Charlie. Shit," Mrs. Duffy shouts, swatting the fire extinguisher out of her hands before throwing the fire blanket over KitKat. "You could blind her," Mrs. Duffy warns, glancing at Charlie who simply shrugs in response.

Silence falls over the class as KitKat drips foam from her chest down, her hair, once just above her waist, now barely past her ears.

Holy fuck.

My heart pounds rapidly in my chest. I didn't...I didn't

mean to do that, I just...

Fuck.

Lacing my fingers together, I brace them on top of my head as I stare at the scene before me. I won't apologize, she's a fucking bitch, stirring up trouble and trying to drag me down, and I'm certainly not waiting around to be lectured by the teacher.

I'm out.

Glancing at Charlie beside me, and she must see my intention, because she nods in understanding. Grabbing my bag off the floor, my fingers trembling, I throw it over my shoulder as everyone glances between KitKat and me, and I hightail it out of there before anyone can say anything.

I refuse to focus on everything that just happened in that classroom, apart from her words. What she said about my dad...I'm going to hurt whoever told her that utter bullshit and lies.

I need to release all this pent-up anger and despair, and the only people who deserve my wrath are out on the football field. Turning on my heel, I bolt in the other direction, running straight for them.

They won't even know what hit them.

My feet pound down the tunnel to the field, leading the way as my mind repeats what just transpired in the science lab. I know everything will go from bad to worse because of it, but she fucking deserved it.

As I step out of the tunnel, I swipe a hand down my braided hair and suddenly realize I still have the fucking goggles and lab coat on. Ripping the goggles from my face, I throw them over my shoulder, doing the same with the coat as I march onto the grass, seeing the football team huddled in the center of the field.

I can't hear the coach from here, but he claps and the guys break off into smaller groups, likely running some kind of drill. Dropping my bag on the sideline, I spy the Allstars together across the field, their helmets at their feet as they casually toss a ball between them.

Picking up my pace, my anger heightening at the sight of them, I clench my hands at my sides as Archie suddenly comes into view.

I don't have time for his shit too. No way.

He raises his hands, but I don't slow down. "Not now, Archie," I warn, and he takes a step to the side as I continue toward the motherfucking assholes who keep fucking with my life. Any other time it would be fucking hot as shit to watch them in their element, but I can't see past my anger right now.

Xavier steps back from Hunter and Tobias, his arm pitched back as he shouts orders to the other two. They spread out, putting more distance between them as Xavier readies to throw the ball.

"Ten, twenty-two," Xavier calls, and Hunter takes off running, leaving me with the perfect target that is Tobias Holmes.

His back is to me as he watches Xavier curve the ball through the air toward Hunter, so I grab his arm and pull it behind him, forcing him to turn and face me. The surprise in his eyes is short-lived as I punch his stomach, his face scrunching in pain as all the air whooshes from his lungs.

He leans forward, a groan slipping from his lips, and I can't help but kick down on the back of his calf, making him wobble and drop to his knees before me.

"What the fuck, Eden?" he wheezes, but he can fuck right off.

Crouching down beside him, my heart pounding in my ears, I glare at him. "Fuck you for telling KitKat, Roxy, and whoever the fuck else you like to spout shit to things about me and my dad. Just fuck you."

"Hey, what the fuck's going on?" Xavier shouts, and I rise to my feet, hearing his footsteps behind me.

As I turn to face him, I catch sight of the other players staring at us, but I don't pay them any mind, my focus on these dickheads.

"And you," I growl, jabbing my finger in Xavier's chest as he stands before me. "I am so fucking done with you and your shit. It was most likely *you* who told Roxy and KitKat lies about my dad while you were telling them all about my long-lost twin brother, but you all get to feel my anger since you guys are just one big happy family." My heart races in my chest and my fury kicks into overdrive. I don't feel any relief from my tension at all.

Staring down at me, Xavier wears a frown on his face as he grinds his jaw, sweat dripping down his scar along the side of his ear. He doesn't say anything, and that only pisses me off more.

I raise my arm to slap him across the face, but this motherfucker's reflexes are quicker than I want and his hand wraps around my wrist. He backs me up a step, his grip tightening as his fingers dig into my skin, and I wince.

Leaning forward, he pulls me in so we are toe-to-toe, his mouth at my ear, then he whispers, "Wanna try that again, Nafas?"

My body shivers as my words catch on my tongue. I'm furious with the fact he can slip under my skin so easily.

"How about you try me, dick face? Let go of my wrist, and I'll slam you to your fucking knees. Well, for you it will be painful, but it'll only bring me great pleasure."

I shove at his chest and he steps back, his brows knitted together even as he smirks knowingly while he thankfully releases my wrist.

"You have some nerve storming this field with a confident, bitchy swagger like it's your territory," Xavier grinds out, and I scoff at the audacity of this guy.

"Well, fuck if I let you rule me like all your other pawns on the table, douchebag," I growl. "And FYI, if you think my confidence makes me a bitch, then I'm going to be a bitch, because I won't change myself. Not for anyone, and most certainly not for you."

Placing my hands on my hips, I search for Hunter, finding him strolling toward Tobias who is still on his knees behind me. Everyone is watching us now, the coach included, but even he says nothing.

"Do I want to know what's happening here?" Hunter asks, concern in his green eyes, but I don't need their soft expressions or fake worry.

"Like you don't know that KitKat and Roxy think my dad killed himself. They said the Allstars *told* them right around the time they *told* me to join him," I snarl, watching as Hunter's eyebrows almost touch his hairline. His mouth opens as he goes to respond, but I interrupt. "Save me the bullshit," I snap, turning my back on them as I try to calm down.

I need to get away from them. The hot sun beating down on me is making my fucking head hurt, and this isn't helping at all. I need to leave now.

"Hey," Hunter murmurs, grasping my upper arm, but that's the wrong move.

Whirling around, I aim my palm at his face, hoping to get at least one of them with my hand, Hunter pushes me away, and I stumble back, his eyes going black as he tracks my movements.

"Don't ever try that again," he grinds out, and my eyes widen at the fierceness in his voice.

Stammering over a response, Tobias finally stands, moving closer to us as Xavier steps forward too, the three of them boxing me in.

They are consuming me, not listening, and playing with my emotions. Goddammit. My palms sweat as my nails dig into them, and it takes everything I have not to squeeze my eyes shut and draw in a big breath.

"The three of you stay the fuck away from me. Do you hear me? I'm done."

"That's hilarious," Xavier comments casually, brushing invisible grass from his shoulder as he looks me over, assessing me, and I can't figure out if it's to picture me naked or wipe me off his cleats like shit. "Maybe in the future, you should actually have your facts ironed out before you charge into our practice session and cause a scene."

"If you think this is me causing a scene, you haven't seen anything yet," I counter instantly, standing taller as I feel the eyes of the players around us watching the commotion we're causing.

He shakes his head. "You need to get over it. If anything, you should be thanking me for cluing you in on some of the secrets that are relevant to you."

Anger courses through my veins as he throws that out there so casually.

"I've never seen someone so handsome act so ugly," I hiss, feeling the words deep in my soul. "You're not heroic. You're fucking tragic."

With that, I turn and head back in the direction I came from, my head held high as I pass through the team. No one says a word, but their eyes remain on me the whole time. I would much rather be inside dealing with the consequences of burning KitKat's hair than trying to speak to these three dickheads right now.

Let's hope fate sends me home. I knew I shouldn't have come here today.

KC KEAN

TEN

Xavier

"She did what now?" I ask again, and Mrs. Duffy just rolls her eyes at me.

"Just...follow me," she grumbles, seemingly fed up with repeating herself, but my brain just doesn't understand.

Eden burned KitKat's hair? How? I mean, I can probably guess why. Her whole show of anger and venom on the field links straight back to the little gold diggers, but to purposely burn someone? That seems a little extreme, even for her, and especially after what she went through yesterday.

Not long after Eden left the field, Coach got a call and practice was cut short so Tobias, Hunter, and I could come deal with the situation. They didn't say what the circumstances were or who was involved, but I wish I hadn't rushed in the shower as quickly as I had. I don't have the patience for the dramatics I know are about to follow.

Moving down the hall, I let Mrs. Duffy take the lead as I glance at Hunter and Tobias on my right. I check to see if they are as confused as me, and the look on their faces tells me I'm not alone as they stare at me in confusion too.

Walking side-by-side, with everyone else still in class, I'm glad it's Mrs. Duffy and not the principal going through this with us. I have no time for his snotty tone and desire to run straight to my mother with everything.

"It really wasn't on purpose, and between you and me, it wasn't entirely undeserved. You know how bitchy and disrespectful those girls can be. They were spouting some gossip shit about her dad and you guys, and Eden just reacted. But when she reached over the desk, grabbing a fistful of her hair so she could pull KitKat toward her, it caught on the Bunsen burner."

Tobias snickers beside me, and I'm surprised to see Hunter swipe his hand over his lips, hiding his amusement as Mrs. Duffy glances at us over her shoulder.

"And where is Eden now?" I inquire, following Mrs. Duffy around the corner to the nurse's office.

As if we need to be dealing with this right now.

"It's like Eden attracts this shit without even trying," Hunter murmurs, and Tobias scoffs.

"Or it's like we put her in positions where she constantly has to defend herself," Tobias adds, glancing at me out of the corner of his eye, but I don't respond, looking straight ahead as Mrs. Duffy stops to knock on the nurse's door.

I don't have time for this. Stepping up to the door, I push it open and stride inside to find KitKat sobbing uncontrollably on the bed, her purple hair singed up to her ears when her hair touched her ass this morning.

Holy fuck.

"That's brilliant!" Tobias laughs, clapping his hands, and KitKat just glares at him before crying even louder. Roxy stands beside her, shooting daggers at him with her eyes. Bitch should be glad nothing else was burned.

"This is not fucking funny, Tobias Holmes. I want that whore expelled. Do you hear me? I want her gone. For good. No second chances, no coming back to Asheville High. Nothing."

She stands with her hands on her hips, her dress barely covering her ass as she pouts, and I almost laugh at her attempt to get what she wants.

"It's a shame you're not the boss around here then, isn't it?" Hunter retorts, rolling his eyes at their whining, and I glance around, looking for the damn nurse.

"Xavier, listen to me, I—"

"We're done here," I interrupt, my body tensing as I avoid having to listen to her beg and attempt to seduce me with her cringy voice.

I hate nothing more than when one of my brothers has spoken and the person thinks they can come to me and I will overrule it. You'd think these gold diggers would have learned by now. That's not how we operate.

When one of us speaks, we all speak.

"What's going to happen to Eden?" Mrs. Duffy questions from her spot by the door, her hand covering her lips as she holds back a laugh, and I sigh as I walk toward her.

"Nothing."

"Nothing?" KitKat repeats with a cry, and I carry on walking. This entire situation is ridiculous, but I'm not going to repeat myself to her.

I hear Tobias's and Hunter's footsteps as they follow me out of the nurse's office when a thud sounds from behind, making me pause.

Glancing over my shoulder, I stare at Roxy, who is now barefoot with one sandal in her hand, and the other...the other is by Tobias's feet as he rubs the back of his head.

Did that bitch just...?

Barging past Hunter, I charge straight back into the room, watching as Roxy instantly backs up against the wall, fear rich in her green eyes as I slam my palms on either side of her head, caging her in.

"I will fucking torture you to within an inch of your life, do you understand me?" I growl, veins protruding from my forearms as I try to rein in my anger. Her mouth moves, puckering like a fish, but nothing comes out, so I slam my fist by the side of her head, making the photo frames on the wall rattle, and Roxy gasps in shock.

"Please, Xavier, she didn't..." KitKat tries to come up with some shit to make me back off, but her voice only grates on me more.

"Shut the fuck up, KitKat, or you'll be fucking praying the only thing that happened to you was a bit of burned hair," Hunter growls behind me, but I don't turn around, keeping my gaze fixed on Roxy.

Leaning closer, I bring myself chest to chest with her, my skin instantly crawling at the contact, but I know how to lead this weak bitch into a false sense of security only to break her all over again. Bringing my lips to her ear, I shush her gently, like a baby, and her hands find my chest, attempting to soothe the fire burning inside me, but little does she know she only makes it worse.

I've felt the touch of the woman I want, and even if I can't admit it, I know the difference. Roxy's hands feel like claws digging deeper and deeper into my flesh, while Eden…Eden feels like silk gliding across my skin and sending every nerve ending into a frenzy.

"Are you listening, Roxy?" I ask, my voice barely above a whisper, and she hums in response. "Good." I stroke my fingers through her hair with one hand, keeping the other braced on the wall.

Arching against me, she practically purrs like a kitten. A slight glance over my shoulder shows me KitKat is no longer crying as she gapes at us. Tobias and Hunter stand side by side with their arms folded over their chests like bodyguards, and Mrs. Duffy is nowhere in sight.

Perfect.

Before she can fully understand what's going on, my fingers tighten in her hair as I drag her head back, and her seductive moan turns into a painful whimper instantly.

"You ever, and I mean *ever*, make a play like that again toward the Allstars, I will be sure to make you regret the day you ever laid eyes on us. One more word from your mouth about Eden, or to her even, and I'll let her rain hell down on you herself and I'll back every single move she makes."

I release her and she slumps to the floor dramatically, her hand to her chest. I turn away without a backward glance, but I don't miss the sound of her whimper. Now I need to find the pain in my ass that just seems to attract drama like a bee to a flower.

She fights me at every opportunity, and after seeing her last night, so close to having a much more serious accident, I still don't know whether to push her around like my mother wants or defy the almighty Ilana Knight and protect Eden with my soul. The bruises around her eyes and the scrapes down her face had me close to burning this damn town to the ground in retribution.

All I know is Eden is the pretty flower, and I am the honeybee, trying to sting her every chance I get, even though I know it may kill me in the process.

Swinging open the door to Pete's, I spot her instantly. She's sitting in *my* booth, across from Charlie, with her head in her hands as Charlie strokes her arm in comfort.

The smell of hot dogs and burgers fills the air as I take a deep breath. My eyes fix on Eden as she runs her fingers over her braid, desperation in her eyes as I remember the anger she held back on the field earlier.

"If you make her any sadder than she already looks, I will pull you into a headlock and squeeze your Adam's apple while Hunter shoves a leg off one of these chairs so far up your ass it will tickle your tonsils. Agreed? Agreed," Tobias murmurs as he shoulders past me, and Hunter pats me on the back, following his lead.

I watch as Charlie leans in farther, her eyes fixed on mine as she glares daggers across the diner. She's probably warning Eden that we're here and heading in her direction, because Eden sits up straight and cuts her gaze in our direction as she rolls her eyes.

Charlie moves around the booth, placing herself next to Eden who sits at the end, creating space and access for us. Hunter drops in first, and Tobias is quick to do the same, leaving me to sit directly opposite Eden.

Her face looks worse today than it did yesterday, probably because all the blues and purples have darkened around her eyes, and the cuts on the side of her face have started to scab.

I hope they don't scar like the mark next to my right ear. Seeing her cut up makes my own scars burn in sympathy, the memory desperate to infiltrate my mind, but I hold it at bay, breaking the silence around us to distract me.

"We just left KitKat," I state, and she bites her bottom lip, refusing to look at me. "I'm hoping you've encouraged the haircut she desperately needed."

Her eyes whip to mine, her mouth falling open as she gapes at me.

Hunter scoffs, breaking our eye contact as he grins. "I apologize. That's Xavier's attempt at a joke. You may be unfamiliar with it since it's rare when he actually tries. Wait until he smiles or laughs, you're going to think there's an alien in the room."

Charlie and Tobias snicker along with him, but Eden says nothing as she fiddles with her hands on the table.

Clearing my throat, I stretch my legs out under the

table, accidentally knocking hers, but she doesn't move away, so I hold my position. The feel of her leg against mine makes me hyperaware of her closeness, and my heart jolts at the fact she doesn't pull away.

"I'm here to call a truce."

Frowning, she glances at Tobias and Hunter, who I can feel staring at me in the same way since I said nothing about this on the way over, but I know I'm not doing the right thing by following my mother's orders. I just don't know any different. The embarrassing fear of her demolishing my dreams of Ohio State got the better of me, but I'm big enough and strong enough not to jump when she says.

I won't give everything up for this girl, it's not in my nature, but I can at least try to do...something. I don't know what, just...more than what I've been doing already. I don't want the strain with my brothers, and I don't want to see hatred in her eyes that's there because of me.

"Do you even know what that means?" Eden asks, finally responding, and I bite back the rude response on the tip of my tongue as she eyes me skeptically.

"You're just going to have to trust me."

"You're going to lure me into a false sense of security all over again, and I don't have time for that," she states with a snort, folding her arms over her chest as she leans forward on the table.

My eyes fall to the swell of her tits, and I fight the need to lick my lips as I take her in. I know Hunter and Tobias will be looking at her just the same, and the brush of her leg against mine has my dick twitching for attention.

God, I wish I could wrap my fist in her blonde locks and watch her fall apart just like she did before we knew what was going on. Feeling her eyes on me as she waits for a response, I pull myself from my internal thoughts and lift my hands in a sign of surrender.

"I said I'll cool it."

She flicks her gaze to Tobias and Hunter who shrug, not wanting to say anything when they are likely as surprised as she is.

Uncrossing her hands, she taps her fingers on the table, and I can feel her brain ticking from here.

"Okay, tell me what your mom wants with me."

Sighing, I slouch deeper into my seat as I shake my head.

"See? All talk and no action," she adds as she stands.

I miss the feel of her leg against mine as soon as she moves, which is the only explanation I have for giving in and responding.

"She wants you to pay for whatever your parents did to her. I don't know any more than that. I'm one of my mother's pawns just as much as you are."

I can practically feel Tobias's eyes bugging out as I seem to lose my filter, and I have to bite my tongue before I tell her any more.

"Right, so it's my fault your mother is upset?" she grinds out, but I simply shrug. Stroking the stray hair off her face, she sighs. "You wouldn't know which parents, by any chance, would you?"

I don't, but I know someone who might have more information on the matter since he knew before I did, but I don't say that. She needs to figure this shit out for herself. I can tell things are difficult with her and Archie, and if I want any chance of redemption, I can't get involved in that mess.

"No," I answer, and she stands.

She doesn't utter a word of acknowledgement as she strolls from the diner without a backwards glance.

Charlie clears her throat, a forced smile on her lips as she slides from the booth and follows after her.

"Well, that went well," Tobias comments with a grin,

and I frown at him.

"Are you joking? She just left," I gripe, and he shakes his head.

"Yeah, but she didn't curse you out before she did."

"That's because she didn't say a word," Hunter reasons, stretching his arms over the back of the booth as we watch her climb into Charlie's Jeep.

"Still, it's progress," Tobias singsongs. "I almost want to tell you how proud of you I am for being a good boy," Tobias adds, and I know he's talking to me.

"Shut the fuck up, Tobias," I grumble. "Where's Linda? I need a fucking burger now," I mutter, changing the subject, and neither of them say a word as I wave her over.

Adjusting my jeans does nothing to calm my cock as I rub the spot where we were touching with my other hand.

She makes me weak. I know it. But fuck if I care right now.

ELEVEN

Eden

The Uber pulls up outside of Charlie's home, the late evening sun shining down on the structure. I offer the driver a half-smile as I step from the car, looking up at the cute house before me. It's still a damn mansion, they all are around here, but it's smaller, quaint, and gated, which surprises me.

The heat is still going strong, and since Charlie lives farther inland, it feels hotter without the sea breeze, which is why I opted to go with my blue and white striped mini summer dress. With its thin straps, plunging neckline, cinching belt, and linen material, it's as cool as I'm going to get without rocking up to Charlie's birthday barbecue naked.

My hair is tossed up on top of my head in a messy bun, with a few loose tendrils around my face, and my sunglasses are firmly in place, offering a shield between the worst of my bruising and the other people here. The scrapes on the side of my face have healed a lot, but they are still noticeable. My arm is the same, but it's just too warm to keep covering it up.

I can hear my dad in my ear telling me the fresh air will do it good, and I roll my eyes even now.

As I step up to the wrought iron gates, they instantly start to roll open. There's no little security booth out here, and I can't see the surveillance cameras, but it must be controlled by someone.

I follow the pathway toward the house where cars are all parked up front. It's a true suburban home with expensive but not luxury cars outside, a paved path lined with perfectly trimmed grass, and the classic white wraparound. It reminds me a lot of White River.

My heart hurts that my G-Wagon is undriveable. Ryan promised he would get a mechanic to take a look at it, and

I was holding out hope. I don't know how much longer I will be able to continue using my Amex card, but more importantly, the G-Wagon was a gift from my dad for my birthday which hasn't even arrived yet, and it's already close to being totaled.

Brushing my hands down my dress, I try not to stress. I need to focus on the here and now. There is enough going on around me to take a lifetime to process and deal with—like the fact I'm once again living in a home where I desperately don't want to see the other people there. Thankfully Richard hasn't changed at all, avoiding me at all costs, and at least Archie has been wise enough to give me some space. I'm not ready to face that shit show just yet.

Surprisingly, I have had no backlash with what happened with KitKat. I haven't seen her or Roxy in school, so it may change when I do, but apparently when Xavier said he was calling a truce, he meant it. I know his sway over the school means he probably chooses my punishment, and I've had none.

If the Allstars think that suddenly makes everything okay with us, then they are truly mistaken.

Other students have gossiped about it, but not directly

to my face since they seem quite happy to give me a wide berth when I'm walking around campus. I'm not sure why exactly, but I'm all for it. Even the Allstars have left me alone. Two whole days of silent bliss with nothing more than a glance here or there, but otherwise, I'm actually being given a second to breathe.

Evidently if I follow Ilana's rules of going to school and living at the Freemont house, my life actually becomes a little easier, but for how long? That's what worries me.

Laughter sounds out in the distance, likely from the other side of Charlie's home, as I step up to the bright red door. Before I knock, it swings open, and I instantly know I'm staring at Charlie's mom.

She has the same brown hair and big eyes behind stylish glasses, even her smile is the same.

"Eden, thank you so much for coming. Charlie has not shut up about you. I'm Elaine," she greets with a smile, and the tension I was feeling immediately eases as her calm personality washes over me.

"It's so nice to meet you. Thank you for inviting me," I reply, reaching my hand out politely, but she pulls me into a brief hug, leaving me a little stunned as she suddenly releases me and turns for me to follow her.

Okay then.

Picking up my pace, I quickly come to walk beside her as we head down the pale yellow hall and step into the kitchen. It almost appears like what I'd expect a cute little farmhouse would look like—wood countertops and cupboards with an island in the middle.

"Everyone is outside if you want to join them. I'm just refilling drinks for everyone, and Charlie is trying to help her dad over at the grill so he doesn't burn everything." The smile on her face shows no real complaint in her voice, only the love she seems to have for him.

"Are you sure you don't want me to help with anything first?" I offer, impressed with my own ability to be polite, but she shakes her head.

"No, don't be silly. Besides, if Charlie saw me putting you to work, she would give me all that unnecessary sass, and I just have no strength for that today." I chuckle along with her as I make my way outside, pulling Charlie's birthday card from my purse to take to her before I drop it on the side.

Charlie made it sound like it would be a small affair, family only. I clearly underestimated the size of her damn family. There must be at least twenty people here. A few small children run around the grass at the far end of the backyard, playing tag, while the adults sit around a huge table, drinks in hand as they laugh and chat amongst themselves.

It's strange to see a home with no pool in the backyard, but it really would spoil the space and the relaxed vibes they have going on. It's so quaint.

Spotting Charlie to the left on the patio with a guy who must be her dad, I head in their direction. As I get closer, I smile at the pink, plastic tiara on her head, bedazzled and all, and when she fully turns around, I spot a huge "18" badge dead center on her purple floral dress.

"Happy birthday, Charlie," I say with a smile, catching her attention as she meets my gaze, and she squeals.

"Thank you, and thank you for coming. It saves me from dying of boredom from these losers." She laughs as her dad fake glares at her. God, they are all so wholesome it's crazy, and it makes me jealous. My dad would look at me like that all the time.

"Hi, Eden. I'm Simon. Please take this grill sergeant away from me," he says with a mock concerned look in his eyes.

His salt and pepper hair frames his face, and his smile

reaches all the way up to his brown eyes. He would definitely be rocking those hot dad vibes if he wasn't wearing a bright orange Hawaiian shirt right now.

"Puh-lease, you would burn the whole backyard down if you weren't supervised," Charlie shoots back instantly, and I can't help but grin along with them, spying the other table filled with a wide variety of side dishes and the birthday cake.

"Seriously, Charlie bear, go away. I even gave you access to the alcohol cabinet, and you're still standing here micromanaging me," he exclaims, his eyes wide as if he's confused about why she's not wasted in a corner somewhere.

Simon looks to me for help, so I link my arm through Charlie's and pull her away, and she follows reluctantly.

"Don't blame me when the food is burned and you can't eat anything," Charlie gripes, but I don't take her on, not missing the shake of her dad's head as he hears her.

"Charlie bear, show me the alcohol," I say with a pout, singing her dad's nickname for her, and she rolls her eyes at me.

With all the shit going on in my life, combined with the sweet, family love in the air, I'm going to need a lot of alcohol to get me through tonight, especially if her grandmother doesn't offer any details.

I'm already on a downward spiral since arriving in Knight's Creek. I silently pray nothing I discover sends me any deeper down the bleak black hole.

We join everyone at the tables lined up under the gazebo and Charlie introduces me, their names going right over my head except when she points out Grandma J, and my heart pounds a little harder when recognition seems to flash in her eyes, but she says nothing as we take our seats—Charlie is the only person between us.

"Food's ready!" Charlie's dad shouts at the top of his lungs, and the table is suddenly overrun with food and people.

Leaning back in my seat, I watch them together. The whole family is in sync with each other, and I feel completely out of place. I remember every time my dad would find an excuse to use the grill, and we would spend hours upon hours outside as a family, laughing, joking, playing cards, and just...being. I miss those moments, even if they did drive me crazy sometimes. Now I regret not doing it even more.

"Psst. Psst."

Glancing to my left, following the sound, I find Grandma J looking straight at me. Her gray hair is perfectly straight to her chin, her face devoid of any makeup as she wears her wrinkles with true pride. Her brown eyes sparkle like she's filled with stories to tell, and I'm open to listening.

She looks at me as Charlie leans over the table, grabbing two glasses of bourbon and offering me one as she falls back into her seat with the other. I definitely won't say no.

As soon as I have the glass in my hands, another glass appears in hers, and she reaches it out for us to clink together, and the second the sound rings in my ears, she leans forward.

"You look just like your granny, girl. She had all this blonde hair and sparkly blue eyes."

My heart almost stops at her statement as she downs her bourbon in one gulp. On instinct, I drink mine down, and the liquid burns my throat as I repeat her words again and again in my mind.

Charlie suddenly falls back in her seat, her mouth full of food as she glances at me, and her eyes bug out of her head, breaking the moment.

"Oh my God, Eden. You need to get food now before it's all eaten. They are savages," she mumbles around her mouthful of food, and I can't help but scoff at her.

"I think it takes a savage to know a savage," I retort, my mind still reeling from Grandma J's words, but when I glance her way again, she's talking to Charlie's mom.

Placing the tumbler on the table, I realize I'm shaking. I need her to tell me more, anything at all. Both of my parents told me my grandparents had passed away. Is that still true, or just another one of their many lies? Either way, I'm desperate for more, wanting to cling to every word that passes her lips.

Charlie thrusts a burger smothered in ketchup in my face, and I reluctantly take it, plastering a smile on my lips as I force myself to eat it. I really need to take better care of myself, especially since it's a little after six in the evening and this is the first thing I've eaten today. Plus, I went for a jog on the beach earlier. Fuck. I'm just not good at remembering to eat when so much is happening around me.

I sit quietly, smiling when needed and forcing a laugh when someone tells a joke, withdrawing from the whole atmosphere here. I'm lost in the memory of my dad as I bask in their family environment. My head hurts. My heart too.

At some point, someone replaces my empty bourbon glass with a Sex on the Beach cocktail, followed by another, and another, the sickly sweet concoction going down easily as Charlie chugs them like water.

Someone is already tipsy, slurring her words and mumbling Archie's name under her breath as she taps away on her phone. It seems like she may be sending him drunk texts, but I don't want to get involved in all of that. We never really got around to the Archie talk, but I know she won't forgive him until I do. I can see the loyalty sparkling in her gaze.

"I'll be back in a minute," she suddenly murmurs, guilt in her eyes, and I know she's going to call Archie, but I don't say a thing as I nod, letting her go. Her mom watches her leave with a hint of concern on her face but says nothing. Instead, she hands me another cocktail, squeezing my shoulder before she continues around the table, taking any empty plates into the house.

Looking into my glass, I become lost in the crazy going on around me. I'm here for Charlie, but it feels like we've barely said two words to each other. I hoped she would help set up a conversation with her grandmother like we talked about, but it seems she's forgotten, and it's her birthday, so

I don't want to be rude.

"You look lost, girly."

Sighing, I sit up straight, only to find Grandma J now in Charlie's seat, her gaze fixed on mine, and my mouth goes dry as all the questions I'd spent the past few hours considering are suddenly forgotten.

Clearing my throat, I take a huge gulp of my drink before I say the first words that come to mind.

"You knew my gran?"

A soft smile plays on her lips as she takes another shot of bourbon.

"I've always known that chick. She was batshit crazy, always surrounded by men, shaking her ass on the dance floor like a queen, and putting the world straight whenever she had one too many drags of her weed."

My eyes widen with each word that leaves her lips. My gran sounded awesome as hell, and the hurt of never knowing her rises within me.

"She sounds badass," I finally respond, and she hums in response, content to sit beside me without speaking, but I need more. I remember seeing a picture of my mom with her parents when she was a child, but they had brown hair, straight and dull, along with permanent scowls on their faces. So I can only assume she was my dad's mom.

"Everyone in Knight's Creek seems to know who I am. Did you know my parents?" I ask, biting the bullet. She may not answer or even know them at all, but at least this way I won't be beating myself up later for not asking anything.

She pulls her gaze from mine, her eyes misting over as if she's lost inside her thoughts until she finally nods, her gaze distant as a ghost of a smile crosses her lips.

"Yes, yes, I knew them."

My heart pounds in my chest, and my hands sweat as I dig my nails into my palms. Her honest answer fills me with hope as I try to remain calm and act casual, even with the alcohol coursing through my veins.

"Thank you for being open with me," I murmur, downing the rest of the cocktail before I meet her gaze again. "You don't happen to know who my parents actually were, though, do you? Obviously I have a twin, and we were both raised by different parents like some kind of *Parent Trap* remake."

She snickers at my comparison as she shakes her head. "Girly, you look just like your daddy, don't play me like that."

I don't blink. I don't move a muscle. I don't think I even breathe as I read her face and eyes, looking for a lie, but all I see is the truth, even in her sassy snark.

My dad was my dad. He had blonde hair, my smile, my eyes…Archie's eyes.

Squeezing my eyes shut, I will myself not to cry. Hearing someone confirm my father was actually the man who raised me is overwhelming in the best possible way.

Taking a deep breath, I open my eyes to find a tumbler almost filled to the top with bourbon. I glance at Grandma J, and she nods at it, encouraging me to drown in the burn. I manage two large gulps before I have to pause, my lips tingling as liquid courage thrums through my veins.

"Someone sent me an obituary about me, saying my mom was Anabel, and I don't know how true that is," I tell her, staring into the distance as I share more information with her. If it catches her by surprise, she doesn't show it.

"Well, she was definitely the one to carry the babies, I do know that."

I almost choke on fresh air as she willingly tells me my history, my story. I feel sick in the pit of my stomach, but I force a smile when Elaine collects my plate, the sound of the children filtering into our bubble as I take a deep breath.

"Grandma J, come help in the kitchen," someone calls out, and she stands.

"Please don't go yet. I have so much to ask, I..."

"I'm sorry, girly," she murmurs, stroking my back in comfort before she brushes her pants down. "You and I both know I said far too much, but I see your pain, and you deserve some of the truth, even if it isn't all joy."

With that, she turns on her heel, links her arm through a family member's elbow, and saunters inside.

Grabbing the glass of bourbon, I swallow down the rest of the glass, ignoring the burn as I eye the actual bottle on the table, opting to fill my tumbler up again.

My mom...isn't my mom.

My mom, my *biological* mom, is dead.

Dead.

Just like my dad.

I'm officially an orphan.

Downing the bourbon, I quickly refill it, not feeling the burn like I was earlier. My whole body is numb with pain and despair, but now isn't the time or place to cry. No. That's for later.

For now, I drink.

Pass me the bourbon.

TWELVE

Eden

"Are you sure you're going to be okay from here, Eden? I can walk you up to the house if you'd like," Charlie's dad, Simon, offers, but I shake my head, the movement making the world sway even more.

"Nope. I'm all good, thank you," I slur before climbing down from his SUV and pushing the door shut with my hip without glancing back. The pretty lights lining the path are the only illumination aside from the full moon in the sky.

Moving to Archie's front door, I manage not to trip

over my own feet somehow as I rummage around in my little black purse for the keys.

Where are they? Where the fuck are the goddamn keys? They must be here somewhere, but I just can't feel them, and it's too dark to see. Even with the porch light on, I'm struggling.

Maybe I should walk around to the back. Do they ever even lock the patio doors? I'm not sure, but I may as well find out instead of standing here messing around for hours. The alcohol coursing through my veins is making things ten times harder.

Glancing over my shoulder, I find Simon still sitting in his SUV, the interior light on as he watches me with concern in his eyes, but I plaster a huge smile on my face as I indicate what I'm doing. Not waiting around for him to stop me, I move as quickly as I can to the back of the beach house, stumbling a little as I go.

As soon as I'm around the corner and out of sight, I slow down, the world feeling like it's spinning on its axis. The lights are on back here, and the sound of soft classical music fills the air, making me pause.

I don't want to run into Richard, not in this state. It's highly unlikely I'll be able to keep my mouth shut, and

I don't want to finally have *that* conversation with him when I've had too much alcohol. I should have stayed at Charlie's, but I know I wouldn't have settled there.

At the last minute, I decide to walk past the steps leading up to the back patio and pool area, and instead, I let my feet carry me farther down to the beach. The second I step onto the sand, I kick off my sandals and stand in place, sinking my toes into it and letting it settle my soul.

I don't see a soul around, not that there would usually be anyone here at this time of night. It's completely quiet except for the sound of the waves crashing against the shore—nature's lullaby. It feels weird that it's Saturday night and it's been quiet the whole weekend. Archie didn't even throw a party yesterday, and I don't know how their game finished either. But they were thankfully away, and I'm forcing myself not to give a shit.

Tonight feels like it went from bad to worse. I finally learned something true about my life, but in learning it I also broke my soul a little. I was prepared to do anything I could, but I forgot the impact it could have, which is why I couldn't stop bringing the bourbon to my lips. Eventually I boycotted the tumbler at some point and drank it straight from the bottle. All the alcohol I've been drinking lately clearly built up my ability to hold my liquor better.

I have no idea where Charlie went, she never came back, but Elaine eventually came to tell me she had passed out drunk on her bed, and that's when Charlie's dad offered me a ride home.

All I can hear in my mind are Anabel's and Jennifer's names on repeat over and over again—my biological mom and the woman who raised me. Neither of which are here right now. My dad is dead, and Richard is upstairs, but he's proved to be about as useful as a guitar with no strings.

I don't realize I've made it to the water's edge until the cold water laps at my feet, making me jump. Shit, that's cold, but I love it all the same. Throwing my purse on the sand behind me, out of the water's reach, I take another step hoping the water will numb my pain just like it does my body.

I can't help but push through the chill that racks my bones, sobering me up as the water hits mid-thigh just below my dress. Tilting my head back, I glance at the clear night's sky, wishing I could see stars twinkling while the moon glimmers above, the lights from the houses along the ocean offering a low glow.

No matter the time of day or what's happening around

me, this is always my happy place, with the sand between my toes, and the water coating my skin.

Nothing on the shore offers me anything but pain, and I just don't understand how to move past all of this. The secrets. The lies. This town.

Taking another step, I shiver as the water hits my inner thigh, my dress clinging to my skin as I push past the waves. I struggle as one knocks me back a step. Another hits just after it, pushing me again, but this time I stumble and lose my footing, and it's the only opportunity the water needs to take me off my feet altogether.

Falling under the tide, I swallow a mouthful of salty seawater before a scream leaves my lips. I flail around and scramble to find my footing, knowing that if I can just get one down, I will be able to stand up, but the waves continue to crash over the top of me, forcing me to swirl around in the water, the current making it impossible to find my footing.

Desperate for air, I manage to feel the sandy bottom with the palm of my hand, and I try to place my foot down beside it so I can rise, but it's much more difficult than I expected.

Why am I actually fighting?

There is nothing here for me, and if I let the ocean consume me, I'll be reunited with my dad. Maybe that's the best thing to do after all. I would be safe with him. But if I was so content with that, then why am I still trying to break through the surface?

My father's words from my dream play on repeat in my mind. *I need you to survive, thrive, and beat the odds. You'll find your way. You always do.*

I hold on to them as I start to weaken, but then all at once, strong hands grip my waist and pull me from the depths of my despair.

Choking and spluttering, I feel someone moving me around, but I can't open my eyes as I continuously retch, my dress completely drenched as the water tries to keep hold of me. The saltwater burns the back of my nose and throat as I manage to stop choking long enough to inhale.

My lungs burn as I continue to splutter a little. Taking another deep breath, I pry my eyes open, coming face to face with someone's back, and that's when I take stock of my body. I must be thrown over someone's shoulder. I grip their waist tightly as I feel their arm banded around my legs as they walk us out of the ocean and onto the sand.

My eyes burn from the seawater, and my hair sticks to

my face, but I'm too scared to let go of my savior to swipe it away.

Suddenly, I'm being pulled from my place on their shoulder, but I continue to cling to them as they move me.

My toes skim the sand beneath us, and I look up through my lashes to find Hunter glaring down at me. I can practically feel his anger vibrating off of him as I tighten my grip on his neck, clinging to him as I stare back at him speechlessly.

"What the ever-loving fuck are you doing out here alone, Eden?" he growls, but all I can do is gape at him. I have no words, none at all, but I don't shy away from the fury in his eyes. Instead, that's all I focus on as I try to calm myself.

My breathing is still erratic, and I suddenly remember how drenched to the bone I am—it's freezing. I shiver under Hunter's gaze, and he sighs when he realizes I have no answer for him. Not right now, at least.

"Let me get you warm and dry, but you have some fucking explaining to do. I can smell the liquor from miles away," he grumbles, lifting me off my feet once more and carrying me bridal style. Keeping my hands firmly around his neck, I close my eyes as I rest against him, soaking in his heat to try and keep my chills at bay.

I could almost fall asleep, but the second I feel him carrying me up some steps, I panic, knowing he's opted to take me back to the Allstars' mansion. I don't have the mental or physical capabilities to deal with the three of them right now.

As if sensing my inner turmoil, I feel the briefest touch as his lips brush my forehead, but it's gone so quickly it almost feels like a dream. The softness of his whisper in my ear, however, confirms his touch.

"Don't worry, love. The others are sleeping."

I relax instantly at his words, opening my eyes just as he unlocks the door to get inside his home with his palm recognition. Kicking the door shut behind us, he remains quiet as he carries me up the stairs before stepping into the room I remember as his when they decided to play tag a few weeks ago.

Hitting the lights, he tries to place me on the bed, but I can't bring myself to release him. As much as I hate the Allstars and everything they stand for, deep in my soul, I know I can trust him. Trust Hunter. Especially since he just pulled me from the water. I'm scared I may drift away again if I let go.

"Just two seconds, Eden. I need to close the door quietly, okay?"

Bringing his hands to my wrists, he slowly tries to pry them apart, and I whimper, not releasing him until I meet his eyes and see that he'll be quick.

The second I let go, he's at the door and back again in a flash, dropping to his knees before me as he tries to look me over.

"You're drunk," he observes simply, his hands braced on the bed on either side of my legs as I look down at him, and I nod. "I'm trying to figure out why on earth you would go out into the water in this state, love, I really am. But I'm coming up blank, and we need to take care of you first. So do you want to have a quick shower or just dry off for now?"

Shaking, I point to the bathroom, hoping a warm shower will help, and he nods in agreement. He holds his hand out for mine, and I stare at it for a moment before intertwining our fingers, then he slowly pulls me to my feet.

He leads me to the bathroom. I stay firmly at his side as he turns the light on and presses a few buttons, the shower suddenly coming to life before my eyes.

It's sleek in here. Charcoal tiles line the walls, floor, and ceiling, making the chrome shower and vanity pop. The whole thing just screams Hunter. The bathtub sits to the left, an open clawfoot one, and if I were in better shape, I would be gushing over the whole thing, but right now, I just need to shower.

Reluctantly letting go of his hand, I peel my dress from my skin, letting it drop to the floor with a slap as I struggle to undo my bra.

"Uh, I don't know whether to offer you help or give you privacy," Hunter murmurs, looking up at the ceiling, and I realize I just casually started to undress without a care in the world.

"Please help me," I rasp, my voice sounding hoarse, and he slowly meets my gaze. I give him my back, and it takes a moment before he undoes the clasp. The stroke of his fingers on my skin sends a shiver down my spine that has nothing to do with the cold.

I strip the straps from my arms and remove my panties, completely unashamed. He's seen everything already since he protected me during my naked walk of shame through school.

"Could you stay while I..." My voice trails off as I point toward the shower, and he nods, giving me a soft smile.

Stepping into the huge shower space, the jets pointing in every direction, with the floor space to easily hold four people, I put my hand under the spray, feeling the temperature, and it almost feels like needles in comparison to my cold hands.

Slowly stepping farther under the spray, I hold my breath, letting the pain of the water ease as my body gets used to the heat. I feel a lot more in control of my body than I did earlier.

"Are you okay?" I hear him ask, and I glance over my shoulder to find him watching me with concern. "Your face is all scrunched up like you're in pain."

"I'm alright. It just feels harsh against my skin, that's all," I murmur, reaching up to try and undo my hair from the messed up bun.

Everything is all tangled together, and I can't seem to get the hair tie out, but with one pleading look over my shoulder, Hunter is by my side in the shower with his hands in my hair, trying to help. I take him in as he works the hair tie through my locks. He's in a pair of jersey shorts, which now stick to his body, a pale blue top, and sneakers. He's completely distracting me from everything else going on right now.

"Magic," he says, holding my hair tie between us with a pleased smile on his face as I feel my hair touch my shoulders. "Are you okay while I get you some clothes?" he asks, bending to meet my gaze. I bite my lip, nodding in response.

He leaves without a word as I turn around, tilting my head back to let the water cascade over my hair as I gently massage my fingers in my scalp. Quickly working his men's two in one shampoo and conditioner through my hair, I rinse and repeat, finishing up just as he steps back into the bathroom in a fresh pair of shorts and a white t-shirt.

He holds out a large, fluffy, charcoal towel spread out wide, so I walk toward him, letting him envelop me in it, and I gasp when I realize it's heated too.

"Thank you," I whisper, securing the towel around my chest before he retakes my hand and leads me to his bed, where there is a band tee and boxers waiting for me.

Taking a seat beside the clothes for a minute, I sigh as my brain slowly tries to catch up with everything that just happened. Hunter takes a seat beside me, not uttering a word as my head falls into my hands and tears track down my face.

I don't know how long I cry, but when he places his

hand on my shoulder and pulls me into his side, I go willingly, the towel still snug around my body. He doesn't shush me or try to get me to talk. He simply holds me while my emotions play out between us.

When my tear ducts dry up and there's nothing left to give, I sit upright, my eyes puffy and swollen.

"I'm sorry," I murmur, wiping at my face as I internally get mad at myself for breaking down like that, but my brain is now fully aware I was very close to dying because of my own stupidity.

"Do you want to talk about what happened? Or would you rather sleep?" Hunter inquires, running his fingers through his blond hair.

I stare at him like an idiot, trying to decide. "I, uh, learned some stuff tonight, things that cut deeper than I expected, which led to me drinking too much, and you saw what happened from there," I admit, my lips deciding to talk before I had fully decided.

He nods in acknowledgment. "You want to talk about it?"

"I guess that depends. Am I talking to the Allstar Hunter or the Hunter who brought me snacks and meds when I was on my period?"

He looks at me with pure sincerity in his eyes, just like the guy who practically took care of me when I was in my crankiest form, and without another thought, I decide to spill every thought and emotion, hoping he'll take care of me like that all over again.

Hunter

The pain in her eyes is what has me approaching her cautiously instead of steamrolling her into giving me the answers I so desperately want. I need to know what in the hell she was doing out there in the water when she had clearly drunk too much beforehand.

If I'd been able to sleep, then I wouldn't have been out on the deck with my guitar at midnight, playing the same tune over and over again. She's beyond lucky I watched her stumble down to the water's edge, and that's when my feet had moved of their own accord, knowing she was in danger.

Now, as she sits beside me on the bed, I want to wrap her up in my arms and make all her troubles disappear.

"Let's get you dressed then. I have water in my mini

fridge, and you can get under the sheets to keep warm, okay?" I offer, and she smiles in appreciation.

I hate that she asked which Hunter she'd be getting. I only want to be my true self around her—no barriers and no secrets—but it's hard in a town like this, especially when Xavier is making choices and decisions for all of us, but he did promise a truce. I'm just going to have to hold him to that now.

Grabbing the shirt, I shake it out before putting it over her head and pulling her damp hair from beneath it. She feeds her arms through the sleeves, her cheeks blushing as I help her dress. Her makeup is mostly off, revealing the purple and blue bruising around her eyes, and the scabs on the side of her face look sensitive.

Standing, she steps into the boxers on her own, and I grab the towel from the bed, waiting for her to finish. The moment she does, I gently use the towel to pat away the remaining streaks of mascara from her face before throwing it into my laundry basket. Eden murmurs her thanks, but I only smile in response. She's vulnerable, almost delicate right now, and I don't want her to feel like I'm abusing my chance of seeing her this way.

Pulling my sheets back, I gesture for her to get under

while I grab two bottles of water from my fridge, and when I turn around and see her lying in *my* bed with *my* t-shirt on, my internal caveman goes fucking nuts.

My heart pounds in my chest and my skin burns to feel her pressed up against me, my desires overwhelming my senses as I see her exactly where I want her—as mine.

She smiles softly at me as I hand her a water and take a seat on the bed beside her, too scared to lie down in case it has her putting her defenses back up, but she surprises me by patting the pillow, telling me without words that she's comfortable with me joining her.

Sinking into my bed, I brace my head on my hand as I stare down at her, watching as the gears in her mind work overtime to find the words to say.

"I found out that my dad was my biological dad, but my biological mom was Archie's mom, Anabel. Well, *our* mom and dad is probably the correct term, I guess. So I realized my biological parents are both dead. Just...dead. Which leaves me with a twin brother who I can't even look at right now and two parents who aren't our parents nor acting like parents should. Does that even make sense?" She sighs, covering her hands with her face as she rambles, and as depressing as her words are, she looks fucking adorable.

"That sounds like a rough blow whichever way you look at it," I finally respond. Parents are a touchy subject for me. I have no love, no care, or affection in that regard, but if it were Bethany, Cody, or even Ryan, I would be broken inside.

Still hiding behind her hands, I stroke my thumb across her fingers until she slowly pulls them away from her face.

"I'm so sorry, I just, all of this is embarrassing," she murmurs, not meeting my gaze, but I tilt her chin up until she meets my eyes.

"None of this is embarrassing, not even a little bit, love. But I need you to tell me what you were doing out in the water." I hold my breath, waiting for her to respond, worrying I've overstepped until she finally nods.

"Honestly, I-I don't even know. Charlie's dad dropped me off, and I couldn't find my key to unlock the front door at Archie's. So I went around to the side, but instead of heading for the patio, not wanting to see Richard, I was just drawn to the water instead."

I watch as she struggles to find the right words, but I keep quiet, giving her time to process, licking her lips as I replay the scene in my head. Fear wells under the surface of my skin as I remember how hard my feet pounded the sand as I rushed to get to her.

"I love the ocean, like l-o-v-e. I would marry the damn thing if I could. As a kid, I always wanted to be a mermaid," she shares, making me smile as she takes a deep breath. "It calls to me all the time, just like tonight, but tonight I wasn't in the right headspace to think clearly, even without the booze. Things just went really bad really quickly when I went too far out."

Dropping my hand from her chin, I stroke her arm, building up the courage to ask her the most important question of all as I swallow past the lump in my throat.

"When I was rushing toward you, there was a moment when you stopped splashing around, like you'd stopped fighting or something." I don't say anything else, hoping she understands what I want to know, and she bites her lip, her eyes downcast as she avoids my gaze.

"I did," she whispers, squeezing her eyes shut for the briefest of moments before she meets my gaze, her blue eyes sparkling with determination. "For the smallest of moments, I didn't see anything wrong with joining my dad. It seemed like the safest option, but there was still this part of me that was desperate to breathe again."

The tension drifts from my body as she speaks the

honest truth. Thank God.

"I'm glad you didn't stop fighting," I mutter, and she smiles.

"Me too. There is still a lot for me to learn about my parents. Drinking excessively and going out into the water wasn't the right way to handle it. I know I overreacted."

"I don't think you overreacted, Eden." Taking a deep breath, I decide she deserves to know a deeper side of me. I *want* to share that side of myself with her. The ocean calls to her, beckoning her closer, and she is *my* ocean. "My parents weren't good people, Eden. Are there worse people than them? Probably, but they should never have been allowed to have children. The whole damn family heritage should have been cut off many generations ago. The things they did to Bethany and me…there aren't any words, none, but I feel completely indifferent toward them. I watched them die right in front of my eyes, and as much as it may have scarred me, nothing scarred me as much as the pain they put me through."

I feel like a weight has been lifted off my chest. I'm unable to refrain from talking about my own pain, trying to convince her that I don't want her to feel like I'm taking her vulnerability and using it against her.

"Oh, Hunter," she murmurs, cupping my cheek as she holds my gaze, our own brands of pain swirling between us. "Is everyone in this town broken?"

"I honestly don't care enough about many others to find out," I answer, stilling as her thumb strokes my bottom lip.

"I think that's enough heavy talk for one night, don't you?" she whispers, and I nod. "I don't want to be alone, and somehow my subconscious knows I can trust you, even when I'm at my most vulnerable," she admits, and I smile.

"It's cute that you thought I was going to leave you alone," I tease, and she laughs ever so slightly before bringing her soft, plump lips to mine. It's over all too quickly as she pushes me onto my back and nestles in against my side, her head on my chest as she relaxes.

My body calms at her touch, relaxing just like hers. One thing I've learned is that she's dangerous when she's hurt. She can easily destroy everything around her, but she doesn't. Instead, she destroys herself.

TOXIC CREEK

KC KEAN

THIRTEEN

Xavier

Taking another sip of my black coffee does nothing to calm the jitters inside me. I'm exhausted, physically and mentally drained, and it's all because of *them*.

It's hilarious how Hunter always tries to quietly sneak out of the house to the back patio when he can't sleep, seemingly forgetting that unlocking the door sets off the alarm on everyone's device, and even though he shuts it off quickly, it's never fast enough not to disturb me.

I wasn't surprised when I heard my phone vibrate as an indicator, the screen coming to life with the night vision showing him, guitar in hand, heading outside. When I heard it go off again, letting me know he was back, I almost hadn't looked, but a part of my brain forced me to, and that's when I saw them.

Wet through to the bone, Hunter cradled Eden in his arms as she clung to him. The vision burned my retinas. What the hell happened in that time he was gone? Every fiber in my body begged for me to go and find out, but I knew deep down I would only make the situation worse.

Whatever occurred, Hunter was clearly there for Eden and whatever she needed.

That piece of information didn't actually sit well with me though. I'd barely slept at all, knowing she was down the hallway. I tossed and turned for hours until I gave up and came downstairs. There had been no other alarm notification, so I knew she was still here, holed up in Hunter's room with him, and that just made me fucking angry at this point.

Why hadn't Hunter sent a message in the group chat explaining her presence? Why the fuck weren't they down here yet? Glancing at my watch again, I clench my jaw as I notice it's now after ten in the morning. My motherfucking Sundays are supposed to be relaxing.

That's why I'm sitting here, *waiting* in the kitchen, *waiting* for someone to make an appearance. The sound of shuffling behind me catches my attention, and when I peer over my shoulder, I find Hunter sauntering into the kitchen without a care in the world, rubbing his hands through his hair as he yawns. I get a barely controllable urge to punch him in the dick.

"Hey," he grunts, his voice gravelly as he bypasses me at the center island and heads straight for the freshly brewed coffee. With his back to me, standing in just a pair of jersey shorts, I stare at him in exasperation, waiting for something, anything at all, but he doesn't utter a fucking peep.

Clearing my throat, I try to calm myself, but I know it'll be harder to do than a simple breath. "Are we going to discuss the elephant in the room?" I finally ask, and Hunter glances over his shoulder at me, confusion in his eyes as he shakes his head.

"What elephant in the room?"

"Well, not this room specifically, but, well, yours." Realization dawns on his face, and he glances to the open doors leading to the stairs. "You do know you never shut the alarm off in time, right?" I add, taking another sip of my coffee, and he sighs.

"Sorry, I couldn't sleep, I—"

"Well, obviously I know that bit. It's the other part I'm more intrigued with," I interrupt as he finishes putting his coffee together, but when he turns around, I spot two steaming mugs in his hands. "Oh, coffee in bed now, huh? She must have tired you out enough last night then," I remark, feeling my temperature rise, but he simply shakes his head and doesn't respond to the fight I'm intentionally trying to pick so he'll fucking spill.

"You don't know what you're talking about, X," he murmurs, walking toward me and placing both mugs down on the countertop. I glare daggers at them like this is all their fault, even if I don't actually know what I'm pissed off about.

"I saw you carry her in last night. She wouldn't cling to you like that if she didn't want to be there with you," I state, and he gives me a pointed look.

"Like I said, you don't know what you're talking about, Xavier," he repeats, and that only seems to rile me up more. This motherfucker knows exactly what he's doing.

"How about you fucking explain it to me then," I bite out, throwing my hands out to the sides, unable to keep my agitation at bay, and he tilts his head back with a sigh.

"It's not really my place to—"

"He saved my life last night, Xavier. Is that enough?"

Hunter's words are cut off by the sound of Eden behind me, my body going stiff as her tired voice washes over me.

I look at Hunter first, feeling out of place. He has his hands braced on the counter with his head down, but he's peering over at her with a soft smile on his lips. Turning to see her, I find Eden leaning against the doorframe in Hunter's top that stops mid-thigh. I clench my hands as jealousy rages through me when she rakes her fingers through her messy blonde hair. She's obviously in this state for a reason, and that reason *has* to be Hunter.

Smiling at Hunter, she turns her gaze to me, and her lips instantly drop, my gut sinking right along with them. In this moment, sitting in my kitchen, watching her look at me with such disdain, I know I have truly fucked up. But I'm a Knight, so I don't apologize, not ever. I'll have to roll with the choices I've made, but maybe there could be a way for her to look at me like she just did Hunter. I've never wanted it before, but seeing them stirs something inside me.

I haven't responded, but I don't really know what to say

either, because I know whatever it is will completely ruin things between us even more.

"He couldn't take me home in the state I was in, and he was nice enough to take care of me when I was at my most vulnerable. I'm sorry that didn't involve running to tell you," she grinds out, stepping up to Hunter's side and taking the mug of coffee he offers her. She murmurs her thanks before she turns back to glare at me.

"Where's Tobias?" Hunter asks, trying to change the subject.

"He went to see his parents," I mutter. As pissed as I am right now, Tobias seeing his parents is never good, and Hunter deserves to be aware too.

Observing them, I watch as Hunter places his hand on Eden's shoulder in comfort and she takes a deep breath. He's making sure she's okay, and they silently communicate with just their eyes. I can't sit here and watch any more of them together, especially with him touching what's *mine*.

We share, we always share, and now I'm nowhere near being able to touch her again, and that fills me with so much frustration and anger.

I slap my hands down on the countertop, and they glance at me as I scrape my chair back on the marble floor, not worrying about leaving a mark as I grab my half empty coffee mug and storm from the room.

I don't need to see them together in any way, shape, or form right now. Stomping up the stairs, I head straight for my room, slamming the door shut behind me before placing my mug on the nightstand.

I should change, go down to the stadium, and put in some training. I need to stay focused on what's important right now, and hopefully, it will help clear my mind and release all the tension that's been building inside me since I saw the footage last night.

I pull my top over my head and drop it at my feet before kicking my shorts off and leaving them carelessly on the floor also. I prefer to dress more appropriately outside of my own personal space. Polished, put together, just as my mother expects.

I wrench my closet door open, and it ricochets off the wall, but I don't give a shit, my anger in full force as I grab a pair of jeans and a Henley.

A knock sounds on my bedroom door, and the interruption only pisses me off more.

"Fuck off," I growl, dropping my fresh clothes on the chair at my desk as they knock again. Marching toward the door, I swing it open. "I just said—"

"Fuck off, I know, but I need to talk to you," Eden interrupts, catching me by surprise, especially since I expected to find Hunter there.

Clearing my throat, I brace one hand on the doorframe and the other on the handle as I stare her down. "I don't know what you need to talk about, but right now really isn't going to work for me. So..." I leave the sentence open for interpretation, encouraging her to back off, but instead, she folds her arms over her chest and glares at me. She's feisty today. I like it.

"I really don't need this shit right now," she murmurs, almost to herself, and before I can throw back any response, she pushes past me, walking into my room like she owns the place, and I don't miss how she glances at the far wall.

Her eyes widen a little in surprise when she finds pictures of her still filling my wall, but she says nothing about it as she turns to face me, and I'm desperate to ask if she saw the new additions, but I don't.

"I want to speak to your mother."

It takes a minute for me to understand what she just said, but there is no way she just...I frown at her, but she doesn't move. If anything, she stands taller, placing her hands on her hips as she waits for me to respond.

"You have got to be fucking kidding me."

"I'm not," she responds quickly, and I shake my head.

"Well, you should be. Ilana Knight is ruthless, and I hid you away the first time you were here. You would be crazy to actually want to meet her in person," I argue, slamming my door shut since she seems intent on staying.

I feel her presence with every inch of my soul, and it takes far too much effort to act like it means nothing to me, especially when she's in my space, my room.

"Xavier, the only reason I'm here, in Knight's Creek is because of that woman, and after last night, I don't want to be walking through the dark anymore. I need to know what she actually wants from me, what she intends to achieve."

I scoff at her statement, watching as she leans against my desk by her photos, crossing her legs at her ankles as she looks to the ceiling. It's on the tip of my tongue to ask her about last night, but I know I'll get nothing from her.

"No."

Her eyes bug out of her head as I lean toward her, grabbing my Henley from the chair, but she catches the other end of it before I can step away, halting my movement.

"What do you mean 'no?'"

"I mean exactly what it sounds like. No, I will not arrange for you to meet my mother," I respond, trying to pull my shirt from her hands, but she pulls back just as hard, so I take a step closer to her.

"But you have to." Defiance shines in her eyes as she challenges me, even though I can see how tired she is, like I'm draining her of all her energy.

"No, I don't."

"Xavier, don't be an asshole. I just told you why I have to meet with her."

"I don't have to do shit, Nafas. Not a damn thing, now let go. I need to get out of here." I tug the top again, and she tightens her grip, her face scrunching with annoyance as she glares at me.

"Xavier, please…"

"What part of no don't you understand?" I growl, releasing my hold on the shirt as I step closer to her, caging her in against the desk as I bend slightly so we're at the same level, my nose brushing hers as I do.

"I understand the word just fine, but it's not the answer I want, so I refuse to leave until you help me. You said you called a truce. I'll believe that when you actually fucking help me out."

She's intoxicating this close, and I can barely think straight as her scent consumes me, but it still doesn't change my mind, even if my cock is straining against my shorts. If anything, smelling Hunter's body wash on her only makes me more determined to get away from her.

"I'm doing you a favor. You just can't see it yet."

"I feel like I'm sitting on death row, Xavier, waiting for your mom to decide when my time is up."

I want to tell her not to be ridiculous, not to overreact, but with my mother, who the fuck knows how true that could be?

I fist my hands on the desk, annoyed that she won't let it drop, so I move to step back, but her hand whips out, pulling on the waistband of my boxers to try and keep me in place, and I freeze.

"Help me, Xavier. Please."

Her words barely register in my brain as I slowly pull my gaze from her blue eyes to where her hand holds me captive. She's holding the waistband off my hips, and my cock stands tall and proud, precum glistening on the tip.

"Fuck," she mumbles, pulling my eyes back to hers, only to find her gaze transfixed on my cock. Her tongue sweeps across her bottom lip, and the movement sends a jolt of desire straight to my dick.

"Eden, I'm going to need you to let go," I bite out, not moving as she slowly slides her gaze to mine.

I remain frozen in place as her icy blue eyes sparkle before me, her hand pulling me closer, and like an explosion, our lips slam into each other.

I don't know who moves first. I don't know whose lips are more punishing as we both battle for control. My fingers thread into her hair, wrapping the long, blonde locks around my fist as I tilt her head back, crushing my lips against hers again, but the sudden bite on my bottom lip has me hissing in an intense mixture of pleasure and pain.

Gripping her hair tighter, I pull her closer to my chest as her fingers tug my boxers down, dropping them to my ankles before her hand wraps around my cock.

"I hate you," she hisses, sinking her teeth into my lip again as she stares up at me with half-mast eyes.

"I hate you too," I growl, and she scoffs, tightening her hold around my cock, and I moan into her mouth.

"You sure about that?" she teases.

I bring my other hand to her core, cupping her pussy as I tug her hair, and she groans. "Damn sure."

"Well, I *really* fucking hate you," she murmurs with less bite to her words as her other hand grips the back of my neck before she crushes her lips to mine. I force her back against the wall.

Tilting her head back, she tries to catch her breath as I lean forward and bite her nipple through her t-shirt. She hisses as she strokes her hand up and down my length in a vise-like grip. Holy fuck.

"You're playing with fire, Nafas." My voice is like steel, covering the emotions she is unknowingly drawing from me.

"Then fucking burn me," she retorts instantly, and my body moves of its own accord.

I pull her to her feet, and she loses her grip on my cock as I grab the hem of Hunter's band tee and pull it over her head, throwing it over my shoulder as I drop her boxers as well. I remove every piece of *him* so I can mark her as *mine*.

She stands before me fully bare, and I watch as her chest rises with every breath she takes, her skin pink with arousal.

We collide, and her legs wrap around my waist as I hold her in place, squeezing her thighs as I move us to the side of the desk and pin her against the wall, loving the sound of her gasp as I do.

My cock brushes against her folds, desperate to stretch her out instead of preparing her, and she seems to be on the same wavelength as she attempts to nudge my dick to her entrance.

"How did we go from——"

"Shut the fuck up, Xavier, and fuck me," she growls, her eyes burning with need, so I tilt my hips back, lining my cock up with her pussy and feeling her desire between her legs. "No mercy, Xavier," she adds, gaping up at me, and I nod.

"No mercy," I murmur before doing exactly what she wants and slamming all the way home.

Leaning my forehead against hers, she moans long and throaty as I scramble to catch my breath, the feel of her tight center sending tingles throughout my entire body like I've never felt before. I don't want to give her a moment to catch her breath, but I need it myself as sweat drips down my face.

Squeezing her thighs, I slowly withdraw from her body until only the tip nudges her entrance, then I slam straight back in, loving how she moans even louder.

I'm not going to last long. All this pent-up tension and

need has me close to coming already.

Pressing my lips to hers, I swallow her moans as I fuck her harder and faster with every thrust, trying with all my might to fuck my anger into her. I feel her tits brush against my chest as I pin her to the wall with my hips, so I can use one hand to stroke her pretty pink clit that's begging for attention.

"Ah, Xavier. Fuck."

Her legs squeeze tightly around my waist as her pussy spasms around my cock, and I watch her fall apart in my arms as her body reacts to mine. The way her walls cling to my cock, riding out every wave of ecstasy, has me tipping over the edge right alongside her. My orgasm tingles from my toes to my fingertips as my mouth latches onto the delicate skin where her shoulder meets her neck, and I bite down—not as hard as I'd like, but enough to leave a mark.

My ears ring as my heart attempts to burst from my chest, and I close my eyes as I try to catch my breath.

Holy. Shit.

Peeling my eyes open, I glance down between us where we're joined, and it slowly dawns on me why it felt so good—no condom. No fucking condom. Eden chuckles, and I pull my gaze to hers.

"The fear in your eyes is excellent," she purrs with a smirk, and my heart freezes at her casual words. "I have the implant," she continues before I can respond, and a breath of air whooshes from my lips.

I nod as her words slowly sink in and calm me down, hoping that's the truth as I slowly walk us into the bathroom, my cock still semi-hard inside her. Placing her on the vanity, I press the buttons on the wall to turn on the shower remotely.

"I'm clean," I murmur before she can grill me. Her eyes search mine, looking for the truth, but I know that's all she'll get.

As I pull from her body, she stands, and I watch as my cum trails down her thigh. I can't believe how hot that looks. I glance back at Eden, and the way her eyebrows are knitted together tells me the moment of sexual bliss between us has passed, even if my cock is rising at the sight before me.

Quickly grabbing a cloth, I run it under the water and offer it to her. She turns to glance in the mirror then glares at my reflection.

"You fucking bit me."

I simply shrug, rather pleased with the red mark on her

neck as she strokes her fingers along it.

"What does that mean? What the fuck does a shrug actually mean right now?" she asks, and I shrug again.

"I don't know what you want me to say."

Pinching the bridge of her nose, she sighs. "What the fuck is this, Xavier? What do you want from me? Before I came to Knight's Creek, I never went back for seconds. Ever. This is the third time we've found ourselves in a situation like this."

I hate that she isn't looking at me, because I can't gauge her emotions with her eyes closed. So instead of baring my soul, I grin, pleased that our bodies know what they want at least, even if our minds are on a different level right now. I feel like I want everything with her, but it seems like she wants to cut my dick off and shove it down my throat.

"You're the one who strolled into town all, 'I won't be around long enough for it to matter,'" I mumble, quoting her own words back at her, and she rolls her eyes. "What do you want me to say? We fucked, Nafas. What more do you want? A promise ring or something?"

She scoffs as she brushes past me, heading for the door to my room. "Only if it means you promise to fuck off," she snaps, and I follow her, watching as she slips Hunter's shirt back over her head and my jaw ticks in annoyance.

"Where are you going now? Back to Hunter? If I'd have known I was loosening you up for him, I wouldn't have let you come yet," I jibe, making her grin at me over her shoulder, clearly recognizing my green-eyed monster.

"Not that I need to explain myself to you, but since you're not willing to set me up with your mom, I need to go see Archie."

Oh. That's not what I expected her to say at all.

She doesn't utter another word in my direction as she opens my bedroom door and saunters out, heading straight for the stairs as opposed to Hunter's room which is what I anticipated.

How the fuck does this girl surprise me at every turn? More importantly, what do I actually do about her wanting to meet my mother?

Fuck.

TOXIC CREEK

KC KEAN

FOURTEEN
Eden

Stupid, stupid, stupid, Eden!
Shit. Fuck. Tit. Wank. Bastard.

I internally berate myself all the way back to Archie's in my newly stolen t-shirt—along with a pair of boxers which I think belong to Xavier—unwilling to admit that being surrounded by Hunter's earthy scent offers a sense of calmness and peace I refuse to decipher.

I want to be fucking irritated at him for being so nice to me, even after he heard Xavier and me which didn't change how he acted at all.

Yesterday had been a complete turning point for me, especially with Hunter. I was at my most broken, literally sinking and drowning in my pain, and he physically pulled me out of the water then gently coaxed me out of the dark hole in my mind as well. He somehow remembered to collect my purse off the beach, but my sandals were long forgotten.

And what did I do? I argued with his friend, basically his brother, and wound up fucking him against a wall without protection. Way to go, Eden. I don't regret it, I just...don't know.

My heart almost skipped a beat when he asked to check on me later, leaving me nodding like an idiot with Xavier's seed still inside me, but he gently stroked my hair behind my ear and kissed my temple.

Stomping through the sand as the water gently laps at my feet, I force myself to calm down, relaxing my shoulders as I take a deep breath. Admittedly, the sex was phenomenal. It's just a shame his big dick energy is literally run by a giant dick.

When I pass an older couple walking hand in hand down the beach, I feel them look me up and down, judging me, but I refuse to give them any attention as I move away from the water's edge, purse in hand, as I slowly take the steps leading up to Archie's pool area.

As I get to the top, I can't help but glance back in the direction I've just come from, and it doesn't surprise me to find both Hunter and Xavier standing side by side, way up on their cliff top, watching me.

I can't even wrap my head around what the fuck is going on there, and this isn't the time to figure it out. Right now, I need to steel my ovaries and find Archie. I can't avoid him forever, and last night, after learning things about my parents, *our* parents, I realized putting this barrier between us wasn't making anything easier at all.

The pool area is empty, which for midday isn't all that surprising, and as I step inside, I find the main floor quiet as well. I don't even know if he's home, but I can't picture him still in bed, so I opt to head down to the game room, walking straight there instead of going to my room first. That'll only give me time to back out, and I can't.

Tiptoeing down to the game room, I see the light shining from under the door, and I instantly question whether I should wait a little longer. Fuck. Even the fact that I'm standing here in the Allstars' clothes can't pull me from this conversation. It needs to happen, no excuses, and it needs to happen now.

Bite the bullet, Eden.

Swallowing past the lump in my throat, I rap my knuckles against the wooden door but push it open instead of waiting for a response. Slowly peeking around the door, I find him deep in a game of Apex, his headphones firmly in place as he leans forward, his elbows braced on his knees.

I quietly shut the door behind me and lean against it, watching him play as I take a moment to gather myself while I look around the familiar space. I don't know who he's playing with, but they are shit. He's practically carrying the team, so I'm not surprised he slams his Xbox controller down when they finish second, a stream of curses falling from his lips as the champion squad fills the screen.

Taking his headset off, he drops it on the desk and runs his fingers through his hair, and I finally speak.

"I'd say good game, but you're only as strong as your weakest link, and, well…you had two of them."

His head whips around so fast I'm sure he pulled a muscle, but as soon as his eyes lock on me, he doesn't move, doesn't even a blink, as if I may disappear if he spooks me.

With a heavy sigh, I move closer and take a seat in the gaming chair beside his, swiveling to face him as I grip the armrests tightly. He looks tired, almost as drained as me, and it makes me wonder how much of his emotions he had to smother around me.

"Hi," I murmur, biting my lip nervously, and he relaxes back in his seat a little.

"Hi."

Glancing around the room, I try to find the right words to say, but basic communication seems to elude me. "I'm mad at you," I finally state, and he nods in understanding.

"I'd be surprised if you weren't, Eden. Especially when I hate myself too."

"I didn't say I hated you. I said I'm mad at you. There's a huge difference," I point out, but he doesn't say anything as he looks down at his lap. "I need to hear everything you know, Archie. No secrets. No lies. Just honesty."

Leaning forward, he braces his arms on his thighs as he hangs his head, his chin hitting his chest as he takes a deep breath.

"I swear, no more secrets, Eden," he murmurs before meeting my gaze. "About twenty minutes before you showed up, my dad called me down to his office acting all urgent and frantic. When I got down there, he simply said a girl was coming to stay with us—a girl who just so happened to be my twin sister." My heart pounds as he looks at me with guilt written all over his face, but he shakes his head and continues. "He was heartbroken, Eden, almost in as much pain as when my mom died, but I had to promise I wouldn't say a word, not a single one, or there would be consequences, even if it did break my heart too."

Fuck. Of course there would be some kind of consequences in this stupid town, and I'm sure it leads back to Ilana—it always seems to. I hoped as much though. I prayed there was a reason he kept this to himself. Although knowing something was held over his head that was clearly more important to him than being honest with me hurts.

"What were the consequences?" I ask, trying to remain neutral, but he sees right through me.

"Cookie, I can see your brain going into overdrive right now, worrying about what was more important than you, and it's almost laughable because even then, before I even met you, the consequences were your safety. Your safety meant just as much to me then as it does now. You heard me tell Xavier, and I will reiterate it for you—I choose you, Eden. I will always choose you over this town and these people. I'm just sorry that in having to protect you, I also broke your trust."

I gape at him. My jaw is practically on the floor as I see the pure honesty in his gaze. He didn't tell me to protect me.

My grip on the armrests tightens as I try to keep my emotions under control. Focusing on his similar eyes, I remember the first day Charlie saw us together at lunch, and she asked if we were related because of our eyes.

Bright blue, like the ocean, wide enough to almost be too wide for our faces, with ridiculously long eyelashes. I see the resemblance now.

Our blond hair is also very similar. His is a little lighter than mine, but other than that it feels like we are simply a guy and a girl. Then my mind wanders to when we mentally seem to understand each other's feelings and emotions, while having similar interests.

"Please say something, Eden," he whispers, pain etched into his features, and I wet my lips, watching as he bounces his leg nervously.

"It's not often I'm lost for words, but now is one of those times," I admit, and it eases some of the tension on his face. "I forgive you, but I can't forget, not yet at least. We aren't where we were, even if it was to protect me. You knew the stress I was under more than anyone, and I can't just let that slide."

"I get it, Eden. I really do. I just want you to actually be my sister and for me to be your brother. I don't know who we actually are other than that. My dad refused to give me anything else, so I'm as in the dark as you," he says, sweeping the hair back off his face, and I stall, needing to tell him what I learned last night.

"Charlie's Grandma J told me who my, *our*, parents are last night," I mutter, and his eyes widen as he slowly falls back in his seat. "Do you want to know, or..."

"Yes, please, yes." Emotion wells in his eyes, and that's the only sign I need to recognize he doesn't know.

Clearing my throat, I force myself to maintain eye contact with him. "My dad, Carl, and your mom, Anabel, were our parents." I struggle to spit it out, my voice seeming to enhance the word "were," and it doesn't take long for the reality to dawn on him too.

Watching the pain and sadness play out across his face has my own emotions going a little haywire, and my eyes fill with tears again, but this time I feel a lot stronger—much stronger than last night—and I know that's a step in the right direction. I feel sad, sad in the pit of my stomach, but I know I'm not alone now.

"Oh, Eden," he whispers before suddenly rising to his feet and scooping me into his arms.

I let him wrap me up, my toes barely touching the floor as he crushes me against his chest. I don't know how long we stand there, emotion thick in the air as I sob quietly into his neck, and I feel his tears too.

We're two broken teenagers with no living biological parents, but we have each other, and we have two other parents that seem to be caught in the crossfire as well. We need to get to the bottom of this, of all of this. It's not just my dad who was murdered now, it's Archie's dad too. He already lost his mom, and I feel like this could open old wounds.

"I'm sorry," I murmur. "I know it's hard, I just needed you to know."

"No, of course, Eden. I'm glad you told me." With one final squeeze, he finally releases me, and we take a moment to catch our breath. "Where do we go from here?"

"What do you mean?" I ask, watching as determination flashes over his face.

"Well, you wanted justice for your dad. I want justice for him too. Whatever you need from me, I'll do it."

Squeezing his arm, I force a soft smile to my lips. "I

asked Xavier to set up a meeting with his mom, but he was very reluctant," I state, skipping the part where we got completely sidetracked and I have no clue if he will actually help or not.

"Whatever you need, okay?" he repeats, and I nod. "And, uh, if you ever want to talk about my mom, please just say so. I need a little time, but I would love to know more about your dad, the person he was, and how he made you the strong woman you are."

"You're being too fucking sappy now," I grumble, unable to take his praise, and he grins.

"Oh, you better get used to it, cookie. I also think it's time we discussed the fact I know you have gross sex toys up in that room. Do we need to have the birds and the bees talk? Especially since I *know* that isn't your top. Can I guess which Allstar it belongs to?"

My face scrunches in disgust as he puts his hands on his hips, staring me down, but he can't hold his laughter in. The pressure in my chest eases, and I greatly appreciate his ability to relax a tense conversation.

"Don't be embarrassing, Archie. It doesn't suit you," I say with a roll of my eyes, my cheeks heating as he snickers. I like how it feels having this normalcy with him.

"Want to grab a drink and some snacks so we can play some games? You saw the team I was dealing with, I could use some help."

I stare at him for a moment, considering his offer, and as much as I can't forget, I *can* relax with him for the rest of the day. At least until Hunter comes over.

"Sure, but you're getting the drinks, and we're focusing on my weekly challenges first. Agreed?"

Nodding like an excited puppy, he rushes for the door before turning back to face me.

"What do you want to drink? Something hard like bourbon or rum?" he questions, and I freeze, taking a deep breath before shaking my head.

"No, uh, just some water please. I had a bad night last night, and I think it'd be a good idea for me to avoid using alcohol as a coping mechanism, at least for a while."

My heart pounds in my ears as I wait for his judgment, but he simply smiles wide as understanding flashes in his eyes.

"Perfect, give me two minutes."

I spin my chair to the other Xbox, proud of myself when he calls out again.

"And don't you be thinking I don't know that's Hunter's

top you're wearing right now. Don't make me go into ultimate big, older brother protector mode."

I roll my eyes even though he can't see me. Asshole.

"We don't know who was born first, it could have been me."

"Please, we both know that would never be the case, let's be real."

Groaning, I cover my face. I already can't deal with him. It's like my dad is right here with his snarky protective ways, and my chest burns with the comparison. This is all a little too heavy. I need a mind-numbing game to distract me, and apparently a brother to play it with as I pick apart similarities between him and our father.

"Oh, and we need lots of photos together to make up for all the time lost. Faces squished together and love pouring from the screen, all that jazz," he babbles as he comes back into the room, two waters in hand, and I roll my eyes.

"Forget it. We are not going to be one of those pairs of siblings who end up on one of those 'siblings or dating' games because we look gross and all lovey-dovey, asshole," I grouse, swiping a water and a bag of flaming hot Doritos from his hand. He acts all hurt with his bottom lip sticking out. I *really* can't deal with him. "You are too fucking much."

"You love it," he counters instantly, and I don't respond.

He's right. The way we gelled from the second we met, and the protective side of him where he's unwilling to leave me to handle everything thrown at me, shows me exactly how much of a brother he's been this whole time.

FIFTEEN

Eden

Charlie: Oh my gosh, Eden. I'm so, so sorry I got wasted last night. I promise to make it up to you. Please tell me you at least got to speak to my Grandma J!

Eden: Honestly, don't stress about it. And I did, she didn't say much, but I'll tell you more tomorrow.

Placing my phone on my nightstand, I quickly redo my ponytail as I change into a pair of booty shorts and my favorite Miami Dolphins jersey.

I don't blame Charlie for letting her hair down and going a little too far. Fuck, I did the exact same thing. We should probably find better coping mechanisms if we want to survive this place without AA meetings further down the line. I also don't want to pry. I know she was messaging Archie, but she can tell me whatever was going through her mind last night if and when she's ready. It's almost seven in the evening, so I'm guessing it's taken her some time to sober up today to be ready for school tomorrow. She doesn't need me grilling her as well.

I already off-loaded all my troubles onto Hunter, and right now, I can't say I'm sorry about it. Yet again, he somehow had a way of making me feel safe, even if we were in the same house as Xavier—but I can't go there with that either. I'll get her up to speed when I see her, I just don't feel the need for a heart-to-heart today.

With a heavy sigh, I grab my phone and try to dial my mom again, but it's no surprise when it goes to voicemail. This time, though, I leave a message.

"Hey mom, it's me. I-I just need to talk to you about something as soon as you get a minute. Please."

Ending the call, I drop the phone onto the mattress

like it's about to catch on fire. As much as I know I *need* to talk to her, it doesn't mean I actually *want* to talk about this whole situation with her. Like, does she even want to be my mom anymore? Not that it feels like she's doing a stellar job of it right now, but still, seventeen years is a long-ass time to be someone's parent.

Straightening my soft, gray bed sheets, I nervously glance around the room to make sure everything is relatively clean. I'm slightly freaking out that Hunter is coming over. It's not like anything is going to happen, but he still somehow has the ability to make me nervous, especially after yesterday. The idea of being in his presence after last night has me on edge, and I can't tell if that's a good or bad thing.

A knock on my bedroom door freezes me on the spot. I wring my hands as I try to miraculously see through the door to check who it is. My nerves don't get long to catch up, though, as the door swings open, revealing Hunter who's leaning against the doorframe as he searches me out. His eyes instantly find mine, and I think I may be sick with the way my stomach churns from doubting myself after he saw a completely different side of me.

"You going to let me in, love?" he asks with a grin

spreading across his face, and my eyes narrow into slits as I glare at him, watching him look me up and down. Seeing him standing before me in a pair of navy board shorts and a loose white tank, leaning against the doorframe, I want to combust into a ball of flames.

Who the fuck is this guy? All sweet lines with a cheeky sparkle in his green eyes? Where the hell is the silent but deadly Hunter Asheville I'm used to seeing? I almost want to ask when the dickish side of him is going to make an appearance, but I refrain.

"What's in the bag?" I finally ask, glancing at the duffel bag in his hands as I try to avoid his gaze, my body flinching as I hear my bedroom door close behind him. The sound of the lock clicking surprises me, and I forget how to fucking act.

"Food," he responds simply, and I pull my gaze back to his as I stand by the bottom of the bed.

"Food?" I repeat, needing clarification, but he simply gives me a pointed look.

"It doesn't really count as watching a movie if you don't have snacks, now does it?"

He drops onto my bed without a care in the world, and I'm reminded of the night he stayed with me while I was cranky and on my period. He makes himself at home just as he did then, and I use the time to really take him in.

He seems completely oblivious as he places his polarized glasses on my nightstand, tousling his blond hair as he does.

God, this man is oh so tempting. But I'm instantly reminded of the fact I fucked Xavier earlier this morning. It may have been filled with hatred, my red-hot orgasm the result of the fire between us, but it still makes me feel a little guilty around Hunter.

I repeat Hunter's first words to me in my mind, trying to calm the stress building within me. *You see, we share, Xavier, Toby, and me. So if you've had one of us…*He must have said that for a reason, and I can tell there is some truth to it.

"Are you going to stand there all day, Eden, and continue to be weird and make this like some awkward first date where you can't make eye contact with me?"

Oh, you asshole. Challenge accepted.

As I pull the heavy curtain across the balcony so the sunset doesn't blind us, I feel his eyes on me the whole time. I dim my bedside lamp, and my thigh almost brushes his, but I make sure to keep my distance as I climb into my bed on the other side.

"I am not awkward, and this is *not* a first date, surfer boy," I grumble as I grab the remote from between us and flip through the movies available on demand.

"Of course not, that was your grumpy crotch night. I saved your life last night so that definitely counts toward a second date, which would make this the third."

His eyes find mine, and a smug glimmer shines through. I literally have no response. Not a single retort or jibe, and that only angers me more.

"Shut the fuck up, Asheville," I murmur, turning back at the TV as I hear him snicker.

"You know I know you address us by our last names when you feel like we're getting too close, right?" he remarks, and my eyes widen as I bite my lip, refusing to glance in his direction, but I know he's on to something.

Thankfully, he doesn't say any more as he unzips the duffel bag and proceeds to pull a variety of chocolates, candy, and chips out. I don't take anything else as I watch him take four bags of my favorite Swedish Fish Tails out, my mouth instantly watering for the pineapple and watermelon ones. The smug grin on his lips tells me he's had help from his sister, because Bethany is the only person who truly knows about my obsession.

When he pulls a can of Dr. Pepper from the bag, I about melt into a puddle of happiness as I quickly snatch it from his hands, loving the hiss as I open it, and gulp down half of the fizzy goodness in one go. Leaning over, I place it on the nightstand on my side of the bed.

"I'm feeling *Avatar* or *Lord of the Rings*. I know they are nothing alike, so please don't question it. Just tell me you like at least one of those," I state, shuffling farther down the bed to rest my head on the pillows, and this time it's his turn to gape at me, his jaw loose as he searches my eyes. "What?" I bite out, glaring at him, and he blinks.

"Will you be the Frodo to my Samwise Gamgee?"

"Baby, my blonde hair makes me Legolas and you know it. I'm not carrying no ring to no Mordor, understand? I'm going to be an elegant as fuck elf with smooth moves. If anyone is Frodo, it's Xavier, although he would make a better Gollom," I say with a pout, and he grins wide.

"Carry on with your attitude and you can be Gimli," he teases, and I can't stop the giggle bursting from my lips.

"Stop," I say with a laugh, hitting play on *Lord of the Rings*, and he lies back on the bed beside me, relaxing in the comfortable silence that surrounds us.

He crosses his arms behind his head, and I try not to

watch every move he makes, his chest rising and falling softly with every breath he takes.

"Who would Tobias be?" I muse out loud, and Hunter chuckles.

"That motherfucker would think he's Aragorn just so he could do the whole opening the double doors scene." I can't help but laugh at how true that is. "Just so you know, Toby doesn't know I'm here right now. So if he calls, I'm not answering."

"Why?" I ask, pulling my eyes from the opening sequence to see him already staring at me. If I reach my hand out now, I could easily trace my fingers over his face.

"Because he would be here if he knew," he responds, like it's completely self-explanatory.

"Is that an issue?" I murmur as my heart rate increases. I'm worried I just talked myself down only for him not to be okay with whatever the fuck this is.

"No, it's not an issue. I just wanted you to myself for a little while longer. Especially after last night," he admits, his voice barely above a whisper, and it washes over me like I've just been sprinkled with fairy dust or something. Butterflies go crazy in my stomach as goosebumps erupt on my arms.

Rubbing my lips together, I remain silent as I train my eyes back on the TV. Last night clearly changed a fucking lot between the two of us. We dropped our walls and offered our more vulnerable sides to each other. Nearly drowning will do that to me, and even though there is so much going on around us at the minute, I can't help but be drawn to him more and more.

Hunter protected me when my clothes were stolen. He raced up the steps midway through a football game to see what was going on when I received my first threatening text message. He even took care of me in my crankiest moment, supplying me with snacks, drinks, and medication. Even when I found out about my relation to Archie, Hunter wasn't in the know. He stood by my side in as much surprise as I was, but ultimately, he stood by his friend, his brother, and if I'm completely honest with myself, I respect that level of loyalty.

Lying on my side with my hands under my face, I watch him out of the corner of my eye as my heart pounds in my chest. Why would he do all of those things? Why would he pull me from the water last night and then after hearing me fuck his friend insist on coming over here? What does he expect to gain? Do I *want* him to gain anything?

"I can practically hear the cogs turning in your mind, love. Are you going to enjoy the movie or lie there stressing the whole time?"

Before I can even process how to respond, my lips are already moving. "I'm trying to figure out why you're here and what you want from me."

When he doesn't reply, I slowly tilt my head to meet his eyes, and even I'm not stupid enough to miss the heat there.

"There is just something about you, Eden, that makes me want to cradle you in my arms and protect how delicate you are, all while watching you fight against everything in this world fiercely, recklessly, but wholeheartedly. It just draws me in. *You* draw me in. With your pretty blonde hair and shimmering blue eyes that are a mixture of pain and need. I find myself wanting to be whatever you need."

Holy fuck.

My brain practically short-circuits again and again as I try to absorb his words, my eyes locked on his. That is not at all what I expected him to say. Not at all. But the truth in his tone as he rocks my fucking world literally leaves me speechless and has my nipples rock hard.

How do I even respond to that?

"Those...were some pretty sweet words, but I still don't know what you want from me," I finally mutter, and his green eyes stare at me intently.

Turning on his side, mirroring my position, he leans closer so our breaths mingle together between us. "I don't know. I just know I want to be near you, I want you to trust me, I want to protect you, but most of all, I want to touch you, taste you, feel you."

Every word coats my skin with need, desire, and as he finishes speaking, he lifts his hand to stroke his finger down my cheek, making me feel cherished and wanted all at once.

"I don't go back for seconds," I mutter, my voice and words weak. He knows I've fucked Xavier more than once, but I gave him the same message too.

"That was before the Allstars, love. We both know it," he responds as my body inches closer to his.

"I fucked both of your friends. Xavier and Tobias. I need—"

"Who are you trying to talk out of this, Eden? Me or you? I already know all these things. I already know Tobias is as hooked on you as I am, Xavier too, we just all have completely different ways of showing it."

He strokes his finger from my cheek to my collarbone, and my skin heats under his touch as he keeps his gaze fixed on mine.

"Last night, you saw a part of my soul no one else has, Hunter. This feels different, it—"

My words are cut off by the brush of his lips against mine, and I instantly moan into his mouth as his hand circles the back of my neck, pulling me closer as my chest presses against his.

His lips are soft, gentle, and demanding all at once as he leisurely explores my mouth. I cup his face, desperate for more, leaving little to no room between us.

I can't think. He consumes me, leaving me gasping for my next breath.

Pushing against his chest, I roll off the bed as he releases his grip on my neck, landing on my feet as I swipe a hand down my face.

I don't let people in, not like this. We fuck, then we go our separate ways. This is all new territory, and it's messing with my mind.

"Fuck," I mutter, instantly regretting the loss of his touch, but it was so much all at once I just needed a second.

"I'm sor—"

"Oh my God, don't apologize, really, just don't," I interrupt, pacing at the side of the bed as I try to calm myself down. "I just need a minute or like five. Or maybe it would be a good idea for me to go masturbate in the bathroom for five minutes then come back, and I won't feel like a fucking pubescent boy who took a Viagra or something," I ramble, and he sits on the edge of the bed, trying to discreetly adjust himself as he smirks up at me.

"Good to know you're as affected as I am."

Wait, what? It worries me to take him at his word, since the Allstars and their words haven't served me well so far. Can I trust that it's changed?

I whirl around to face him, but my hand catches on the can of Dr. Pepper on the nightstand, and in slow motion, it lands in Hunter's lap. We stare in shock as the fizzy liquid continues to pour all over his shorts and the gray sheet beside him.

"Fuck, fuck, fuck. I'm so sorry," I blurt as I finally grab the can, but it's pretty fucking pointless when it's practically empty now. It doesn't help when he just continues to fucking sit there, staring at the mess I've made.

When he finally lifts his eyes to mine, I'm relieved to find only humor in his gaze, but I still need to find something to clean him up, especially the puddle of Dr. Pepper around his fucking crotch. Shit. Following my gaze, he huffs out a laugh before I remember to fucking look for something, but then Hunter suddenly cups the liquid in his hand and pours it down my top.

There is Dr. Pepper down my motherfucking favorite Miami Dolphins jersey.

Looking back up from the spillage to glare at him, I find his gaze ready and waiting for mine as he raises his eyebrow, the challenge clear on his face. Before I can retaliate, he grasps the back of my thighs and pulls me toward him, and my ass lands square in his lap, the liquid seeping into my booty shorts and wetting my thighs.

I turn to gape at him in surprise, but I don't realize how close he is until my nose brushes his. My arms wrap around his neck, holding on for safety with the momentum.

The full, megawatt smile stretching from ear to ear on his face melts whatever was left of the barrier I was holding between us as I crash my lips onto his again. My eyes fall closed as I rake my fingers through the back of his hair, teasing his lips with my tongue, but when I try to grind my hips against him, the sticky substance pulls against my skin.

"Ah, shit. Fuck, we need to wash this off," I complain

as I slowly move from his lap, and he rises along with me, circling me in his arms.

"Lead the way, love," he whispers against my lips, and I shiver at the touch, nodding in agreement as I bite my lip.

He laces his fingers through mine, and I glance down at our hands for a moment before finally remembering to head to the bathroom. I pull him along behind me as I feel his eyes on my ass with every step.

He releases my hand as I quickly turn the shower on and step back for it to warm up, but Hunter has a completely different idea in mind, nudging me into the open shower space that the water doesn't directly fall on.

Threading his fingers in my messy bun, he turns my head to face him, and the move sends jolts of desire straight to my core. He must see it in my eyes, because he tightens his grip.

"Fuck. The things I want to do to you," he mutters, releasing my hair to pull his t-shirt off as I stand and watch. His face is full of desire as he watches me in return.

"Don't tease me, Hunter, just do them," I respond, and he pauses, his eyes searching mine and darkening when he sees I mean it.

"You don't know what you're saying," he grinds out,

his hands flexing at his sides, and I grin.

"Why don't you let me be the judge of that?" I counter, but he shakes his head.

"I like it rough, aggressive, and having you completely at my mercy. Like I said, you don't know what you're saying."

Holy fuck. Yes, please.

"Yes, I do."

"See, you say that, but I want you naked. I want to drop you to your knees so you can lick every drop of soda off my cock as I control the pace with my hand in your hair," he growls, his voice full of challenge, and it's about the hottest thing I have ever heard.

Wordlessly, I slip off my jersey and quickly kick my booty shorts to the floor, hearing them splat with the soda, all with my eyes trained on his face as he watches me strip. His hands flex at his side again as his eyes freeze on my taut nipples, and I use his distraction to drop to my knees before him, the sound of the shower the only noise in the room.

Placing my hand on his thigh, just above his knee and slightly under his shorts, I peer up at him through my lashes as I squeeze his leg slightly, waiting for him to make the next move. He continues to search my eyes for a moment, but when he sees only need in response, he tightens his jaw and nods. His green eyes deepen to a dark emerald as I slowly untie the waist of his shorts and watch the material drop to the floor.

Holy fucking shit. I've died and gone to big dick heaven.

Steam slowly begins to fill the en-suite with the shower running, making me even hotter. What the hell is with these Allstars and their big dick energy completely backed up with literal big dicks? And why the fuck are they almost always commando?

The vein protruding up the length of his shaft begs for me to run my tongue along it, while the purple head implores to be licked like a lollipop. Before I can decide where to begin, Hunter stays true to his words and laces his fingers through my hair as he guides my mouth to his cock. I open willingly as excitement courses through my veins.

When the tip of his dick brushes against my lips, I sweep my tongue out, slowly dragging it along the underside of his length and enjoying the feel of his vein throbbing with need. Retreating from my mouth, he tests how much I can take, edging farther forward with every thrust, and I hum against his cock.

As he starts to nudge the back of my throat, his touch

becomes a little gentler as he prepares for me to gag, but when he sees no resistance, his eyes widen. Taking it as a challenge, he suddenly tightens his grip on my hair, holding me in place as he pulls his cock almost all the way out, resting the tip against my tongue, then slamming as deep as he can.

My eyes water, even though I don't gag, and I fucking love the feel of the stretch. I swallow around his thick length, and he groans uncontrollably—a gentle reminder that he may have set the pace, but he isn't in charge here.

Heat rises on my chest and neck as every thrust of his cock hits the back of my throat, and it feels like heaven not to feel worry or fear, just red hot sexual chemistry.

Stroking my hands up his inner thighs, he squirms under my sensitive touch, and he suddenly pulls me away.

"Fuck, Eden. Fuck," he pants as I catch my breath, saliva dripping from my lips as I stare up at him, my chest heaving as my pussy screams for attention.

I slowly slip my fingers between my legs, but my intention is cut short when Hunter wrenches my arm away, pulling me up to my feet in one swift move.

"I didn't say you could touch yourself," he murmurs, his voice hoarse with need, and it has me desperate for more.

"What are you going to do about it?" I tease, and he

clenches his jaw as he searches my eyes. I nod, not truly knowing what I'm accepting, but needing it all the same.

Nudging me farther into the dry shower space, without the water actually touching me, he twirls me around until he's standing behind me, the spray hitting his back as he presses against me. His cock nestles between my ass cheeks as he whispers in my ear.

"Bend over and grab your ankles."

A shiver runs down my spine at his words, and I find myself leaning forward, stroking my hands down my legs until they are wrapped around my ankles. My ass is in the air, giving him a direct view, and a part of me wonders if I should feel embarrassed for being so exposed, but if anything, I love it even more.

His fingertips stroke from my neck to the bottom of my spine, and I practically moan, even though he isn't touching me where I want it most.

"So pretty and pale, love. Imagine how hot it would look all pink and sensitive," he says loud enough so I can hear him over the shower while palming my ass cheeks, and I understand exactly where his mind just went.

"Please."

I don't need to repeat myself. His right hand suddenly

leaves my body, the anticipation alone setting my body on fire until his palm connects with my skin, and a moan tumbles from my lips as his hand comes down at an angle, stopping me from falling over at his touch. Taking my response as the only answer he needs, he does it again on the left side before his fingertips slowly drag along the marked flesh.

Holy fuck. It feels so damn good. He repeats the action—one slap to each ass cheek followed by a gentle caress—and every nerve ending in my body ignites, my pussy begging for more.

"Please, Hunter, I need more," I beg, and he grips my waist tight as he curses.

"Fuck, I didn't bring anything, Eden, I—"

"I have the implant, Hunter. Tobias and Xavier have done the same, but no one else. Not ever before, but it's your decision," I state, still bent over with my ass in the air, and he suddenly steps back, my heart sinking as I try to remember if I actually have any left after Tobias was here.

Before I can tell him to check the drawer in my nightstand, Hunter pulls me upright by my hair, tilting my head back to meet his gaze as he stares down at me.

"Fuck it," he mutters, before spinning me around to

face the privacy glass, my hands landing on the panel in preparation as he kicks my feet apart.

Swiping the steam from the glass in front of us, Hunter trails kisses along my collarbone as he slowly rubs his cock between my thighs, gliding easily with how wet I am.

"Goddammit, Eden. What you fucking do to me. I want to treasure you, touch you with soft caresses and passion, but I want to ruin you more. Claim you. Make you the center of the Allstars with my marks to prove it. I want to fuck you so hard you're going to feel me for days."

Oh fuck. Why does that sound so good?

"Ruin me," I plead, glancing over my shoulder as I tilt my sensitive ass up in his direction, and it's like releasing his true carnal self.

One hand grips my waist as the other strokes over my collarbone and circles around my neck, tightening as I moan at the touch. Bending his legs ever so slightly, he lines the tip of his cock up perfectly with my entrance, and then he thrusts hard and fast into me as I cry out with pleasure.

"Fuck," he grunts directly in my ear as I lift one of my hands off the glass to squeeze his hand tighter around my throat. "You're going to be the death of me, love," he bites out before squeezing a little more and thrusting into me again and again.

My airway feels restricted, but it's the restriction that has me close to an orgasm so easily and quickly. I know if I pushed him back or shouted, he would release me in a second, and that only seems to heighten the pleasure building inside me.

Dragging my hand down my body, trusting him not to loosen his grip on my throat, I pinch my nipple as I squeeze my breast, enhancing all the feels I have right now. His cock is unrelenting, slamming into my pussy over and over as my core only tightens around him, loving every second of his onslaught.

Sliding my hand down farther, I brush the pad of my finger against my clit, and the orgasm rips from my toes without warning, a scream burning my throat as my body is racked with my climax.

"Fuck, Eden! Fuck," Hunter growls, his cock pulsing inside me as we ride the waves of our orgasms together, the pleasure lasting forever as I fall into a blissful state, even as my arms give out, and I slump into the glass, the weight of Hunter behind me.

Trying to catch my breath, I feel the sweat between us virtually gluing us together. I rest my head on the glass, and a soft giggle falls from my lips, followed by another, and I can't seem to stop.

"Why are you laughing with my dick inside you?" Hunter mumbles, a touch of amusement in his tone, and I grin.

"I don't even know. I just feel so calm, free, and full of bliss," I respond truthfully, and he kisses my neck just below my ear, and it has my skin tingling again.

"Let's shower then, so you can enjoy all those feelings while we watch the movie."

Humming in response, I turn around to face him, his cock slipping from my core as I circle my arms around his neck. "We're going to have to restart it, and I definitely need pizza or tacos, or preferably both. Snacks aren't going to be enough with all the calories you just helped me burn off."

He grins down at me, his blond hair swept back off his face as he cups my cheek and places a gentle kiss to the corner of my lips.

"I would agree to just about anything you said right now," he replies, my chest warming as I lean in to kiss him just as he did me.

I don't know why I feel like this, all carefree and full of

light, but it has to do with this man before me. Surrounded by all my drama and darkness, this little glimmer of light is like magic, and I can't deny it—I'm addicted.

TOXIC CREEK

SIXTEEN
Eden

The radio plays another hyped dance track that everyone is obsessing over as I fiddle in my seat, desperately refraining from skipping the song. This isn't my car, so I don't get to make the music choices, even though I did let him have control of the radio in my G-Wagon on occasion.

Archie grins from beside me in the driver's seat, strumming his fingers on the steering wheel to the beat of the song, rubbing salt in my wounds as I fold my arms across my chest, ignoring the challenge in his eyes. The motherfucker turns the damn thing up, and I have to look out my side window, watching the sun peek through the scattered clouds, but the chuckle coming from his lips tells me he knows how much he's annoying me.

Stupid fucking brother.

God, that's weird. And I still can't seem to settle those words in my mind, but I'm here and I'm trying.

As we cruise through town, I'm surprisingly impressed with his driving skills. I glance at all the little shops and cafes, but my eyes focus on the record store just like they do every time we pass by—a reminder that I need to stop by, but I'll be there all day, so I need to plan accordingly.

I've been desperate to know why his dad let him drive again ever since I saw his car parked outside of Bethany's home, but it wasn't anywhere near as exciting as I hoped. Richard had simply felt sorry for him after the ball was dropped about our extended family surprise, which completely baffles me because this asshole knew before I got here and he's still the one who gets some form of apology. All I get is radio silence. I guess that's for the best.

Lame.

Propping my foot up on my seat, I tighten the lace of my white Converse, a new sense of nerves tingling under my skin at the prospect of today. Being back at school and seeing the Allstars is fucking with me. Yesterday with Hunter was…something, I just don't know what specifically, but it had me paying a little more attention to how I look.

After he ruined me in the bathroom, we cleaned off and he restarted the movie. While we waited for tacos, he massaged some oils into my sensitive skin, and I loved it almost as much as the earth-shattering sex. I don't know how Hunter has the ability to get under my skin like he does. He's all soft, deep, and almost sensitive, but I'm not oblivious to the cold-hearted motherfucker I've seen him be around school. And on the field last week, when I was filled with rage and lifted my hand to him, his words and tone struck me to the core.

We fell into a comfortable silence, watching the entire first movie in the Lord of the Rings series before he kissed me sweetly and left. Just. Like. That. I almost fucking asked him to stay. Stay. Like it was so casual and totally natural, when it was the complete fucking opposite. The uncertainty, and admittedly, the fear of rejection, had me holding the question in instead, and I think that's what has me out of sorts. Reminding me of my first boyfriend all over again and why I don't do more than fuck and run.

I don't kiss people goodbye, and I don't relax with them after fucking. I don't do *any* of this shit, but here I am stressing out about what outfit I'm wearing. It took forever for me to settle on a pair of high-waisted denim shorts with a frayed hem and a ribbed, pale pink crop top, which sits just above my belly button.

My hair is an organized messy bun on the top of my head, and my sunglasses are firmly in place. My bruises and scabs are barely evident now, so I enhanced my features with a bit of makeup. What's causing me the most stress right now, though, is how I'm supposed to fucking act when I see them.

Dammit, Eden. Get a grip.

I don't need to be acting like some pussy-ass bitch. I just need to act natural. Whatever that is.

As Archie begins to sing along to the music, I pull my phone out to distract myself, scowling at him, but he pays me no mind. My phone lights up, and I see a text from Lou-Lou.

Lou-Lou: Girl, hit me up with your address. You know I'm not going to miss your birthday. Do you want me to get there on Friday or Saturday? Either way, you better

be ready to party.

I can feel her energy through her words, and it sparks a little bit of excitement in me too, making me smile.

"Hey, do we have any spare rooms? A friend from White River wants to come up on the weekend for my, sorry, *our* birthday." I turn to glance at Archie to find him nodding as he turns the music back down.

"For sure, there are two guest rooms. I'll make sure Stevens sets one up for them. Are they of the female variety, or do I need to prepare to deal with the Allstars going all fucking caveman over a guy?"

Rolling my eyes, I can't help but actually feel a sense of truth in his words.

"Lou-Lou has the best tits I've probably ever seen, but also the biggest fucking balls, so it depends which way you look at it," I say with a grin, and he chuckles. "Also, Stevens, I haven't fucking seen that dude since the day I showed up. Where in the hell has he been hiding?"

"He lurks in the shadows, cookie. He's practically the man of the house, taking care of literally everything," he responds, a smile on his lips, and I roll my eyes at him again. "Also, I was thinking of kicking the parties off again this weekend, you know, with our birthday."

He sits silently, waiting for my response, and I feel the question in his words.

"You don't need my permission to throw parties at your own home, Archie." The expression on his face tells me he does, and I sigh. "Throw the parties, Archie. Honestly, they are actually decent, and I love a good time. If it gets to be too much, I'll slink off to my room. You know I'm good at that."

"Perfect," he murmurs in response, his shoulders relaxing as he turns at the light.

Glancing out of the window, I see the school up ahead and fire off a quick response to Lou-Lou.

Me: I'll send you the address now. Archie is throwing a party on Friday if you want to be here for that.

I slip my phone into the bag at my feet just as Archie turns into the school parking lot, heading straight for the front where his allocated spot is, and my eyes find the Allstars instantly.

What time do they actually fucking get here? I have never shown up here before them, and it can't be for practice because Archie is with me this morning.

Standing side by side, they look hotter than ever with their matching aviator sunglasses making them look way cooler than they actually are. Surrounded by the football team, they stand out for all the right reasons—the hot, bad boy jocks every girl dreams about. Pity they are actually assholes on the surface. Underneath may be different, but I just might happen to like it.

Their eyes are all on Archie's red Mercedes Benz SLR McLaren as we pull into the spot, but my focus is more on the fact that the cleat chasers are standing on the grass on the other side of the walkway.

"Let's go, cookie," Archie murmurs, swinging his car door open, and I follow after him, taking a deep breath as I round the front. I hitch my bag higher over my shoulder, and my mouth dries as Hunter takes a step forward, shouldering a teammate out of the way. "Hmm, seems a certain Hunter Asheville caught some feelings when he came over yesterday."

"Shut up," I hiss, elbowing him in the side, and he grunts in pain as I spy Charlie standing at the top of the steps leading up to school. When I give her a quick wave, a relieved smile covers her face as she brushes her brown hair behind her car, her gaze flickering between Archie and me.

Glancing at Archie, I see him looking in the same direction. "Did she drunk dial you Saturday night?" I ask, and he nods, staring down at his feet, and I hum.

"Please go and convince that girl you're not the complete asshole we know you are," I mutter, and he gapes at me in surprise. "Archie, you have got so much making up to do it isn't even funny, but it's not just me who needs you groveling on your knees."

Pulling me into his side, he gives me a one-armed squeeze and kisses the crown of my head. "You're the fucking best, cookie," he states, and I grin, slightly embarrassed with his sudden public display of affection, but I refuse to search out all the eyes I feel on us.

"I know, I know. Now go get your girl."

Squeezing my shoulder, he rushes for the steps, saluting the Allstars as he passes. As I near Hunter, his lips curve up in a grin, but a guy suddenly steps between us with a sneer on his lips as he glares down at me. I have no clue who this guy is. He looks familiar, but I don't know his name.

"It's fucking disgusting how you parade around with your fucking brother on your arm. Is he good in bed too? Stupid fucking wh—"

Before I can even comprehend what's actually happening, Hunter whirls him around and plants his fist straight in this guy's face. I gape at Hunter, my irritation rising, as the guy falls to the ground. I have never spoken to this motherfucker in my life, but he has the audacity to come at me with some lame-ass rumor?

Giggles and laughter to my right have me glancing at the cleat chasers, and that's when I look at KitKat for the first time since the accident. She's glaring at me, and her purple hair has been cut into a short bob that sits just below her ears. I almost want to tell her to get her fucking roots done since her natural blonde color is growing more obvious than the purple now, but there's no time since the guys are causing a scene in front of me.

Turning back to the Allstars, I'm startled to find Tobias and Xavier now standing behind Hunter as he looms over the guy on the grass, a chuckle on Tobias's lips and blood dripping from the asshole's nose. The rest of the team stands around watching as the Allstars hold their ground over this dick.

Slowly crouching down, Hunter grips the neckline of this shithead's t-shirt and pulls him closer as he growls, "If you ever fucking breathe in her direction again, I'll blow your fucking brains out."

Feeling everyone's eyes on us, I glance around, spotting Archie frozen on the steps with Charlie by his side as they observe the whole thing unfold, not knowing what to do, and I'm right there along with them.

Is all of this actually necessary? This isn't the first rumor or taunt I've heard, and I'm sure it won't be the last.

"I am sick to death of people defending this bitch!" Roxy yells, and I find her to my right, all legs and tits in her black mini skirt and deep V-neck top as she stands with her hands on her hips, glaring at me with her lips snarling and her nose wrinkled. She must have marched toward me while I was looking at the players.

Excellent. This is all just fucking great.

My fight-or-flight instincts thrum under the surface of my skin, but it's all cut off as an arm wraps around my shoulders, pulling me in closer to a warm, masculine side, and I stall when I find it's Hunter. His grip on my arm tightens as he attempts to comfort me, but I don't need his comfort. I don't need anyone's comfort, especially not over something so ridiculous. None of this actually upsets me, I'm used to brushing it off.

"If you're done playing caveman, I'd like to head to

class," I say, raising my voice loud enough for the others to hear. All three of the Allstars look at me in surprise. "What? This shit doesn't excite me, and his comment was boring as fuck," I remark with a shrug.

"Anybody else got anything to say?" Hunter grinds out, forcing himself to sound unfazed, but I feel the tremor in his touch, and it makes me fucking hotter for him as he looks around at the crowd.

It shouldn't, it *really* shouldn't. But having Hunter flash his alpha side in public gives me tingles, even if it is some lame attempt to protect what doesn't need protecting. The reason why aside, I could ride him here and now, public or not.

Everyone nearby stands and stares in shock at Hunter defending me, and a few even edge away under his glare when no one responds. Not even Roxy says anything, although she practically shakes with anger, standing alone as all the other cleat chasers only put more distance between us.

Hunter nudges me forward, keeping his arm over my shoulders, and I gulp at the unfamiliar touch as everyone watches us, but I keep my gaze straight ahead as Tobias falls into step beside me with Xavier on his other side.

When we're far enough away from everyone, walking toward the steps, Tobias elbows me gently to get my attention.

"Hunter has been extra calm and chill. It's obvious now you had something to do with it, especially if the glare on Xavier's face is anything to go by," he comments with a grin, and my eyes widen with innocence, but he clearly knows there's been a shift.

I search Xavier out, finding his expression really is like thunder, his jaw tight and his eyebrows scrunched as he attempts to keep his emotions off his face, but he's doing a shitty job of it.

"Fuck you. There's nothing going on with my face, asshole," Xavier growls as we reach the bottom of the steps.

Tobias scoffs. "Don't mind Xavier, love. He's just all bent out of shape because he got a hate fuck, and I got hot, toe-curling sex and a movie. He'll get over it eventually." He grins down at me, and I have to fight the blush trying to take over my cheeks at his words.

"I knew it. You motherfuckers! How has all this actually been fucking going on without me? I feel mistreated. Bubble, why are you wasting your time with these butt knuckles when I would happily ride away into the sunset with you right now?" Tobias pouts as he rushes up the steps so he can reach the top first and hold a hand out to me. "But I must say, I'm very impressed you have Hunter showing any public displays of affection. It makes me wonder what the hot, toe-curling sex involved," he teases with a wink, and I roll my eyes. My hand instinctively reaches out for his, but Hunter pulls it back at the last second, making me glare at him.

"Shut the fuck up, Toby," Hunter grumbles, a grin on his lips.

"Is it because she let you stick it in her ass? I know you're a crazy motherfucker. Did he stick it in your ass?" Tobias whispers, glancing between us as he rubs his hands together, and it's Xavier who pushes him away. A burst of laughter slips from my lips at his candid mouth. I cover my giggle with my hand, and Tobias grins at me knowingly.

Instead of heading straight for the doors, Hunter moves me to the center of the balcony at the top of the stairs, overlooking the parking lot and walkway, then he drops his arm from around my shoulders to turn and face me. I squint up at him, but I can't tell what he's thinking with his eyes covered, so I push his aviators up on top of his head.

His green eyes sparkle with a new kind of mischief I only usually see in Tobias's gaze, but it's mixed with determination as he cups my chin.

"You ready to make a statement, love?" he asks, and I frown up at him. Before I can even respond, his lips are on mine as he pulls me into his chest. It takes me a moment to catch up, shocked by the intimacy in public. When he presses his lips firmer against mine, I go willingly, molding my lips to his like I've wanted to do since he left yesterday, especially with his little alpha performance back there, my hands fisting his top as I do.

"Hot. As. Fuck," Tobias murmurs before Hunter's lips are torn from mine.

Startled, I blink my eyes open, unsure when they actually closed. Tobias stands before me, stroking his hand down my cheek, and I'm surprised by how soft his touch is.

"Please let me kiss you too," he murmurs, and the fact he always wants reassurance from me strikes me in the chest. He never takes anything from me without my permission, and I can't deny I'm as addicted to him as I am to Hunter, just in a completely different way.

Rising up on my tiptoes, I bring my lips softly to his, and he tentatively explores my mouth, not caring that everyone is watching me make out with more than one guy. But if it's a statement they want to give, then it's a statement I'm all too willing to be a part of. My arms wind around his neck, my fingers instantly finding the hair at the nape of his neck under his hat, and I let go of any inhibitions I have of other people seeing me like this.

They already call me a whore, what's the worst they can do?

As I slowly pull away, my body desperate for more, I refuse to look down at the other students who will undoubtedly have something to gossip about now. Looking toward the door, I find Archie staring at me with raised eyebrows while Charlie grins.

"What's it going to be, X?" Tobias asks as he steps back, and I turn to face them again.

"N—"

"Eden, this is about more than just your feelings right now. It's about control and showing everyone we mean it when we say you're ours and under our protection," Hunter murmurs, the tension in his arms and his fisted hands emphasizing the truth to his words, and I sigh.

Xavier moves to stand in front of me, his jaw tight as he glances down at me.

I don't know how things have slipped from sex, to sex and movies, and now publicly claiming me. My brain wants nothing to do with it while my body is desperate for more. I can't lead with my fucking pussy, that's not going to keep me safe.

"I get it, but one, I don't need your protection, and two, would you want to kiss someone who looks this fucking mad about it? I'd rather—"

My words are cut off again, but this time by Xavier's lips. Kissing isn't really our thing, so it catches me by surprise when his soft, full lips gently taste mine. His hands grip my waist as my fingers tentatively find his shoulders before sliding up to his neck.

Wow.

My brain short-circuits as my nails dig into his neck, and my body turns to jelly in his arms as he holds me so delicately—a complete contrast to the hard hate fuck yesterday.

All too soon he pulls away, and I'm left panting. Looking over the three of them, completely different from each other yet melding together so perfectly, I know I'm in trouble.

No matter what the people of this town throw at me,

including the Allstars, I can't seem to stop myself from ending up back in their arms.

Glancing over the balcony and seeing everyone staring up at us, I feel the true power of the Allstars. Tobias stands to my left, with Xavier on my right, while Hunter stands directly behind me with his chest pressed against my back as he grips my waist and rests his chin on my head. I spot the guy who caused all of this shit to begin with still wiping blood from his face with his jacket sleeve.

I feel like I'm surrounded by kings looking down at their people. I just have no fucking clue who I'm supposed to be, both with the Allstars and Knight's Creek in general, and a part of me hates that I want to stick around long enough to find out.

SEVENTEEN

Tobias

So Eden finally let Hunter between her legs, and yet she's still standing. Fuck, this girl was made for us. I've seen that guy fuck. The quiet man everyone is used to vanishes, leaving a dominant male in his wake. I can't deny I wish I'd been there to watch her fall apart in his arms. I need details, but the looks on both their faces tells me I'm shit out of luck.

Since we've been surrounded by classmates, Hunter, Xavier, and I haven't really spoken, but as we step out onto the field for football training, I know we will hopefully get at least five minutes to ourselves to make sure we are all on the same page.

Loving the feel of my football cleats sinking into the grass, I carry my white helmet in my hand as I straighten my black beanie the best I can with the other. Laughter rings out from behind me, drawing my attention, and I find the girls spilling out onto the field for either cheerleading or track.

My eyes instantly find Eden walking side by side with Charlie as they head to the edge of the field. Fuck, she's beautiful, with her perfect hourglass shape and tanned skin. I'm excited by the prospect that Xavier may have finally pulled his giant fucking dildo out of his ass so we can get back on track with my bubble.

Eden catches me staring and curls a loose strand of hair behind her ear, attracting my gaze to her bare, slender neck. Teasing me. I want to bite her, mark her, and kiss her all over her neck, branding her as mine. I've never felt this way about someone. Ever. I never want to see another pussy in my life except for her pretty pink folds. The thought doesn't even scare me, which has me wondering.

"Hey, Hunter," I murmur, glancing to my left to find him and Xavier standing together, watching Eden walk by us in the distance without even glancing our way. "If you're not going to tell me how kinky you got, can you at least tell me how you marked her? Because we both know you did," I say with a grin, but he just gives me the middle finger. Fucker. "I mean, you can tell me, or I can shout the question to Eden now, it's your choice." I shrug, making Xavier glare at me too. "X, don't tell me you don't want to know. I can see the need in your eyes."

"Fuck's sake, Hunter, just tell him because I'm not pissing her off. Well, not purposely anyway," Xavier grumbles, patting Hunter on the shoulder as he, too, waits for the naughty details.

"You're both douchebags, you know that?" Hunter grouses, glancing around to make sure no one is in earshot as he steps up to my side. "And it was her ass while she was bent over with her hands holding onto her ankles before I pinned her to the shower wall and fucked her with my hand wrapped around her throat."

"Fuck."

I don't know if that was me or Xavier, but the smirk on Hunter's face as he steps back tells me he wanted to rile us up, and he definitely did. My cock strains in my tight pants, my jockstrap making it painful as I try to rearrange myself, but what surprises me the most is the way Xavier storms a few feet away, running his hands through his hair.

"You're just as much of a dick as we are, Hunter. Now go calm the green-eyed monster brewing inside of him before he starts beating us into the ground the entire practice," I say with a laugh. Hunter rolls his eyes and walks toward Xavier as I search out Eden again, but her track coach has them deep in a group huddle.

"Okay, Allstars, round it up. If we're going to make a statement against the Vipers this Friday, then we need to train our asses off and make sure we are at the top of our game," Coach Carmichael calls out, and we all gather around.

I reluctantly join the group, standing in a circle around the coach as he goes over the drills we're going to do, and he's quick to put us through our paces. In no time at all, we're pushing through box drill sprints, shuttle drills, and shuffle runs before we start going through his plays, listening to him call out number after number until we hit it perfectly every time.

My gaze continues to stray to Eden several times, and I can't wait for this to be over so I can see her. Sweat trickles down my back as I catch the water bottle Xavier throws my way while Coach repeats his usual speech about being determined and driven as a team, and all I can think is how *I* want to be determined and driven as part of a team to make Eden ours.

With a clap of his hands, Coach takes off toward the building, and the rest of us disperse. I'm watching everyone head inside as the track team continues to run when my eyes fall to Billy, and it makes me pause.

"Hey, Hunter. What did Ryan do with Billy's older brother after he tried to run with Eden?" I ask, my eyebrows knitting together as I realize my focus hasn't been on anything but her since she arrived. Usually I would demand to be a part of whatever went down, but knowing she's safe offers a little peace of mind. I have no clue what Ryan actually does, but I have to admit, it has me intrigued.

I don't want to follow in my parents' footsteps, so I could always bug him to let me follow in his.

Clearing his throat, he glances in Billy's direction, who looks over his shoulder at us with a glare. "He's no longer an issue."

Hmm. Good.

Everyone knew we ran out of the game to save Eden, especially since Coach chased after us, and when he addressed the team, grilling us even though we protected her, he let it slip that Graham was the one who had her, so Billy has been eyeing us ever since.

"Well, we may need to keep a watchful eye on Billy then. It seems he's not too happy about his brother being missing," Xavier murmurs, and I nod in agreement. "But as sad as dead family members are," Xavier continues with a bored tone, "how about we discuss more pressing matters, like Hunter making grand statements on his own. Again."

I can't help but scoff at his bullshit as he stares expectantly at Hunter who simultaneously looks at me with a *what the fuck* expression as we head indoors.

"I'm not being funny, Xavier, but I'm all for the decisions Hunter makes for the group without any prior discussion. It's nothing like the shit you fucking decide, asshole."

Dismissing whatever's about to come out of his mouth, I turn and head straight for the lockers. The quicker I get in there, the quicker I'll be ready. I want to be ready and waiting for Eden when she gets out of the locker rooms so I can walk to calculus with her like some lovesick fucking puppy.

I catch her gaze as I'm leaving the field, winking as I go, and I'm pretty sure she rolls her eyes at me, but *any* reaction is still a reaction at this stage, and it fills me with excitement.

Rushing through the motions of showering and dressing, I secure my black hat on my head, the scar on my scalp burning stronger than ever today. I fix my white t-shirt and shake my head, ridding the memory from my mind as I lace my sneakers.

"Fuck me, Toby, what's crawled up your ass and got you running around like crazy?" Archie asks, but when I glance over at him, the knowing smirk on his face tells me he knows exactly what, or rather *whom*. Motherfucker.

I simply grin in response as I throw my bag over my shoulder and head for the door, not even waiting for Hunter or Xavier. The hallway is pretty quiet, but when a group of girls steps out of the girls' locker room, a perfectly orchestrated grin from me with my Allstar persona has them confirming Eden is still inside within seconds. Perfect.

Leaning on the wall opposite where she will exit, I prop my foot up behind me as I glance at my phone, ignoring the missed call from my mother. She can forget it. I made an appearance over the weekend, and that was enough to scar my soul just as it does every time I visit. I don't need their brand of torture again anytime soon. If my father threatens to place me in prison one more time, I'm going to walk myself in and throw away the key just to shut him the fuck up.

"Will it make an ass out of you and me if I *assume* you're waiting for me?" I hear Eden murmur, and I quickly pocket my phone as I lift my gaze to find her standing before me in her denim shorts and pale pink crop top. She looks like a fucking wet dream.

"I would do just about anything to see your ass, bubble, so what answer is the correct answer for me to get closer to doing just that?" I counter with a grin, making her shake her head with a chuckle.

"Walk me to class and I'll think about it," she flirts back, her teasing going straight to my cock, and I groan.

"Whatever you say, milady."

"Don't be cheesy, or I'll go on my own," she responds, a pointed look on her face, and I seal my mouth shut, offering a smile instead as I throw my arm over her shoulders. Watching Hunter do it earlier made it all too enticing not to, and when she doesn't throw me off, I mold my side to hers, loving how good she feels beside me and the scent of coconut coming from her.

I hate how quickly the math classroom comes into view,

ruining the moment, even if everyone is fucking watching us, but I don't pay them any mind. I almost consider asking her to skip, but she slips from under my arm and steps into the class before I can say a word.

Fuck it. Calculus it is.

Glancing over my shoulder, I find Xavier and Hunter marching down the hall, glaring at me as I walk into the classroom behind her. I watch her ass sway in those itty-bitty shorts, and I have to refrain myself from biting my knuckles.

I need some time, just her and me, I don't care what we even do, but knowing Hunter got to spend some alone time with her makes me taste the sour jealousy on my lips—it's a lot like Xavier must feel on a daily basis. Any sense of jealousy toward my brothers is strange, but she's fucking worth it.

Slipping into the seat beside her, I drop my bag to the floor and quickly pull my phone from my pocket while Mr. Price sorts through some papers on his desk.

Me: On a scale of one to ten, how close am I to touching your bubble butt?

From the corner of my eye, I see her pull her phone

out and swiftly glance in my direction before tapping away on her screen as Hunter and Xavier take their seats on her left.

Eden: You're sitting right next to me.

Me: That isn't an answer, bubble.

Eden: Seven.

Me: Just a seven? Holy fuck. You're ruthless, Eden.

I hear a soft bubble of laughter, a sound I could definitely get used to, and it surprises me how little she actually laughs.

Eden: If you want me, you have to earn me, Tobias.

That is hot as fuck. Hot. As. Fuck.

Tobias: Noted, bubble. How about a little date? You have yet to attend any of our pep rallies. Ready to make an exception?

It feels like it takes an eternity for her to respond. Mr. Price stands, ready to speak to the class, when my phone finally vibrates.

Eden: Okay. But don't make me regret it.

Biting my bottom lip, I try not to squeal like a fucking schoolgirl. Mr. Price begins talking, but I don't register any of it, my focus solely on Eden. I turn to look at her, but I pause when I find her staring down at her phone in horror.

"Hey, Eden...Eden?" I murmur, confused over what the hell just happened in a split second, but when she doesn't even glance my way, I quickly stand and hover above her, instantly finding the cause of the pain and shock written all over her face.

A picture nearly fills the entire screen. A man's face. Sleeping. Pale. Whiter than white. With a bullet wound dead in the center of his forehead.

Who is that?

Glancing to the top of the screen, I find words that will likely haunt me for the rest of my life.

UNKNOWN: LOOK AT HIM. YOUR

FATHER LOST ALL HIS COLOR THE SECOND HE LOST HIS LIFE. DO YOU THINK YOU'LL DO THE SAME?

She finally turns to look at me, the color drained from her face, and then she stammers before taking a deep breath and wetting her lips, her phone clattering to the table.

"Get me the fuck out of here right now."

TOXIC CREEK

KC KEAN

EIGHTEEN

Eden

I don't see anything, I don't hear anything, and I don't feel anything except Tobias as he gently grabs my arm and helps me to my feet before wrapping his arm around my shoulders and pulling me toward the parking lot without a backwards glance.

I think I'm going to be sick. Nausea churns in my stomach as I try to comprehend what the hell I just saw, but I can't look again for clarification. No fucking way.

My fingers curl into the back of Tobias's white top as he flings open the main doors and directs me down the steps as rapidly as he can. The sun blinds me for a moment as my senses slowly filter in, but I let Tobias lead me. I don't realize Hunter, Xavier, and Archie are with us until we reach the bottom and Hunter takes my bag from my hands while Xavier swipes my phone from the back pocket of my denim shorts.

Looking to the other side of Tobias, I see Archie, his eyes filled with concern as I hear them all talking, but my brain can't process their words, unable to understand what they are saying. My defensive walls are high, blocking everything out, yet Tobias's touch helps keep me grounded.

Archie comes to a stop right in front of me, forcing me to halt, and I feel the tension between them heighten when he refuses to move, bending his knees to meet my eyes with a sad smile on his lips.

"Eden, I need you to focus for a minute, okay?" he whispers, moving to brace his hands on my shoulders, but Tobias pulls me closer to his side, making Archie glare up at him. When he brings his gaze back to mine, I finally nod, and he continues. "I can take you home or wherever you want to go—"

"I just told you, I've got this," Tobias hisses, and I grip his shirt tighter as he speaks.

"I'm giving her a choice, asshole," Archie growls. I place my hand on his chest.

"Please, Archie," I murmur, feeling Tobias's arm slip away as I step into Archie's side. I focus straight ahead as I let him guide me to his car.

I can hear the Allstars growling behind me, but I'm too shaken for it to register as more than background noise.

"Are you actually fucking joking?"

"Shut the fuck up, Xavier, it's bad. Fucking bad, man."

Wordlessly, Archie opens the passenger side door for me, and I drop into the seat, effortlessly securing my seatbelt as he rounds the front of the car and slips into the driver's seat.

"I'll get us home in no time, cookie, okay?" Archie says as he puts the car in drive and pulls out of his spot.

My head falls back onto the headrest as I attempt to take a deep breath, but it's no use. Prying my eyelids open, I look out of my window, and my gaze falls to the side mirror where I find the Allstars still standing where I left them.

My heartbeat slows, each thump racking my entire body as I feel lightheaded.

Ba-boom. One. Ba-boom. Two. Ba-boom. Three.

"Stop the car," I shout, unclipping my seatbelt before he jerks to a stop, confusion etched across his features. "I'm sorry, Arch. I need them right now."

My eyes dart between his, not wanting to deal with any judgment when my soul is pleading for them. But surprisingly, he simply nods with a sigh.

"Whatever you need, Eden. As long as you're okay," he finally murmurs, and I jump from the car, holding the doorframe as I answer him.

"I'm fine, Arch. I just need to clear my head. Will you explain to Charlie? I just..."

"Of course, Eden," he assures me with a reluctant sigh before putting the car in reverse but not actually moving.

Glancing over my shoulder, I find the Allstars staring at me with a mixture of confusion and hope, and with a single nod of my head, they are rushing to my side as Archie steps from the car, completely disregarding how the car is parked right now.

"If a single hair on her head is—"

"We fucking know, Archie," Xavier interrupts, dismissing him as he strides to his SUV, seemingly inconvenienced by the whole thing. I offer a forced smile over my shoulder as Tobias walks me to the rear passenger door.

Sliding in, Xavier gets behind the wheel, and I expect one of the others to climb in beside him to sit in the passenger seat, but I'm surprised when Hunter and Tobias both slip into the back seat on either side of me, nudging me into the middle as they sandwich me in.

"You had me worried there for a second, bubble," Tobias mutters with a soft smile, but I don't respond.

"Just drive around for a bit, X, she needs the distraction," Hunter suggests, and I catch Xavier's nod in the rearview mirror. He holds my gaze for a moment before slipping his sunglasses from his head to his nose and putting the SUV in drive.

Hunter strokes my knee gently to my left as Tobias curls his hand around mine, and I try to relax, wishing for the image to disappear from my mind and never return, but that's *never* going to happen. Who the fuck takes a picture of a dead person's face, my *dad's* dead face, or any part of them for that matter? His sullen eyes, his tight lips, his pale skin. I could practically feel his cool touch through the screen.

It's sick and twisted, and I know it'll link back to this damn fucking town, tainting everything like it always seems to.

"Please put some music on," I mutter, and without a word, Xavier presses a few buttons on the touchscreen infotainment system, and his Spotify playlist pops up on the screen, instantly continuing where he left it. "Flames" by Mod Sun and Avril Lavigne filters through the speakers.

Fuck, that shit's ironic. Any other time, I'd be rolling around with laughter, but right now the lyrics hit my soul, perfectly describing whatever the hell is going on between the Allstars and me.

"Do you want me to turn it up?" Xavier asks, and I nod, needing it loud enough to silence my mind, and he does just that.

My eyes close as I squeeze my fingers around both Tobias's and Hunter's, letting the lyrics distract me. I never thought I'd say this, but I'd rather be diverted by the Allstars than the latest threatening message.

The motion of the SUV, combined with the music playing in the background, lulls me into a sense of calmness, but along with it comes a strong feeling of just... emptiness. God, I wish I had the magic I had the other day when nothing mattered but chasing my orgasm alongside Hunter.

I'm sick of letting the people of this town bleed me dry.

I have nothing left to give.

The feeling of nothingness begins to fade as frustration builds within me, and I pull my hands from Hunter's and Tobias's and run them through my hair, gripping my scalp as I try to take a calming breath.

I hate showing weakness, being vulnerable, and this feels completely different than the other night, especially since all three of them are watching me crack. My palms sweat, my heart races in my chest, and tears burn behind my eyes.

"You're not distracted enough, love," Hunter states from beside me, and he's right. As soon as the calmness washes over me, something else pops into my mind that riles me up all over again. My emotions are a complete rollercoaster of fuckery.

"Where's my bag? I want to take one of those tablets you gave me," I murmur, hoping it will work its magic just like it did when I was a PMSing bitch. Hunter grabs my bag from the footwell and dives inside without question, pulling the St. John's Wort out along with a bottle of water, and I manage to smile in thanks.

Gulping it down, I try to take another deep breath, but the agitation still burns inside me.

"Tell us what we can do, Eden," Tobias pleads, and I turn to face him, the helplessness within me clearly bleeding out through my eyes as he looks me over.

"What is anyone supposed to do when someone sends you a picture of your dead dad?" I mumble, at a total loss, and he grips my chin.

"I refuse to let this break you, bubble. So I'm going to ask again—what do you need from us? I can distract you, I can try and make you forget, or I can be crazy and stupid to force a smile. I can literally do whatever you need, but I need you to tell me what that is."

I've never seen desperation in Tobias's bright blue eyes. I've never seen it on any of their faces for anyone other than each other, let alone for me, and it leaves me almost as speechless as the message did.

What do I need from them? What has the potential to ease my pain, anger, and frustration? The answer instantly falls from my lips.

"I need you to make me forget. Make me feel the magic like I did the other day, when none of this mattered and I was just whole," I answer, holding Tobias's gaze before glancing at Hunter and watching as understanding flashes across his face. His expression goes from quiet Hunter to alpha Hunter in a blink of an eye.

"Xavier, head for Mount James," Hunter orders, making Xavier grunt, but I assume he does as he says, my eyes sliding back to Tobias.

His fingers stroke my cheek as he slowly runs his hand into my hair, searching my eyes, and I wet my lips in anticipation. The drag of my tongue against my bottom lip is the only action Tobias needs to lean in closer and press his mouth to mine.

I suck in a breath, lifting one hand to his neck as the other squeezes Hunter's thigh.

"Of course I'm fucking driving," Xavier bites out, the sound of a hand slamming against the steering wheel accompanying his complaint.

Hunter brushes his fingers up my arm, leaving a trail of goosebumps in their wake, but I need more. Tobias nips my bottom lip, making me moan into his mouth as he deepens our kiss. His hand finds the edge of my denim shorts, and he slides a finger under the material, teasing me.

"Please," I beg against his lips as Hunter unbuttons my shorts.

Releasing my mouth, Tobias stares at me with a heated gaze, then he bites his bottom lip before turning me to face

Hunter, who captures my mouth in a demanding kiss. Holy fuck. This is exactly it. This is exactly what I need. My body sings under their touch, building toward a blinding orgasm to override my mind.

I tilt my hips off the seat, and my shorts and panties are discarded as we hit a dip in the road, pulling my lips from Hunter's. I try to catch my breath as I glance out of the front window. Everything is a blur since my mind refuses to focus on anything other than what's inside the SUV, my head fogged with need.

Thankfully the back windows are tinted. I look down at my bare legs before a sound to my right catches my attention, and I turn to find Hunter moving the front passenger seat forward so there is more leg room back here.

Kneeling in the space he just created, Hunter turns to face me, pulling me into his vacated seat and spreading my legs before him as Tobias moves over also.

"Whoever makes a mess over those seats can pay for the fucking cleaning," Xavier warns as I watch him adjust himself in the driver's seat, his hard length noticeable through his jeans as Tobias's lips find my neck.

"Challenge accepted," Hunter responds without looking at Xavier, heat in his gaze as he stares at my core.

"Agreed," Tobias whispers against my neck, the sensation making me gasp with desire as his hand strokes up my thigh.

I close my eyes and my head falls back as Hunter beats Tobias to my center, lazily stroking his tongue from my entrance to my clit as he holds my legs firmly apart. It's like my body instantly recognizes the safety with him, even with Tobias, and I practically melt into the seat at their will.

Hunter grazes my clit with his teeth, and I gasp again with pleasure, hearing Xavier curse from the front seat before Tobias covers my mouth with his. He sucks my bottom lip into his mouth as Hunter slowly inserts two fingers into my pussy, and my back arches as my body tingles.

"I fucking hate you guys," Xavier growls, which only heightens how I feel.

Having both Hunter and Tobias touch me at the same time is electric. They work in sync on my skin, leaving me desperate as Xavier's gaze keeps flicking between the road and the rearview mirror.

Air sweeps across my chest, forcing my eyes open. Tobias is holding my crop top up to reveal my breasts, tucking the cup of my bra down to flash my nipple in his direction, the bud tight and needy.

He breaks the kiss, hovering over my chest before looking up at me. I probably look like a mess with my eyes completely blown from their touches, but the sultry heat in his gaze before he swipes his tongue across my nipple tells me he likes what he sees.

Just as my head is about to fall back again with all the pleasure, I catch sight of Xavier in the rearview mirror, his jaw tight as he takes in my bare skin—it only enhances how I feel. Watching him squeeze the steering wheel while Hunter and Tobias caress me hits me straight in my core.

The world moves around us in a blur as Xavier continues to drive, all while Hunter fucks me with his long, thick fingers, and Tobias bites down on my nipples.

Another moan falls from my lips as my mind goes completely blank, leaving nothing but desire and heat burning through my veins.

"Let me watch you fall apart, Nafas," Xavier murmurs, his mouth slightly open as he observes my skin reddening under their skilled touches.

I grind against Hunter's face as he laps at my core over and over again, and my eyes fall to half-mast as my spine begins to tingle.

"You heard him, love. Come for us. Come for you," Hunter whispers against my nub.

My chest heaves as my heart races, and my eyes fall to Tobias as he cups my breasts and returns his lips to mine.

"Do it, Eden. Let me see you."

Hearing the encouragement from all three of them is too much, and the first wave of my orgasm smashes through my body, wringing me tight as I slowly fall apart again and again before them.

My hair is a tangled bird's nest, and my pussy is on display for all to see with my tits bursting from my bra while sweat drips down my temples. I'm a hot mess, a total hot mess, but the best kind.

As I slowly come back down, Tobias moves back over to his seat, encouraging me to move over with him while Hunter falls back into the spot on my right, wiping my juices from his face. Before I can acknowledge what's going on, fingers swipe against my wet folds and I shiver, watching as Xavier raises his hand to his mouth and tastes me as he licks them clean.

Holy fuck.

Staring at him, I am speechless, but when his gaze

indicates for me to look to my right, I glance over to find Hunter's cock out as he palms himself, his fingers still glistening with my orgasm as he does.

As if I didn't just explode under their touch, I'm desperate for them, my pussy yearning for friction all over again. I lean toward his cock, but Hunter shakes his head, causing me to halt my movement. Confusion and embarrassment consume me until he lifts his chin, gesturing for me to look behind me.

"He needs you more, Eden."

Glancing over my shoulder, I see Tobias with his shorts pushed down to his thighs, his dick in his hand as he squeezes his balls, but the burning need in his blue eyes is what catches my attention. I shift my hips, and his eyes widen as I move toward him—I want to give him more than my mouth.

I even fucked Xavier more recently than Tobias, dammit, and Xavier is a douchebag. My body yearns for him. Swinging a leg over his hips, I line his cock up with the apex of my thighs, and sink down on his hard length in one swift motion. The way he freezes, his fingers digging into my hips as he tries to slow the movement, makes me grin, even as my own breath hitches, my eyes fixed on his.

"Eden, fuck. Fuck, fuck, fuck," Tobias chants, trying to catch his breath, but I want all of him, and I want it now. I asked him to get me the fuck out of there, and he did without question, without even looking at the other two Allstars.

Bracing my hands on his shoulders, I grind against him, dragging my clit against his cock and hitting his pubic bone just right as I repeat the motion again and again. He grasps my hips, holding me in place, and rises up to slam into me.

It's hot. It's fast. It's everything I need as his grip tightens and our movements become erratic, reaching our climaxes together. Hunter grunts beside me, pulling my gaze toward him, and I watch as cum shoots from his cock, his eyes fixed on Tobias and me.

Tobias covers me in a smattering of kisses across my chest and neck as he comes down from his own orgasm, and my forehead falls to his as I try to catch my breath.

"You are something else entirely, bubble," Tobias mutters against my skin, and I hum in response.

"You're fucking telling me," Xavier adds, and I can feel the tension dripping off of him without even looking.

Slowly removing myself from Tobias's lap, I find

Hunter shirtless as he holds his top out for me. "Let me clean you up, love," he whispers, and I simply nod in response, remembering how much he loved taking care of me after he spanked and then fucked me.

Falling back into my seat, my head resting on the cushioned back, I catch my breath as he cleans me—even Tobias's seed that drips from me—while Tobias rearranges my bra and top. Hunter offers me my panties and shorts, I lift my ass so he can pull them up my legs, and I smile in appreciation.

Finally looking outside, I frown when I realize we're still driving around, Xavier continuing to move as we fucked in his backseat. But when I see the bright red metal up ahead, I lean forward.

"Pull over," I murmur, and Xavier frowns at me as he continues to drive. "Xavier, pull over," I repeat, and this time he listens, pulling the SUV to a stop. Before any of them can say anything, I'm climbing over Tobias to get out.

As soon as I step outside, my feet move of their own accord, taking me to the edge of the red bridge I almost went over when the SUV rammed into me. God, how different things could have been if it happened just a few feet earlier.

I stand there for what feels like an eternity, only the sound of the highway in the distance and the birds singing filling my ears. Xavier comes to stand beside me, his hands in his pockets as he casually looks down at the deep ravine as the water flows under the bridge.

"I can't imagine how you must have felt that day. All I remember thinking as I drove toward you was how I had been a total cunt to you and that threatening you might have been the last words I'd left between us."

I look to my left and meet his gaze, his sunglasses on his head. I'm stunned at his admission. Completely speechless.

"I know you hate me, I don't even blame you, but you have to know I will do whatever it takes to stop you from being that close to death ever again, because I lied when I said I hate you too."

I can't seem to pick my jaw up off of the ground as I process what the almighty Xavier Knight just fucking said to me. I don't even need to ask if this is a joke, because his hazel eyes are raw and full of truth.

"You fucked things up so badly, Xavier, all to save your own skin. You haven't groveled on your knees and begged for forgiveness, and I can't picture you doing it either," I finally respond with a sigh, looking back down at the water. "I'm not usually an ultimatum kind of girl, but you seem to pull that side out of me, so this may all be completely nothing, but you need to decide if you choose me. Otherwise, you simply lose me. I'm not a backup plan, and my worth is too valuable to be a second option."

"I'll take that into consideration," he murmurs, and I can't help but grin at his classic Xavier response.

"Of course you will," I say with a nod. "How deep is the water down there?" I ask, my heart pounding wildly in my chest as I look over the barrier, the water slowly flowing under the bridge with a grassy bank on either side.

"The water is like twenty feet deep, I think. Why?"

"Is that a safe enough amount of water to catch me from this height?" I continue, not answering his question as I continue with my own, and I sense him frowning at me.

"Probably, but I've never—"

I don't hear the rest of his words as I climb over the edge of the barrier and jump off the ledge. Adrenaline rushes through my veins as I sail through the air, plunging into the water feet first. Everything happens all too quickly, but when I float near the bottom of the ravine, I get my answer.

Yes. Yes, it is enough water to catch me.

The sound of another splash fills my muted ears, and when I push up off the bottom and break the surface of the water, I come face-to-face with a dripping wet Xavier Knight.

He jumped in after me. This motherfucker is crazier than I thought.

"You are so fucking infuriating, woman." Glaring at me as I kick my legs lightly to keep my head above water, he swipes his brown hair back off his face. "I choose you, okay? I choose you."

KC KEAN

NINETEEN

Xavier

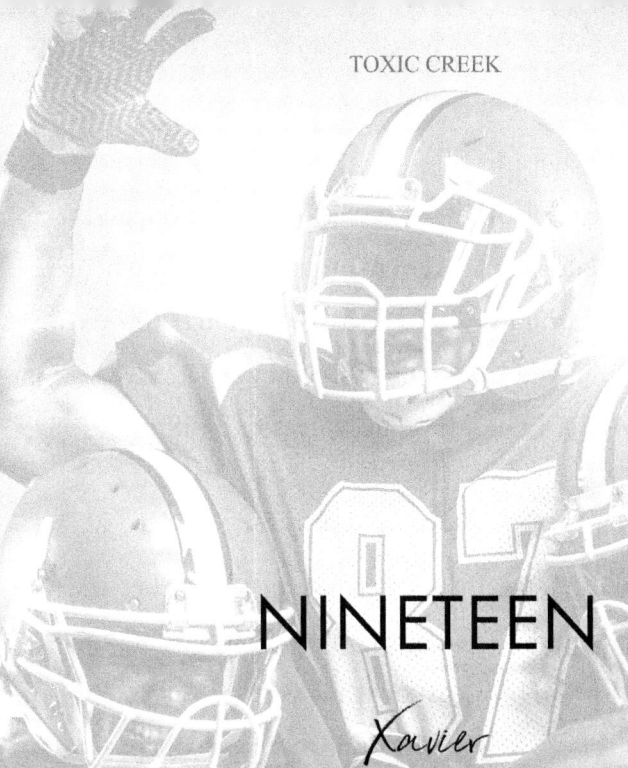

I don't know what I fucking did to deserve this level of batshit crazy from the woman who suddenly holds all of my attention, but fuck me, she is next level.

I just spent the better part of nearly thirty minutes watching them fuck in the back seat—on my freshly detailed cream leather, I might add—and I said nothing. Nothing. Well, nothing asshole-ish. I might have ground my molars into dust, but I managed to hold my tongue. My dick was screaming for any scrap of her attention, but the moment she retook her seat, legs spread, I couldn't help but get a taste of her myself.

Then, in the blink of an eye, her eyes glazed over, and I realized all too late where we were and there was nowhere for me to turn around. As soon as she spotted the red bridge, demanding for us to pull over, I knew I had to, even if I didn't want to. I knew her emotions were still raw, the crash still fresh in all our minds.

Eden stood and stared down at the ravine for what felt like an eternity, the three of us trying to give her the space she needed, but enough was enough. If I wanted to man the fuck up and be a part of whatever was developing between her, Tobias, and Hunter, this was my chance.

Because I lied when I said I hated you too.

That was the understatement of the century, and as I look down at her, where she sits by my side in the back of the SUV, I wish I'd been able to explain better. But that's always difficult when you're the kind of person who only ever expresses anger and acts indifferent.

"I can feel you staring at me," Eden mumbles, glancing up at me with her blonde hair wet and plastered to her head, and I shrug in response as a shiver runs through my body.

"Can you also feel me shivering from the fact I jumped

into the ravine after you?" I retort, and she gives me the most innocent look she can muster, but we both know it's bullshit.

My words were overwhelming her, I know that now, but it's not like I had any control over them. They just tumbled from my lips. now I can think back and see the distress in her eyes and the blush that crept up her neck after my confession, however, so when she said choose her or lose her, I jumped straight in after her, leading with actions instead of words for once, and so far, it was working in my favor.

I can't pinpoint what it is about her that holds me captivated Maybe it's the sway of her hips or the constant sass that spills from her lips. But deep down, I know her soul touches mine in a way I can't explain, just like it did the first moment I saw her when she took my breath away.

After watching her fall naturally in sync with Tobias and Hunter, I can almost admit she completes us. Almost. Now, I just need to convince her to give me a chance.

Feeling Hunter glare at us, I grin. Fuck, I forgot how good he is at lecturing people, and damn did he practically rip me a new asshole for being so stupid to jump into the water. His words were almost as harsh as he grilled Eden too, but she had simply risen on her tiptoes and placed a gentle kiss on the corner of his mouth, and he shut the fuck up.

It's beyond lucky I had a few blankets in the trunk, otherwise we would be freezing to death.

"It's so fucking cold," she whispers, tightening the blanket around her body as Hunter drives and Tobias flips through his favorite playlist from the passenger seat. The dance tracks filter through the sound system as I uncover one of my arms to pull her closer, and she comes willingly. Her head rests against my shoulder, and I stiffen in surprise at the contact before forcing myself to relax and propping my chin on her head as I take a deep breath.

"You literally just jumped into the grossest water I've ever seen, yet you still smell like coconuts," I murmur, squeezing her shoulder, and she hums in response. Tilting my head down, I bring my lips to her ear. "Are you going to explain why you did that?" I ask, and she peers up at me through her lashes.

"Did what?"

I don't respond. Instead, I raise my eyebrow at her, giving her a pointed look as I wait patiently for her to give in, and as if by magic, she sighs, sitting up, and I instantly miss her closeness.

"I wanted to know what it felt like to fall through the air, adrenaline pumping through my veins as I plunged into the water. I was wondering what it would have felt like if I was trapped inside my G-Wagon."

Wow. That's...that's not what I was expecting her to say. I smother my shock and sadness at her admission, knowing what this town can do to your mind, but I won't share that I've felt similar thoughts over the years.

"Have you had a near-death experience before?" I ask, feeling like an idiot the second the question leaves my lips, but she shakes her head.

"Not really, but ever since I arrived in this damn town, I just seem to find myself in those types of situations."

I hate how true that is for her, how true it is for so many of us as others dictate how we act and what we do. I have done nothing but add to all her drama, but there isn't anything I can do about that now. There's no changing the past, I can only make a difference going forward. I just need to play it safe and continue in the role expected of me while protecting her and my brothers at the same time.

But first, Hunter told me sharing my past with her, showing her I can be a little vulnerable as well, could make a difference. And as much as I can feel the bile rising at the back of my throat, I swallow it down and bite the bullet.

"I've almost died," I divulge, and her eyes shoot to mine, and as hard as it is, I hold her gaze.

"When?" Her blue eyes dart across my face, looking for any signs of emotion, but I can't let my mask fall. Not even now.

"Which time?" I reply, and she balks at my words, glancing at the guys up front who nod solemnly. "We've all danced with death, Nafas. All at the hands of the people in this town, and all intentional. We have roles to play, so we continue to play them accordingly."

I don't mention that Hunter's situation changed completely when Ryan came onto the scene, altering his course along with Bethany's because he went through so much fucked up shit before then. It's still an internal battle to get up in the morning for all of us.

"Wait, what?" The color drains from her face, more so than when she recalled her own brush with death, and it surprises me. She continues to stun me in the most random ways possible.

I clear my throat, not wanting to share any stories about the other guys, but I think giving an example that affected all three of us would be the best option right now.

"Have you seen Holmes Correctional Facility yet?" I ask, and she frowns in confusion as she shakes her head before glancing over at Tobias, but he says nothing. "It's on the other side of Mount James. It's the local prison."

She turns to Tobias and surmises, "I'm guessing it's called Holmes Correctional to mark something in the town with your family name?" Tobias nods in confirmation. Someone clearly explained how everything works around here with all the stupid landmark naming shit. "What does that have to do with your near-death experience?" she continues, looking back at me, and I sigh, catching the sign that'll lead us back toward the beach.

"Holmes Correctional Facility has two sections, the juvenile facility and the adult prison, and sadly, it's *our* experience. Our parents feel it's appropriate to place us in there when we don't act accordingly," I answer blandly, and somehow her frown deepens.

"Please explain."

"There isn't much to it. We all know Ilana runs this town, above the mayor and all, but Tobias's mom works for the government. She placed his father as the warden of Holmes Correctional. I've been placed in the juvenile wing four times, Hunter twice, and Tobias...well, Tobias..."

"Eleven. I've been forced in there eleven times."

Eden's eyes almost fall out of her head as she stares at the three of us.

"Nobody knows apart from our parents because they cover everything up. But one of those times, when we were all in there, they were extremely unhappy with the fact we had signed up to play football." I pause, nearly feeling the memory like it's happening this very second. I can sense Hunter ready to take over the story, but I have to show a part of myself that I let very few see, and I will.

"My mind can't comprehend what their issue is with you playing football. You're amazing."

"Oh, they know we have talent. They just didn't like us signing up for high school football without their permission, not that it was needed. So if we wanted to make decisions like men, we were to be treated like men, which led to a two-week stint at fourteen. The first night we were pulled from our beds and forced to the outdoor gym area where there were eight young guys, barely old enough for the adult section, waiting for us."

Any sense of being cold has vanished. My skin is hot with anger and aggravation, and I can tell Eden's shivers have subsided as she practically vibrates with fury.

"Do I even want to know how it ended?" Eden rasps, her voice much weaker than earlier, and I almost regret being open with her when I see how much it actually affects her.

"They beat us to a pulp. We can hold our own, Ryan taught us, but not when we're outnumbered, outsized, and completely caught off guard in the middle of the night," I answer honestly. "We spent the rest of the two weeks recovering from our injuries in our cells. It's actually where I got my scar, but at least we got to play football."

The positivity we hold onto from that experience does nothing to calm Eden as she shakes her head.

"There are no words for how diabolical that is."

"There never is, love. But we do what we need to so we can survive and leave this place behind," Hunter murmurs, but she doesn't get it, and I can understand that.

Nobody says anything for a while. We all sit in silence as we process what we're actually dealing with, watching the world pass us by as Hunter drives along the coast, the sun bouncing off the ocean in the distance. I almost jump out of my skin as something strokes my fingers on my lap.

I glance down, my breath catching in my throat as

Eden intertwines her fingers with mine, caressing her thumb against my knuckles. I lift my gaze to meet hers, but she's watching the world go by through her window.

What is this?

Is this sympathy? Support? Pity?

I look up, meeting Hunter's eyes in the rearview mirror, and he nods with a grin, making me frown as Eden gently squeezes my fingers. I don't know what the fuck this is, but right now, I don't care. Her touch somehow soothes me while her mouth infuriates me. She's like playing with fire.

"Do you want me to drop you off at home, or would you rather head back with us?" Hunter asks, my anger returning as she pulls her hand from mine.

"That isn't my home, but yes, please take me to the Freemont house. I'd rather change into my own clothes, and I need a minute or five." A refusal is on the tip of my tongue, but her eyes fixate on mine like she expects me to overrule her. "Don't say a word. All this emotional whiplash you're giving me is causing a fucking headache. I can't think when I'm around any of you. I feel like I'm abandoning all my morals and values for some dick."

"But it's some good dick, right?" Tobias interjects, pouting at Eden over his shoulder, but she just does it back.

I know we're cracking through her hard exterior, even if she doesn't see it herself. I can be patient.

"The appendages between your legs are excellent. The problem are your personalities, which smell like cheesy ball sacs. I don't know how to deal with the negatives in this situation," she retorts, eliciting a laugh from my chest without warning, catching her by surprise.

The SUV comes to a stop outside of Archie's house, and as much as I don't want her to leave, I know I'm the main source of all her uncertainty, so I swallow my pride and open my door.

"You can go, but you have to leave this way," I tell her with a grin, patting my lap, and she arches an eyebrow at me.

"I can just get out of my side," she counters, and I bite my lip at her sass.

"You could, but you love a challenge, Nafas, admit it."

Huffing, I watch as the determination sparkles in her pretty blue eyes as she drops the blanket from her shoulders, revealing her wet shorts and cropped tee, her bra visible through the material, and I have to hold in a groan.

Slowly, she shimmies across my lap, rubbing her ass against my denim-clad cock. I desperately want to pin her to me, but today isn't the day.

"I'll be thinking of you," I whisper against her ear, and I feel her shiver before she drops from the SUV as Tobias holds her bag out to her.

The three of us stare at her as she secures the strap over her shoulder before clearing her throat.

"Well, this is awkward with all of you watching me, so I'm just going to go now." Turning on her heels, she whirls around, but before she even takes a step, she spins back to look at us. "Thank you. You didn't have to get me out of there like that, but you did, and I appreciate it."

"I'm going to run some checks when I get back. If I find anything, I'll let you know. It wasn't Billy's brother, that's for sure," Hunter informs her, and she nods absently.

With that, she turns again and actually leaves this time, closing the front door to Archie's house behind her with a quick glance over her shoulder.

The second Hunter begins driving away, I instantly regret not making her come with us.

"I'm almost mad Xavier didn't go all caveman and force her to come with us," Tobias says with a chuckle, a hint of truth in his words, and I hum in agreement.

"Is it too late to change my mind?" I question as we

round the corner to our driveway, and my heart instantly drops. "Never mind, everything happens for a reason, right?" I bite out as my mother leans against her SUV, tapping her fingers expectantly.

"What do you want to do, X?" Hunter murmurs, but I don't respond. I need to drop every ounce of vulnerability I just put on display for Eden and fast. My mother will see it as a weakness, and I don't need her looming over me any more than she already is.

Hunter parks the car on the other side of the stone steps that lead up to the front door, and I finally answer him.

"You two head inside. You don't need to deal with her."

"That's not how this works, Xavier. We're a team, even when it comes to *her*. You trying to protect everyone and placing the weight of the world on your shoulders is what caused the issues with Eden in the first place, and I won't go back to that," Tobias replies, and I reluctantly nod before the three of us slip out of the SUV.

There's nothing I can do with my wet clothes, and having the blanket on will only give her some form of ammunition, so I round the corner as I am, tossing the blanket blindly, and sweep my hair off my face.

She lifts her sunglasses up off her nose as she stares me down. Dressed as impeccable as ever in her navy pinstriped pantsuit, she sneers at me with utter disgust, ruining her latest round of Botox, but I say nothing. It's always the best way with her; let her say her piece and hope she fucks off.

"Do you care to explain why you aren't in school?" she demands, her voice grating on me, but I continue to act unfazed.

"Not really, no."

Running her tongue over her teeth, she tries to rein in her anger, but her brown gaze is practically venomous already.

"Don't think I don't know you left with the Grady girl. It seems as though you've forgotten our little agreement. I can take it off the table if you'd prefer."

Every fiber in my body screams at me to tell her to fuck off. She'll find another reason to stop me from going to Ohio State anyway. Fuck the agreement. Fuck her. Fuck her shit. Fuck it all. But I know that won't help us right now. So instead, I take a deep breath as I stare her down.

"I'm having a little issue with the fact someone else seems to be pushing her buttons too, which results in her literally running from the school. I find she doesn't feel humiliated by childish classroom bullying anyway, so we went after her. I'm not drenched just for the sake of it, you know," I growl, and she tilts her head, trying to decipher how much is the actual truth from my lips.

When she knows she isn't going to get anything else from me, she nods, taking a step closer as Hunter and Tobias continue to stand on either side of me.

"Don't fuck with me, boy. If you're lying, I'll find out. As for the other person playing with her, don't you worry about it. Maybe focus on sticking to your end of the bargain. Understood? My run for mayor is picking up momentum fast, and I want everything perfectly in place when it happens."

Before I can utter a word, she turns to her SUV. The back passenger door opens before she fully approaches, and then she slips inside, the tires screeching a little as they drive away. We remain in place, watching her leave with her security detail.

When the SUV is finally out of sight, I hang my head, sighing as I feel a headache coming on.

"What the fuck are we going to do, X?" Tobias asks, and I shrug.

"Fuck if I know, but we'll figure it out. We have to. These people don't get to win. No matter what." Feeling the resolve deep in my soul, I turn my gaze to Hunter. "Tell Ryan I'm willing to do things his way," I murmur, catching the flash of surprise and relief on Hunter's face as I finally give in.

We've never made a move against my mother because I asked them not to. But now? Now I don't see any other way to survive my mother and this town, especially if I want Eden to be safe right along with us.

This is how it has to be.

TOXIC CREEK

TWENTY

Eden

The bell rings and everyone's chairs scrape across the floor before it's even finished, and I'm right there with them. Mrs. Leach rambles on about the English assignment due on Monday, but I already did it yesterday, so I'm barely listening. My grades are solid, thank God—I don't need to deal with that on top of everything else.

Charlie's arm loops through mine, and we head out into the hall, our feet carrying us toward the cafeteria before our brains can even catch up.

"Girl, I'm starving," she murmurs as we pass the

cheer squad walking in the other direction. Their eyes are narrowed as they sneer at me, looking me up and down, but there is no KitKat and Roxy for a change, so they don't actually say anything.

"Me too," I respond, staring them down as they pass while following the crowd heading in the same direction.

I've been on high alert, the image of my father still flashing in my mind as I scan the crowd. Hunter found the cell phone that sent me the picture in the cafeteria lying in the trash , and Ryan dusted the device for fingerprints, but he came up with nothing. I know they are still trying to gain access into the cell and are playing with the sim card, but any further details looks slim.

I know there is someone watching me at Asheville High, likely for Ilana, but I'm more anxious that whoever it is will try to make a grab for me again like Billy's brother did. Could it be Billy? He hasn't done anything to create suspicion, but he could be involved in the same things as his brother. I don't know, but I need to be extra vigilant.

It's been quiet in class and in the halls since the football team, band, and cheer squad are all out of classes today as they prepare for the huge pep rally tonight. I've only ever known pep rallies to take place at the start of the season, but apparently, here in Knight's Creek, they also do it the afternoon of their game against their local rivals—the Vipers.

The buzz and excitement are practically humming throughout the school, and I have to admit that even I can feel the energy today, or maybe it's just because classes finish early to accommodate the pep rally.

Stepping into the cafeteria, I follow Charlie as we join the line, my eyes gazing over the menu as I feel eyes on me.

It's been like this since I got to Knight's Creek, but it's grown worse since I was seen storming from the school with Tobias's arm around my shoulders and the other two Allstars and Archie hot on our tail. Apparently, that isn't something they have done before. At all. Which now only seems to add fuel to the fire where the cleat chasers and their ring leaders are concerned.

But the Allstars...they've been surprisingly quiet, focusing on the game coming up, and giving me enough space to figure shit out like I asked. I think it's the space that surprises me the most. It almost feels like the Allstars are running interference because I've had no shit and no one in my face demanding things from me. Maybe the public claiming actually worked?

I know it's not going to last much longer, it never does, but I'm definitely going to enjoy the peace and quiet as long as I can.

"Are you ready for tonight?" Charlie asks, straightening her glasses, and I stare at her with wide eyes.

"Which part?"

"Well, you've got the pep rally, the game, or the party afterward to celebrate yours and Archie's birthday. So all of it really," she says with a chuckle.

I roll my eyes as I glance around the cafeteria, waiting for the line to move. "I just want to curl up in bed and watch some movies if I'm being honest," I admit, and she gapes at me. "But I'm obviously not going to do that," I quickly add, almost reconsidering my words as she glares at me in mock disgust.

I'm definitely up for the game. I want to see the Allstars tear into the Vipers, and I kind of want to spend some time with them that isn't controlled by someone else's actions or attack toward me. How am I supposed to have any other opinion of them if we never just...be?

"I bought the cutest peach dress for the party, and Archie asked me to wear his jersey to the game tonight…" Her voice drifts off nervously toward the end, but before

I can respond, we are interrupted by a woman calling us forward to grab our food.

Opting for tacos, I swiftly grab my tray and head toward our usual spot, falling into my seat and placing my bag at my feet as Charlie drops into the seat across from me. I can feel her purposely looking anywhere but directly at me, and I remember what she said a few moments ago.

"Charlie, you know I'm not going to be upset that you and Archie are figuring things out, right?" I start, taking a bite of my pork taco while I wait for her to reply.

She glances up at me guiltily. "Uh, I'm not all that sure, to be honest. After he kept such a huge secret from you, I don't know." Tucking a loose strand of hair behind her ear, she nibbles her bottom lip, ignoring her food, and I feel bad.

"Charlie, I'm happy for you guys. I was surprised when you called things off to begin with. I don't ever want my relationship with Archie to affect yours as well. He's my... brother, and if I know anything at all about siblings, it's that they have the ability to piss each other off," I answer honestly, remembering how Lou-Lou and her brother used to scream at each other like crazy.

"I just don't want Archie to come between us, Eden."

"And he won't. Everything is all good. I promise," I insist, leaning closer to squeeze her hand before taking another bite of my lunch.

Nodding in understanding, she finally takes a bite of her sub, and when I think we're going to relax into a comfortable silence, she grins at me with a gleam in her eyes.

"So, what jersey are you wearing tonight?" she asks, and my eyebrows knit together in confusion.

"Huh?"

"There's my little bubble butt. What's going on?" Tobias calls as he appears out of nowhere, taking the seat to my left as Archie, Hunter, and Xavier join him.

Running my eyes over each of them, I have to bite my lip to stop myself from drooling. Tobias is in his usual beanie, with his Allstars jersey and a pair of shorts, and Hunter is wearing his jersey with a pair of straight-cut jeans and a black jacket. Xavier takes the seat to my right, and I hungrily take in his painted on black skinny jeans and jersey.

They are hot as fuck and driving me crazy as hell.

I feel a few eyes looking our way as they settle at our table instead of sitting with the rest of the football team in the center of the room. The murmuring picks up, but Xavier leans forward in his seat, practically blocking the cheer squad from view as they enter the cafeteria.

His gaze holds mine, the green in his hazel eyes shining a little brighter today as he licks his bottom lip, staring straight at my mouth as he does. I refrain from rolling my eyes again before they actually fall out of their sockets.

Sitting back in my seat, I see Archie murmur in Charlie's ear. Whatever he says makes her smile, and the corner of my mouth lifts too. Hunter takes the spot beside Tobias, and I can barely think about anything else other than the wild moment in the back of Xavier's SUV.

How do they consume me so much?

"I think her ears are broken," Hunter mutters with a grin on his lips as a few cafeteria staff members approach the table, dropping plates stacked high with chicken and vegetables in front of the four guys before darting off again.

"My ears aren't broken, you just overwhelm me," I counter, but the lift of his eyebrow tells me he likes that answer way too much. Douchebag.

"You're still coming to the pep rally this afternoon, right?" Tobias questions, his mouth full of chicken, and Xavier leans around me to shove his shoulder with a grunt.

Something about a gross caveman with no table manners.

"I'll be there," I answer, returning my attention to my own food as the table falls into a comfortable silence, but I don't miss the gazes we're still garnering from the other students in the cafeteria. All of them are watching to see what drama will transpire today.

As if in slow motion, one by one, the Allstars edge toward me in some way. Tobias slides closer so his thigh presses against mine, his bare leg rubbing against mine since we both have shorts on. Xavier's hand gravitates to my other thigh, stroking lazy circles on my skin. Hunter relaxes his arm behind Tobias's chair to rest it across the back of mine, his thumb dragging over my exposed shoulder as well.

Fuck. Fuck. Fuckity fuck.

If I thought they were overwhelming me before, that was nothing compared to now. My mind flips back to Xavier's SUV, my skin prickling with desire as my heart races, leaving me almost jittery.

It takes everything in me to continue eating, acting unaffected by their touch, but I know I'm being completely obvious, especially judging by the grin on Charlie's face, and when she clears her throat and rests her hand on

Archie's shoulder, I know she's up to no good. I flip her the finger before she even opens her mouth.

"So, before you got here, I was asking Eden what jersey she would be wearing tonight."

I curse under my breath as I force myself not to hide my head in my hands, but without a moment's pause, Tobias claps his hands.

"Well, since someone put her in his jersey at the last game," he begins, glancing at Xavier with a raised eyebrow while wagging his finger, "that leaves Hunter and me. We decided she can wear mine at the pep rally and Hunter's at the game."

I gape at him before glancing at the others who all nod in agreement, then I splutter over a response.

"She is sitting right here, you know. Do I not get a say at all?"

I squeeze the edge of the table before me, not really all that mad when I consider it, waiting for someone to answer.

"If it's because you just want to wear my jersey, Nafas, just say the word. I—"

"Ignore Xavier, love. That's his lame-ass attempt at being funny," Hunter interrupts with a roll of his eyes, and the sass almost makes me laugh, but I'm too focused on the gasps from the table and surrounding students.

Chancing a glance at Archie, I find him and Charlie staring open-mouthed at Hunter and me, and I instantly know it's because he called me love. Jerks. I feel my cheeks flush the slightest bit, but I refuse to let everyone's attention on Hunter's new nickname cause me any discomfort.

"You're not going to turn me down like that, right?" Tobias murmurs, brushing his fingers against my cheek, and I swallow hard past the lump forming in my throat as he stares into my eyes. "If you need me to get you off to make you say yes, then just say the word, bubble, and I'm in," he continues, leaning in close to my ear, and I shiver at his ridiculous words that nobody else seems to hear, thankfully.

"I'll take a pass, thanks," I mutter in response, hearing a snicker or two around me, but my focus is on my lap, watching as both Xavier and Tobias touch me, and Hunter's caress on my shoulder only adds to the tingles spreading through my body.

"We could make it a quickie," Tobias offers, and I chuckle.

"You mean a normal?" I retort, laughing at my own

joke as everyone at the table does the same while Tobias pouts. His gesture makes me desperate to sink my teeth into his plump lips.

"You take that back, Eden Grady," he says louder before moving closer to bite my earlobe. A moan slips from my lips, making me slap him away as my eyes dart to Archie who is covering his ears and turning a little green.

"No, no, no, no, no. Nope. No way. That is all too much," Archie whines, and I agree it's weird in the company of others, but this fucker is overreacting.

"Don't act like you didn't go through my fucking toys the first day I was here," I say, and he cringes as Charlie spins to stare at him with wide eyes.

"Archie, that's gross," she chides, and I stick my tongue out at him. The normalcy of it all catches me off guard, pulling me from the moment.

"What just happened?" Hunter asks, making me face him. He stares at me expectantly, waiting for me to respond, but I'm completely lost. "You went from smiling and joking to the color practically draining from your face. Obviously, something affected your mood."

Asshole. Why does he see through me so much? If he's willing to call me out surrounded by everyone here, then I should have the balls to answer honestly.

"I hate that you offer me a false sense of security. That my mind simply forgets the shit you already did to me without actually seeking revenge or bringing you to your knees. I hate that your touch matters and that you want to make it okay, forcing me to hate you less and less."

I'm almost panting with each breath as I look from my left to my right to stare at the three of them. Archie and Charlie sit tight-lipped as the Allstars freeze in place.

Just as I'm about to rise from my seat and put some much needed distance between us, Xavier cups the back of my neck and brushes his lips against my earlobe as he leans closer.

"Break me. Break *us*. We deserve it. But you deserve the kind of loyalty we don't offer to anyone but each other. You deserve us bending over backward to protect and please you. I meant it when I said I choose you. I did things your way, offered you the space you seemed to need, but time's up now, Nafas. Time's up."

His lips gently caress my cheek, and my eyes flutter closed as I drown in his words and touch. Then, all at once, he's gone. When I finally blink my eyes open, I find only Charlie sitting across from me, the expression on her face showing she's just as confused as me as she glances toward the door they must be heading to, but I don't turn.

"Do you still want to go ahead with the plan?"

"I do," I murmur, clenching my hands.

"You're so fucked, Eden," Charlie comments, tapping the table, and I couldn't agree more.

I am totally and completely fucked.

TWENTY ONE
Eden

The gymnasium is filled with bodies, the voices echoing around the room as everyone waits for the pep rally to begin. White and green balloons and streamers decorate all surfaces, and half of the students in the crowd have the same colors painted on their faces. Charlie looked at me earlier when we saw them all doing it in the girls' bathroom, the question clear on her face, but the second she saw my eyes widen in panic, she knew it was a no-go for me.

I've never been in the gymnasium before, especially since the games always take place at the town's actual stadium, but it's surprisingly big, and by the looks of it, we actually have a basketball team also. Who knew? Clearly, we can't be known for our other team sports or they don't get the same level of backing as the football team does.

Charlie convinced me it was a good idea to sit in the front row so we had a perfect view of all the action, and I already know I'm going to regret it at some point.

The coach's shoes squeak against the hardwood floor as he walks out to the center of the basketball court, and everyone seems to get more excited, their conversations growing louder as they anticipate the whole team spirit celebration we're about to partake in. The whole room is a mixture of freshmen, sophomores, juniors, and seniors, so it's embarrassing that I barely recognize any faces.

"I'm so ready for this," Charlie exclaims, clapping beside me as we rise from our seats, the lights dimming as Coach Carmichael clears his throat into the microphone.

"Asheville High, let's give it up for the band and cheer squad who are going to be opening today's pep rally. Then, we're going to show some love for the Allstars, have a couple of games, and make sure we're all riled up for tonight," he announces in his monotone voice, his eyes flitting around the room as he speaks. "As a reminder, there will be school buses available to run students over to the stadium if needed. But for now, enjoy the show."

The crowd claps and whistles, and the guys standing behind us jostle me forward slightly, but when I turn to glare at them, they quickly calm down.

Swiping my hands down the front of my shorts, I retake my seat as the coach steps off the court and the drums from the band instantly pick up. I recognize the tune as the rest of the band joins in, covering the open space before us as they play "We Will Rock You."

I clap and stomp my feet when needed and smile when Charlie catches my eyes, but my resting bitch face stays in place the whole time. I usually love these things, but my earlier discussion with the guys still plays on my mind.

They have fucked me over. I don't give a damn what excuses or justifications they may have, they screwed me over. I see the change in them, the need to prove themselves, but why would I suddenly become such a pushover, letting them take what they want again and again without giving me anything in return?

No matter what I think, there is still a part of me that's drawn to the darkness inside them. Their cutthroat mindset completely resonates in my soul. Maybe we're destined for each other, to tear each other's souls out and return them all damaged and broken. But first, they need a reminder that I'm my own damn person.

The band finishes playing after only one song, and a little part of me is grateful I don't have to listen to instrumental covers of old tunes for a change. But the second the cheer squad replaces them, I take it back. Anything is better than watching these bitches.

"Oh fuck, here she goes," Charlie murmurs, confusing me, but the second I hear Roxy's voice through the speakers, I cringe in understanding.

"Hey boys, girls, and...whores," she greets sweetly, her gaze falling to me as she sings the last word. I almost want to applaud her for her balls, but instead I throw her the peace sign as I stick my tongue out, playing up to the title she seems to have given me.

It doesn't surprise me when no teacher calls her out, it seems to be the general fucking status quo around here. Especially since the Allstars always seem to be the ones to control discipline.

"I would make her my whore," a guy shouts from across the gym. I don't see who, but the gasps and whispers that follow tell me he didn't get the reaction he wanted.

His words don't affect me, not even a little, except I know they'll somehow get back to the Allstars and they'll start taking matters into their own hands. Again. I can already feel my stress rising from it. A reminder is definitely needed.

"Thanks for that," Roxy grinds out, a fake smile on her face as she continues, looking anywhere but at me now. "Let's feel the team spirit tonight, people, and put your hands together for my girls."

She steps back from the microphone, and I watch as she inches her skirt up higher, displaying the bottom of her ass cheeks. I refrain from scoffing at her desperate attempt to gain attention as the entire cheer squad starts clapping and spreading out across the court, encouraging the crowd to join in.

Charlie nudges my arm when I don't instantly participate, and with a roll of my eyes, I reluctantly clap my hands, giving her a pointed look as I do. She grins, which only seems to irk me. She's riling me up on purpose.

The second the cheerleaders start their chant, I stop clapping, watching as they move in sync while a few do some crazy handsprings and cartwheels.

"Dance for the Allstars." Clap. "Let's show them what we've got." Clap. "Gooooo, Allstars." Clap.

Wow. I'm quite sure my father's funeral had more fucking spirit than this. Apparently, though, my thoughts are in the minority since the entire crowd goes crazy, stomping their feet, clapping their hands, and cheering at extreme levels.

It feels like an eternity before everyone calms down and Roxy returns to the microphone, lapping up the love until it dies down.

"Are you ready to feast your eyes on our men?" she asks, leaning forward and cupping her ear to encourage everyone to be louder, and I want to barf as the rest of the squad shouts along with her. I know I'm acting childish, I just can't seem to give a shit. "I saw our Allstars practicing today, and boy, were they h-o-t, hot! So let's put your hands together and get ready for the Allstars."

The music system kicks up in the background, pumping Riton, Nightcrawlers, Mufasa, and Hypeman's "Friday" through the speakers, and even I have to admit how much of a feel-good vibe this has.

Spotlights suddenly turn on, brightening the room, as Roxy starts calling out each player's name. Everyone claps as each guy comes out, dancing for the crowd before joining a line and clapping along with everyone else.

Some guy drops to the floor, sliding across the court on his knees, and I can't help but laugh, annoyingly feeling the excitement myself. The anticipation continues to build as they go through the team, and when Archie steps out, leaving only the Allstars to join us, he starts shaking his legs and hips like he's Elvis.

Charlie throws her head back with laughter, loving his little show, and I quickly pull my phone out and record a snippet before he ends his minute in the spotlight. Glancing back at Charlie, all I see is love in her eyes, and witnessing the emotions on her face makes me pause—they definitely match Archie's.

Fuck me. This is the kind of thing I should be chasing, some high school sweetheart romance, not the three fuck heads who drive me crazy. But maybe that *is* the kind of high school romance I'm destined for.

"It's time for the Allstars of all Allstars!" Roxy shouts, and I cringe at the overuse of the word "all" in her damn sentence, but my heart rate picks up and I bite my lip as I watch for them.

Hunter strides through the doors at the far end, his steps strong as he glares straight ahead, and I almost laugh at how predictable he is, until he stops in the center of the room, places his hands on his hips, and gyrates.

What the holy fuck?

Everyone screams when they see the usually quiet guy letting his hair down and shaking his ass. I bring my hands to my mouth, joining in with them. His eyes find mine, and he grins for a moment until he realizes I'm not wearing a jersey, never mind Tobias's like they wanted, but he just joins the line of football players without giving me any further indication of his thoughts. His grin, though, has slipped to a frown.

Before I can consider how that makes me feel, the song repeats again, and Tobias swings the doors open, letting them smash against the walls as he shakes his hips with every step. The smile on his face is infectious, even to me, but the second he gets to the middle of the room, his eyes fall to mine, and he spots my crop top. Determination instantly fills his features, and not a moment later, he's working his way toward me, forcing me to swallow my nerves.

His grin widens as he stops in front of me, thrusting his hips at my face as he slowly pulls his jersey over his head, his beanie remaining in place as he reveals a white tank top underneath, and I don't miss a glimpse of his abs too. Holy fuck. That's hot. Too hot. He twirls the green and white material above his head like a cowboy, and I hear the crowd around us laugh and cheer louder at his antics as my cheeks redden at the public attention.

He holds the jersey out for me to take, and I arch my eyebrow, not moving a muscle as I remain lost in his gaze.

"Don't leave me hanging, bubble. I might cry in public, and nobody wants that," he murmurs with a pout as he leans forward.

I sigh and take the fabric from his hands as my heart beats faster at his closeness. "I'm not wearing it," I manage to say, and he simply grins at me.

"I figured as much, but I'll take this as a small win. I'd only think something was wrong if you didn't make me work for it, Eden."

Leaning forward, he quickly pecks my cheek before jogging off to join the other team members. He stands out like a sore thumb without his jersey on, and I hate to admit my blood boils from knowing everyone is looking at what is ultimately...mine.

Fuck. Jealousy isn't me, not at all, but it rages through my veins uncontrollably. It makes me want to scream and kick something, to claim him, but instead I sit as still as a statue.

"And last, but certainly by no means least, is our quarterback, our knight, our final Allstar. Please put your hands together and make some noise for Xavier Knight!" Roxy screams through the microphone, derailing my train of thought as I turn my gaze to the doors expectantly like everyone else.

Two girls from the cheer squad open the door for him, treating him like the royalty he isn't, and he strides into the hall full of swagger, a dark grin on his lips as the gym goes wild. I can't hear a single thing with all the banging, clapping, cheering, and screaming. Fuck, it's crazy in here. Seeing the Allstars in all their glory is something else.

When he raises his arms in the air as he walks to the middle of the room, I can't help but shake my head at his arrogance, squeezing the jersey in my hand as I do. Xavier's eyes meet mine and he winks, licking his lips. I gape at him in surprise. Please let that be all he does. I can't deal with him channeling Tobias right now. It's already too much seeing him flirt with me so publicly.

He barely shakes his ass before joining the others, but when he does, the song instantly changes, and they start doing the fucking renegade dance everyone is obsessing over, which has the noise levels kicking up to a level where

I think my eardrums might burst.

Charlie squeezes my arm, jumping up and down excitedly with everyone, and I let her pull me along as I stand with her. If anything is going to get the school pumped up, this will do it. Please just tell me this is the end.

When I catch sight of the cheer squad, I stall. I was too lost in the trance of the Allstars like everyone else to notice the cheerleaders lined up opposite them, and in slow motion, they all step forward and thrust cream pies into every single one of their faces.

I fucking hate the cleat chasers, but this is excellent. The shock on the football players' faces tells me it definitely wasn't planned, and that makes it all the better—until the cheerleaders step forward to help clean up.

The second someone stands near Archie, Charlie is up and out of her seat in an instant, not caring who's watching as she shoulder barges the girl out of the way and wipes the cream from his face. All while I stand watching KitKat brush up against Hunter, while Roxy licks the cream from Xavier's face as another cleat chaser helps Tobias.

All three of them saw Charlie jump to Archie's aid, and they swing their gazes to me, waiting for me to do the same. But they are not mine. As much as my heart is pounding and my palms are sweating, they are not mine. My body and soul crave them, sure, but my mind knows the shit they've done. Jealousy burns through my veins, but my resolve wins this time.

I guess it's up to my heart to decide, but it's as dark as theirs. Fuck. I know I still want to fuck with them later—they deserve it. I'm never going to be exactly what they want, I'm only going to be me, and they can take it or leave it. They'll never fit into the box I imagined for my perfect guy either. Instead, he's spread out across the three of them, forcing me to fall for the good along with the bad.

With that, I place Tobias's jersey on my seat and leave the gym, pushing past everyone as I refuse to look back at them.

I want them, but they haven't earned me yet.

Xavier

Turn around, Eden. Turn the fuck around.

Watching jealousy flash across her face, I thought she was going to be up on her feet and crossing the court in seconds, so I remained still, letting her finally come stake her claim. But instead, her face suddenly wiped clean of any emotion as she headed for the doors, Tobias's jersey on the seat she just vacated.

Disappointment fills my veins as I will her to turn around, but she doesn't.

Roxy presses up against my side, bile rising in my throat from her licking the cream from my face, and I push her away.

"Fuck off, Roxy," I growl, swiping the cream from my face. She lifts her hand to my cheek, and I bat it away as anger builds inside me. "Are you deaf or desperate? Touch me again and I'll snap your fucking fingers," I snarl, hearing her mumble something under her breath as she storms off, but I pay no attention to what shit she actually says.

"Get your skanky ass away from me, KitKat, and while you're at it, fix your fucking roots, your hair is a mess," Hunter bites out, and I almost laugh at his harsh words, but my mind is too focused on Eden's departure.

Wiping at my face one more time, I look around for the guys, only to find the three of us standing alone in the middle of the court while everyone else laughs and jokes around us.

"She didn't like that," Tobias murmurs, staring at the

door Eden left through.

"She didn't do anything about it either," I add, and a sense of sadness falls over us.

"We have a lot of fucking making up to do," Hunter grumbles, and I nod. Clearly, I'm more of an asshole than I thought, but I'll do whatever it takes.

"Hey, guys, do you want to check this video before it circulates?" Archie asks, joining us with Charlie at his side.

Taking the phone from his hand, I see two girls standing nervously behind him. They must be freshmen or something, because I don't really recognize them. Glancing down at the screen, I watch the video play as the cheer squad throws cream pies in our faces, and then I see my disappointed expression while Roxy licks my face and Eden leaves. It continues to play out, moving in closer as I push Roxy away, and Hunter's words to KitKat are just noticeable before she storms away too.

"I'll get them to delete it," Tobias murmurs, his face scrunched up in disgust from observing the gold diggers hanging all over us, but I raise my hand.

"No, no, I want it everywhere, and you're going to show it to Eden, Charlie."

"I am?" she says with her eyebrows raised and a pointed

look on her face, but I just stare back.

"Yes, you are. I want her to see that we fucking pushed them away."

"After clearly baiting her to claim you in a setting you know she never would have."

She's not wrong. I know that. Brushing my hair off my face, I take a deep breath. "Please, Charlie," I say, ignoring all the noise and the crowd around us as I try to convey how much I need her to do this, and with a sigh, she nods.

"Look at that. You do have manners. But fuck this up again, and I won't help with shit."

With that, she grabs the phone from my hand, turns on her heel, and walks off with Archie hot on her tail as they approach the girls together.

Figuring out how to get Eden to be with me is some next-level shit. Usually, they are all fighting over us, so of course I find myself falling for the challenge. It seems we all do.

TWENTY TWO

Eden

Sitting in a sea of black and red, with Bethany and Charlie on either side of me, I feel every ounce of anticipation in the air. The away team still has a reserved section across the field, but the best seats are definitely saved for the home fans, that's for sure.

I'm a mixture of nerves and excitement for the game. I don't know how long it's going to take those motherfuckers to notice we aren't in our usual seats, nor how long it'll take for them to find us in the away team seats.

We've received quite a few looks and stares from those

around us, wearing our whites and greens, but Ryan made it a point to send some guys to sit with us because he's apparently all for me making a stand, but he wants to protect us from the situations our crazy statements can get us into.

My phone pings in my pocket, and I take a quick look to see it's a message from Lou-Lou.

Lou-Lou: Hey, girl. Just about to leave the halfway snack stop. I can't wait to party! It's been way too long.

Me: I can't wait to see you! I should be back at the house in time after the game, but message me when you're close so I can make sure.

I put my phone away as Bethany giggles beside me as she glances down at her phone. Just being back in her presence calms me. Glancing across the field, I spot Ryan sitting in our usual seats with Cody beside him, and I almost feel bad for separating them from Bethany, but she seemed excited for some girl time even if it is sitting with the Vipers' fans.

"Girl, are you ready for this shit show?" Charlie asks, nudging my shoulder with hers, and I roll my eyes. "Wait, have you seen the video yet?"

Scrunching my nose in confusion, I shake my head. "What video?"

She pulls her phone from her pocket and presses a few buttons before thrusting it in my face. "The video of what happened after you left," she murmurs, but my focus is on the screen.

I recognize the moment I couldn't sit and watch anymore and left the gymnasium, but I can also tell when I leave by the looks on the Allstars' faces. It shocks me how disappointed they were, but I don't know what they expected from me.

Just as I'm about to hand the phone back to her, not wanting to watch these motherfucking cleat chasers pawing all over them, I see Xavier push Roxy away. When she moves toward him again, whoever is recording steps closer, picking up more sounds as they go.

My heart pounds in my chest as I watch him growl down at her and she moves away from him, but it's Hunter's voice that suddenly holds my attention.

"Get your skanky ass away from me, KitKat, and while you're at

it, fix your fucking roots, your hair is a mess."

Gaping at Charlie, I hear Bethany laugh beside me, and I realize she's been watching along with me.

"You didn't see how mad they were when they wanted you to throw down on those bitches but you just got up and left. You must be wielding some magic, because they actually respected your space and didn't come bulldozing you down like I expected," Charlie remarks as I hand her the phone back.

That's true, and I'm almost impressed. I'm sure I'm going to tip them over the edge when they come out, though, but it's all for an important cause. I'm my own woman. I'll do what I want, when I want, *wearing* whatever fucking jersey I want.

"There's time for all that yet," I finally respond, and Bethany laughs.

"I think Charlie and I should place bets on who is going to pick a fight first."

"Dibs on Xavier. He's the worst," Charlie says quickly as I look between the two of them in bewilderment. They appear excited by the prospect.

"No, definitely Hunter. He always thinks with his fists first when he's annoyed," Bethany argues, and I start to second-guess my decision a little. "But I must admit, I love your determination, Eden. Those little assholes deserve it."

"They aren't going to behave like fucking heathens because I'm sitting here. They may be pissed off, but they aren't going to start brawling," I reason, but it's almost a question, and the fact that they both laugh at me in response is all the answer I need.

I'm not responsible for them acting like idiots. Not at all.

The crowd around us jumps to life, cheering and chanting as the Vipers step onto the field. I haven't looked up their stats or skills, but they are all built like beasts. Even from here, they all seem like they are seven feet tall and four feet wide. It's definitely a good thing I believe the Allstars' skills outweigh theirs, although I'm reconsidering how much of a distraction I may be.

The Vipers hover on the field as the music changes. "The Violence" by Asking Alexandria blares through the speakers as the band goes crazy on the drums and the Allstars enter the field, led by Xavier who is flanked by Hunter and Tobias. Their presence instantly dominates the turf, and I get chills of excitement. This is going to be an epic game.

I track the Allstars' every move, watching them look up to the stands in confusion as Hunter offers a small wave to Cody—he waves back like a lunatic, and it melts my heart. A quick glance to Bethany and I see her smiling at her little boy, her unconditional love for him shining in her eyes.

The Allstars pause, glancing between one another, searching the crowd, making my heart pound in my ears as the whistle blows and they slowly join the rest of the team, ready to start the game.

We observe in silence, fully engrossed in the coin toss as the referee signals for the Allstars to start. After one final huddle, Xavier points, ordering everyone around, and like a well-oiled machine, everyone moves into position. The whistle blows, Xavier calls out the number for the play, and the action all happens at once.

The fullback blocks as Xavier hands the ball to Archie, who takes off like a bolt of lightning between the Vipers' defense. My eyes dart around the players holding back the Vipers, giving Archie just enough room to get the first down just as the Vipers' middle linebacker wipes him out.

"Shit," I hiss as Charlie hides her face to hide the view from her vision, but Archie sits up in mere seconds.

"Those were some fast moves," Bethany comments,

smiling at Charlie as she turns back around, and Charlie relaxes her shoulders at the compliment for her man.

Watching as Tobias leans down to help Archie to his feet, patting his helmet as he stands, I can tell they are talking amongst each other. Hunter and Xavier come to stand in front of them, likely planning the next play, when all of a sudden Archie is pointing a finger in our direction, and I have to will the blood not to rush from my cheeks as the Allstars turn in slow motion to stare at us.

I hate that they are wearing helmets, that I can't see their emotions on their faces as I hear Bethany mumble a sharp, "Oh s-h-i-t," under her breath.

The only sign I get that they've actually found us is the clenched fists at each of their sides. They don't move a single muscle, not even responding to the coach calling out their names, and that's when I know I definitely have their full attention.

Sitting in a crowd of red and black, I stand out in my green and white shirt, just as I wanted it to. With my hair up in a bun, the back of my jersey is easily visible, and I hope they get the message. Turning to show them the name ironed onto my jersey, I watch Bethany grin beside me as Charlie reaches over and high-fives her.

It doesn't say Asheville like they arranged. It doesn't say Holmes like they wanted for the pep rally. It doesn't even say Knight like the one Xavier slipped over my head at the last game I attended.

Memories flash through my mind of every time they've fucked with me, pushed me, or punished me for something that actually had nothing to do with me.

"We share, so if you've had one of us…"

"Archie is your brother, your twin brother."

"Fuck you out of my system."

The video of me walking naked through the halls.

All of it is why I find myself with my back to the field, straightening my jersey with my heart in my throat.

There, in thick, white block letters reads, "GRADY."

Because that's who I motherfucking am.

Hunter

She's sitting in the motherfucking away stands. The. Mother. Fucking. Away. Stands.

And she somehow managed to get my sister to go with her, which only tells me we deserved it.

I'd been excited this morning, all riled up for our rival game and the vision of her wearing my jersey while we pummeled them. But the second we mentioned it at lunch, I knew none of it would happen, especially after she didn't wear Toby's at the pep rally.

When the cream hit my face, a classic pep rally surprise, I watched with envy as Charlie rushed to Archie, and I prayed Eden would do the same, but we should have known better.

Instead, she left, and we didn't get to see her until now. My heart stalled when she wasn't sitting with Cody and Ryan, but when Tobias mentioned it to Archie as he lifted him off the grass, he pointed straight in her direction.

"What the actual fuck?" Xavier growls, his body coiled as tightly as mine.

"Can somebody please tell me why my girl is sitting with the fucking Vipers?" Tobias grunts as he stands frozen in place to my right, just as she slowly rises to her feet, her green and white jersey making her look like an angel amongst devils in the middle of all the black and red Vipers jerseys.

Watching as she slowly turns, giving us a show, I can't help but scoff. "I think she's in the Vipers' pit to prove a point that little Miss Eden Grady is indeed her own woman." As much as I wanted her in an Asheville jersey, I must admit she looks hot as fuck wearing her confidence as a second skin in her Grady one.

"Couldn't she have done something that didn't fuck with my head when I needed to focus?" Xavier bites out, and I raise an eyebrow at him even though he can't see it.

"Unfortunately, Xavier, she would argue that we never really gave a shit when we fucked with her, so it's all fair game really."

Archie chuckles under his breath as he steps back, leaving the three of us to get a grip.

"If she's sitting in the Vipers' pit, that means she cares, guys," Tobias murmurs, and the zap of hope that swirls inside me fuels me up.

Things have changed for us, I know that, and everything was going good until we fucking seemed to overwhelm her with our bullshit. I won't apologize for it. I have no shame in asking for what I want, and now I think it's officially time to claim her as ours.

No more confusion. No more power plays. No more feeling like I'm being held at arm's length.

"What's up, pussy boys, ready to forfeit already?"

Dante, the Vipers' team captain, goads as he steps in front of us, flanked by his cuntish teammates, and my blood instantly simmers just beneath the surface. I can't stand this asshole.

"We're good. Let's go," Xavier says before turning to the team and grabbing the ball. Wordlessly, Tobias and I follow his lead, ready to get this shit over with.

The coach growls our names, and when we glance in his direction, I'm surprised to find him red in the face with spit frothing on his mouth, and all his annoyance and anger seems to be aimed at us. Apparently, someone didn't like us stopping to sort our shit out. Tough luck.

"This one's for her, X," I murmur, walking past him to take my position, and he nods in understanding. Perfect.

"Twenty-one. All in twenty-one," he hollers so the whole team hears, and we fall into place, ready for the counter play he wants to go with.

Xavier is the king of misdirection because he can realign his body in a split second, leaving everyone to wonder what the fuck just happened, and a twenty-one tells me I need to be ready.

Breaking from the scrimmage, I watch from the corner of my eye as Xavier lines up as if he's going to throw to

Tobias. Everyone covers him as planned, but at the last millisecond, the ball is whirling through the air towards me, and I catch it perfectly in my arms before I take off sprinting down the field.

Not a single Viper is ready, especially since we've been working on switching this move up from play twelve. Putting one foot in front of the other, I pound the grass, feeling someone approaching from my right just as a teammate wipes them out, and I continue on, just managing to escape their grasp.

Seeing the end zone right in front of me, I run harder, feeling my lungs burn as I count the steps it'll take to get points, but just as I near the line, I'm hit from the side and dropped to my back. I hold still, letting the Viper land on top of me without a fight, stretching my arm out with a deep breath.

As soon as the ref blows the whistle, I know it was all worth it. Opening my eyes, I find the ball *just* over the line, and I smile in relief. It would have been a shit run to dedicate to someone for it all to fall short, that's for sure.

The Viper curses as he rolls off of me, and I jump to my feet as quickly as I can. My eyes instantly find Eden's, and since we're aiming her way, I'm closer than before, close enough to see her nibble her bottom lip.

Without a second thought, I point up at her, letting everyone know who that was for. I don't miss my sister clapping and jumping up and down like a damn seal as Eden forces herself not to hide behind her hands.

Game on, love. You can be who you want to be, and I'm still going to be here.

"Who's the pretty blonde in our pit, Asheville? Have you loosened her up for me?" Dante shouts, his lizard-like tongue sticking out as he wets his lips. Watching his green eyes sparkle as he tries to sexualize Eden, I know I'm at my limit.

Catching him to my right, I don't hesitate to charge toward him, aiming straight for his waist as I wrap my arms around his middle and knock him to the ground. We're a clusterfuck of arms and legs as we grapple to be on top, but as big as this guy is, he has no chance against me.

Hovering over him, I hit the motherfucker straight in the gut.

"Don't even fucking look at her, you dumb cunt," I spit out as I feel people trying to pull me off of him, and I hope it's his teammates so they can all have a taste of my fury too. I love the feeling of cracking skulls when I'm this pissed off.

"I'll cut your fucking dick off and shove it so far down your throat you'll choke on it," I growl as Tobias pulls me against his chest.

Xavier steps in front of me, leaving the Vipers to circle us, but it's obvious they aren't really up to the challenge.

The coaches and referees run over to us, separating the teams as a bottle of water is thrust in my face. Looking back up at the crowd, I find Eden staring down at me with her hands covering her mouth, and I grin.

Slowly, I raise my arm, pointing directly at her again.

That one was for you too, love.

TOXIC CREEK

TWENTY THREE
Eden

I definitely made my statement at the game, and they still won, thank God. The Allstars destroyed the Vipers 31-9, which only brings me joy. The heart palpitations I had when Hunter knocked that guy to the ground almost had me passing out, but it was naïve of me to think he wouldn't come out on top.

The way he pointed to me afterwards, just like after he scored his touchdown, told me it was for me. That guy must have said something to piss him off, and it was probably about me. If it's true, the guy fucking deserved it.

I've practically had hot sweats ever since. It's not like I need him to defend my honor, not even a little bit, but he looked so fucking sexy doing it.

I run my fingers down the front of my khaki green, silk, off the shoulder wrap dress and smile. It accentuates my chest well, and the slit up the front makes it perfect for the beach. I paired it with my favorite leopard print sandals and beach curled hair, going a little heavier on the makeup tonight and painting my lips a deep red.

I've held back, making my statement, but now I hope Xavier's words are true. *Time's up, Nafas.* It's not officially my birthday until Tuesday, but I'm not against any early birthday presents that come in the form of dick. I can practically feel my soul laughing at me. It's more than sex. It has to be. I've never struggled so much with staying away from a guy, never mind three of them, but I'm just not ready to accept that.

Not now, maybe not ever.

"For fuck's sake, Eden, what's taking so long? We're dying out here," Lou-Lou yells, laughter in her voice as Charlie giggles along with her. "You owe me deets on the guys in this town and what's been going on with you," she adds, making me roll my eyes as I hear Charlie snicker.

"Girl, she's in deep," Charlie chirps.

"I am not!" I shout, running my fingers through my hair as I hear them laugh.

"Eden, have you found yourself a man?" Lou-Lou calls out teasingly, and before I can answer, Charlie beats me to it.

"Just one? Try three."

Stepping into the bedroom from the walk-in closet, I find them both preparing to take a shot, and as much as I feel left out, it's better that I keep my distance from the liquor. I mean I jumped into a ravine the other day without a drop in my system, and I can't bear to think what I did the last time I *did* have a drink.

"You guys need to stop," I grumble, making them both giggle like children.

"Who are these guys? Tell me more," Lou-Lou presses before they take their shots, cringing as the harsh liquor goes down their throats.

"They are the Allstars. Absolute assholes if I'm honest with you, Lou-Lou, but that only seems to encourage her," Charlie says with a grin, winking at me as I shake my head.

"Not true."

"Oh, so true, don't play coy, Eden," Charlie teases, and

I feel a slight blush heating my cheeks.

"Eden Grady, have you gone and caught feelings?" Lou-Lou exclaims, gasping with her hand to her chest in exaggeration, and I turn my back on them, refusing to entertain them anymore. "Fine. Charlie, let's do another shot," she says, taking the hint, and I appreciate it.

Tonight is still going to be fun though. I don't need alcohol to have a good time, to laugh, or to dance, and that's exactly what's going to happen.

I glance between them. It's crazy how I attract such different people. Lou-Lou is street-smart, edgy, and screams sexy as sin with her heavy makeup, her short, tight red dress, and her sleek blonde hair up in a bun. Charlie is beautifully understated with little makeup, her hair braided to the side, and her flowy peach colored dress which falls just above the knee.

They look like the devil and the angel sitting on my shoulders.

"You are too fucking hot, girl," Lou-Lou praises with a grin, checking out my dress, and I roll my eyes at her. "Are you sure you don't want to do a shot with us?" she asks again, and I shake my head. Neither of them knows or understands my need to put some distance between me and the hard stuff, and now just really isn't the time to explain.

"I'm definitely sure. I'm just not comfortable with being out of control at the moment," I offer in response, and they both nod, thankfully leaving it there.

"Well, that just means more for us then, right?" Charlie grins, and Lou-Lou laughs as she pours them another.

"Please tell me you've left some hot guys available here. I'm in desperate need of a good time that doesn't involve drama," Lou-Lou states with pleading eyes, and I raise my eyebrows.

"There wasn't drama when I left," I say as subtly as possible as I add a pair of hoop earrings to my ears, enhancing my ensemble, and she rolls her eyes dramatically.

"Girl, I can't even, but that's a discussion for another time. Tonight, I want to forget all about it."

The beseeching expression on her face tells me not to push for more, and I know how it feels to be on the other end of that look, so I feign zipping my lips and throwing away the key, and she sags a little with relief.

"Eden, oh, Eden! Where are you?"

Tingles zip through my body at the sound of Tobias's voice coming from the balcony, and I rush to open the curtain as quickly as possible, only to find all three Allstars out there.

"Holy motherfucking shit tits. They are some damn fine men," Lou-Lou whispers as my mouth becomes dry.

My mind feels like it's going into overdrive as I try to take them in all at once, still not actually opening the patio door as I feel their eyes on me.

Tobias grins knowingly at me, wearing denim jeans with a fitted, white V-neck top and an open, pale blue shirt over it with his black wool hat firmly in place. Hunter stands with his hands in the pockets of his distressed black jeans, his worn gray top tight against his body like it's been painted on.

Xavier causes my breath to stutter. He stands before me in jeans and a fitted navy top with his hair swept back off his face, his tanned skin looking lickable. But what holds my attention is the actual emotions visible on his face.

For the guy who is always closed off, with nothing more than anger and privilege emanating from him, but tonight he's looking at me like I hung the fucking moon. Desire, need, and hope swirl in his eyes, and that's what has me stepping forward to unlock the door.

"Lou-Lou, I love you, but if you touch any of my men,

I won't be responsible for my actions," I warn, keeping my gaze on the Allstars through the glass, and I hear her intake of breath.

"Wait, did you just say...men?"

"Yes, yes, she did," Charlie answers, a hint of defensiveness in her tone, but she doesn't know Lou-Lou.

"Holy fucking shit, you lucky bitch," Lou-Lou responds with a chuckle as I slide the door open.

Hunter steps forward first, lifting me off my feet. I yelp in surprise, but the kiss he plants right where my neck meets my shoulder has the sound turning into a moan.

"You and your damn stubborn tendencies, love. If I ever see your ass in the away stand again, I'll fucking spank it," Hunter whispers against my ear, and I shiver.

"Tempting," I murmur in response as he lowers my feet to the floor.

"Are you done proving a point with us now, bubble? We are insufferable fuckers—we know, you know, everyone knows. Now can we please go back to you at least semi liking us?" Tobias says as I turn to face him. He wears his classic pout on his lips, and I can't help but grin. Before I can answer, Xavier steps in front of him, consuming my vision as he crowds me.

Bending his knees slightly and bringing his face to mine, he cups my chin, seemingly unfazed by everyone else as he crushes his lips to mine. My hands instantly go to his shoulders, holding on for dear life as he devours my lips, and I fight for dominance, my grip tightening on his shoulders as I press my lips firmer against his, but it's pointless.

His other hand trails down my spine, resting on my lower back as he pins me against him. Reluctantly, he releases my lips, my eyes fluttering open to find him looking right back at me.

"You're your own woman. You're in charge, blah, blah, blah. But you can do all that as mine." His eyes search mine, and I frown as he waits expectantly. "Say it, Nafas," he murmurs, and my brows knit together even more as he pulls me tighter against him, holding all of my attention.

"I have no—"

"Say you're mine. Say you're ours. Don't give me any excuses or any bullshit either. Don't lie to me, to us, or to yourself. Just. Say. You're. Ours."

I gape at him, aware of the silence as everyone stares at us.

"I still haven't forgiven you." I try to step back, pushing

against his chest to put some space between us so I can think clearly, but he doesn't budge.

"We know that. You can accomplish your revenge, express your anger, or whatever else you have planned for us while you're ours. Say it," he insists as my heart pounds in my chest, and my fingers tremble.

I feel someone move up behind me, and my breath hitches as Hunter kisses my neck in the exact same spot he kissed earlier while Tobias steps up to my side and tilts my gaze from Xavier. Having them crowd me, with their woodsy, earthy, and spicy scents mixing together, is giving me sensory overload, yet I feel safe all at the same time.

Nobody says anything, nothing at all. I have a pair of dead parents, a mom who hasn't been in contact with me for what feels like an eternity, Ilana determined to control and ruin my life, a twin brother, and the Allstars—who have gone from trying to tear me down to using all of their resources to build me back up again.

Everything is wrong in my life, and they sat back and watched me make a stand for myself, not interjecting or stopping me, just letting me be me, and *that* is what I need, more than anything, from those around me.

This may be crazy, I may be foolish, and this may all

blow up in my face, but I take a deep breath and relax in their hold.

"I'm yours." I should be frightened by how right those words feel, but a soft smile curves my lips instead.

"Yes, girl. You get 'em. Slay the cocks, baby. Slay. The. Cocks. This is all hot as fuck, but I need to go find myself a stiff pole to dance on, if you know what I mean," Lou-Lou calls, breaking the tension in the room, and it makes me smile.

Hunter steps back a little, and I do the same, extracting myself from their touch as they all stare at me with a mixture of surprise and need.

"I'm yours, you're mine. Now come have fun with me before I remember a reason to be pissed off at you," I say, and Tobias grins, his hand on my ass as he guides me toward the door.

"You are so fucking made for us, bubble. I love it. Let's go."

Lou-Lou and Charlie laugh as they lead the way, and I latch on to the little bubble of happiness inside me.

Lou-Lou was right. Tonight is a night to forget. To forget everything and just be Eden Grady.

I sway my hips on the clear, makeshift dance floor over the pool as "Bed" by Joel Corry, RAYE, and David Guetta pumps through the speakers. The campfire burns on the beach, illuminating the night's sky, and there is mood lighting around the deck, making it a little brighter up here as well.

Watching tipsy Lou-Lou and Charlie dance beside me is strange when I'm sober, but the music rocks through my body, and the smile on my face, for the first time in the longest time, isn't fake. It's a genuine, natural smile. It almost feels foreign, and my jaw aches, but it's totally worth it.

Sweat trickles down my back as I slow my movements, my legs aching since we've been dancing for the better part of an hour while the guys sit around the campfire with Archie and a few others from the football team.

I feel their gazes on me the whole time, and my eyes constantly slip over to them. I joined Charlie and Lou-Lou, leaving the Allstars down on the beach alone, to prove that I do what I want when I want, but now I'm just punishing myself. I'm drawn to them.

"Hey, I'm going to go sit down for a bit," I shout over the music, and Charlie instantly links her arm through mine to join me while Lou-Lou shakes her head.

"I'll join you when I actually have a dick of my own to sit on."

Scoffing at her words, I turn for the steps leading down to the beach, sidestepping a few people as we go. I subtly try to look for KitKat or Roxy, and I spot them hovering near the drinks table farther down the beach closer to the water. They are too caught up in whatever conversation they are having, and I heave a sigh of relief knowing I don't seem to be on their radar tonight, which surprises me since the party is technically for my and Archie's birthday.

Charlie stumbles on my arm a little in her tipsy state, so by the time we get over to the guys, I happily let Tobias pull me down sideways into his lap. His arm bands around my back as he squeezes my thigh, purposely inching his fingers under the slit of my dress to feel my bare skin, and I shiver at his touch.

"Hey, bubble, what are you drinking?" he asks against my ear as he presses his lips against my cheek.

"Soda or water, I'm not fussy," I murmur, prepared

to stand, but he pulls me tightly against him as he hollers for Billy.

I cringe internally at Billy's closeness, especially since I can now see the resemblance between him and Graham, and it sends a shiver down my spine.

"Get three beers and a bottle of soda," Tobias orders, barely lifting his gaze to acknowledge Billy, but my eyes stay on him the whole time, watching as he frowns at Tobias before glaring as he takes me in.

"Billy, did you not hear him?" Xavier growls from two seats down. Hunter is the only person separating us, since Charlie sits on Archie's lap the next seat over.

"I was talking about football with the guys, can't it wait a minute?" Billy whines, but that doesn't go down well with the Allstars.

"You can talk about football with the boys when you get back or take a little trip to the ER, Billy, it's completely up to you," Xavier bites out, clearly disliking being disobeyed, and with a curse under his breath, Billy storms off in search of drinks.

Hunter rolls his eyes dismissively at Billy's retreating form before returning his gaze to me, starting from the tips of my toes and slowly caressing my body all the way up to the loose wisps of hair framing my face. I practically feel breathless from his eyes alone.

"Cookie, we still haven't decided what to do on our actual birthday," Archie shouts, breaking the moment as I shift my gaze to his. Charlie is snuggled up in his arms, and I smile at how sweet they look.

Thankfully, the music isn't as loud down here, but the roar of the fire makes up for it.

"I'm not sure, what did you have in mind?" I respond, trying to shift my position in Tobias's lap, but he makes it impossible when he doesn't relax his hold on me.

"I think we should try to go to Pete's for breakfast, then play video games and maybe watch a movie."

"So you're saying we should spend the day like we spend our Sundays," I state, and he shrugs unapologetically. I already know I'm skipping school on Tuesday, but I'm down for whatever.

"Do we spend our Sundays doing exactly what we want to do?" he counters, and I can't help but grin because we definitely do.

"I want to go to the record store in town at some point too. I keep meaning to, but it keeps slipping my mind."

"I'll take you there, Eden," Hunter interjects.

Tobias scoffs in response. "Hunter could guide you around that damn record store with his eyes closed. He loves it so much. That's why Bethany and Ryan bought it when it was on the verge of closing, just to make poor, sweet little Hunter happy. Isn't that right?" He grins, looking down at me instead of at Hunter, but he just tells him to fuck off in response.

"Seriously, love. I'll take you."

I meet his gaze, and the lightness sparkling in his green eyes fills me with excitement.

"I'd like that," I answer, nibbling on my bottom lip as he offers me a half smile before bringing his nearly empty beer bottle to his lips and looking back at the flames.

"You're going to have to think of something to do with me too, Eden. You can't be throwing these one-on-one dates out so casually without including me," Xavier says as he stands and stalks toward me.

"Fuck off, X. She's mine right now," Tobias gripes, and I stare at him until he amends, "She's her own, but she's on *my* lap right now." As if to prove his point, he somehow manages to hold me tighter, and I feel like my eyeballs are going to pop out of their sockets. The feel of his cock hardening beneath me is too intoxicating for me to complain.

"Tobias, this isn't a pissing contest, and you're about to make my brain explode, please stop," I grumble, and he instantly releases his hold a little, wearing an apologetic, guilty smile on his lips as he does, but I can't seem to be mad at him.

Knowing I'm not going to move out of Tobias's lap just yet, Xavier turns back, grabs his chair, and drops it right beside us, his hand falling to my exposed thigh beside Tobias's.

I squeeze my eyes shut as I try to contain myself, my body instantly reacting to his and Tobias's touches, and I hear Xavier's soft chuckle. It startles me, and I open my eyes to find him smiling at me. I have to bite my tongue to stop myself from telling him to fuck this party and leave with me right now.

"I want to take you to an NFL game. Just you and me," Xavier murmurs, and I find myself nodding before I even realize what I'm doing.

"If you take me to a 49ers game, you can count me in," I tell him, tucking my hair behind my ear, and he nods in response.

"You have yourself a deal, Nafas."

"What about—"

A bottle is thrust in front of Tobias's face, which he wordlessly takes, before Billy silently hands out drinks to Xavier and Hunter as well. He circles back to finally hand me the soda in his hand, and I barely manage to refrain from rolling my eyes at his shit.

"Anything else?" he barks, and I watch the anger flash across Xavier's face as he sweeps his tongue along his teeth.

"Nope, you're done," I answer, sliding my gaze to his, watching as he glares down at me.

"The fuck did you just say?" Billy growls, fisting his hands at his sides, and I just smile wider at him as he stands frozen in place. Between his fucking attitude toward me, and his brother's attempt to abduct me, I have no time to be nice to this asshole.

"I said you're done. Go back to your friends and chat about football like a good little boy, or we can have the all-important football conversation here if you'd like," I offer, refusing to look anywhere but directly at him as I speak.

He doesn't give me the same courtesy though, flicking his gaze from one Allstar to another. They must offer him the same expectant look I do, because when he looks back at me, he rolls his eyes.

"You wouldn't know shit about football, but whatever," he sneers with a huff, turning to leave, but nobody gets to make a remark like that and walk away without question.

"Darlin', I know more about football than you do about the logistics of a woman's cunt, that's for sure," I sass, and he turns back to me with a growl, but before he can even open his mouth, Xavier and Hunter are both on their feet trying to separate us, and it's almost laughable.

It feels like Billy glares at me for an eternity, weighing the pros and cons of coming at me right now, before he finally shakes his arms out to relieve the tension building inside him. Stepping back, he glances down at my lap before turning to leave, and I frown in confusion, tracking his gaze, then I freeze.

"Fucking stop him," I snarl, and Hunter looks back at me with wild eyes for the briefest of moments before doing just that.

Billy grunts in confusion as Hunter restrains him. "What the fuck man?" he hisses, but nobody responds because they have no idea what I want. Hunter just followed through blindly, trusting my judgment, and if I wasn't on autopilot right now, it would likely warm my soul.

Tobias must feel the anger emanating from my body,

because when I go to stand, he doesn't try to hold me in place as I clench my fists, trying to shake the unnerving feeling coursing through my veins.

"Where is Lou-Lou's purse?" I ask, peering under the seats they've been sitting in all night, and I spot the sparkling silver purse under Hunter's chair.

"What the fuck is going on?" Archie and Xavier both ask at the same time, but I'm too busy rifling through her purse to answer. My shoulders relax the second I find what I'm looking for.

I push my bottle of soda into Xavier's hands, and he holds it even though he's looking at me like I'm crazy. When I quickly rip open the packet and pull the strip from the foil, realization slowly washes over his face, and I see him pale for the first time ever.

The bottle lid unscrews easily, making the tension within me rise as I place the testing strip into the soda for ten seconds, then I lay it down flat on Hunter's vacant seat as everyone stands around me, watching in silence as I do my thing.

"Now we wait," I announce, my eyes flickering over everyone's but settling on Billy's. "Unless you have something you'd like to say sooner," I add, watching as the flames from the fire highlight just how pale he seems to have gotten, fidgeting against Hunter's hold.

"Is this a fucking joke?" Tobias growls, his hands fisting at his sides. He looks like he's about to tear Billy limb from limb.

Billy instantly starts squealing like a pig. "I-I d-don't know what it is. Honestly. They just said it would be a bit of fun. I-I..." He trails off, knowing he's only making things worse for himself as I fold my arms over my chest.

"Who are *they* exactly?" I inquire, and he looks away nervously. "I won't fucking repeat myself," I say calmly, even though my skin feels like it's only getting hotter with rage.

"I don't know, I don't—"

His words are cut off by Xavier stepping in front of him, his fist connecting with Billy's face lightning fast, and he slumps back against Hunter's body while he holds Billy's arms behind his back.

"How much longer does this thing take?" Archie asks, glancing down at the strip, but it's not really necessary now. Not when he's openly admitted someone said it would be "fun."

I take a deep breath as the reality of it sets in. Someone

tried to drug me. Roofie me.

"What was the plan once I was lying limp and helpless on the ground, hmm?" I muse, my voice much calmer than I expected. I stare him down as I process just how close that actually fucking was. If he hadn't glanced down, I wouldn't have noticed.

"Nothing. Nothing at all," he rambles, blood dripping from his nose as he shakes his head.

"Don't fucking lie to her," Hunter growls in his ear, and I feel the razor blades in his voice from here.

Billy drops his chin to his chest and shakes his head nervously. "I honestly don't know. Roxy said she would take care of it when it got to that stage."

The world goes silent as I listen to my heartbeat pound in my ears, my breath lodging in my throat at the level these bitches are willing to go to.

Without a moment's hesitation, I take Xavier's spot in front of Billy, pull my hand back, and hit the motherfucker square in the nose with my palm. His head whips back with the impact, and just as I think that's enough for him, I hear a snap.

My head whips up to Hunter, but he's staring down at Billy's hands behind his back with an emotionless glaze over his green eyes. Following his gaze, I look at the awkward position Billy's hands are in, and as Hunter lets him drop to the ground, I gape in surprise when I realize he just snapped his fucking wrist. He went from my calm, quiet Hunter to a cold motherfucker in two seconds flat, but the fact he did it to defend me is what has me appreciating the move rather than fearing it.

"Eden, why don't you get Charlie and Lou-Lou and go up to your room? We can take care of this," Xavier murmurs as he comes to stand behind me, his chest heaving against my back as he strokes his fingers down my arm protectively.

"I want those fucking bitches to pay, Xavier," I growl, looking around in a blind rage, but it's Hunter who grips my chin to make me stop.

"They are already long gone, love. We weren't exactly quiet when we started interrogating him," he murmurs, and he's right, I know he is, but my blood still boils with anger. Even the soft smile he gives me as he tries to remain calm does nothing to help.

"Don't let them ruin any more of your night, Eden. Take the girls, and we'll cover some ground. We'll meet you at Pete's tomorrow, okay?"

"Okay," I sigh, hating that he's right.

This damn town is going to have me looking over my fucking shoulder for the rest of my life.

TWENTY FOUR

Eden

Heading downstairs, I run my fingers through my damp hair as I hold my phone in the other. Last night was a total mind fuck, and I didn't do much sleeping because of it. The thought of what could have been and what might have happened when I left repeats in my mind. So when the sun blasted through the crack in the curtains, I threw myself out of bed and into the shower, trying to wash away the icky feeling that coated my skin.

Date rape drugs aren't new, we've always known about them. We even had it happen to people at parties I've been at, which is why I knew to look in Lou-Lou's bag. We've tested our drinks before, but they've never come back positive.

Technically, I didn't wait around long enough last night to find out if that one did, but Billy said enough to confirm it. I thought I might have heard from one of the Allstars or even Archie, but there's been nothing, and I don't really know what I'd say if I called them. I was just hoping for some form of update I guess.

I need a distraction, preferably in the form of food, but first I need to see if anyone else is actually awake. Charlie went to Archie's room last night, but I don't know if he joined her, and Lou-Lou took the spare bedroom.

I stop at the bottom of the stairs, and my curiosity about everyone's whereabouts is answered when I find both Lou-Lou and Charlie lying on the huge, U-shaped sofa. They both offer the smallest acknowledgement of my arrival with a nod, and as I step closer to them, I understand why.

With no liquor last night, and the fact I've showered and slipped into an olive green and white polka dot summer dress with lantern sleeves and a tie front , I look as fresh as a daisy. These two, on the other hand, look a little worse for wear. They're dressed in their pajamas, with sunglasses covering their eyes and the curtains still closed, and I don't know who feels more sorry for themselves.

"How are your hangovers treating you?" I inquire as I take a seat on the sofa with them as they groan in response. Pulling my damp hair off my face, I twist it into a bun at the top of my head and secure it with the hair tie from my wrist.

"Shut the fuck up, Mother Teresa. Don't come down here looking all fabulous and shit, smugness does *not* suit you," Lou-Lou grouses, and I grin. Fuck, I've missed her brand of crazy.

"What she said," Charlie murmurs, encouraging Lou-Lou, and I like how these two get along, like my two worlds are colliding, even if it is to team up against me.

"Did Archie come back last night?" I ask Charlie, and she shakes her head gently as she wipes a hand down her tired face.

"No, but I did wake up to a message saying he was okay and not to worry."

"Oh, how fucking ominous of him," I grumble, but even though a part of me is glad she's heard from him, the other part wants to know what the fuck he's been doing. Is he with the Allstars? Fuck.

Asking myself the same questions over and over again isn't going to get me any fucking answers. And sitting here isn't a distraction. I need something more.

My phone vibrates in my lap, and when I flip it over, I find Bethany's name flashing across the screen.

"Hey," I answer immediately, bringing the phone to my ear, and I instantly hear Cody laughing in the background and it warms my soul.

"Hey, Eden. I was just calling to make sure you were up. We're like two minutes away with Ryan's early birthday present for you. So get your ass outside." She ends the call, leaving me confused as I stare down at a blank screen.

"What's up?" Lou-Lou asks, frowning at me, and I shake my head.

"Oh, nothing. Bethany is nearly here, and she told me to wait outside," I reply, rising to my feet and doing as she instructed.

As I swing open the front door, my heart stills and tears prick the back of my eyelids.

My G-Wagon.

My hand covers my mouth as I stand frozen in shock, watching as Ryan pulls my G-Wagon to a stop in the driveway. Bethany pulls in right behind him in her car, and

I still can't believe my eyes.

Ryan opens the driver's side door and steps down, a tired smile on his face as he dangles the keys in his outstretched hand in my direction. Without thought, I run at him, my feet leaving the ground as I wrap my arms around his neck and squeeze him tight, my legs dangling.

He just revived the very last thing my dad ever gave me. Ever. And with some form of magic, he put it all back together or at least got someone to do it.

His arms slowly wrap around me as I see Bethany jump from the car with tears welling in her eyes as she places her hands on her chest, and I hear Cody squealing from the back of her car.

Overwhelmed with emotion, I can't pinpoint exactly what I'm feeling, but I know I love the three of them like I loved my dad. These people are my family.

"Thank you, Ryan," I whisper, squeezing him extra tight, and he makes a slight choking sound but doesn't actually say a word. I take the hint, though, and relax my hold around his neck.

Placing me back on my feet, he wordlessly grabs my hand and places the car key in my palm, closing my fingers around the metal.

"You're welcome, Eden," Ryan replies as Bethany appears at his side with Cody in her arms, and I quickly wipe away the tear that drips from my eye as I clear my throat.

Bethany and Cody step forward, wrapping me in their arms as I bite my tongue, forcing myself not to cry in front of the little guy, and it works for the most part.

"Have you seen Hunter?" I ask as Bethany releases me, Cody reluctantly clinging onto his mom as she takes a step back to give me some space. I don't miss the nervous glance she throws Ryan's way before she focuses on me.

"They, uh..."

"They needed a hand, and we just got a little caught up with some other things, so yes, we've seen them, and they are all good," Ryan finishes, when Bethany stalls.

I release a relieved breath, nodding slowly. "Are they the reason you look like you haven't slept yet?" I ask Ryan, and he simply winks in response, not answering my question. That's as much of an answer as I'm going to get, and I know it's because of Billy. I wonder if they managed to find the bitches who encouraged him to fucking do it.

"Thank you so much, you guys," I repeat as my heart slowly starts to calm down, and I shake my hands out.

"There are really no words for how I feel right now. You have literally just made my life. I thought it was totaled and I'd lost the last piece of my dad," I murmur as I stroke my fingers across the hood in disbelief.

"You deserve it, Eden," Bethany says with a soft smile on her lips, and I lean in closer to caress Cody's cheek as a way to distract myself before I cry again. "Anyway, we'll leave you to it. I just got a little excited when I knew it was done, and we just couldn't wait until Tuesday to give it to you."

I hug her once more, and when I step back, Ryan grumbles, "I'd just like to add that this is *my* gift to you. Betty gets zero credit for this," he says with a smile, and I roll my eyes, laughing at their antics.

"Well, thank you the most for being awesome to me," I respond, patting his arm, and he grins.

"Hey, I know you, you're Ryan Carter," Lou-Lou suddenly shouts, moving from watching through the window to standing in the open doorway. "My brother's talked about you before," she adds, and I frown, my gaze flicking between them, but Ryan just offers a tight smile and a nod, which makes Bethany roll her eyes at him.

I almost want to ask how on earth she knows Ryan, but

I don't care enough to move my focus from my G-Wagon.

"I need sleep, and lots of it. If you need us, you know where we are, or give us a call, alright?"

I nod at his words as the three of them climb into Bethany's car, waving as they leave, and I don't move from my spot until they've driven off and are completely out of sight.

Turning the keys in my hand, I look back at the house, finding both Lou-Lou and Charlie in the doorway, and I take a deep breath, needing a moment to appreciate the people I have around me.

I definitely need to get out of here now, and I *definitely* need to take my baby for a spin.

"Do you guys want to head to Pete's?" I ask, opening the driver's side door as I hear Lou-Lou yell in response. I want to go even if we haven't heard from the Allstars, and I have my wheels back.

"Give me ten fucking minutes to shower and change and I'm with you, bitch."

Watching her run up the stairs, I glance back to Charlie who looks a little sick. "I'll be as quick as I can, but I'm going to need more than ten minutes, okay?"

I smile at her, and she follows after Lou-Lou as I slip

behind the wheel of the G-Wagon. My hands tremble a little as I stroke the steering wheel, remembering the last time I was in here, but I'm surprisingly excited to be behind the wheel again. It looks exactly as it did before the accident. But none of that matters, and nothing in this world will stop me from driving her again.

Ilana and her twisted fucking mind have taken enough from me already. She doesn't get this, or anything else for that matter.

Stepping into Pete's, it's busier than I've seen it before. The crowd is a mixture of families, couples, and friends sitting at the tables and outside patio, but by some miracle, the booth I've always sat in is empty. It's almost like it's freaking reserved or something. Probably for the Allstars.

"Hey, girly," Linda calls as she approaches us, wearing a wide smile on her lips as she fiddles with her short blonde hair at the front.

"Hey, are we okay to take the booth?" I ask, and she waves us over in that direction.

"Of course, give me two minutes and I'll grab your orders."

I smile in response as she heads toward a table where a family sits. Making our way through the tables, I relish the chaotic sounds of everyone chatting, cutlery scraping against plates, and the TV on the wall playing sports news. The atmosphere is always perfect in here. It's just enough going on to distract me from my mind and from wondering what's happening. I hate feeling out of the loop.

"What's good here?" Lou-Lou asks as we take a seat, her and Charlie scooting in first while I take a spot on the end.

Glancing at the time, it's just after ten in the morning, so I decide to recommend something for breakfast. "What about pancakes and syrup? Or do you need something heavy to absorb all that liquor you consumed last night?" I say with a grin, and she flips me off before picking up the menu to decide for herself.

I already know what I want, so I stare out of the window, watching the ocean glisten under the bright sun until Linda returns to take our orders.

"What am I getting you, girls?" I let the others order first, deciding on carbs to soak up their alcohol, before Linda turns her gaze to me.

"I'll take the breakfast wrap and a water, please."

Nodding, she jots it down on her pad before looking back at me. "No boys today?" she questions, and I almost cringe.

"Not so far," I murmur, and she scoffs.

"They'll be coming in no time, girly. I've seen the look in their eyes," she comments with a grin before heading back to the kitchen while I fight the blush trying to creep up my neck as Lou-Lou arches her eyebrow at me.

"What's there to do around here then? I have to leave by four, but I want to do something before then," Lou-Lou mutters, and I feel a little sad knowing she isn't here to stay.

Before I can offer a response, the back of my neck prickles as the main door opens, and my gaze swings in that direction, my breath catching in my throat as I watch the Allstars and Archie stroll in. Did Linda see them in the fucking parking lot or something?

They head straight toward us, Xavier leading the pack as always, and I slowly realize they are still in yesterday's clothes. As Xavier nears the table, he waves his finger, indicating he wants me to move farther around, but I don't catch on quickly enough, so he takes matters into his own hands. He pulls me from the booth, and I go effortlessly into his arms, loving the feel of his hands on my hips as he lifts me into the air.

My eyes are locked on his, watching as the hazel coloring goes from being predominantly brown to an emerald green. I rest my hands on his shoulders, and neither of us say a word as our lips naturally gravitate toward one another.

His kiss is punishing, as if he's trying to commit the touch to memory, and I let him take control without question for a change, submitting to his mouth as he teases my lips, but I can't pinpoint what makes me give in so easily.

Before my fingers can curl in the hair at the nape of his neck, I'm being lowered to the booth again, completely manhandled by Xavier, until I find myself sandwiched between him and Tobias on the other side of me. I almost feel disoriented from the shift around the table. Archie sits on the other end of the booth with Charlie beside him, followed by Lou-Lou then Hunter completing the table.

"How have you been? Everything okay?" Hunter asks with a smile on his lips as he places his forearms on the table. Xavier strokes my bare shoulder, and Tobias squeezes my thigh.

"Nothing has really happened at all, except Ryan and Bethany brought my G-Wagon to the house," I tell him, and he leans past Tobias to intertwine his fingers with mine.

Every single one of them is touching me right now, and I feel like I may combust. Being on this level with them, feeling like there is a general understanding between us, makes me more relaxed, and I can tell they are relaxing too.

"They did a good job with it, didn't they?" he remarks, talking about the G-Wagon, and I smile and nod in response.

"Amazing," I murmur, and the table falls silent as everyone ignores the huge elephant in the room, so I take it upon myself to get straight to the point.

"Did you guys sleep yet?" I ask, glancing at Xavier to my right before turning my gaze to the others, including Archie, and they nod.

"We managed to get a couple of hours in, but we headed straight here as soon as we were done," Archie answers, kissing the top of Charlie's head and making her smile.

"Done doing what?" I press. Archie glances at Xavier, who looks down at his lap, while Tobias sighs and Hunter clears his throat. "Listen, we're either going to be totally fucking open about everything or nothing at all. I refuse to keep doing this back-and-forth bullshit with you when it comes to things that involve me," I bite out, not controlling my emotions at all.

"We were with Ryan," Tobias answers, and I force myself not to sigh since I already know that much from the look on Ryan's face earlier.

"Doing what?" I prompt, my response a little blunt as I turn to face him. He searches my eyes for God knows what before he finally replies.

"Dealing with Billy, running tests on the soda, hacking into phone records and surveillance footage, and missing you," Tobias murmurs, keeping his voice down as he bops me on the nose, and I can't even bring myself to glare at him.

"Please don't tell me you think that's giving information, Toby," Lou-Lou chimes in with a pointed look on her face as she glares at the guys, and I smirk.

"I don't know what you mean," he says in confusion, and I shake my head.

"She means you gave the simplest answers possible. I want to know the details. Like *what* did 'dealing' with Billy include? *What* tests did you run on the soda? *Whose* phone did you hack into and why? And *what* surveillance footage are you talking about?"

"Ah, uhh, well...Xavier or Hunter will tell you that."

I give him the stink eye, the wimpy little asshole, but to my surprise, Xavier squeezes my shoulder and does just that.

"Dealing with Billy involved beating the shit out of him and having Ryan's team patch him up because Hunter said killing him wasn't an option." He rolls his eyes so casually that I just gape at him. "We ran tests on the soda to see what exactly was in it and hacked into both KitKat's and Roxy's phones to see who they got it from." He watches me with a slight grin on his lips as if he's pleased with himself. "Is that good enough for you?"

I feel like he knows the effect he has on me. I can barely think straight right now, but I nod in response, knowing in my gut he's giving me the truth.

"Did you guys manage to find anything?" I inquire, but Xavier points at Hunter.

"We'll make it a group effort, shall we? Hunter can finish this off." Cocky fucker.

Hunter runs his thumb across my knuckles as I stare at him expectantly, and he grimaces.

"It was definitely a date rape drug in your soda, and neither of their phones brought up anything, which leads us to believe they may have a burner of some kind, but I'm not sure. The surveillance footage was from Archie's house, which gave us nothing, so they are going to scan through other surveillance cameras because they got that shit from somewhere and we want to know where. Be it before or at the party."

Nodding along with every word he says, I don't know whether I'm more stunned by what they were up to while I was trying to sleep or the fact that they told me.

"So it's still a waiting game?" Charlie speaks up just as Linda approaches with our drinks, bringing the conversation to a halt.

"See, I told you these little shitheads would find you soon, didn't I?" Linda says with a wink, and I grin along with her. "I guess these boys want feeding and watering too, huh?" she adds, and they all nod, giving her their orders as she whips her pen and pad out, winking at me again before she walks away.

Tobias grabs my water, gulping half of the glass down quickly before turning to me with a smile. "I'll share mine with you, bubble," he says with a grin, and I roll my eyes.

"But yes, it's back to the waiting game. I think that means we have to hold off on going after KitKat and

Roxy right now," Xavier murmurs, and I whirl my head around so fast to stare at him I almost get whiplash. The disappointed look on his face catches me off guard, but he continues, "I know you want to, Eden. Believe me, we do too. But I think it's important we know who they got it from first."

My eyebrows knit together as I stare at him in confusion, trying to process his words. As much as I understand what he's saying, I still want to fucking disembowel them the second I see them.

"I get it. I do, but—"

"My gut is telling me my mother has something to do with this," he blurts out, cutting me off, and I wait for him to explain. "I have no proof, none at all, but there is just something about all of this shit that has her name all over it. I know she has people watching me at school, feeding her information, and I wouldn't put it past those two to be her bitches, especially when my mother thinks she's running for mayor instead of Roxy's father."

Well then.

Searching his gaze, I see the truth in his hazel eyes, and it doesn't go unnoticed that he's sharing his gut instincts with me. Even if it is his mother, he's being open *and* honest with me. With a heavy sigh, I look around the table as everyone digests what he just said, and I finally nod.

"Okay then. We wait. I can do that. But there has to be a time when I get to fucking ruin them."

"Agreed," Charlie adds before everyone else murmurs their agreement.

A heavy silence falls over the table, draining any fun and happiness we had going on until Tobias claps his hands together.

"Screw them. They don't get to fucking wreck our weekend. They've done enough," he declares, sweeping his gaze around the table as he talks. "I say we eat our food, change, and head to Mount James. It's a nice day. We can relax, go swimming, and enjoy the sun. Just the seven of us—no phones, no social media shit, just us. What do you say?"

He's asking the table, but his gaze is focused on me, and I find myself nodding instantly. Apparently it's not just me who needs the distraction. Everyone else does as well.

"Let's do it."

TOXIC CREEK

TWENTY FIVE

Tobias

Jumping out of Xavier's SUV, I rush over to Eden's G-Wagon, which is already parked, and swing her door open. I had the great idea of us all coming out here for the day, but I didn't consider the fact we would have to separate for a little while before getting to Mount James, and I'm not embarrassed to admit I fucking missed her.

After last night, I just want to be in her presence in any way possible. I hate that she was so close to being drugged, and if she hadn't spotted it, things would have gone much worse.

Reaching across her, I unclip her seatbelt before looking at her expectantly, waiting for her to give me the go-ahead, and she nods with a roll of her eyes, making me grin, so I lift her from her seat.

"You're like a giant Labrador today, Tobias. All bouncy and shit," she mutters with a smile as I kiss the corner of her lips. She strokes the back of my neck before running her fingers along the rim of my black beanie.

"You fucking love it, bubble," I retort, tightening my arms around her waist as her long, slim legs dangle above the ground, looking hot as hell in her cute fucking green dress.

"Hmm, don't flatter yourself!" Eden's friend Lou-Lou shouts as she jumps out of the passenger side of the SUV, fake gagging, making Charlie and Archie chuckle as they climb out of the back.

"She would love my peen, wouldn't she, Eden?" I tease, waggling my eyebrows, and the smile I expect to see on her face is nonexistent as she frowns at me.

"No, she wouldn't because it's mine," she whispers in my ear so no one else can hear, and the territorial tone in her voice has my cock hardening instantly.

"I love it when you lay claim on me. Do it again, now,"

I whisper back, and she scoffs before pushing on my chest, so I place her on the gravel, but before she steps back from me, she rises up on her tiptoes and whispers in my ear.

"You wish."

With that, she turns on her heel, grabs her tote bag from the cargo space, and waltzes off in the direction of the waterfall with her arm linked through Lou-Lou's with Charlie and Archie following behind.

I watch her eyes fix on Xavier and Hunter, who grab the towels and cooler from the SUV, and I want to stomp my foot at the wink she tosses their way.

"Hey, asshole, fucking help," Hunter demands once Eden has walked past him, and I rush to assist with the cooler, picking up speed so I can stay behind Eden, not caring where Xavier or Hunter are as I head off without them.

I saw enough of them last night when all I wanted was to be deep inside of Eden, or even just lying beside her, but all of my plans were fucking ruined by some sadistic fucks trying to drug my bubble.

After she actually listened and went up to her room, Hunter dialed Ryan's number, and he was at Archie's house in record time. We told Archie to stay at home, but none of us could really argue with him when he was adamant about helping keep his sister safe, even if it meant venturing into the dark side with us.

Watching him step up to her side now, with Charlie on his other arm, he ruffles Eden's hair. I can't believe none of us saw the resemblance before. The shape of their blue eyes and the shape of their faces is so noticeable now.

Is it possible to be jealous of the fact he got to spend nine months in the womb with her? Like, I don't want to be related to her, but fuck, I want to spend every fucking second with this girl.

Laughing off my crazy thoughts, I swipe a hand down my face and get a grip on reality. I'm just so fucking tired after last night. We watched hours and hours of footage, scrolled through Roxy's and KitKat's phone records, and literally kicked the shit out of Billy because Ryan said we couldn't damage our hands for football—no punching allowed. It was necessary and worth our time and effort, but it just wasn't what I wanted to be doing.

I hear the waterfall before I see it, the sound of the flowing water like music to my ears. Following the dirt path the others take, I stop in my tracks when I see the water spilling over the ledge about twenty feet off the ground and falling into the crystal clear pool below. The pool has a rocky bottom and is completely surrounded by trees, bushes, and boulders, giving it a serene atmosphere.

The sun beats down, glistening off the water, and I take a deep breath. It's so peaceful out here. It's the best place to unwind, and that's exactly what we all need to do today while we wait for more information on who is behind this. I mean, we know it's fucking Ilana, but you get nowhere without proof in this town, and even if you have it, you don't tend to get very far.

Eden stops by a large boulder, placing her towel and bag on it before slipping her sandals and dress off, revealing a white drawstring bikini underneath, and any chance of my cock deflating goes out of the window. She is just too fucking beautiful.

"Keep up, man," Hunter says as he passes, blocking my view of our girl, and it takes me a second to realize I actually stopped walking to stare at her.

"You've got it bad," Xavier remarks as he stops beside me, and when I flick my gaze to his, I find him staring at her just like I am.

"I'm not the only one," I reply, and he nods once, his jaw tight as he agrees. I just want to protect her and make all her troubles go away. Glancing over her shoulder as Hunter strokes his hand down her spine in passing, she gives us a soft smile. "We do whatever it takes to keep her," I add, and to my surprise, Xavier's stance relaxes.

"Whatever it takes," he repeats before stepping toward her.

Breathing deeply, I take the final steps to join everyone as they all spread out their towels and belongings, placing the cooler in easy reach of our group.

I blindly grab the closest empty bag and shake it out, making everyone look at me as I speak. "Everybody, please place your phones, smartwatches, and whatever other shit you have on you that gives you access to the outside world in this bag right now. For the rest of the afternoon, we're shutting off."

Lou-Lou rolls her eyes, but everyone wordlessly places their phones and devices in the bag as I grin. There isn't anyone else at the waterfall right now. A few people are hiking past us, but this is just ours for the time being, and I hope it stays that way.

Charlie pulls out a mini speaker, waving it in my direction, and I glare but relent when she connects her phone up to it and relaxed beach vibes begin to play. No lyrics, just instrumental melodies. Okay, I can totally deal with that.

Relaxing against the massive rock behind me, I fold my arms behind my head and look up at the sky, letting the sun heat my skin. I hear Eden's giggle, and it draws my attention to her as she lies beside Hunter with his arm propped up behind her as her head falls back with laughter. It surprises me how much I like seeing him make her laugh and actually seeing him smile too.

Fuck, if anyone here deserves to smile, it's him, but that doesn't mean I can't be jealous as shit.

Deciding she's spent enough time with him, I rise to my feet, kick off my sneakers, and throw my shirt down beside me. Heading in their direction towards the edge of the ledge we're on, ignoring the rest of the group as my eyes are solely fixed on her. Coming to a stop in front of them, I can see the knowing look in Hunter's eyes instantly as Eden smiles up at me, my shadow blocking out the sun over her.

"Bubble, come swim with me," I say without a pout, instead giving her my best impression of puppy dog eyes, and she nods in agreement. It almost has me giddy when she places her hand in mine and lets me pull her to her feet. "Are you ready for some fun, bubble?" I ask, and as she's about to open her mouth, I grab her waist and rush her to the edge, dropping her into the water before she can say a word.

I hear Xavier and Hunter grunt at me, but the others laugh, which only fucking encourages me, so before she can resurface, I dive into the water beside her. It's cooler than I expected, but still the perfect reprieve from the hot sun, and when I break through the surface of the water, I find her already glaring in my direction.

"And the crowd goes wild as Tobias Holmes makes the tackle of the season," I cheer, grinning at her as I repeat her own celebration from when she tossed me into Archie's pool, and she smiles as she remembers.

"You're a shithead, Tobias Holmes," she says with a smirk as she moves toward me, her head just above the water as she moves on her tiptoes, and I pull her into my arms as I try to rearrange my beanie on my head.

Seeing me struggle to multitask, she reaches up and straightens it for me, and I instantly recognize the question in her eyes, but if she wants to ask, she has to say the words. I'm not going to offer that information willingly, I can already feel my heart beating faster just thinking about it.

Her fingers hover around my face, slowly stroking

across my cheek as she searches my eyes, and I see the moment she's built up the nerve, but I still wait.

"Is there a particular reason why you always wear your hat?" she inquires, and I take a deep breath, feeling a little light-headed even though I knew she was about to say those words.

"Yeah." I close my eyes for a moment, trying to remain calm, but it's difficult whenever it comes up in conversation.

"You don't have to tell me, I just wondered, that's all," she soothes, but I shake my head. We're all about sharing our dark and wicked stories with her at the moment, so what's one more?

"I can tell you, just, privately," I murmur, glancing around, and my eyes settle on the waterfall. I know there is a huge ledge under there, and it would be private enough for us to talk.

Looking back up at the others as they relax, listening to music and chatting. Xavier watches me with concern in his eyes, noticing we're not laughing and joking anymore, likely seeing the distress firing inside me. I point my thumb behind me, indicating the waterfall, and he nods.

"Follow me," I tell her as I lace my fingers through hers, and she falls into step with me, wading through the water at my side that hits her collarbone.

I can't tell if my palms are sweating or if it's just the water, but when we get right in front of the cascading waterfall, I happily release her hand and dive under the spray, tugging my hat off as I do.

Coming up on the other side, I swipe my hair out of my face and toss my hat onto the damp ledge five feet away as I wait for Eden to appear, and like a fucking siren, she emerges from the water. I watch every drop of water trickle down her face and neck as she blinks her eyes open.

She takes a moment to glance around the private space we're now in, and this time it's her who holds out her hand to me. It's completely foreign to me how easily our fingers intertwine, like two pieces of the same puzzle, and as she leads us to the ledge, I find myself more and more ready to open up.

Not wanting to get out of the water just yet, I brace my arms on the rocks, staring at my hat in the distance. My head burns with the reminder as Eden stands quietly beside me, not rushing, but somehow showing her support.

"The first time I went to the Holmes Correctional Facility, I was eleven," I murmur, letting the words leak from my mouth as I slowly relax, having overcome the initial hurdle of starting the memory. Eden says nothing but squeezes my fingers gently, encouraging me to proceed at my own pace. "I didn't really understand what I had done wrong. I spent the entire time trying to piece together what I did that made my parents so upset, but it wasn't until I got a little older that I realized I was never the one actually in the wrong to begin with."

Closing my eyes, I feel as though I'm right back in the dark concrete enclosed space again. Alone, but too headstrong to be afraid.

"I'm so sorry," Eden whispers, her breath fanning over my shoulder as she speaks, and I shake my head.

"There's nothing to be sorry for, Eden. I was trapped in a situation I had no way of getting free from because the only people who could save me were my parents, and they were the ones putting me there in the first place."

I remember researching what the meaning behind the word parent was once. "One who gives birth to or nurtures and raises a child." I must have typed it ten different ways, but every time it came up with a meaning I had no connection to. My mother and father never nurtured or raised me properly. I always wondered why they even bothered having a child at all.

"The first time I went in was the day after my eleventh birthday. I had no birthday party, no celebration or cake, but I came home from school the next day and Mrs. Duffy had made me some chocolate chip cookies and a card since I had let it slip the day before that I had nothing—no parties, no presents."

I see the recognition on her face as I mention the teacher who was so sweet to me as a child. Now, she gets away with saying whatever the fuck she wants to any of us because we know she is worth a thousand of anyone else in this town—Eden excluded.

"That's why she's cool as shit, because she had to put up with you for so long," Eden concludes with a smile, and I grin in response.

"Yeah. She's cool. But when I came home that day with the treats, my father, Grant, took one look at them and flipped the fuck out. My memory is a little sketchy from there if I'm honest, but he beat me like he did when I was misbehaving, only this time it didn't stop with the punches to my torso. I remember his college sports trophy swinging toward me in his hand as my mother, Moira, stood watching from the doorway. The next thing I knew I was waking up in a juvenile correction center with twenty-two stitches in my head."

Wrapping my hand around her wrist, I slowly lift her fingers to the scar that runs from the back of my skull to my right ear. The jagged raised skin is as prominent now as it was the day it happened since it was roughly sealed shut, without care or expert precision, because my father wanted it to remain under wraps. I watch her eyes widen as she feels the scar from end to end, but her expression softens.

"I can only assume it was because he felt I had shamed the family by taking a gift from Mrs. Duffy, but it was never spoken of again, so I never truly understood," I add, trying to distract myself from her touch.

I can feel her trying to look deeper into my eyes, wanting to read my emotions, but I locked that shit down a long time ago. Taking a deep breath, I finally meet her gaze for the first time since I started talking. I expect to see pity or sympathy, so I'm surprised to see something else entirely. It feels like she cares, like she sees me in a different light, but one of strength and appreciation.

Lifting her hand to my cheek, she keeps her gaze on mine as her other hand remains in my hair.

"You are far more than they raised you to be, Tobias

Holmes. I respect wholeheartedly that it's a part of you that you want to keep private and hidden, but don't you ever let it define you. Even when you piss me the fuck off, there is always a piece of me that craves you and the way you make me smile, or how you light up a room with your smile and personality. None of that comes from them, and they don't get to take any credit for the person you are, remember that."

I think my heart is about to pound out of my chest, and I barely hear her words through the ringing in my ears because nobody has ever told me anything remotely close to this. Ever. Yet here comes some girl from out of nowhere, wearing a clear target on her back as she stands strong against it, refusing to be trampled or broken, with the kindest words I've ever heard.

How could I ever think anyone else could contend with that?

"You're something else, Eden Grady," I rasp, completely lost in her.

"And you are still so fucking fine my eyes hurt," she counters with a grin, making me smile, and I don't miss the fact she played me at my own game. Seeing that I had reached my limit on the topic, she brightened the mood with a light-hearted comment.

Her hands stroke down to my chest as she looks up at me through her lashes. Water droplets still creep down her temples, and I trace one with my finger, her mouth falling open slightly as the air around us heats.

Slowly, I lean forward and tilt her chin up, bringing my lips to hers in a tantalizing kiss. I feel every inch of her mouth against mine as her hands press against my bare chest, her nails digging into my skin in the best way possible.

I need her closer. I need more. I just need her to consume me like she always does.

Trailing my hands down to her waist, I spin us and slowly push her backward while staying chest to chest with her until her back reaches the ledge, then I bend and lift her into the air. I love that her legs open for me automatically before wrapping around my waist as my grip tightens on her hips.

Eden's head falls back on a moan, separating our mouths, so I leisurely drag my lips down her neck, flicking my tongue against the goosebumps rising on her flesh. I stroke up her rib cage, resting my thumb just below her perky tits, and I love how she instantly constricts her legs around me, wordlessly begging for more.

Her hands cradle my face, and I hold my position as she searches my eyes for a moment, trying to get a read on me, and I don't know why until she moves. Tilting my head to the side, she brushes her lips against my scar, kissing from the back of my head to my ear, each touch sending a shiver down my spine.

No one else has ever touched it with their lips except her.

"Bubble, if we don't stop now, I'm not going to be able to stop at all," I admit, and she grins in relief as she looks back at me, her eyes practically blown as she meets my gaze.

"Don't you dare fucking stop."

Kiss.

"I need you."

Kiss.

"Right now."

Kiss.

"You don't get to share a part of your soul with me and not fuck me into oblivion afterward."

Kiss.

"That's not how this is going to work if I'm yours, Tobias."

Kiss.

Fuck. This girl is everything. "I don't think there is anything I wouldn't do for you, Eden," I rasp, and she nods ever so slightly like she gets it. This new level of understanding between us has me burning for her more than ever. "You have to be quiet because I don't know how much they can hear over the waterfall, but I don't want anyone to disturb us. This is just you and me right now. Agreed?"

She licks her lips, remaining silent, and pulls on the string at the back of her bikini, followed quickly by the ones around her neck. Eden throws the scrap of material aside, and my gaze falls to her breasts, but before I can stroke my thumb across her nipple, she's rising to her feet with a seductive smile on her lips.

I stand as still as a statue as I stare up at her, watching her drag her bikini bottoms down her thighs, revealing her glistening pussy. Who the fuck made this girl? She's one of a kind, and I'm never letting go.

Bracing my hands on the ledge, I push off of the bottom of the pool and quickly swipe my tongue along her pussy, leaving her gaping down at me in surprise. I pull myself out of the water and drop my shorts in record time, drawing her close to me, my cock pressing against her stomach as I capture her lips again.

"Sit down on the ledge, legs in the water, Tobias," she orders, and I happily oblige. Turning to face the waterfall, I make sure no one can see us from here. The cascade is too thick to catch even the smallest glimpse unless someone specifically swims under.

Leaning back on my hands, I watch as Eden drops to her knees, straddling me with her tits close to my face as she glides her wet pussy along the length of my cock, and I groan in pleasure.

"You have to be quiet, Tobias, remember?" she teases with a smirk, and I love it. I could come just from watching her with her walls down as she takes what she wants from me.

She positions herself with my tip notched at her entrance then sinks down onto my dick, her tight center squeezing my cock so damn hard I almost draw blood from the imprint of my teeth on my lip.

"Fuck," I grunt as she slowly grinds against me, and when I bring my hands to her waist, she bats me away.

"You keep your fucking hands where they are or this stops," she warns, the desire in her eyes shining brighter with each word.

"You've spent too much time around Hunter, bubble," I murmur, propping my hands behind me as I lean farther back and let her take control. Grinding her hips again, I fight to keep my legs in the water, desperately wanting to flip her over and fuck her hard, but giving her what she wants is far more important. "You better make yourself come on me, Eden," I growl, already feeling my body tingle under her touch.

She's completely bare, in every sense of the word, and I want every part of it. With one hand braced on my shoulder, she slips the other between her legs, and I stare in pure amazement as she strokes her clit while rocking against me.

Struggling to stay upright, I surge forward, sucking her nipple into my mouth, and she cries out, her movements becoming stuttered.

"Fuck. Fuck. Fuck. I-I'm...I'm coming. Fuck. Yes. Yes," she pants in pleasure, her back arching, and I bite down on her nipple as her pussy grips me like a vise and she rides me harder than ever as she crashes into her orgasm.

My toes tingle, and I try to hold off, but the gentlest of shivers from her as she sinks onto my cock has me bracing myself on my hands as I thrust into her, my own moan falling from my lips.

As the pleasure rolls through my body, I curse as I finally wrap my arms around her, pinning her to me. When it seems we've ridden every wave of ecstasy, she slumps against me with a soft sigh on her lips as I slowly lean back and let her lie on my chest.

I have never felt closer to another person than I do right now at this moment with her. She wrecks me to my core in the best possible way. The feel of her heartbeat against mine almost lulls me to sleep until she leans up to look me in the eyes.

"How are we supposed to clean up?" she hisses with a laugh, and I shake my head. Without a word, I pull us into a seated position and throw us into the water, making her yelp in surprise.

"All clean," I singsong, and she whacks my chest with a roll of her eyes as I slowly pull out of her body, instantly feeling the loss.

"Tobias, how will you feel now that your cum is in this pool, ready to impregnate anyone who enters?" she inquires, her voice stern, and I freeze.

"For real?" I ask, my face paling, and she throws her head back with laughter. "Oh, you sneaky bitch," I say with a grin, tugging her closer and scattering kisses all over her face as she hums in approval.

"Thank you," she murmurs, leaning back to meet my gaze, and I frown in confusion. "For telling me something private. For trusting me," she clarifies, and my heart swells.

"I told you there isn't anything I wouldn't do for you, bubble. Whatever it takes to keep you safe is my top priority." No truer words have ever left my mouth, and there are the other words I know to be true, deep in my soul, she isn't ready to hear yet. One step at a time, and this girl will be ours forever.

TWENTY SIX

Xavier

"Fifty-five...fifty-six...fifty-seven..."

"Count in your fucking head, Tobias," I grunt. Trying to do my reps on the weights while he fucking counts his push-ups out loud drives me insane, and he knows it. Hunter runs on the treadmill, his earphones securely in place as he blocks us out. Asshole.

We made sure to have a big enough gym put in at the house so we could all work out comfortably, but Tobias is still all up in my face while I'm trying to work out.

Placing the barbell back on its rack, I chug down my

water as Hunter's ringtone fills the room. Before he can even stop the machine and jump off, I'm grabbing his phone and answering the second I see Ryan's calling.

"What have you got?" I question, panting slightly as I bring the phone to my ear and place my hand against Hunter's chest as he approaches, ignoring his grunts.

"Nice to speak to you too, Xavier," Ryan replies in a bored tone, and I refrain from rolling my eyes. Idiot. "I was just calling *Hunter* to keep you guys all up to date."

"Go on then," I demand bluntly. I don't have time for niceties right now. I want to know more so I can have more control of the situation. I hate feeling like we're standing still, and when it feels like control is slipping through my fingers, I get antsy and act much more rashly.

Hunter drops to the mat beside me, pushing Tobias to the ground and stopping his push-ups, but even Tobias seems more concerned with the phone call than his exercises at the moment.

"Nothing new in regard to who supplied the girls with the drugs, unfortunately, but I'm kind of hovering over some information about your father, and I was wondering if you wanted me to send it over to you?"

His words make me pause, and my gaze darts to the

guys who must be able to hear him because they stare at me with wide eyes, their jaws slightly dropped.

"What information?" I finally respond, rubbing the back of my head as I consider what the hell my father's been up to.

"I think it's best that I send you the details. Give me thirty, and I'll have everything for you."

The phone goes dead without any form of warning or goodbye, just how I like it. I hate saying more than what's needed, but I don't want to wait thirty fucking minutes either.

"What do you think it could be, X?" Hunter asks, taking his phone back from me, and I shrug. As much as I hate to admit it, I have no clue.

"We'll find out when Ryan pulls his finger out of his ass," I scoff, grabbing my own phone from the bench beside me and heading for the door.

If he can't tell me now, I may as well shower, because we need to leave for school soon.

Heading upstairs, I enter my room and go straight for the bathroom, turning the shower on to warm up while I brush my teeth. My mind wanders to Saturday again and how carefree and relaxed we all were up at Mount James.

It was special seeing Eden in a completely different setting.

I knew the second she and Tobias came out from under the waterfall that they'd fucked. It was written all over both of their faces. The pair of them basked in their happy glow as Tobias rearranged Eden's bikini top. At the same time, though, there was a new level of understanding between them, and as she fixed his hat, I could tell he had told her the story only a few people knew.

Fuck, she was getting under our skin, and I loved the feeling of her there. I just still have a nagging feeling that my mother is going to come between us and fuck this all up.

With a heavy sigh, I force myself to put that thought to the back of my mind, focusing on yesterday instead. After Eden waved her friend Lou-Lou off, we convinced her to come back here with us. We did nothing but eat and watch movies together, and she stayed the night. Well, we all fell asleep on the sofas and continued the movie marathon into Sunday.

It was the most normal twenty-four hours of my life and exactly what we all needed. Being together, without drama or tension, was perfect. I hated that she went back to Archie's last night. I wanted to make her stay, but I'm trying to fucking listen to her. Now, we have to head to school and face all the shit from Friday night's party with no further details.

I'm already stressed out about running into Roxy and KitKat, so I know Eden is going to be even worse, but if there is any chance of linking this back to my mother, we need that first before we destroy them.

Quickly showering, I wrap a towel around my waist and head for the closet, glancing at the time and increasing my speed. We have practice this morning, so I need to get a move on.

Dressing in my black skinny jeans and plain white tee, I grab my duffel bag and rush downstairs, finding Hunter and Tobias ready to go. Wordlessly, I unlock the front door and they follow me out, the three of us in our heads as we climb into my Jag and I engage the security system for the house from my phone.

Hunter takes shotgun as Tobias slumps in the back seat, and as I slowly start to pull out of the driveway, my phone vibrates in my pocket and I hit the brakes. I pull it out, and my eyes burn the photo on my screen to memory as I press the call button on the steering wheel.

Thankfully, my phone has already connected, and the

ringing sounds throughout the car as I start driving again, tapping my fingers against the steering wheel as I hand the phone to Hunter. I hear him curse and pass the phone back to Tobias who does the same.

"Xavier," my father murmurs, answering the phone, and I grip the steering wheel as tight as I can, my jaw grinding with anger at the simple sound of his voice.

"So, I'm trying to decide if Mom knows where you're going and this is all part of her plan, or if you have your own dirty little secrets too," I state, referring to the picture Ryan just sent, waiting quietly for him to respond.

"Xavier, you may think you know everything at play here, but let me tell you, you certainly don't."

"That tells me she doesn't know, how interesting," I muse, my mind kicking into overdrive as I process how to handle this.

"And it's in everyone's best interest to keep it that way, Xavier," he grinds out, finally showing some emotion.

"I can keep it a secret if you give me access to that house tomorrow."

"No!" he shouts, and I hear Hunter curse to my right as Tobias slams his hand down on the leather seat in the back.

"You give me access to the house tomorrow or I go straight to her right now," I growl in response, and he goes silent. The only sound I can hear in the background is the blinker in his car, which means he's likely on his way there or back right now. Perfect.

"I'm going to need you to do stuff for me too, son," he murmurs, and I shake my head as if he can see me.

"Not a chance."

"I don't think you realize how much I do for you behind the scenes with your mother. If you want this, then you'll come for dinner in two weeks' time with your mother and me, and bring Roxy Montgomery with you."

"Not a fucking chance," Hunter growls, but putting up with them for one night is nothing in the grand scheme of things. Not if it gives me access.

"Fine," I bark, feeling both of the guys glare at me, but it'll be worth it. It *has* to be worth it.

"Fine," he responds, reminding me of myself, and I end the call, stopping at the next set of lights and sagging back in my seat.

"Why the fuck did you just agree to that?" Tobias demands, and I glance at him in the rearview mirror.

"You know why," I mutter, taking my phone and

swiping the photo off the screen. "Nobody says a fucking word. Not a single one until I figure this shit out," I order, and they both nod in agreement. The only reason I know they'll follow through is because the outcome is for Eden.

I just need to get through today and put the agreement in the back of my mind, because the thought of dinner with the three people I dislike most in this world is not good for my fucking brain, sanity, or wellbeing.

Eden

I don't know what bug crept up Xavier's ass since I saw him yesterday, but I want to throat punch the moody asshole so badly. He's been like this all day, barely speaking to me, but I refuse to ask him about it in school. I don't want any form of discussion with him to be so public, we don't need any more fucking drama.

It's getting close to the end of the day, and I have definitely had enough of walking on eggshells. Between him and the fucking cleat chasers, I'm at the end of my rope.

I can't say shit to KitKat and Roxy, even after they

tried to drug me and have spent the better part of the day glaring at me, and I can't say anything to Xavier, so forcing everything to fester inside me is not helping.

Hunter and Tobias have been completely different. It's like they are trying to compensate for Xavier, which tells me they know what his fucking issue is.

As I head down the hallway toward calculus with Hunter's arm tossed over my shoulders and Tobias walking on my other side, I feel everyone watching us. Officially being the Allstars' girl has suddenly had eyes on me for a totally different reason.

Everyone seems wary and cautious around me. The rumors have seemed to dial down, unless KitKat and Roxy are near, then it kicks up a notch and I have to act like nothing's wrong. Xavier's words from this morning run through my mind.

"We have some details, but nowhere near enough. So we act normal and ignore them completely until we have a more solid plan in place, and to do that, we need proof."

He mumbled that out at me before stalking off, and I've barely seen him since.

"Bubble, are you going to come to our house tonight?" Tobias asks, brushing the back of his hand against mine as we walk.

"I have to catch up on all the homework I didn't do this weekend, never mind all the crap we've been given today," I murmur, and he shakes his head.

"You can do all that at our place too," Hunter reasons, and I raise my eyebrow at him.

"Wait, you guys actually do your own work? I assumed you paid somebody to do it," I say with a smirk, and he pulls me closer to his side, kissing the crown of my head as he does.

"If I wanted somebody else to do my homework, I would scare them into doing it, not waste my money, love."

I roll my eyes at him as Tobias laughs, stepping into the classroom just as Roxy says my name.

"...Eden is a fucking whore, a fucking leech, and it's beyond embarrassing. There is no room in this school or this town for her. I know it, you know it, we all fucking know it. So why isn't anybody doing anything about it?"

I stop in the doorway, Hunter and Tobias staying with me as I feel a hand squeeze my hip, and when I glance over my shoulder, I find Xavier looking down at me. There's annoyance in his eyes, but it isn't directed toward me this time.

I don't see Charlie or Archie yet, and I'm glad because they've had enough of the bullshit surrounding these bitches too.

A few of the people in the classroom glance my way, but Roxy pays them no mind as she continues. "We can make her go away. My daddy has covered up worse shit than the possibility of some overdosed little whore, but it's got to be a team effort. Look what she did to KitKat, I won't allow it. I need a show of hands for all those willing to work together to destroy this slut once and for all."

Stepping out from under Hunter's arm, I'm surprised when Xavier releases my hip, but I'm also thankful because my blood is boiling so badly I'm about to cut the bitch.

Nobody says a word as they watch me approach, their mouths falling farther open with every step I take, rage coursing through my veins at the words spilling out of her stupid fucking lips. KitKat is standing beside her, and she glances over her shoulder first, spotting me, but before she can alert Roxy, I move in.

"Count me in!" I shout as I raise my hand. She whips around to see me, but I'm already smacking her across the face before her eyes can widen.

My hand stings with the impact as my heart pounds in

my chest, watching as Roxy sticks her hands out, catching her fall as she leans against the table to my left. Out of the corner of my eye I see KitKat move towards me, but lightning fast, Tobias is blocking her path in an attempt to protect me.

"I don't think so," he growls, flexing his hands at his sides, and all I can think about is how much I hate men hitting women, but in this case, I'd fucking allow it. She's done more than enough to deserve it.

More than anything, I want to know who is fueling them, encouraging them. It *has* to be Ilana, I know it. I just need proof first, but even then, I don't know what I'll do—my mother's safety is still at the forefront of my mind.

As Roxy pushes up off the table, I grab the back of her hair and pin her to the desk as Mr. Price walks in, trying to fight his way through the crowd that's formed around us. I only needed two more minutes to beat this bitch up, I don't need any interruptions.

"What's going on in here?" Mr. Price yells, but I ignore him. No one here has ever paused to help me, and I don't plan to let them do it for Roxy now.

Roxy throws her elbow back, trying to hit me in the stomach, but I'm just out of reach. Pulling her up off the table by her hair, I glare at her as she grins maniacally at me, a pink mark glowing on her cheek from earlier, her make-up smudged, and her hair a mess.

"You can build your little army against me, I don't give a fuck. Not one. But your days are numbered, and you are not going to be ready for me when I come for you. Because. I. Will. Come. For. You. I'm here because I have to be, you're here because you have nowhere else to go, and you'll eventually learn you are nothing outside of this town. You're barely anything in it," I growl.

With that, I release my hold on her, and she instantly shoves my chest, knocking me back a step or two, but when I move to charge her, I'm tugged into Hunter's chest.

"That's enough, love," he murmurs. Anger blurs my vision, but I don't miss the expression on Roxy's face when she hears Hunter say "love." The look of disgust takes over her face, and I grin.

"That's enough. Anyone on their feet can get out right now."

With a deep breath, I try to calm myself as I glance around the room, finding only Roxy, the Allstars, and myself standing, and I shake my head. As Hunter drops his hands from my body to grab his bag off the floor, I step forward and stick my foot behind Roxy's as I push her back, watching in slow motion as she falls flat on her ass. A few students laugh and gasp around us, loving the constant fucking drama.

"She's not standing anymore, she's good to stay," I mutter, straightening my hair as I turn to face Mr. Price who looks at me with total shock in his eyes. "But don't worry, I was just leaving anyway," I add, heading straight for the door, bag in hand, but it's not until I'm halfway down the empty hallway when I look over my shoulder and find the Allstars walking toward me, a mixture of anger and concern written all over their faces.

Not waiting for them, I head out to the parking lot, annoyed and frustrated with how today has turned out. I thought if I followed the rules like they asked there wouldn't be any more issues, but clearly I was wrong.

When I reach the bottom of the steps, I whirl around to face the Allstars.

"You guys don't have to stay with me. If anything, I'd prefer to be alone, and I know you guys have practice after this."

"You don't have to be alone, Eden, we—"

"I know I don't have to, Tobias, but I don't suddenly

know how to lean on you for everything just because I said I was yours. This is how I deal, how I process. I'm going to go back to Archie's, change into my running clothes, and hit the beach. Honestly, it's fine." I wave my hand around, dismissing any further concern as I sigh.

Hunter steps closer, tilting my chin up so he can look into my eyes. I can feel him searching for something, but I take a deep breath as my eyes instinctively close. His lips touch mine softly, sending a zap of electricity through my body which actually helps relax me a little, but before I can get any ideas about where this could lead, he's stepping away.

Before I can pout, Tobias takes his spot, stroking my hair behind my ears as he kisses me. "I'm just saying, you were hot as hell in there. I'm going to need a cold shower before training, that's for sure," he teases with a grin, making me scoff at him, and then he steps back, fixing his hat like always, leaving me to face off with Xavier.

"You've been a dick today, ignoring me and putting walls between us, and don't even get me started on your fucking attitude. I thought we were past all this, and it's infuriating as hell that we actually aren't," I state, folding my arms over my chest while holding my ground as he moves to stand right in front of me with a sigh.

"You're right," he murmurs, and my eyes widen in surprise at the fact he just agreed with me. "But I do have a good reason for it, I swear. You're cutting school tomorrow, I know that. I just need your afternoon to be mine, okay?" he whispers against my lips, honesty shining in his eyes, and I find myself nodding in response.

"You better have your shit together then." I can't deal with his crap on top of what just happened in there, so for a change, I back off instead of pushing him for more.

"I will, Nafas. I will."

He presses his lips to mine, and I grip his shirt as I force him to give me control over our kiss, and after a moment, he does, letting me delve my tongue between his lips before raking my teeth against his bottom lip, and he groans.

"Tomorrow," he murmurs, and I nod again, butterflies fluttering in my stomach like I didn't just smack a bitch in rage.

"Or tonight. I'm free, bubble," Tobias adds, and I shake my head with a grin.

Turning my back on them, I quickly climb into my G-Wagon, and when I get comfortable in my seat, I find they haven't moved at all. Instead, they remain exactly where I left them, watching me leave.

Pressing the gas pedal, I leave school early, *again*. The fact that I let Roxy get under my skin so fucking much annoys the shit out of me, but I also hate how my sense of calm from moments ago is suddenly gone because I'm not around the Allstars. They have me addicted to them.

Paying no mind to the town or the scenery as I make my way back to the beach, I find myself pulling into the driveway in no time. As I climb out of the SUV, I pull my phone from my pocket to find a text message from Charlie.

Charlie: Girl, what did I miss? You're not here, and Roxy looks like she's about to turn into the Incredible Hulk.

I almost laugh at her comparison, quickly typing out a response as I step into the house.

Me: I wouldn't be surprised if someone recorded me. Again. I just let her get under my skin, like an idiot.

Putting my phone in my pocket as I rush up the stairs, the house as quiet as ever, I find my door slightly ajar which is odd, because I know Stevens cleans the house and shit, but my door is always closed. Always. Standing frozen in place, I listen to see if I can hear anything, but there's not a single noise.

I push the door open with a jab of my finger, and I notice nothing out of the ordinary, but it isn't until I close the door behind me and walk toward my bed when I see the envelope with "Eden" written across it in scratchy handwriting.

Taking a seat on the bed, I stare at it in confusion as I slowly open the envelope to reveal what's inside.

A small Post-it Note falls out with the same handwriting scrawled across it. I flip it over, and my heart sinks as my palms sweat.

To Eden,

I'm sorry I offer you nothing in the way of answers. I'm doing my best for you, for Archie. Looking at you is like looking at her too, and it hurts my heart. One day I'll make everything okay for you. But for now, I thought you deserved this more than I. Happy birthday.

-Richard

What the fuck?

I tilt the envelope to look inside. A slim card is all that fills the space, but when I pull it out and turn it over, a sob leaves my lips as my fingers shake, and my eyes squeeze shut.

Right there in front of me is the photo of all photos. It's dated September twenty-first, eighteen years ago.

Two babies, one bundled in blue, the other in pink, are cradled in the arms of Anabel Freemont. With my dad, my mom, and Richard surrounding her as she sits in her chair.

Their smiles are wide, and the joy and happiness visible on all of their faces is too much.

They were all happy about our arrival.

All of them.

So what the fuck went wrong?

TWENTY SEVEN

Eden

My eyes flutter open, but the light shining in through the balcony curtains makes me shut them again just as quickly. I feel like something disturbed me, but when I don't hear anything again, I flop onto my back, huffing in frustration at being woken up.

"Happy birthday, cookie," Archie sings, bouncing on the bed, and I almost fall off in surprise.

"What the fuck, Arch?" I grumble in response, double-checking I actually have fucking pajamas on right now, and he rolls his eyes. He's too fucking awake for this time of morning, and it's already annoying.

"Happy birthday to you too, Archie. The number one best twin in the whole world," he says with a smile, completely ignoring me as he holds out a little box between us.

"Happy birthday, Archie," I murmur, swallowing past the lump in my throat as the words leave my mouth. This is the first birthday where we know we aren't an only child anymore. Twins. Fucking twins. Quickly fumbling for my phone, I scan the time, and I'm surprised it's almost nine-thirty.

When Archie had gotten home last night, he'd come blasting into my room, waving around an exact replica of the photo that had been left on my bed. He looked as shocked as I felt, and once he finally left, lost in his own emotions, I showered and curled up into a ball under the sheets.

My first birthday without my dad.

Another birthday without my biological mom, and the first without my mom as well.

What a life to live.

"Don't be sad, Eden. This is our first birthday together. We may not have any parents in our lives, but we have each other, and that's enough for me. You, as my twin sister, will always make me happy."

His smile softens as he searches my eyes, and I sit up in bed, slowly wrapping my fingers around the velvet box in his hand. Peering inside, I'm surprised to find a pretty, delicate necklace.

"Thank you," I say softly, running my finger across the heart pendant as I take it out of the box. It's a solid gold heart with a small diamond in the center, and it's absolutely beautiful.

"It was Mom's," he murmurs, and my heart stops as I stare down at the piece of jewelry that instantly went up in value at his admission.

Lifting my gaze to his, I search his eyes, and he nods as if understanding I need him to confirm that information.

"Archie, I don't even know what to say. It's everything," I whisper, my eyes squeezing shut as I tighten my grip on the pendant.

"Would you like me to put it on for you?" he asks, and I find myself nodding in response, refusing to open my eyes as I let the emotions wash over me. Happiness beats so hard in my chest it hurts, while the sadness creeping in makes the reality of the situation all the more real.

It takes me a moment to release my grip on the necklace, but I eventually let him take it from my hands as I hold my hair up off my neck. The second I feel the weight of the pendant on my chest, a sob leaves my lips, and Archie wraps his arms around me.

This is way too emotional for me right now. I can't believe he's gifted me something so special. It represents a woman I'll never get to meet. The woman who nurtured us in her body, yet I have no recollection of a single thing about her. It only makes me more determined to understand what my history is. How did my dad and Jennifer end up together when he and Anabel had us? Why were Archie and I separated, and why was our dad murdered? *Our dad.*

Rubbing Archie's arm to loosen his hold, I jump from the bed, swiping the tears from my cheeks as I rush to my walk-in closet and grab the gift I wanted to give to Archie.

As I sink down onto the bed, the heart pendant bounces lightly, and it brings a sad smile to my lips. Shaking my head, I clear my throat and hold the wrapped present out to him.

"You didn't have to buy me anything," he says with a huge grin, ripping at the paper like a kid at Christmas, and I roll my eyes.

"I didn't," I mutter just as he looks down at the material, his eyes widening in surprise.

"This is not a signed Jerry Rice jersey," he whispers in awe, and I can't help but smile.

"It is. Dad had two, one I wear all the time with RICE printed on the back, and one with GRADY printed. If I didn't almost live in the Rice one, I would have given you that instead of the Grady one, but it makes me feel close to him, and I just wanted to offer you something similar too."

Sitting back down beside him, he peels his Freemont jersey from his back and slips the new one over his head, and it falls perfectly over his shoulders. Staring down at himself, I watch as the smile on his face stretches from ear to ear as I wait silently for him to say something.

"I was wrong," he murmurs, lifting his gaze to mine. "*You* are the best twin in existence."

Trying to contain my emotions, I cross my legs as another tear tracks down my face, but when I glance at Archie, I'm shocked to see him in the same state.

"Archie, are you okay? I didn't mean to make you cry," I mutter, leaning forward to stroke his arm, and he fake glares at me.

"My eyes are just wet, Eden. I'm not fucking crying,"

he grumbles, and I scoff at his nonsense.

"If you're both done crying, I want to see her now," Xavier shouts from behind my closed bedroom door, and I frown in confusion.

"You have some visitors. I somehow managed to convince them I deserved to see you first, but I think that had everything to do with Bethany glaring at them and not because we're siblings," he explains, shrugging before rising from the bed. "I love you, Eden."

It almost feels like his words settle over my soul. Archie is my family now. My "blood is thicker than water," and I'm going to do whatever it takes to keep this guy in my life.

"I'm really lucky to have you here, Arch. I can forgive you for the secret when I see how hard you work at being my family. I love you too," I say with a smile, and with a tilt of his chin, he acknowledges me before opening the door and exiting like he didn't just make me say the three words I've only ever uttered to my mom and dad before. But the unconditional love between us is a whole new experience, and I can't even describe how that makes me feel yet.

"You took more than two minutes, Freemont," Tobias grumbles, waltzing into the room and diving onto my bed. He's followed quickly by Xavier, Hunter, Bethany, and

Cody, and I feel a little overwhelmed with everyone in my personal space.

Tobias looks hot as hell with his gray shorts and white tee, his smile wide as he gets comfortable. Xavier is dressed in a navy polo top, skinny jeans, and a black jacket—he looks just as stressed out as he did yesterday, excellent—while Hunter looks as relaxed as ever in gray sweats and a matching hoodie. He's absolutely sinful.

"'Appy birday, De-de," Cody shouts, clapping his hands as he rushes toward me, bypassing the Allstars, and I catch him in my arms and lift him into my lap. He wraps his arms around my neck, and I almost laugh when I glance over his shoulder to find all three Allstars glaring at the back of his head. Fuckers.

"Why don't you show Eden what you made, Cody?" Bethany suggests, handing me an envelope, and I mouth my thanks as Cody takes the piece of paper from her other hand and instantly gives it to me.

"Wow, what is this?" I ask, turning the paper to find a handmade drawing of four people. On closer inspection, I locate names dotted below each one.

"It's us, De-de. Look." He points to the smallest person in the middle and the girl with the yellow hair to the right, and I notice the two drawings to the left are labeled Mom and Dad.

"I love it, Cody. Thank you so much," I say, placing it on the bed and giving him another squeeze as my heart swells.

"Where was my picture when it was my birthday, Cody?" Hunter grumbles, sticking his bottom lip out, and I have to hold in my smile as Cody waves his finger around.

"You not a-zerve one, Uncy Tee-tee."

Tobias and Bethany burst into laughter, making Hunter glare at them, while Xavier covers his mouth. I shake my head at them all.

Hunter suddenly pulls Cody from my lap, laying him over his shoulder as he starts to tickle him, and Cody laughs and giggles, filling the room with his happiness as Bethany nods at the envelope in my hands.

Taking her hint, I rip through the seal, pulling the card from the envelope as Tobias places his hand on my thigh, stroking little circles into my skin, and I shiver under his touch.

"Happy 18th birthday, queen. May you not remember what you drank, but know where you slept."

I can't help but grin as I open the card. Scrawled inside

is an invite to a girls' weekend of my choosing, and I find her gaze, immediately nodding in agreement, and she smiles wide at me.

"Thank you so much. That'd be awesome."

"I was thinking we could do a city or a lake or a theme park, literally whatever you want. I will be there for it," she exclaims, pulling Cody from Hunter's arms with a raise of her eyebrow, and I nod. She's like a superwoman and the best damn mom to Cody. She deserves a break too, to just be Bethany, and I'm beyond excited.

"I will honestly go and do whatever you want," I say with a smile, and she nods, glancing at her watch.

"I'm sorry to pop in and dash, but I have to work today, and Cody needs to go to daycare," she tells me, kissing my cheek before heading for the door.

"Thank you," I call out as she closes the door behind her, and I flop back on the bed, already tired and exhausted by the day.

Tobias's hand creeps farther up my thigh, and a gasp catches in the back of my throat when I feel someone knock his hand away with a growl.

"We don't have time for that," Xavier grunts from beside us, and I almost stick my bottom lip out like Hunter did just moments earlier. A bit of hot sex would help calm my mind right now, and sex that involved all three of them would definitely have me falling into a sex-induced coma, which I'm not opposed to—I think.

"Fuck, fine," Tobias mumbles as Hunter holds his hand out to pull me back into a sitting position, and I go willingly.

"Happy birthday, love," he murmurs before rushing for the door. He steps out into the hallway for a moment and returns with a fucking ribbon wrapped guitar. Ribbon. Wrapped. Guitar.

I gape at him in shock as he circles back around to my side of the bed and gently places the acoustic guitar in my lap. My fingers trail over the wood as I stare at the instrument with excitement. My dad could play the guitar, but I never let him teach me. No matter how much he begged, it was just never for me. But now, now I want to learn every note.

"Hunter, I have no words. Thank you," I whisper, tilting my head back, and his lips find mine.

"You're welcome. With you wanting to go to the record store, I thought it might be something you'd like. When we go to the store, we could look at learner sheets and everything," he suggests against my lips, and I smile, quickly kissing his mouth once more before he pulls away.

"You guys are wasting time," Xavier complains again, and I twist Tobias's arm to check his watch. I mean, it is almost ten in the morning on a school day, but they'd be late already, and I wasn't going in since it's my birthday, so I don't see what the problem is.

"Ignore him, bubble. Happy birthday, these are from me. Well...they are from Xavier, really, but he'd have kept them to himself, and that's just not fair," he says with a grin, but a quick glance at Xavier tells me he has no fucking clue what Tobias's talking about.

Like a bad magician, he pulls a brown envelope from beneath his t-shirt, emptying the contents into his hand before holding out what looks like photos. I can sense Xavier reaching for them, but I quickly spin and stand from the bed, turning my back to him before he can snatch them away.

There are three photos in total. One of me sitting on Tobias's lap from the night of the party, sitting around the bonfire, when I led him upstairs and he touched me for the first time. Our eyes are filled with arousal, and a sense of happiness and anticipation surrounds us.

The second is of Hunter and me standing on the balcony at the top of the steps at school as we look into each other's eyes just moments before Hunter brought his lips to mine. I can't even remember exactly how I felt at that moment, but in this photo, I look like his whole world.

And the third, well, the third is of me lying in my bed with my body covered only by my sheets as Xavier lies beside me. Both of us have glassy eyes as he holds the camera up in our direction. It's from the first night I was here when nothing mattered except the pain of losing my father, and he offered the perfect distraction.

I don't recall a single photo being taken. Not one. But that's not the only thing these pictures have in common. The underlying theme in every single photo is the look in my eyes. There's no sadness, no guilt, no shame, just need, excitement, hope, and passion.

I hate to admit it, but these three are my emotional enhancers. I seem to feel more when I'm around them. With a look, a kiss, or a word, they make me react. Sometimes it's with anger and annoyance, but others it's with want and desire, and when they make me feel like that…fuck.

Turning back to see the guys, I falter when I find only Xavier remains. Dammit, how did I not hear them leave? I was so consumed with the photos in my hands.

"Where did—"

"That's irrelevant," he mutters, cutting me off, and I glare at him. Sometimes he can just be such a fucking douche.

Pinching the bridge of my nose, I sigh. "Xavier, I really don't—"

"Get dressed, we're already behind schedule."

I wish he would stop fucking doing that. "I'm not going anywhere with you right now," I grind out, placing the photos on my nightstand and clenching my hands in annoyance, but he just shakes his head.

"You'll get in the fucking car, or I'll pick you up and place you there myself," he threatens, and I frown.

"What the fuck is your problem, Xavier?" I ask, almost defeated, and I watch his shoulders rise as he takes a deep breath and walks toward the door. As his hand wraps around the door handle, he turns to glance at me over his shoulder, and the determination in his gaze tells me not to fuck with him right now. But not specifically with anger, there is an array of emotions washing over his face.

"Eden, I need you to get dressed, get your ass downstairs, and meet me in the SUV. None of this is for my benefit,

I swear." Glancing down at his watch, he opens the door. "You have ten minutes. Oh, and happy birthday, Nafas."

The words have barely left his lips and he's already gone, completely out of sight, and as much as I want to stomp my foot and cause a fucking scene for talking to me like that, I know whatever he's up to must be important, because it always seems to be the most intense circumstances that bring out his asshole-ish tendencies.

I just wish I had time to ask what occasion to dress for.

TOXIC CREEK

KC KEAN

TWENTY EIGHT
Eden

Tapping my fingers on my crossed arms as I stare out of the window, my body tilted away from Xavier's, I watch the world go by. I don't know how much longer I can sit in this awkward silence. It's driving me fucking insane, but I don't know how to address the storm brewing inside Xavier without arguing, and I *really* don't have the energy to argue. Not right now, not today.

We've been on the road for close to two hours now, heading north, and it looks like we're following the signs for Bakersfield. Feeling the car slow, I look forward as Xavier pulls off the freeway to stop at a gas station.

I have no clue what's going on and no idea why we're in a rental as opposed to his Jag, but he's been a closed book ever since we set off. He's evaded or ignored every question I've asked, so I've given up.

Pulling the car to a stop, he sighs and grips the steering wheel until his knuckles turn white before jumping from the car and slamming the door behind him. I gape at his retreating form, biting my bottom lip in annoyance.

I grab my phone, find Tobias's number, and hit the message button, tapping out a quick text as I rub my forehead in frustration.

Me: Hey, can you please tell me what the fuck is going on with Xavier? I'm about to punch him in the dick for his shitty attitude, and I'm not going to feel any remorse for it!

Within seconds, I see the message has been read, and three little dots appear at the bottom as Tobias responds.

Tobias: Make him talk, bubble. He's trying to do the right thing, but there is a lot to consider and understand. Things are never

straightforward in this town, but it's even worse today.

What the fuck does that even mean? Spying Xavier walking back to the car, I put my phone away and take a deep breath as he slides into the driver's seat and hands me a little bag. I take it from him and peer inside to find a bag of Swedish Fish Tails and a bottle of iced tea.

When I flick my gaze to his, he's already staring at me, and this only makes me more confused. He just stopped to get me snacks? He's got his aviators in place, but the tightness of his jaw tells me he's serious.

"What the fuck is going on, Xavier?" I ask, pulling my drink from the bag as he puts the car in drive. When he doesn't respond right away, I can feel myself becoming more annoyed, so I turn to glare at him. "Xavier, it's my birthday, and today of all days I don't care for your shitty attitude. You have me all stressed out, and I told you yesterday to figure it the fuck out, but here we are."

"I don't really know how to explain it, and deep down I don't know whether I'm doing the right thing or not because I know it will build you up and break you all at once," he confesses softly, and it catches me off guard because I expected his usual growl.

My eyebrows knit together as I stare at him in confusion. He's still not making any sense, and I don't know whether that's better or worse than the silent treatment.

"Xavier, I don't know what you're talking about. What could possibly make me happy and hurt me at the same time?" I question calmly as I attempt to process what he's trying to say.

"We're like two minutes out, I just needed a minute which is why I pulled over," he murmurs, glancing at me before looking straight ahead.

"So, to clarify, your mood is reflective of where we are going? I fucking hate it when you ignore my question and don't answer me," I grumble, squeezing the bottle in my hands as he offers a stiff nod in response. It's like drawing blood from a fucking stone. Communication shouldn't be this hard. What the hell has him so worked up he can't find the right words?

Pulling off the freeway again, he navigates through traffic, driving into a rundown part of town. Derelict buildings with shattered windows and graffiti cover the neighborhood we're driving through. Broken-down cars are parked along the road, some with flat tires while others are propped up on cinder blocks. Front gardens are overrun with unkempt grass and weeds, and I'm unsure if people even live here anymore. It almost reminds me of the parties in White River. It wasn't this bad, but it really wasn't far off either.

I have no idea where we are, so when Xavier pulls over to the right, coming to a stop in front of a semi-habitable house with shuttered windows and doors, it makes me frown.

Chancing a glance at Xavier, I watch him take a deep breath as he squeezes his hands together, his fingers red from the tight grip he has on them.

"I need you to trust me, Eden," he finally says, his eyes fixed straight ahead, and my eyes widen in surprise. "We can't rock the boat here. This is for you, we're risking it all for you. Today isn't the day for us to play saviors, that won't keep anyone safe. I just need you to know that when we leave, we leave as just you and me."

I can feel my heart pounding in my chest, even though I have no clue what he's fucking saying. Where the fuck are we? None of this makes sense at all, and I never truly know where things are heading with Xavier, especially not based on my past experiences with him.

"Xavier, you're talking in fucking riddles. I don't know anyone here, and what do you mean about other people's safety? Don't you think we have enough going on for ourselves? The only other person I'm concerned about is my..."

My stomach drops as I whip my gaze to the house before looking back at Xavier, and the expression on his face confirms it. I don't know whether to rush from the car or beat more information out of him, but instead I find myself frozen in place, tripping over my tongue.

"Xavier, I...you...is..."

Taking a deep breath with my hand on my chest, I try to calm my racing heart as my mind goes into overdrive. He reaches over the center console to lace his fingers with mine, leaving me to just stare at him expectantly.

"Listen, when Ryan was digging into the drugs and everything, he found something else entirely. Something I'm not fully aware of myself, but I need you to not ask any questions." He runs a hand through his hair, and I can feel his stress from here. "The shit I'm going to have to do because of this is punishment enough." The strain on his face is obvious, and instead of my anger rising, it simmers down as my concern overwhelms me.

"Xavier, is my mom in that house?" I ask, my heart pounding in my ears as I wait an eternity for him to respond.

"I believe so, yes. The footage Ryan found showed my father here, and after speaking to him yesterday morning, I learned my mother knows nothing of this. Which tells me, for some crazy and insane reason, my father is hiding your mother from Ilana. I haven't figured out if that's a good or a bad thing yet, but the positive is she's safe."

I'm speechless. Completely and utterly speechless.

"I know it's a lot, Eden. Bringing you here is kind of risking everyone if my mother finds out, hence the rental, but I just wanted to bring you here, today especially," he murmurs, reaching across with his other hand to stroke my cheek. "We don't have much time, an hour at most, but you have to remember she is safer here no matter what we might think, Nafas."

Nodding, I swallow past the lump in my throat as I search his hazel eyes. "Take me to see her, Xavier. Please."

"I'm not coming in with you, Eden. This is for you. I can't imagine the questions you might have, and I know you've learned some things since being in Knight's Creek, but she still raised you, loved you, cared for you in her own way, and I want you to have that time together."

I can't sit here and process his words any longer, I just need to get out of this damn car and find my mom.

Pulling my hand from his, I fumble for the handle, swinging the door open before stepping out. I don't even bother shutting it behind me as I blindly rush for the entrance.

Just as I'm about to slam my fist into the wooden door, it swings open, and my mom stands before me with a tired smile on her lips as she throws her arms around me.

My mom is holding me.

My *mom* is fucking holding me.

Circling my arms around her middle, I pull her in tight, feeling her shoulders shake as she sobs. Her embrace feels so familiar. If I close my eyes, it almost feels like we're back in White River before everything changed. I'm too stunned to cry, laugh, smile, or be angry right now as she steps back and pulls me inside, closing and locking the front door behind me.

I take a deep breath, still at a complete loss as to what's actually happening right now, as my mom nervously rubs her hands together. Her blonde hair is pulled back off her face, her clothes hang loosely from her body, and she wears no makeup. How is this my mom?

"Can I get you something to drink?" she asks, and I glance at my hands to show her my iced tea, but I'm empty-handed. I must have left it in the car.

I nod, and she moves deeper into the small house, heading straight for the kitchen as I glance around. It's not modern or anything inside, but at least it has the basic necessities. A brown sofa sits in the center of the room, a small flat-screen television is set up in the corner, and a rolled up yoga mat leans against a pine coffee table.

Sinking down onto the sofa, I cradle my head in my hands as I try to keep up with where the fuck I am and how this is all possible. I can't get swept up in emotions here. I can't. I had so many questions I was ready to ask when she called next, but my brain is scrambling to remember them all now that she's actually in front of me.

I don't hear my mom return to the living room until she places my bottle of water on the coffee table, and I look up to find her hovering above me awkwardly. I guess after the initial shock of seeing one another, she remembered the bigger picture like I did.

"Is it true Xavier's dad has you here?" I question, and she frowns at me for a moment before nodding.

"Reza has me here, yes, but this is the safest place for me to be right now," she answers, and I nod, hating that she's trying to placate me with her words and avoiding giving me a straight answer. "Are you well?"

"I'm fine," I reply dismissively as she sits beside me, running her hands over her jeans as she stares at me. I don't bother to ask her the same question, I can clearly see she's doing okay, and she's apparently not in as much danger as I thought. But I'll have to take her word for it.

"So," she murmurs, clearing her throat, and I shake my head at how she can't even seem to adult enough to lead the heavy conversation we need.

"So you're not my mom," I state, getting straight to the point, and her eyes widen in surprise like she's forgotten who I am and how I act.

"That's right," she whispers, tears welling in her eyes, and I almost regret Xavier bringing me here to deal with her usual victim routine. This is all she's given me since I was forced to go to Knight's Creek, but she quickly shakes the sadness away and focuses on me.

"How does that make you feel?"

How does that make me feel? I don't fucking know. I haven't had time to process any of the bombshells that have been dropped on me since the minute I left White River.

"I honestly don't know. There has been so much information, facts, and lies thrown at me, I almost feel numb to it all," I admit.

She nods like she understands, but does she really? I've seen the picture. I know she was there when I was born, but what role did she play? None of it really makes sense.

"Why was I separated from Archie?" I ask, trying to relax back on the sofa, but my body remains stiff.

She shakes her head and tilts her head to the left, her eyes sliding in the same direction, and I follow her gaze to a small black camera in the corner.

Fuck these nosy motherfucking assholes.

"It's like Big Brother everywhere I go," I growl. "Who the hell is watching, and why can't they hear you tell me why I was separated from my twin brother? Why is satisfying these sick fucks more important than telling me, your so-called daughter, why her past is turning out to be so shitty?"

I stand, pacing in frustration in the small space as my heart pounds in my chest and anger runs through my veins as I try to remain calm.

"We can't rock the boat, Eden," my mom murmurs,

looking up at me helplessly, and I stop mid-step as I turn to glare at her.

"Why does everyone keep fucking saying that?" I bite out, remembering Xavier saying that earlier. Looking out of the window through the slightly drawn blinds, I see the black rental exactly where it was when I left it, but I can only assume he's still sitting in there. Waiting patiently.

"I'm sorry, Eden. We never wanted any of this at all. But things were taken out of our hands, and we did what we felt was right to keep everyone safe."

"But now anyone who is still living isn't safe, so it seems pretty fucking pointless right about now. It's like the severity of the situation currently falls on my shoulders instead of yours like it originally should have," I tell her, and she tilts her head back, a sigh on her lips. She doesn't even argue with me, which just leaves me frustrated. What was the point of Xavier bringing me here?

She doesn't give me an answer because I'm fucking right. Whatever my parents thought they were doing to protect themselves only made their problems mine. Not even Archie's. Why is that? Why isn't Archie facing the same kind of fate as me?

I run my hands through my hair, my body tingling with

all the built-up emotions going wild inside of me.

"What the hell happened to make Ilana act this way?" I muse to myself, but the sound of my mother clearing her throat lets me know she heard it. "I wish you would stop protecting yourself by pretending to protect me. None of these secrets keep me safe, they keep me cornered and at a complete disadvantage."

Taking a deep breath, I dig my fingers into my temples, wanting to relieve the pressure, but she still sits there and says nothing. Nothing at all. It's fucking infuriating. Glancing over at her, I watch as tears trail down her face, but it's not good enough.

"Will you answer me? Say something, anything at all, just stop giving me the silent treatment. Do you have no desire to be my mom anymore now that I know—"

"No, no, of course not. You will always be my daughter, I will love you for all of eternity, but you don't understand," she pleads, rising to her feet and placing her hands on my shoulders.

My anxiety calms a little at her words, but like always, we never progress. "Then give me something, Mom, please," I beg, my hands wrapping around her wrists as her eyes search mine.

"Eden, Ilana, well, she—"

The front door suddenly swings open, slamming against the wall as a man appears in the open space. He's dressed head to toe in black, with matching sunglasses on his face, and his arms are folded across his chest.

"Time," he grunts, interrupting my mom, and her hands drop from my shoulders as her face pales.

"Five more minutes," I blurt out, but he's already shaking his head.

"No, now. Reza will be here in a minute, and the rule was for *her* to be gone by the time he returns."

Who the fuck is this guy? I take a step toward him, ready to give him a piece of my mind, but Xavier beats me to it.

"Watch your fucking mouth," he growls, shouldering past the asshole as he searches me out. As soon as his eyes fall on me, trying to get a read on the situation, my pounding heart eases a little. "Nafas, I'm sorry. This douche is right, he just doesn't have a polite execution with his words." He glares at the guy who doesn't react, and I feel myself sinking.

"But, Xavier, I—"

"Eden, I need you to remember what we agreed on

before you got out of the car. I know you hate it, and it makes me hate it too, but I promise it's the right thing to do," he says calmly, reaching his hand out to me, and I just stare at it.

"You have to go now, Eden," my mom murmurs, trying to push me toward Xavier, and I bite the inside of my lip in frustration.

"Xavier, she was just about to tell me what happened with Ilana—"

"I don't think she was, Eden. With the way this guy came flying around the front of the house, I can only assume she said something that triggered the security, and now here we are." His voice is soft, like he's worried how I'll react.

I turn my gaze to my mom, but she doesn't meet my eyes as she looks down at her feet. When the fuck did my mom become such a weak bitch? They want me to leave. They all do. So what am I standing here willing to fight for? Clearly she doesn't want me to fight for her, and she doesn't look all that poised to fight for me either.

With my hands clenched at my sides, I close my eyes and take a deep breath, and when I open them, I find Xavier with his hand still outstretched in my direction.

Ever so slowly, I reach my trembling fingers out to his, and his hand wraps around mine tightly as he pulls me in close and kisses my temple.

Refusing to look like I'll have to be dragged from the house, I put one foot in front of the other and tug Xavier toward the door. When he's opening the passenger door for me, I hear my mom's voice. Glancing over my shoulder, I freeze in place as she stares at me with pleading eyes.

"Happy birthday, Eden."

Why do her words feel like they're too little too late? No hug, no I love you. If I didn't feel so numb right now, her actions would gut me.

Dropping Xavier's hand, I climb into the passenger seat, letting him shut the door and jog around to the driver's side. As he falls into the seat beside me, an SUV parks in front of us, and I hear Xavier curse under his breath, but he doesn't slam on the gas pedal and speed away like I expect him to. Instead, he stares at me.

His hazel eyes search mine, and it almost looks like his hands are trembling as he continues to gaze at me.

"I'm sorry, Eden. I brought you here to make you smile, to help you forget about all the shit and just give you time to see your mom and make you smile on your birthday.

You're so brave, so strong, and I don't want this to play any part in hurting you."

"It's not your fault, Xavier. Let's just go," I murmur, but he doesn't move.

I feel numb, completely numb. My emotions are shutting down because I don't want to acknowledge how hurt I feel. It's better to feel nothing than the pain and hurt caused by those who are supposed to care. So I feel nothing.

"I will do whatever it takes to make everything right. We'll come back for her, Eden. I swear it." I'm not sure if he's trying to convince me or himself, but I offer him the slightest nod as I look down at my lap. He tilts my chin up, forcing me to meet his gaze as he takes a deep breath. "I will do whatever it takes, Eden, because I love you."

He what?

As I fall back into my seat, Xavier's fingers slip from my face. He stares at me, waiting for a response, but what do I say to that when I know it isn't true?

With a heavy sigh, I turn to face him. "Xavier, you don't love me. Loving someone means giving up control, compromising, and that's just not who you are," I murmur softly, clasping my hands in my lap as he gapes at me.

"I'd give it all up for you, Nafas. All of it," he whispers in response, and I sigh.

"Why does it already feel like we have?"

I've already given up everything in my life, and for what? Nothing.

TOXIC CREEK

KC KEAN

TWENTY NINE

Xavier

It's been over a week since I took Eden to see her mom, and as much as she says she's okay, I know she's not. She's been distant and withdrawn. I can't stop thinking about it. The whole day in general was a complete mindfuck.

Even now, while we're running plays on the field, I can't get my head in the game because I'm wondering what the fuck went wrong behind that closed door. She's been tight-lipped about what happened with her mom, only saying that Jennifer offered no explanation or knowledge with regard to the minefield Eden is trying to get through with my mother and this town. It infuriates me that her mother seems to be no better than mine.

"Knight, get your head in the game. Let's work on your arm," Coach growls, and I shake my head, trying to clear my mind, but it's difficult when she's out here running track off to the right, looking as beautiful as ever.

We spent the weekend together, with Charlie and Archie too. We were trying to keep everything low-key and relaxed for Eden, but as much as she tried, she was still lost in her thoughts.

"I've got you, man," Tobias murmurs, patting my arm as he heads down the field with a ball in his hand, ready to throw in my direction. We're all feeling the distance with Eden, but I saw the pain on her face before she masked it, and it's stuck with me ever since.

"I'm going to run sprints, shout if you need me," Hunter says, and I nod.

Flexing my shoulders, I try to relax as I ready myself for the ball. Tobias sends it sailing through the air, and it lands perfectly in my arms as I prepare to return the throw. After I send it back, I know I was a little heavier with the power behind the ball when Tobias pulls it into his chest and folds in half from being winded.

Fuck.

The message from my father this morning is making everything worse as well. There is so much shit at every corner, but he wanted to drop a simple reminder that I had obligations to meet since he gave me access to Eden's mom last week. The text replays in my head as if it's on a loop.

Dad: *Are you at home or away this weekend with football? Either way, I expect you at dinner on Saturday evening. You know the drill, and you know who to bring. No excuses.*

A part of me just wants to yell a huge fuck you because I didn't get to see the happiness on Eden's face like I expected. It all went to shit, and when I couldn't contain my feelings and told her I loved her, she told me I was wrong.

Fucking wrong.

Have I ever loved someone before? Hell no.

Do I know what love is? No, but does anybody truly know?

But am I willing to do everything in my power to keep Eden safe, even if it means sacrificing my free will to my mother's rules? Hell yes.

There is a feeling in the pit of my stomach that I just can't get rid of. Anytime I look at her, feel her, smell her, or even fucking think of her, I lose my breath. She literally takes my breath away, and now that I've finally got my shit together and figured that out, she tells me it isn't possible for me to love.

God fucking dammit.

Lost in my own mind, I hear Tobias call my name at the last second, and I manage to catch the ball he's thrown my way, before it smashes me straight in the face.

I hate being unfocused. I feel like I'm out of control—which I don't like, just like Eden said—but I'm willing to feel like this for her. Why can't she see that?

"Yo, chuck the ball, X!" Tobias hollers, and I swipe a hand down my face before tossing it in his direction. He's ready for my unnecessary anger this time and catches it without injury as sweat trickles down my spine with the afternoon heat.

Fuck, my head feels like it's all over the place.

How the hell am I supposed to go to dinner with my parents and take Roxy instead of Eden? She will literally gut me with a rusty knife and let me bleed out while Hunter and Tobias watch. I can already feel it, but I'm scared to tell her about the agreement because then she'll insist on coming with me, and I don't want to put her right in my mother's path. I don't even know what she's truly capable of.

"Again," Tobias calls, and I prepare for the ball much quicker this time. I wave for him to move farther back, and he goes willingly.

I haven't told the others what I said to her, so I definitely didn't tell them how she shut me down. In that moment, I knew in my soul she was lost in herself, overwhelmed with so many different emotions all at once. I watched her turn her emotions off. My subconscious clearly thought I could bring her back by saying those three words, but I was wrong.

I hate it. I hate it more than not being in control, but not as much as I hate not being able to fix it. And that's how I know I love her.

I roll the ball in my hands as I search for her. It doesn't take long, and I spot her off to the right, completely focused as she paces herself, outrunning everyone else near her.

How do I get her to open up to us? Or to at least one of us? Possibly Hunter maybe? He can get all deep and shit, draw her troubles out of her and cleanse the pain from her soul. That's what I want. But there is a nagging part of me that knows I fucked everything up so much to begin with that she's never going to see how I really feel. The second I recognized her surname and decided to make her our toy, I fucked it all up.

I just can't seem to settle myself. I take a deep breath, but my chest feels tight and my body is tense from head to toe. Fuck. How do I shift this agitation? I know it's because we're at an away game tomorrow and we won't be back until Saturday, which is when my father expects me to visit, and I feel too fucking chicken shit to tell her about the dinner now—even if it was for her.

"Throw the fucking ball, X," Tobias shouts, and it only seems to wind me tighter. Pulling my arm back, I throw it toward him with everything I have, a grunt breaking from my lips as I do.

I know I've overthrown it when he starts jogging backwards, but I don't realize how far until it's too late and he stumbles into the fucking cheer squad's pyramid or whatever they call that shit.

The girls' screams and whines hold everyone's attention as they get to their feet, Tobias amongst them, and I watch in slow motion as KitKat purposely throws herself on top of him, lying on the grass before he can get up.

"Shit," Hunter grumbles, coming to a stop beside me and pointing to the right as Eden marches toward Tobias and the cheerleaders.

I instantly start striding in the same direction, adjusting myself in my pants as I watch the anger grow on Eden's face because it's hot as fuck.

Eden

Inhale, left foot. Exhale, right foot.

In. Out. In. Out. In. Out.

Pinky and Perky, aka KitKat and Roxy, are close to being knocked the fuck out. It feels like it's been ages since they attempted to drug me, and I've continued to ignore them as agreed, but I'm at the end of my rope with them.

Ryan doesn't seem any closer to linking them back to Ilana, so I want to say fuck it, let's give them what they deserve regardless of who supplied them and played the bigger role. Apparently, I'm outnumbered in that respect, but Ryan promised if we don't find anything soon I can do things my way instead.

My promise not to fuck with them is close to going to hell, though, since every word out of their mouths is meant to rile me up. I don't know what they expect to happen when they push me too far, but they are close to finding out.

As I approach their end of the field, they increase their volume so I can hear every word they are saying as they stand huddled together.

"But have you seen the size of Tobias's cock? Girl, I could ride him for days," KitKat says, fanning her face as she gossips with the cheer squad, and I have to grind my teeth to keep my mouth shut.

"Girl, that's nothing," Roxy inserts. "Maybe we should remind them exactly what they are missing while wasting their time with that whore. Daddy says Xavier's going to ask me to marry him soon, and I'm all for sowing your oats and all that shit, but enough is enough. I can't make myself come the way he does."

I regret casting my eyes her way as soon as I do, because I find her smiling in my direction, and I hate letting her get under my skin like that. Anger simmers through my veins as I bite my lip to hold my jealousy in.

Following the track, I turn away from them and head

back in the opposite direction as I try to clear my mind, counting my steps and breaths to calm myself until I hear screams and yelps.

Flicking my gaze over my shoulder, I slow to a halt when I see the cheer squad flat on the ground in a pile of limbs, and I almost grin until I spot an all too familiar jersey and black hat. What the fuck is Tobias doing in there?

Searching for Hunter and Xavier, I see them staring at Tobias in shock. The ball is over in the pile of bodies too, and I realize what happened. I almost continue with my run, but then I watch KitKat practically throw herself on top of Tobias. A growl rips from my throat as I feel my feet moving of their own accord.

Marching in their direction, I clench my hands at my sides, feeling my strides getting longer as my body tries to get me to Tobias as quickly as possible without actually running.

"Back the fuck off, whore," Roxy bites out, blocking me from KitKat as she lies on top of Tobias, literally grinding her hips against his dick, and all I see is red.

Gripping her left arm and digging my fingers into her skin, I shove her to my left, dismissing her as she stumbles over her own feet and lands on her ass. These bitches are determined to get on my fucking nerves, that's for sure.

Approaching the pile of cheerleaders still trying to stand after Tobias knocked them down like fucking bowling pins, I climb over two of them to get to the biggest hoe of the hour. It's almost laughable that she's had her hair redone since Hunter said something about it, but in the same breath, it pisses me off. I hate watching her try to catch Hunter's attention. He's mine. They all are.

Tobias looks beyond confused with a "what the fuck is going on" expression as KitKat lays her body flat against his, pressing her tits into his face. That's the final straw.

I pay no attention to the rest of the cheer squad as I bend down, wrap my fingers in her purple hair, and pull her toward me sharply. Her cries of pain only fill me with sadistic joy.

"Get the fuck up, Tobias," I growl, and he looks up at me with wide eyes as I keep a grip on KitKat's hair. Nodding, he quickly jumps to his feet and dusts off his jersey in disgust as I tighten my hold and swing KitKat around to face me.

"Get the fuck off of me, you stupid cunt," she hisses as I tilt her head back, and I can't help but scoff.

"You're fucking done, do you understand me? I'm

done with your shit, and I'm done with Roxy's shit—all of it. I've done as everyone else desired and said nothing to you while you continued to fuck with me, but enough is enough," I murmur, glaring down at her, but it only seems to make her smile wider.

I know people are looking at us, but I have no idea where anyone specifically is, and I'm guessing this will somehow end up on social media as a video later. I just don't give a fuck, my focus solely on this bitch in front of me.

"You are so fucking screwed, bitch," she says as she tries to pull my hand from her hair, but I shake my head.

"You aren't so big and strong when you're not hiding behind others to do your work, are you? I don't give a fuck about you coming for me, but you don't get to fucking touch what's *mine*."

She laughs as I vibrate with anger, her neck straining as I continue to pull her head back, getting angrier with every second she thinks this is funny.

"Nothing here is yours. Not. A. Thing. So why don't you just do us all a favor and drop dead? It's inevitable that it'll end that way, so why not get the fuck on with it?"

I hear scuffling behind me, but I have tunnel vision on

this bitch right now. My face feels like it's on fire as my anger consumes me. Lifting my right arm back, my knuckles fisted, I whip my hand forward, and smash the bitch straight in the face as I keep her up by her hair with my left hand.

The momentum unbalances me slightly, so when she swings her arms around in defense, she hits me in the arm and leg before I can block her. Stupid bitch. Pulling tighter on her hair, she hits me in the chest, my boob throbbing as I swing my leg around and hit her calf, knocking her to the ground.

Keeping my hand firmly in her hair, I tumble with her, but I somehow manage to land on top of her in the scramble, and it's only now I hear the chants and gasps, a mixture of reactions to two girls fighting over a fucking guy—because that's apparently what I'm doing.

"Get the fuck off her!" I hear Roxy yell, but she can suck my nonexistent dick.

Strong arms band around my waist, trying to pull me from KitKat's screaming body, but I refuse to let go.

"Come on now, love, I've got you," Hunter whispers in my ear. Hearing his voice makes me pause, but these fucking bitches deserve more than a beating. So much more.

"I'm done playing the waiting game, Hunter. They

have to pay for all of this shit," I snarl, still gripping her hair while she digs her blunt nails into my arm, but with the way Hunter is holding me, my other hand can't reach to punch her again. Fuck.

"They will, Eden."

"When? Fucking when?" I growl, feeling angry tears starting to form in my eyes, and I *hate* how much everyone is seeing me meltdown right now.

I finally release KitKat, and she instantly retracts her nails. I fall backwards into Hunter as he holds me close and blindly brushes my hair off my face.

I know he's trying to help calm me, but I feel smothered.

"Hunter, put me down," I mutter, and he places me on my feet as I take a deep breath, my hands braced on my hips as I look down at my feet.

I can feel so many eyes watching me right now, but focusing on that won't help me. I don't really know what will. I feel like I'm on an emotional rollercoaster, my heart rapidly pounding in my chest as I become a little light-headed.

Whoa.

Taking another deep breath, I try to ease the adrenaline rush that must be causing me to react this way. Finally looking up, I see the entire cheer squad, track team, and football team watching me with wide eyes—all except the Allstars, Archie, and Charlie, who have a mixture of appreciation and concern on their faces.

"Are you done fucking staring now?" I growl. I want to get out of here, but I feel like I always find myself in situations that require me to leave without a word, and this time I refuse to go quietly. These people here who allow shit to happen are all part of the reason this town is so fucked up.

Then there's the queen cunt Ilana at the top of the pyramid to contend with. I really need to convince Xavier to let me sit down with her, but now isn't the right time.

Tobias steps up to my right, placing his hand on my shoulder as he stares into my eyes. "I do believe, Princess Bubble, that you just might have defended my honor," he murmurs with a cheesy grin on his face, and the tightness in my chest begins to loosen.

This motherfucker and his ability to calm the situation.

"I plead the fifth," I respond, swiping my hair out of my face as I keep my eyes focused on him.

"You can plead the fifth all over my dick whenever you're ready," he counters, and I squint in confusion.

"What the fuck?" I mutter under my breath as Xavier comes to stand in front of me with a shake of his head.

"I think it's one of his euphemisms for a hand job, Eden. Ignore him," he says, giving Tobias a pointed look.

I glance around, but I can't see past the three Allstars, each of them blocking me from the crowd, and I'm not ashamed to admit I appreciate their brand of protection when it gives me a moment of peace to shut my eyes and take a calming breath.

"Xavier is just jealous you defended my honor first, bubble. Want me to take you home and show you how much it turned me on watching you finally fucking claim me in public?" Tobias whispers, leaning in so his lips brush against my ear, and I shiver.

Fuck.

Yes. Yes, I do.

THIRTY
Eden

Pulling my G-Wagon to a stop outside of the Allstars' home, I throw my head back on the headrest behind me, unable to drop the stress and anger still burning within me.

Tobias jumps down from Xavier's SUV, a glimmer of desire still flashing in his bright blue eyes as he stalks toward me, and I can't help but grin at him. When I agreed to come home with him, he seemed shocked, expecting me to decline and storm to the Freemont house, but he didn't like it when I refused to let any of them drive with me. I needed a few minutes to myself to calm down from the fight and sort my feelings over publicly claiming my Allstars, but it looks like my time is up.

Swinging my driver's side door open, he braces his hand on the frame and the corner of the door, his arms tense as he cages me in. He wets his lips as he looks me over, his gaze lingering on my chest, and I have to bite my lip to contain myself.

I can't see the others when I try to glance past him, Tobias holds all of my attention as he slowly leans across me and unclips my seatbelt. His fingers caress my thigh as he moves back, and my hips flex with the sensitive touch as he grins down at me, knowing exactly what he's doing.

Reaching across the center console to grab my bag, I squeal in surprise as Tobias pushes his arm under my thighs and grabs my waist, pulling me out of the G-Wagon before I can even sit upright.

He whirls around, and my car door slams shut as Hunter appears on our left, taking my bag from my hand as Tobias carries me inside the house bridal style. I can't see Xavier, which tells me he was the one to open the door, and he likely stormed off with the green-eyed monster present as he did. It doesn't surprise me. But it was these guys who said they shared, not me, and now they have me addicted to it.

Tobias carries me inside, pausing in the hallway as he tries to decide where to take me.

"Tobias, take our girl out onto the patio. I want to see her spread out on the table," Hunter murmurs, the order clear in his tone, and I shiver in Tobias's arms as I remember what Hunter is referring to.

He still doesn't likely know that we could see him watching us, but that makes the moment even more sacred. I'm getting hotter just thinking about it, but the blush creeps up my neck as Tobias heads straight for the kitchen and wordlessly unlocks the door, the sea air hitting us the second he steps outside. I've never needed to cool down so much in my life, but even the slight breeze does nothing to dampen the heat I feel.

"Oh, I'm so ready to see a bossy Hunter with you, bubble, so fucking ready. But it was my ass you claimed in public today, so he doesn't get to make *all* the demands. Understood?"

With my jaw practically on the floor, I nod in response, making him grin wide as he lowers my ass to the table in the exact same spot as last time. Still in my track shorts and tank top, I feel the cool surface through the Lycra as I lean back on the palms of my hands, my legs spread as I stare up at him.

"Make me relax, Tobias," I purr, needing someone to take away all the mixed feelings inside me. I want someone to take control, leaving my mind blank and my body blissed out with pleasure so I don't have to stress over the fact I was publicly fighting a bitch over a guy.

"You're so fucking beautiful, Eden. You know that?" he comments, trailing his finger down my cheek, and my mouth goes dry with anticipation as he steps between my legs.

"Why are you still wearing so many clothes, love?" Hunter asks, appearing beside us with a tube of lube in his hands, and my eyes widen under his intense stare, which is full of promise. I rack my brain for an answer, but I fall short, my mind focused on nothing but the need to strip bare for him like he wants.

Leaning forward, I grab the hem of my tank top, ready to pull it over my head, but Hunter's hand lands on my arm, stopping my movement. Freezing under his touch, he shakes his head slightly, and pats Tobias on the shoulder with his other hand.

"You don't strip yourself, love. We do it," he murmurs before climbing on the table, his legs falling on either side of me as he presses close to my back, securing me between his legs.

I instantly feel his hardening cock against my back, making my spine arch with desire as he trails his fingers up my thighs.

"Ah fuck," Tobias rasps, dropping to his knees before me and untying my sneakers as Hunter slowly lifts my tank top, his fingers ghosting against my rib cage as he does, leaving goosebumps in his wake.

As he pulls the top over my head, he kisses the side of my neck, and my eyes fall closed as his hands squeeze my sides just below my sports bra, leaving me desperate for more. I feel like I could combust at any second.

I hear the thump of my sneakers hitting the ground, my socks going with them, before I feel Tobias's lips at the top of my calf. Everything feels sensitive, so fucking sensitive.

My head falls back onto Hunter's shoulder as he maintains his hold, lifting me ever so slightly so Tobias can pull my shorts and panties down my body. I try to pry my eyes open, watching the hunger in Tobias's gaze as he discards my clothes, his eyes focused on my core as Hunter places me back on the table.

Tobias strokes up my thigh, and the anticipation builds inside me as I prepare for him to graze my clit, but just before he reaches the apex of my thighs, Hunter blocks him.

"What the fuck, Hunter?" I grumble, making Tobias nod in agreement as he looks pleadingly at my pussy, but Hunter grins against my cheek as he brushes kisses against my skin.

"Undress him, Eden," he murmurs, caressing his fingertips against my stomach, and I shiver under his touch.

Tobias steps forward without hesitation, grabbing my hands from Hunter's thighs and slipping them under his jersey so I can feel his solid abs. Shit. It turns me on more than anything that we didn't waste time changing before we left, so they are still in their jerseys and all sweaty from working out.

Slowly trailing my hands up his chest, the hem of his jersey rising along with them, I watch as his abs twitch under my touch. When I grip the material to pull it over his head, he ducks down, making it easier as Hunter's fingers slip under my sports bra.

A moan escapes from my lips as he brushes his fingers

against my nipples while I toss Tobias's jersey aside, letting him step out of his sneakers, leaving him only in his shorts before me.

Just as I'm about to slip my hands inside his shorts, Hunter pulls my sports bra over my head, lifting my arms and twisting the material as it reaches my wrists to hold me in position.

Tobias steps back, admiring Hunter's handiwork with a grin, and I love how empowered I feel watching them react to my body, to me, and my teeth graze across my bottom lip.

"You're something else, bubble," Tobias mutters, his eyes roaming from my spread thighs to my outstretched arms.

"I need someone to fucking touch me," I beg, trying to rub my thighs together to gain friction, but Hunter stops me with his other hand. The way he grips my thigh, attempting to hold me in place, has his thumb pressed against my clit, and I try to rock my hips against him, but he makes it too difficult. "Please, Hunter," I implore as he trails kisses down my throat.

"Do you trust me?" Hunter asks, and I try to look over my shoulder at him, but he pulls on my arms to keep me in place. "Do you trust me?" he repeats when I don't answer quickly enough.

"Yes, yes, I trust you."

"Good, because I want to be inside you at the same time as Toby. What do you think about that?" His breath brushes against my skin as his words wash over me, and my blood spikes with need.

"Where?"

"Here," he murmurs, finally stroking my pussy, and I moan in pleasure. "And here," he whispers, ghosting his finger across my ass, and I shiver under his touch.

"I haven't done that before, but I want to," I answer, watching Tobias's blue eyes widen with excitement as Hunter smiles against my skin.

"Like you've never done anal before, or never both at the same time?" he inquires casually like he's asking what the weather is like outside, and if I wasn't desperate for it to happen, I would probably say something.

"Either," I admit, but with their hands on my body, I don't feel out of my comfort zone. God, if the shower sex with Hunter is anything to go by, I'll definitely be into whatever he has to offer.

"Fuck, that's hot," Tobias says with a grin, leaning in

to cup my chin as he holds my gaze. "I get her ass, Hunter. Your dick is too thick for her first time, you'll split her in half." There is a teasing tone to his words, but they both nod in agreement, and I'm in no position to argue.

"Can someone just fucking touch me? I feel like I'm about to explode," I plead, needing more than their teasing touches and words.

"That's all they do, Eden. Tease you with a good time but then fall short when it matters most."

whipping my head to the right, I find Xavier standing at the end of the table, his eyes squinting slightly as he looks me over, desperation written across his face with the sun in his eyes as I watch his fingers twitching to join us.

"Come show them how it's done then," I goad before Tobias and Hunter can defend themselves. They pause at my words, staring at Xavier just as I do, waiting for him to storm off like usual.

"He can fucking watch then," Tobias grumbles under his breath when Xavier doesn't move, but it's like Hunter's words ignite something in him, because in the next second, he's stepping between Tobias and me and crushing his lips to mine.

I moan against his lips as Hunter grips my thighs and

forces me to keep my legs spread when I desperately want to wrap them around Xavier and grind the fuck out of him.

"Just because you decided to show your face doesn't mean you get to keep her all for yourself, asshole," Tobias complains as Hunter releases my legs to cup my breasts, pinching my nipples. My back arches as I finally press my core against Xavier, feeling his rigid length straining beneath his shorts.

"Shut the fuck up, Tobias, and get a fucking sun lounger," Xavier growls, not fully removing his lips from mine as I circle my tongue against his open mouth, watching his hazel eyes darken above me. "If I do this, you don't get to change your mind about us next week, next month, or next year. This is it," he warns, staring at me, and I frown in confusion.

"I don't understand," I murmur, and it's Hunter who responds as Tobias drags a sun lounger toward us.

"Xavier doesn't share like this with T and me, it's not his usual thing."

"But I can't stand to see them touching you without me again. Not after the car, not when I saw them shatter you into a million pieces all over my leather. I want to consume you with them." His words leave me gasping for breath, but when he continues to watch me expectantly, I understand what he's waiting for.

"I won't change my mind," I whisper, feeling no regrets as the words leave my mouth, and I'm instantly rewarded with his fingers sinking into my pussy.

My head falls back on Hunter's shoulder as he bites down on my neck, and my mouth forms the perfect O as I try to take a deep breath, but the second my body starts to relax again, Xavier slips his fingers out before thrusting them straight into me, swirling his digits to hit my G-spot, and my ass lifts off the table as I groan long and throaty.

My eyes turn to slits as I try to keep them open, but my body is overwhelmed by the sensations. Xavier's touch, Hunter's scent, and the soft moan from Tobias's lips are too much.

"That's enough," I hear Tobias murmur before Xavier withdraws his fingers.

I'm lifted into the air and dropped onto the sun lounger as my sports bra falls from my wrists. I try to lift myself onto my elbows, but it proves difficult as Tobias widens my legs and leans forward to swipe his tongue from my clit to my center in one sweep. I tremble under his touch, feeling my nerve endings screaming for friction with all the teasing they've been doing.

"Please don't stimulate my clit any fucking more unless you're going to bring me to orgasm," I growl, having had enough of their little fucking touches. I want to fall apart because of all three of them at the same time. Especially now that Xavier is here, I want it more than ever.

"She's not coming until she's on my dick," Hunter says, a warning in his voice, and I almost consider riding the fuck out of Tobias's face just to prove a point, but I stall when I find Hunter naked. When the fuck did that happen? Before I can make a move, Tobias grabs me under my arms and pulls me forward, allowing Hunter to lie on the sun lounger behind me.

"I'm not a fucking rag doll," I bite out, getting angry with the constant moving around when I just want to fucking come.

Xavier chuckles, and I turn to glare at him as he slowly walks around the back of the lounger. "Hunter, rile her up. She fucks so fucking good when she's mad," he taunts with a grin, and my jaw falls open as Tobias huffs a laugh from behind me.

"Is that so?" Hunter responds almost too casually, and

that should have been my warning. Grabbing my waist, I happily let him throw me around like a rag doll when he positions me above his dick, and the second I feel his head at my center, I slam my body down, taking all of him in one delicious, burning thrust.

"Fuck," Hunter grinds out, baring his teeth as I brace my hands on his chest.

As I rise up on my knees, preparing to do it all over again, Hunter gapes up at me with a shake of his head, and it makes me grin. Mr. Dominant is a little lost for words. Perfect.

"We can't let Hunter have all the fun, now can we?" Xavier murmurs, pulling his jersey over his head as he comes to stand on my left, and I reach for the outline of his cock before he's even close enough. He's like a fucking Greek god, and I'm desperate for more. He's most likely Hades, but fuck it, send me to hell.

"Tobias, you better prepare her quickly before it all ends too quickly," Hunter rasps as I sink down on his cock, slower this time, enjoying the stretch as his hands find my waist. The pads of his fingers dig into my skin, and I pray he leaves a smattering of bruises as a souvenir.

Grinding against him, I slow as I feel Tobias behind

me, his hand stroking down my spine, and I shiver under the caress.

"I've got you, bubble. I'm going to make you sing. Just relax," he whispers near my ear as he slowly teases my ass.

"I can distract you, Nafas, don't worry," Xavier offers, finally lowering his shorts just enough to reveal his cock. He aims it toward my lips, and I open my mouth willingly, loving the weight of him on my tongue as Hunter thrusts up into me and Tobias drips lube down my skin.

Fuck. Fuck. Fuck. Fuck. Fuck.

It's all too much. Feeling them all at once is beyond overwhelming in the best possible way. Grinding down on Hunter with one hand on Xavier's waist and the other braced on Hunter's chest, I let him control his thrusts, and like a fucking magician, he rubs against my clit so fucking good. But the second Tobias circles my ass, inserting a finger to stretch me, I lose all control.

My orgasm catches me completely off guard as it washes over me again and again as I fall apart between the three of them. I try to sag forward, but Hunter holds me upright as Xavier continues to fuck my mouth, and when Tobias continues to stretch me, my skin instantly heats again.

"It looks like we have ourselves a little anal bunny,

don't we, Eden?" Tobias murmurs against my shoulder as Hunter grins at his words.

"We'll see if that's true when we're both deep inside her," he responds, and the thought alone has me ready to come again.

"Do it," I mumble around Xavier's dick, digging my fingernails into his thigh, but when I look up at him, he's completely unfazed.

My movement falters when Tobias teases his cock against my ass, his bare thighs nestling behind mine, and the confidence I had from moments ago wavers.

"Relax, Eden," Hunter soothes, stroking his fingers up my chest as Tobias pushes in, and the feel of them both inside me almost melts me into a puddle. "Push back on him, love. I promise it'll be worth it."

Trying to take a deep breath proves difficult around Xavier's unrelenting cock, his hand twisting into my hair as I do as Hunter says until I'm fully seated against Tobias as well as Hunter. Even Xavier calms his movements for a moment, letting me get my bearings. My eyes fall closed as I try to breathe through the pain, and they all seem to wait for me to make the next move.

I attempt to rise up on my knees, but Hunter holds me

in position when I sit halfway up his length, slowly pulling out until only the tip remains then slamming up into me. Gasping, I feel his cock bury deep inside me right alongside Tobias's, and Xavier takes that as his cue to fuck my mouth again.

"Fuck me, Eden. You're so damn tight," Tobias growls, moaning, and I groan along with him.

We fall into a rhythm, my body burning for more of them. I freeze when I hear a phone begin to ring, but Xavier grips my hair tighter.

"Fuck. Not right now," Hunter hisses, and I couldn't agree more, not when I'm so close to climaxing and falling into a sex coma. No way.

My eyes shut when Tobias moans deep in his throat as he continues to thrust, but Xavier's voice cuts through the fog in my mind.

"Mother, right now isn't the best time," he grumbles, still slamming his cock into the back of my throat as the guys fuck me.

My eyes widen in shock, but when I stare up at him, the hand in my hair tightens, and he seems to fuck my mouth harder.

"I'm aware of what my father has planned for this

weekend, yes," he mutters, not meeting my gaze as I whimper around his dick, lost to the feel of both Tobias and Hunter inside me, fucking me even harder since he answered the call. Every part of my body aches, but I still crave more.

"Fuck," Tobias groans, and I'm glad I'm not the only one too lost in pleasure to care about the call.

Why the fuck is no one stopping while he speaks to his mother? Ilana. That bitch. Oh, he thought it would be okay to answer her phone call while he fucked my mouth? Not a chance.

Tightening the suction of my mouth around his cock, I drag my teeth against the throbbing veins, hearing his sharp inhale as he pulls my hair tight, but I continue until I suck hard on the head of his thick length.

Humming in response down the phone, I love pushing him further than he expects as he stares at me in surprise. I swallow him down, and his cock hits the back of my throat as Tobias thrusts into me. I moan loudly around his dick, the vibrations making his cock pulse in my mouth.

"I'll be there, yes, with a guest. I have to go."

I'm not even sure if he presses the red button to end the call as he drops it into his pocket before he grabs my hair with both hands and fucks my mouth hard and fast. His movements stutter as he tenses, his cum hitting the back of my throat as he throws his head back with pleasure.

"Fuck, Nafas."

Before I can finish swallowing his cum, Tobias pulls me back, forcing Xavier to release my hair, and his cock slips from my mouth as he pushes me down to lie on top of Hunter.

Gripping my ass cheeks, he takes full control of the thrusts, making my breasts rub against Hunter as I hold on to him for dear life. I can't control the moans and groans that slip from my lips, my body tensing as I come hard around them.

"God, oh God," I chant as I hear unintelligible sounds coming from both Hunter and Tobias, but the ringing in my ears is too loud for me to hear them properly.

My muscles spasm around them, and I instantly feel them throb inside me, curses falling from their lips as I drag them over the edge with me.

I collapse limply against Hunter's chest as I try to calm my racing heart, the rhythmic tune of his heartbeat almost lulling me to sleep. I whimper as Tobias slips from my body before Hunter slowly rolls us so I'm beneath him. As he steps away, kissing me on the forehead, I'm surprised to find Xavier standing beside him with a wet cloth and a towel.

Wordlessly, he takes a seat at the bottom of the lounger and drags the cloth against my exposed, sensitive skin. It almost feels more intimate than the moment we all shared. When he finally glances up at me, I see the storm brewing in his eyes, and it instantly reminds me of his mother's call.

"What are you hiding from me?" I ask, and he raises his eyebrows.

"What makes you say that?" he hedges, and I give him a pointed look, making him sigh as I grab a jersey off the ground and throw it over my head.

I feel the need to cover up while he finds the balls to explain what's going on.

"To get you to your mom, my father made me agree to do something. I agreed without question because I wanted to give you the time with your mom that I thought you needed. But now I realize it probably didn't go to plan like I expected."

I say nothing, wanting him to tell me without me pushing and forcing it out of him. He looks distressed enough, his body tense and his hands fisted at his sides.

"My father mentioned that he apparently runs a lot of interference between my mother and me, so I agreed to go to dinner with them on Saturday after I get home from the away game."

Oh, well, that isn't so bad, right? But when he swipes a hand down his face, I know there is more to it.

"Just spit it out, Xavier," I murmur, and he bites his bottom lip as he strokes my leg.

"The agreement was that you got to see your mom, and I had to go to dinner...with Roxy."

An array of emotions surge through me as I gape at him. Anger and hurt are at the top of the list as I frown at him. "No. Hell no. Fuck no. Over. My. Dead. Body," I growl, and he shakes his head at me like he expected me to react like this.

"I have to show up there, Eden. I have no choice."

"You always have a choice, Xavier. Take me." Standing, I look down at him with my arms folded across my chest as he continues to shake his head at me.

"Eden, I can't—"

"Yes, yes, you can, Xavier. I asked you to set up a meeting with her, and you said no. Now is the time. I deserve to know what the fuck is going on."

Sighing, he runs his fingers through his hair. "It's not as simple as that, Eden."

Wrapping my arms tighter around my body, I stare him down, making sure he can see how fucking serious I am right now. "Xavier, you either make it as simple as that or I can't do this. I can't choose you when I tell you what I want and you continue to play a part in keeping me caged up."

With that, I turn on my heel and grab my bag as I rush through the house. Thankfully, I don't catch sight of Tobias and Hunter as I go. Hopefully they caught on to the situation and decided to give us a minute.

I hate ultimatums, yet I also seem to be tossing them around a lot when I'm at this house.

Fuck.

If he takes her, I'll never forgive him.

Never.

THIRTY ONE

Eden

Pulling away from Archie's house, I rub a hand down my face as exhaustion consumes me. After storming from the Allstars' place yesterday, I fell into bed and didn't wake up until this morning, fatigue getting the best of me.

It doesn't seem to have done me any favors, because I still feel like fucking shit, but I don't know whether I had a brain and body overload, causing me to feel like this.

I laid fucking claim on them yesterday, getting myself into a stupid cat fight with KitKat, and that was how Xavier chose to treat me? Fuck that. Fuck him. I understand him agreeing to the dinner to give me a chance to see my mom, but there's no fucking way he's taking Roxy. This is a deal breaker for me, and no matter how many hours I've slept, that hasn't changed. All the pent-up anger I got to release yesterday is back again in full force.

My stomach churns, adding nausea to the fatigue I feel, and I almost regret leaving for school this morning. I feel like death, but I hate staying in that house when I know only Richard is home. I'm still not ready to see or talk to him, which has me reconsidering my plans for tonight since Archie will be staying over in Santa Monica for the away game with the Allstars, and the rest of the team.

I turn the stereo on low, taking the next turn through town and driving the long way to school. Archie left early this morning to go to practice, and I miss his presence in the G-Wagon. Him taking over the music and being goofy now provides a sense of calm.

I straighten the sunglasses on my face, already feeling overdressed with too many layers on, but I just want to hide away from the world today. My period must be due, and Xavier's confession yesterday only made my crazy hormones worse, so I opted to wear an oversized Papa Roach t-shirt, the hem hitting just above my knee, with a pair of yoga pants and Converse.

I didn't even make the effort to put makeup on this morning, rocking the fresh face look instead. But the sun is blazing, and it almost feels like it's giving me a headache, so I plan to wear my sunglasses all day.

Turning into the school parking lot, I park in Hunter's spot like he's been telling me to, especially since he and Tobias have designated spots yet never fucking drive themselves to school because they ride with Xavier.

I spot the three of them standing with the other football players, but their attention is solely on the G-Wagon as I pull up, waiting for me to step out. But I feel my stress levels rising with the determination in Xavier's eyes and the tightening of his jaw that I can see from here.

Fuck my life.

With a heavy sigh, I grab my bag and step down from the G-Wagon. Before my foot has even touched the ground, Tobias is standing in front of me, slipping my bag from my hand. Deep down, my independent mind wants me to argue that I can stand on my own two feet, but I just don't have the energy right now.

"Hey, bubble. Are you okay?" he murmurs, stroking my arm and intertwining our fingers as he stops to face me. I hum in response, but it doesn't satisfy him. "You have me all stressed out because you didn't text me back last night, and now you show up looking pale. I mean it, are you okay?"

I move into his side, and he swings his arm around my shoulders as I fall into step with him.

"Honestly, I just feel run-down and a little queasy. I'll be fine," I answer honestly. "Are you ready for the away game tonight?" I question, trying to change the subject, but he doesn't take the bait.

"I won't be going to any away game if you feel like this, Eden," he states as we come to a stop in front of Hunter and Xavier, the pair of them staring at us in confusion.

"What's up?" Hunter asks as Xavier's hands fist at his sides.

"She's not feeling well, so I'm going to pass on the game. I—"

"No, you are not," I interrupt, glaring up at him, and he gapes at me.

"Eden, I don't want you to be alone if you're unwell."

"I'm. Fine. It's probably just my hormones, I'm used to it. It's nothing to worry about, and definitely not something to stop you from playing," I respond, and he sighs, looking to the others for help, but I shake my head. "Honestly, I just feel tired and sick, but it's probably because I crashed when I got home last night, and I haven't eaten since lunch yesterday," I admit.

"Are you sure?" Tobias whispers into my hair, and I nod.

Hunter cups my cheek as he lifts my glasses from my face to see my eyes, searching for God knows what, but eventually he drops them back down on the bridge of my nose and leans forward to kiss the corner of my lips before Xavier clears his throat.

"Coach actually has us out for the rest of the day because he wants us to leave this morning and practice out there," he mutters, his wary gaze meeting mine.

"You guys should go then," I say, tucking a loose piece of hair behind my ear.

"Are you sure you don't want to come?" Hunter asks, and I force a smile onto my lips.

"I'm sure."

I don't ever want to be that girl who travels with them. It'll just make me look insecure, and although I'm ridiculously new to this exclusive shit, that is one rabbit hole I am not jumping down.

"If you need anything, just call or text. Beth was also hinting at reaching out to you when she called this morning," Hunter says with a smile, and it makes me smile for real this time. Maybe speaking to Bethany is a good idea. Besides, I need me some Cody snuggles.

"Thanks. Be safe and score all the points," I murmur, placing my hand on his chest as I lift up on my tiptoes and press my lips to his. This kiss is slow and languid, and when I pull away, I regret it instantly, but Tobias is there right away, our lips melting together as he gently holds me.

When they step back, it leaves me facing off with Xavier. Awkwardness builds around us, and it makes my nausea kick up a notch. My hand falls to my stomach as he stares me down, my discomfort growing as he searches my eyes.

"Give me two minutes with her, guys," he mutters under his breath, and Hunter and Tobias reluctantly head for the coach where the rest of the team is now gathering.

We both watch them saunter off in that direction, neither of us wanting to be the first to talk since we're both so stubborn. But I refuse to give in.

With a heavy sigh, Xavier turns to face me head-on, forcing me to look up at him as he rubs the back of his neck.

"I'll do whatever it takes to protect you, that's what I

promised you. If it makes you hate me, I can deal as long as you're here and alive to fucking do it."

His words are likely meant to calm me, but they only rile me up more. "You're not seeing me and what I want or need in this situation. This is my life, Xavier. Mine. You might be able to play God with everyone in this town, but you definitely don't get to play God with *my* life." My heart beats erratically as annoyance builds within me, and I fold my arms across my chest, creating a physical barrier between us.

"No, you aren't seeing what this woman is capable of, Eden," he growls, keeping his voice low as he stares pleadingly into my eyes. "I just want to keep you safe, Nafas. I mean this in the nicest way possible, but your dad is dead, and we both know my mother played a part in that. There is more going on here if my father, who is still married to Ilana, is hiding your mother from her. I can't keep you safe when you're directly in her line of sight. Can't you see that?"

I don't know how he manages to keep his voice low as his face reddens with desperation, but I can't bring myself to look away to see if anyone is listening.

"I do understand all of that, Xavier. I do. But I feel

like there is a noose around my neck, and I can't continue with all the secrets and lies Ilana controls. I want to ask her to her face what the fuck she wants with me." My chest heaves with each breath I take, but I don't stop. "I told you how this made me feel, and that isn't going to change. I know you did it to take me to my mom, and I can't thank you enough for that, but this is important to me." My annoyance rises as I feel tears trying to prick my eyes.

Silence stretches between us as we stare at each other. I want him. Fuck, I want him. I want all of them. But this is a hard limit for me.

"I don't know if I can do that, Eden," he answers honestly, peering up at me with his chin resting against his chest.

Nodding, I lick my lips as I take a step back.

"Don't run away, Eden. Give me tonight to think."

"I already gave you time to think, but we obviously spent the whole time hoping the other would compromise," I scoff. "You know what? Don't worry about it. I'll figure it out on my own," I add blandly, forcing myself to sound like I don't care, even if I want to cry.

I turn toward the stairs leading up to the school, but I don't even take a full step before Xavier grabs my hand

and spins me back around to face him. My mouth opens to yell at him, but he crushes his lips to mine. I don't respond to his touch straight away, angry at his constant need for control, but I can't help myself. Kissing him back harder, challenging him for control, I sink my teeth into his bottom lip, and he groans against my mouth before pulling away.

As I open my eyes, not recalling ever closing them, I clear my throat and gather my thoughts. "This is what I meant when I said you didn't mean those words you said," I murmur, bile burning the back of my throat as my own feelings for him bounce around in my mind. "This need for control you have is ruining whatever this is between us. I hope you know that," I warn, unable to stop myself from rising up onto my tiptoes and kissing his cheek before I head for the steps, and this time, he doesn't stop me.

I search for Charlie, but I can't see her in the crowd as I rush up the stairs. I hear a few girls mutter, "Whore" under their breaths as I pass, but I have no energy to deal with them.

Pulling out my phone to text her, I stop in my tracks when I see an unopened message from a random number on my phone, and my heart stills as I read the start of the text visible in the preview. Taking a deep breath, I press the message icon, my eyes devouring the words as it fills my screen.

Unknown: Your outfit of choice today doesn't look like the best option for your wake, now does it? Left unprotected, now there's no one around to interfere. How many lessons do you think you'll get through before you finally get to see your dad? I'm watching. Are you ready?

Glancing around, I search to see if anyone looks out of place or is acting differently, although being surrounded by so many students and teachers heading to class offers me no clues. But I'm not sticking around to figure this shit out. I already don't want to be here, and this just gives me the perfect excuse to leave.

Moving back down the steps, I take my time, trying not to appear scared as I weave through the people walking in the opposite direction. Seeing the school bus pull out of the parking lot, I consider reaching out to one of the Allstars, but I decide against it.

These are my problems to handle in my own way. Climbing into my G-Wagon, I click my seatbelt in place and get the hell out of the Asheville High parking lot. I make a split-second decision as I reach the intersection, turning right toward Beth's house instead of Archie's.

Constantly watching my rearview mirror, I calm a little when it doesn't look like I'm being followed, but the sickness in the pit of my stomach only seems to worsen. I try to call Bethany's phone, but it goes straight to voicemail, yet I hear Ryan's words in my mind as I continue toward their house anyway.

"This is a safe place for you, Eden."

They won't turn me away, and still knowing the access code for the security, I find myself turning onto their street in record time.

This is what I mean when I say to Xavier that I can't carry on like this, letting his mother dictate my fucking life. Making me glance over my shoulder with every step I take. I need to know what I'm truly up against once and for all.

As I slow at the gates of Bethany's property, the system instantly recognizes my license plate number, so I continue rolling down the gravel, and the pounding in my chest subsides a little when I see Bethany's car parked outside the front door.

Taking a deep breath, I try to calm myself down. I hate

that I just ran instead of standing my ground, but I can admit that I don't truly know what Ilana is capable of.

I step down from the G-Wagon and throw my bag over my shoulder as I head toward the front door, my phone vibrating with an incoming call from Bethany, and I smile in relief.

Before I can answer, the front door swings open, and I find Bethany standing in the doorway in a blue dress with concern written all over her face as she frowns at me.

"I'm so sorry. I got another random threatening text message, and I didn't really know where else to go," I admit, and she wraps me in her arms without question. It makes me feel better instantly, and my heartbeat slows with every breath I take as she unhurriedly leads me inside.

Directing me straight to the kitchen, she places me on a stool at the island, giving me a moment as I try to gather my thoughts, and that's when I realize how much I'm shaking. Fuck. I hate giving them a reaction like this. Even if they can't see, it almost feels like their attempts to break me are only getting stronger.

"Where's Cody?" I ask, dropping my bag and phone onto the countertop as she grabs a jug of iced tea and pours me a glass. Heading back over to me, she places the glass in front of me as she swipes my phone up off the table. Tilting it in my direction for facial recognition, she unlocks the phone and finds the message.

"He's having some daddy time with Ryan, thankfully," she answers, frowning down at the phone. "What the fuck is this, Eden? This is getting ridiculous. You did the right thing coming here. I'm just going to call Ryan and send this over to him, okay?"

I nod in agreement, and she squeezes my arm as she passes by. I sit in silence, trying to get a grip on my imagination. What does Ilana expect to achieve from all of this? What minions does she have trying to scare me off? I'm sick to death of having more questions than answers all the time.

Wrapping my fingers around the glass of iced tea, I bring it to my lips, but the second I get a whiff of the smell, I gag. I push the stool back, slam the glass down, and rush to the sink, making it just in time to spew my guts up.

I hang over the kitchen sink, vomiting until I'm left dry heaving, my eyes watering and my hands fisted tight as I retch. What the fuck? A towel is thrust in my face, and I dry my mouth off, taking a moment to catch my breath as I stand upright before turning the faucet on.

"Are you alright?"

Glancing at Bethany, I smile apologetically as I nod. "Yeah, I'm so sorry, I don't know what came over me," I tell her, taking the bottle of water from her hands. I sip it slowly in case I'm sick again.

"Have you eaten anything off or something?" she inquires, taking a seat at the island as I follow, trying to steady my breathing.

"No, nothing. I've just felt tired, achy, and nauseous since yesterday evening," I murmur, bracing my head in my hands, the urge to nap overwhelming.

Nervously tapping her fingers on the countertop, she stares at me contemplatively. "Eden, you couldn't be, uhh..." Frowning, I wait for her to continue, completely lost, and she sighs. "Like you couldn't be pregnant, could you?" she murmurs, and a bubble of laughter escapes my lips.

"Bethany, don't be ridiculous. I have the implant. I must have a bug or something," I answer, waving my hand dismissively, but she continues to watch me.

"Probably. But you don't seem like you're actually ill. You have aches, pains, and sickness, which are more like symptoms. I have some tests in my bathroom if you change your mind." I shake my head, and she does the same. "Ignore me, sorry. I'm sure you've had your period lately anyway, so don't stress." Leaning across the table, she squeezes my hand as I remain frozen in place.

I had my period a few weeks ago when Hunter left the party to keep me company, stealing the first snippet of my soul then and there and forcing me to see the relationship I have with men differently.

That was, well, that was...five weeks ago.

KC KEAN

THIRTY TWO

Xavier

I watch the scenery outside of the bus window pass by in a blur, my brain and heart still hurting from what I have to do today. Dinner with my parents is at the bottom of my wish list. It'll never be something I actively want to do, but I still can't bring myself to tell Eden to come.

I understand her wants and needs, and I understand wanting to know everything, but taking her to dinner with my mother is practically the same as dropping her into a snake pit. I hate that Eden's angry with me, but can't she see how much I'm trying to protect her?

We have another thirty minutes of sitting on this bus before we'll be back at Asheville High, and I either need to call Eden or Roxy. I really don't want to call the latter. She is the absolute tipping point of a bad time with my parents, and I can admit it feels like betraying Eden.

"Have you figured your shit out yet, X?" Tobias asks, glancing over his shoulder from the seat in front where he sits beside Hunter. Neither of them has given me their input on the situation, which only tells me they are as torn as I am—torn on wanting to protect Eden but also wanting to give her what she wants—but I'm the only one who has the balls to fucking say something to Eden. Assholes.

"I could give you a list a mile long with all the reasons why I shouldn't take her, but the only reason it makes sense to take her is if my mother actually fucking explains. It's just really not that likely that she will, and Eden can't see that," I reason, worried about Eden's temper, too, as Hunter glances over his shoulder at me as well.

"I get wanting to protect her, Xavier, but at the end of the day, Eden is the strongest person I know besides Bethany. She's headstrong, independent, and a force to be reckoned with. Maybe what you need to remember are the words she gave you the last time she stormed from the house," Hunter suggests, and I sigh as I rest my chin on my chest.

"You are either on my side, by my side, or in my fucking way— I'll let you decide."

I haven't forgotten those fucking words since they left her lips. The only future I have ever seen is getting out of this town and finding myself at Ohio State. Simple. There was never supposed to be a girl or all the fantasies and hopes she comes with.

But here I am. Now, I have to decide where I want to stand. I am *always* going to be on her side going forward, no matter what, even if it means doing things she doesn't like. Her protection is paramount. Is that enough? My heart tells me it's not. I want to be by her side, and if I want to remain there I have to understand and listen when she tells me this is a deal breaker for her.

Squeezing my eyes shut, I press my fingertips into my temples before leaning back in my seat and looking at my brothers in front of me.

"I can't take Eden on my own," I admit, and Tobias offers me a sad smile.

"We'd never expect you to."

Nodding at his words, I pull my bag from the foot well

and dump the contents on the empty seat beside me.

Most of the team is asleep since they partied after the game last night. We won 28 to 21, which is a fucking miracle since my head wasn't in the game, and I know Hunter's and Tobias's weren't either. Archie practically carried us, thank God. But while they all had a good time, Hunter, Tobias, Archie, and I headed back to our rooms. Tobias bunked with Archie, leaving Hunter to deal with my mopey attitude, and the second the alarms went off this morning, I was already packed and ready to go since I didn't sleep very well. I tossed and turned all night, trying to figure the situation out in my head.

Glancing around to make sure no one is paying us any attention, I pull my phone from my bag, noticing the unanswered messages I sent Eden last night, and I add another.

Me: Meet us at school. We'll be there in thirty minutes. Be ready to meet the dragon herself.

I almost want to add an "I love you," but I know that won't go down well with her just yet, so I hit send before hesitating over my mother's name.

I hit the call button before I can change my mind, and the ring fills my ears as I swallow past the lump in my throat. She leaves me until the last ring, and I prepare to leave a voicemail just as her voice comes through the phone.

"Xavier, your father was just telling me you decided to bring Roxy to dinner. I must admit, I'm shocked, but I'm glad you're finally listening to what is required of you."

No hello. No pleasantries. Just straight to the point as always. Perfect.

"Yeah, about that, I changed my mind. Hunter, Tobias, and Eden will be joining me instead." I keep my tone relaxed, almost bored, not wanting her to see how affected I am, and the silence that follows has my leg bouncing and my palms sweating.

"You will come to dinner with Roxy as you previously agreed with your father, Xavier. You don't get to pick and choose who you bring," she grinds out as I swipe a hand down my face.

"It's highly amusing that you thought I would *want* to bring Roxy moments ago. I don't think so. If Dad wants me to come to dinner, I've decided I'll bring someone who suits me and not the Knight family."

I feel Tobias and Hunter staring at me as I keep my

voice low enough so no one else can listen.

"Do you want me to tell your father you're going against your agreement?" she snaps, and I clench my fist in an attempt to calm myself.

"Do you want me to tell you what he gave me in exchange?" I respond before my filter can kick in as I scrub my hand against my forehead. I hear my father in the background demanding I hold up my end of the deal as my mother replays my words in her head.

"Your father and I don't have any secrets, Xavier."

"Are you sure about that?" I retort, which only seems to anger her more, and I have to bite my tongue and lower my tone before I draw any attention our way.

"I brought you into this world, Xavier, and I can just as easily wipe you from it. Don't underestimate me and the knowledge I have. You may have gone to see Eden's mother, but I know everything. I've allowed your father to play savior, Xavier. It's me who allows everything. You'd do well to remember that."

Fuck. Fuck. Fuck.

I glance at Tobias and Hunter, who stare expectantly when they see the look on my face.

My father goes silent in the background, and I have

a feeling this information comes as a surprise to him too. Excellent. Maybe that might overshadow me for not following the rules, but I know it's not likely. I'll never understand how their relationship works.

"If you want me to attend dinner, it will be with guests of my choosing."

"I set the rules, and if you choose not to follow them, then it'll be your own fault when you have to face the consequences. I told you I despised Jennifer Grady and Eden Freemont. I told you she was a test. A test you are dramatically failing. It's almost embarrassing, Xavier."

I don't bother to ask what the consequences will be, I know it'll be Ohio State, I just know it, but Eden's worth it.

My heart pounds in my chest, and there's a slight ringing in my ears as I find the right words.

"Eden may have been a game, a test to you, but she isn't to me. She never will be. You can throw your weight around, you can hold the family business over my head, and even risk Ohio State, but it won't stop the inevitable. She's mine," I growl, watching the world go by through the window, refusing to glance at the guys.

"You forget the pull I have in this town, Xavier. Have you heard from her since you left yesterday? I heard someone may have threatened poor little Eden, and I'm going to make sure you don't get to protect her," she says with a knowing tone, and I can picture the manic smile on her lips in my mind before she ends the call.

Staring at my cell, my eyes flick to the guys as her words set in. "Have either of you heard from Eden since we left yesterday? I just assumed she was giving me the cold shoulder for being a douche, but Ilana just hinted at another threatening message."

The pair of them shake their heads in response. "I thought we were all getting ignored because of your argument," Hunter replies as Tobias pulls his cell out, dialing Eden's number and bringing it to his ear, concern growing on his face.

The three of us become more panicked when it goes straight to voicemail.

"What else did Ilana say?" Hunter presses, and my heart sinks.

"She said, 'I'm going to make sure you don't get to protect her.'"

Eden

Xavier: Meet us at school. We'll be there in thirty minutes. Be ready to meet the dragon herself.

Thirty minutes wasn't much time for me to figure my shit out, so I climbed in the G-Wagon without changing out of my yoga pants and one of Hunter's t-shirts he'd left at Bethany's house that I put on after I was sick.

I was sluggish, achy, and queasy as hell, so when I mentioned Xavier's message to Bethany, she was reluctant to let me out of her sight, but I deserved answers, and she understood that.

I just needed to make sure I got a minute to speak to them myself before we went anywhere. Privately.

Nibbling on the ginger biscuit Bethany forced me to bring with me, I glance down at my lap, emotion welling inside me again. I fan my face as I glance out of my open window, taking a deep breath. I feel like my head is screwed on backwards. So much has happened since they left. Ryan has been tracking down the message while Bethany has taken care of me.

You've got this, Eden.

I've avoided every call and text message from the Allstars for a very good reason, but mainly because I have no words to express what the fuck is going on, and now he drops a text like that which has me all riled up.

Spying the school bus driving down the road, heading toward the school parking lot where I wait, I untie the bun in my hair and run my fingers through it before I secure it on top of my head again. I want the bus to hurry up and park, yet I also want it to turn around and never come back all in the same breath.

Climbing down from the G-Wagon, I wrap my arms around my chest as I walk around to the front, closer to where the bus will pull in. I think I'm going to be sick. Watching the bus slow to a stop, I see Tobias, Hunter, and Xavier through the window. They stare at me with wide eyes as they urge everyone to move out of the way so they can get off.

I lean against the grill of my G-Wagon, waiting. Every inch of me is petrified, but my internal meltdown is interrupted by the sound of sirens filling the air. Glancing over my shoulder, I'm surprised to see three cop cars speeding down the road, but it stuns me even more when they turn into the parking lot.

What the fuck is going on?

"Eden! Eden!" Xavier shouts, and I glance back in their direction to see the three of them rushing toward me with fear and confusion on their faces.

The cop cars screech to a halt right beside me just as Tobias rushes to a stop in front of me, wildly searching my eyes as he cups my cheek. I feel lost in this moment with him. All the sirens, the red and blue flashing lights, the people, my thoughts, none of it means anything right here as I stand before him and look into his worried blue eyes.

As I lean to look around him, searching for Xavier and Hunter, I gape in shock as two police officers pull Tobias from me and begin to place him in handcuffs. Glancing around in shock, I find Xavier and Hunter struggling against two other cops, and my heart pounds wildly in my chest.

"What the hell is going on?" I shout, stepping up to Tobias, but one of the officers pushes me back.

"Don't fucking touch her," Tobias growls, all dark and menacing, and it surprises me, but he stops resisting the officers, becoming more compliant.

"Eden! Eden, you have to run," Xavier yells, and I turn my gaze to his, my eyebrows knitting together as I try to understand what's going on. "Eden, do you hear me? This is my mother's doing. I need you to run, leave Knight's Creek, and never look back. Answer me," he shouts, but I remain frozen in shock as I watch the cops start to drag them toward the cars.

Hunter looks resigned and not at all surprised by the fact they are being treated this way, and it hurts my heart as I remember the stories they told me about that place. They can't go back to that. I won't allow it.

"No, no. Let them go. They've done nothing wrong," I shout, rushing toward them, but one of the officers holds me back.

"I'm sorry, miss. I can't let you do that," he murmurs, but I ignore him as I try to shake out of his hold.

"Get your fucking hands off her right now," Hunter bites out, his green eyes wild with rage as he pulls against the cop's hold. When the officer holding me releases his grip on me, Hunter allows them to continue moving him.

I glance to the other players, desperately looking for help, but one of the cops has them all on the bus, blocking the exits so they can't help. I spot Archie, his mouth wide open as he watches the scene before him, the other players holding him back as he tries to get to me.

In the blink of an eye, car doors are being slammed shut, each Allstar in a separate one, and the cop cars don't waste any time hitting the gas to get out of here.

Watching each car go by me, I feel utterly helpless. To anyone else, the expression on Hunter's face would look impassive, but I see the anger beneath the surface. As Tobias goes by, my heart sinks when I catch sight of the pain in his eyes, knowing they'll be taken to the correctional center. But what frightens me the most is the desperation on Xavier's face as he mouths, "Run," to me again.

Rushing out into the middle of the parking lot, I stare as the three cop cars drive off into the distance, leaving me alone. Alone with my thoughts. Alone with my fears. This town is worse than I thought, more than I could have ever imagined.

Those cops didn't even give a reason as to why they were arresting them. What am I supposed to do now? Nausea churns in my stomach as I rub a hand down my face. Things aren't the same as when they left yesterday. Standing all alone, I feel weak and vulnerable.

I need to figure something out. For me. For *us*.

Gazing down at my trembling hands, I swallow past the lump in my throat. Bethany said the words would be easy, so I taste them on my tongue with only the wind to hear me.

"I'm pregnant."

TOXIC CREEK

KC KEAN

EPILOGUE
Tobias

The guard scans his key, and the telltale sound of the door clicking open bounces around the small space we're in. Rubbing my thumbs together, I stare down at my new orange jumpsuit. I'm not scared of where I am. I've grown, changed. I'm just scared of the nightmares from my past coming back to haunt me like they always do.

The metal from my handcuffs digs into my wrists, fitted extra tight like always as we follow the guard down the corridor. The white cement walls with the bright lights burning down on us is all that greets us as we continue down the hallway. We've been to the adult section of the Holmes Correctional Facility before. They should just give us a cell number and we could escort ourselves there.

We've been stripped and searched, hearing the same old Miranda rights, and for what? The assault of Graham Brummer. What a load of shit. There is literally no reason for us to be here. It's exactly like Xavier said. This is Ilana's doing, and she always makes sure to punish Hunter and me along with Xavier, and we wouldn't have it any other way. But that fucker is dead. D-e-a-d. Dead. If they are going to arrest us, maybe make it believable or, at the very least, the truth.

My mind just can't stop playing Eden's face on repeat as she watched it all happen. She knew how fucked up this town was, but only by how it treated her, so she was stunned to see it all unfold. My fucking soul burns for her, but she should do what Xavier said and run. There's nothing here for her, and we can't protect her from jail.

Xavier clears his throat, causing me to look up from my feet as we approach the last room off the hallway on the right. They've put us in the general population wing, which has a yard overrun by gangs. Perfect.

The guard unlocks the door, and Xavier steps inside,

completely calm, cool, and collected as we all are. Your skin hardens once you step through these doors, there's no other way to describe it, but we know the score.

Hunter and I follow him inside, and it doesn't surprise me to see three metal beds with thin mattresses, limited storage, a toilet, and a sink. They love nothing more than to strip us down to nothing. Even the window is smaller than all the rest, looking over the garbage dumpsters.

"Hello, son," I hear from behind me, and when I turn, it takes everything I have not to scrunch my nose in disgust at the sight of my father. Coffee stains his creased white shirt, and his brown hair is a mess as he wipes at his nose, likely from the cocaine he sniffed before coming down from the warden's office to grace us with his presence. "Get comfortable, boys. Ilana Knight wants you here for a while. Sleep with one eye open."

With that, the guard steps out, leaving Grant to slam the steel door shut behind him.

Well, fuck.

AFTERWORDS

Whaaaaaaaa! What the hell was that ending? Where are the rest of the words? Who the fuck even is this author? LOL. 0/10 would not recommend this bitch haha!

Cliffhangers give me life, even as a reader, so as an author, when you scream at your reading devices it gives me joy haha!

But seriously, this book was huuugeee! I love hitting over 90k words for a book, so when I reached 106k for Tainted Creek I was so giddy! Especially since it topped Your Bloodline's word count and is now my fattest book yet <3

I want to say I'm sorry if you're mad, but that would be a lie LOL Eden went on one hell of a rollercoaster ride in this book, but our girl can handle anything thrown at her…right?

We'll find out in Twisted Creek! Roll on September 14th <3

THANK YOU

I'm totally obsessed with thanking everyone LOL but by now if you've read this far, you know I gotta start with my homeboy and our offspring. LOL. They keep me stable, they keep me sane, but most of all, they keep me topped up with all the love in the word <3

Next, my bestest friend, Valerie. You are the perfect partner in crime, and you work so hard alongside me to give everyone the best version of Eden possible, even if I do leave you on constant cliffhangers when alpha reading LOL Thank you for taking a chance on me over a year ago, I wouldn't be here without you.

My BETA queens, Monica, Jessi, Catherine, Amy, and Hope. You each bring something completely different to the team, making sure the quality and love is real, and you've done it again with Tainted Creek <3 You rock ladies.

To my co-dependency bubble. It is impossible for me to work without you. I'm addicted. Here's to deadlines and dreams. And all of the fucking noodles.

To BellaLuna again, look how beautiful these freaking covers are. You're awesome sauce.

ABOUT KC KEAN

KC Kean is the sassy half of a match made in heaven. Mummy to two beautiful children, Pokemon Master and Apex Legend world saving gamer.

Starting her adventure in the RH romance world after falling in love with it as a reader, who knows where this crazy train is heading. As long as there is plenty of steam she'll be there.

ALSO BY KC KEAN

Featherstone Academy

(Reverse Harem Contemporary Romance)

My Bloodline

Your Bloodline

Our Bloodline

Red

Freedom

All-Star Series

(Reverse Harem Contemporary Romance)

Toxic Creek

Tainted Creek

Twisted Creek

Printed in Great Britain
by Amazon